THE DEPARTMENT OF RARE BOOKS AND SPECIAL COLLECTIONS

THE DEPARTMENT OF RARE BOOKS AND SPECIAL COLLECTIONS

EVA JURCZYK

WHEELER PUBLISHING
A part of Gale, a Cengage Company

LIBRARY OF CONGRESS CIP DATA ON FILE.
CATALOGUING IN PUBLICATION FOR THIS BOOK
IS AVAILABLE FROM THE LIBRARY OF CONGRESS.

ISBN-13: 978-1-4328-9457-3 (hardcover alk. paper)

Published in 2022 by arrangement with Poisoned Pen Press, an imprint of Sourcebooks, LLC.

Printed in Mexico
Print Number: 01   Print Year: 2022

For Matty and Hank

For Mary and Jack

1

From the first spin of the lock, she knew she wouldn't be able to open the safe. What does a librarian know about safecracking? Standing in the office of the venerable Christopher Wolfe, in front of that safe, the combination to which was only stored inside Christopher's broken brain, she began to stammer excuses. The university president himself stood over her as she spun the dial again and tried her old combination again and failed to open the safe again.

Before Christopher's brain had set itself on fire, he had lacked a talent for details and had been reliant on Liesl to keep him to schedules and plans. Which was why, despite the fact that she was on sabbatical and had no official responsibilities at the library for a full year, she had called Christopher three weeks ago to remind him that the combination to the safe was scheduled to be changed. He was supposed to call her back once it was done and tell her the new code because it was prudent to make sure it was stored in more than one place. But Christopher and details being what they were, the call had never come.

Liesl wanted to suggest to Lawrence Garber, the university president in question, that perhaps the priceless object wasn't in the safe at all so he would begin hunting around the office in panic rather than standing over her in panic, but she saw how that was unlikely to be helpful. He hovered; she spun the dial of the safe.

Christopher's office smelled of cigars and vellum, and President Garber smelled of sweat and eucalyptus. She had been in this office hundreds of times but had never noticed the smell of cigars so acutely. Smoking in public buildings hadn't been legal in decades. She had never chided Christopher for the state of his office and had never questioned his commitment to rules about things like smoking, but she thought that when he woke up and returned to work, she might need to have a gentle discussion with him about tidiness and the consequences of embers for priceless papers. Liesl hated a cluttered desk. If she had to work in here, as Garber had suggested she should, she would ask to have all of the scattered volumes reshelved to create some space.

Christopher had been the director of the Department of Rare Books and Special Collections since the department had moved into its current building in 1969. He shook hands and bought lunches and poured Lagavulin and behaved in ways both atrocious and effective at soliciting millions of dollars of annual donations, both in cash and gifts in kind, to grow the library's collection. The contents of the safe were his latest triumph. Or so they would confirm if they could get the thing open.

The valuable title had been courted, acquired, paid for, and delivered all in the weeks while Liesl had been at home working on her own book. There were rumblings that the university's rivals in Boston wanted it and that the British Library wanted it, but when the day came, neither had bid, and Christopher had easily won the auction, competing against mid-tier schools who made half-hearted efforts at securing the prize for below-market value. At half a million dollars, it was a steal. A contact at Christie's had grumbled about Christopher scaring off other bidders, but there was no proof of anything like that.

Christopher had scarcely had the opportunity to inspect his prize before disaster struck. The call to Liesl's home, summoning the assistant director back to work and ending her sabbatical though it had barely begun, came late on a Sunday as she and her husband, John, were settling in with their port and weathered paperbacks for the evening. Lawrence Garber told her she was an angel, sent to maintain the appearance of order until Christopher regained consciousness, an angel who would keep the ship steadily on course. Liesl wasn't fond of the mixture of biblical and nautical metaphors, but Garber had been an economist before becoming university president, so she was willing to overlook it. They had bigger problems than poorly deployed literary devices. The donors were arriving to see what their money had paid for, and Christopher had been the only one who knew the new combination.

The book inside the safe was a Plantin Polyglot Bible. Some of the money for its volumes had come from the library's endowment, but most of the cost was covered by a group of donors who were gathering at the library that very afternoon to cup the balls of their new prize horse. The auction house, the shipping department, and several staff had confirmed the Bible's arrival at the library. But before their insurer could add it

10

to their policy and allow it to be placed on the shelf, it could only be in the very room where Liesl stood. Guidelines dictated that the uninsured book be secured in the safe in Christopher's office, and presumably one of the last things Christopher had done before a blood vessel that carried oxygen to his brain had burst was to strictly adhere to guidelines.

During his forty years as director, Christopher had frequently forgotten to do important administrative tasks, and Liesl had no choice but to suppose that the period of restricted oxygen to the brain had somehow made him more responsible. She would have expected to find one of the volumes lying open on the desk where Christopher had been poring over its pages in awe, the others stacked up alongside. She suggested to President Garber that they call off the donor meeting.

President Garber planned to do no such thing. He marched around the office. He hadn't yet removed his bicycle helmet or the reflective Velcro strips around his ankles that prevented his cuffs from entering the gears of his bike. While walking his laps, he would occasionally drop to a crouch and yank at the handle of the safe as though he could force it open with his 150-pound

11

frame and sheer will. An economist, a university president. He had authored books, shaken hands with prime ministers and more than one member of the Saudi royal family. Liesl could see in his eyes that this was a problem he considered solvable. It was unclear to Liesl whether the cycling accessories were part of Garber's imagined solution.

The book needed to be appraised for insurance, separate from the general collection, which is why it was in the safe in the first place. The donors would understand, would be impressed by the level of care with which the library was treating the new acquisition. Liesl suggested again that they call off the meeting and tell the donors the truth. They had already been briefed about Christopher's stroke and knew that he would not be the one greeting them.

"We'll show them the Plantin as soon as the safe is open, and until then, they know it's secure," she said.

President Garber was typing something into his phone. She thought he was acting on her suggestion, so she went on. "Everyone knows that these acquisitions take time, and think how nice it will be to pair the first viewing with good news about Christopher's health as he's recovering."

Garber continued to type into his phone, and looking at him and waiting for a reply, Liesl could see his jaw clench. Presumably the tension of his jaw against the strap reminded him of the bicycle helmet, and he finally snapped it off.

"Just think," she said. "With a little bit more time to plan? We could bring in a scholar to talk about the book's importance."

Garber looked up from his phone. He was not smiling. Liesl straightened some papers on Christopher's desk. Garber put his phone in his pocket. Crossed his arms. Uncrossed them. "For God's sake," he said. "There are no circumstances under which we are canceling today's meeting."

"Why shouldn't we? If it means time to get the book, time for Christopher to improve, time to plan a lecture?"

Once she had said it, she went back to the safe to give the handle a yank herself, a feat of force to disguise her self-consciousness at the stupidity of the suggestion. *A lecture?* she chided herself.

"To hell with a lecture," Garber said. "They don't want to write a thesis on the book; they want to be the first to see the book."

"I'm sure if we explained . . ."

"This is day one, Liesl. I brought you in to assure donors they can have confidence in us. How can we screw up so badly on day one?"

"If we just explain," she said. "They'll feel informed." Still crouched by the safe, she wished it would open for no other reason than to allow her to crawl inside and disappear.

"These are major donors. They don't want to feel informed. They want to feel important. They need to be the first to see it."

"We have expertise enough to deliver a lecture today, and there are probably photographs," she said. She regretted it immediately, but couldn't stop the ill-conceived suggestions from coming. She stood up and wiped her sweaty palms on her trousers, stepping away from the safe to find her head.

"Photographs?" Garber pulled his phone back out and resumed typing. "They didn't donate hundreds of thousands of dollars to look at photographs." He walked over to the safe and gave another yank.

"Another book then."

Another book was what Christopher would have proposed. Liesl was sure of it. As sure as she was that Garber didn't want a creative solution from Christopher's second-in-command. He wanted Christopher.

"What other book?" he said. He tapped his phone against his chin. "Go into the stacks and get them something that no one ever gets to see, something Jesus or Shakespeare or Marx used to wipe his chin. Something transcendent." He left the room still typing into his phone, his bicycle helmet dangling from one wrist.

2

That first morning, in the swampy heat of early September, exactly three minutes after Garber exited the library and just as Dan Haberer was about to hit Play on the secondhand Discman that he lorded over adherents to more convenient forms of technology, Liesl took him by the arm and asked him to retrieve the Peshawar manuscript. As an afterthought, she told him to bring a couple of book trucks to Christopher's office to gather various scattered volumes for reshelving.

Dan made an offended display of removing his headphones. Liesl waited until they were all the way off — wrapped in their cord, placed gingerly upon the Discman — and the middle-aged man clad in head-to-toe denim was face-to-face with her before repeating her request. While waiting for the headphones and listening to Dan's vague grumbles about book request slips and policies and work he had planned for the morning, Liesl had plenty of time to reflect on how unusual Dan's heavy-denim-and-combat-boot ensemble was in the academic library. Corduroy slacks that stretched over thick thighs. Well-polished loafers concealing collapsed arches. A short-sleeved polo on a hot day, occasionally. These were the uniforms for their battalion. To be confronted with the workman's ensemble over Dan's slender frame as he ambled, for Dan always ambled, toward the elevator to get the Peshawar for her and the donors was a contradiction so acute that Liesl never quite trusted her eyes.

It was the too-obvious choice, the Peshawar, for the show-and-tell with the money. She could have been creative, could have asked some of the library's people, could have phoned up a dealer for a one-day loaner. But Liesl wasn't up on doing things just for the sake of appearances on her very first day of the number one job. Besides, she assumed that this accumulation of money-loving people would appreciate being in close proximity with these pages that had contributed to the invention of modern mathematics. You can't have a bank balance with eight zeroes unless someone first invents the zero.

She flipped through an old exhibition catalog that featured the Peshawar. Finance money, pharma money, family money — she was looking for the angle they'd feel at the front of their trousers. She wasn't an expert in Sanskrit, mathematics, or early writing, and while that hardly mattered when she was talking to undergraduates, she worried that this group might see through her. This group that flexed their fortunes to acquire pages like these. That, coupled with Garber's lecture that morning about the need to convince the donors that the library was in stable hands, had her feeling like a schoolgirl about to sit for an exam. Had Christopher been there, he would have done the talking. It all made her rather doubtful of her own level of knowledge and nervous to even touch the book when Dan finally rolled it into the office on a book truck.

Then there was another thing. The pages of the Peshawar looked like garbage. The library had been playing a shell game for years, using photos of the leaves in lieu of the real thing. The photographs were just easier to read; they hadn't been darkening over the decades like the birch leaves had. But Garber had been clear; photographs were going to do little to make this group feel important, so even if the real thing was barely legible and even if the lack of legibility might raise some questions, she was going to have to bring up the real thing. Dan left her alone in the office with it, and she opened the album. The Plantin volumes that were, at that moment, trapped in the safe in Christopher's office, while finely bound and historically important, were not totally unique — there was a handful of sets in library and private collections. The Peshawar, on the other hand . . . Nothing like it existed in the whole world. She decided she would let them touch it if they wanted, stroke the leaves. That would have to be enough to get them off.

"Francis," Liesl said when she walked into the workroom. "Can you be a bit late picking up your grandson today and give a bit of a talk on the Peshawar this afternoon?"

Francis strove for a personal presentation that resembled an MI6 spy and almost succeeded except, pity for him, for being older than and not as handsome as the well-known filmic representation of a British spook. He exaggerated his dark features: dark-brown eyes, yes, but a dark-blue button-down and his still-dark hair, which was worn slicked back when he was feeling rakish and to the side when he wasn't. At this moment it was back. When he replied to Liesl, his Eton accent was much stronger than you'd expect from a man who'd left the isles behind nearly forty years earlier.

"You know I'm happy to leave that terror waiting in the playground until morning," he said. "But seems an odd day to be pulling out the Peshawar."

"Indeed. But all the same we've pulled it out. You'll do it then?"

"You know I hate to miss my weekly appointment with that vile child, but I suppose I'll have to. Can you tell me why? You all right?"

"The Plantin's in the safe. The safe is locked. Christopher is the only one with the current combination. So we're substituting the Peshawar."

"The donors aren't going to like that."

"They might if you make it sound appealing."

Francis leaned his chair all the way back. He was considering, or negotiating.

"Quite a mess they've dragged you into," he said.

"It's fine."

"Is it? I suppose it's better than being the one with the stroke."

"That's a bit cold, Francis. I'm here to help in any way I can. I'm surprised you're not happy to do the same."

"Don't chastise me, Liesl. You're meant to be asking me a favor."

She wasn't, though. Only asking him to do his job. But she kept her tone gentle.

"You know the Peshawar better than anyone. We're trying to present a picture of a fully functioning library to the donors. It seems simple to me."

"It's not to me," he said. "Chris is my best mate. I don't like being asked to stand in for him like he's already dead."

"That isn't the intention. You know it isn't," Liesl said. She pulled a chair up to Francis's desk and sat next to him. "I don't want Christopher's job. But I want his job to be recognizable to him when he comes back. That means we have to keep things moving in the meantime."

"Why don't you ask Max?" Francis said. "He's always been better than I have at glad-handing the donors."

"A Catholic priest is not the right tool to get their minds off a missing bible."

"Former priest," Francis said. "It's not as though he'd be wearing his collar."

Liesl didn't think that Max had Francis's compunctions about not stealing Christopher's job out from under him. But she didn't say so.

"I want them to feel special, like they're getting to see something unique. I think you're the one to do it."

"And you think the Peshawar is the right book?"

"It's one of a kind. Fragile. We rarely pull it out. We never let it travel. How many people in the last hundred years have stood in a room with it? I think it's perfect."

"Not much to appeal to the eye, though."

"You'll sell them on its scarcity."

"The invention of mathematics," he said in a booming ringmaster voice.

"You'll do it then?"

"If you think it's the best thing for the library, for Christopher, of course. I wouldn't mind some time with the old book myself. It's been years."

"You wrote that article about it just last spring."

He looked pleased that she remembered.

"With Chris, I did. But we used the photos for our research. Easier to read."

"Don't bring that up in your lecture."

"Yes, Boss," Francis said with an ironic salute. He went back to his work, and Liesl went back to Christopher's office to do power poses until the donors arrived.

The donors arrived. When she walked into the reading room, which wasn't really a reading room but a space that photographed well and was often used for events, she was pleased to see that whoever had ordered the catering had allowed budget for macarons and wine. Both would be useful. Enough wine and a scattering of well-chosen graduate students and she might be able to remove the focus from the books altogether. Percy T. Pickens III, the chair of the library's advisory board and the donor most responsible for making the acquisition of the Plantin possible, was already in the room. She had hoped to beat him there.

"I hear there's a problem," Percy said.

"Is someone getting you a drink?" she asked.

"Listen, Liesl," he said, leaning against the makeshift bar. "These are big shoes you're stepping into. The advisory board is here to guide you in any way you need. Some of us have been involved with the library for as long as Chris was. So what's this problem with the Plantin?"

"There's no problem with the Plantin."

"If there's no problem with the Plantin, then why aren't I looking at it?"

"It's in the safe," she said. "For insurance." She wasn't sure what to do with her hands. Percy's attention made her feel conspicuous.

"Like hell it is."

"It has to be insured apart from the main collection," she said, hands clasped in front, but then no, because that made her look childlike, and it was necessary that Percy recognize her new authority.

"I'm not proposing you send it out on a mall tour. I want to see what my money paid for."

"I understand that, Percy. Christopher didn't have a chance to arrange the insurance before his illness. The safe is fireproof and waterproof, and the Plantin is priceless. It stays in the safe until we have insurance."

"I didn't come here to drink bottom-shelf Jack Daniel's and make small talk. I came to see the book."

"I appreciate the value of your time. And I won't be wasting it. We're bringing out something very special, a cornerstone of our collection. A building block of civilization." Arms crossed in front of her but then no, because that made her look defensive.

"The others are going to be upset when they arrive."

"No one's time will have been wasted. But with your passion for travel and your keen interest in history, I'm hoping you can help the others see the importance of the piece we'll be showing." Hands in the pockets of

24

her trousers, but then no, that made her look suspicious.

"It's more than an interest, Liesl. My work might involve the oversight of my family's ranching interests, but I would hope you know that during my studies I worked on archaeological digs. I'm not *interested* in history; I've had history under my fingernails."

"The Orkney Project, isn't that right? I've read about it."

"History is more than books, Liesl."

Liesl didn't grimace. "Ranching interests" was a way of saying that the Pickens family owned land they mined for oil and metals and anything that could be sold to a foreign dictator. The Orkney Project had been funded by Percy II as a summer job for his son when even nepotism couldn't secure a spot in a respectable graduate school. She poured him a drink.

"Well," he continued. "Who's the understudy this afternoon?"

"We've brought up the Peshawar manuscript."

"What is that, a Quran?"

"No. It notes the first use of a zero in mathematics."

"But it's in Muslim? We came for a bible, and that's what you're bringing us?"

"It's written in Sanskrit. The manuscript likely predates the Arabic language."

Percy might have been handsome if his square jaw wasn't obscured by layers of chins, Liesl thought. She considered his face. His skin was pink and smooth, but quick to sweat. His hair, thin and yellow, was blow-dried into a swoop meant to obscure his scalp. No, she decided. Even if he weren't fat, Percy Pickens would be ugly. Francis rolled in the manuscript on a book truck.

Liesl braced herself. She was ready for abuse. Directed from Percy at Francis, from Francis at herself. She wanted to go to her office, not Christopher's office but her own, where there were potted plants and framed prints of orchids, and lock the door.

"Percy Pickens." Francis strode over and shook Percy's hand. The two men looked happy to see each other.

"Francis," Percy said, and they stayed locked in the handshake for longer than was necessary.

"Has Liesl told you what we're showing, then?"

"Something Indian. Not a bible."

"Something fewer than a dozen men have clapped eyes on in almost fifteen hundred years."

"Basically a virgin, right?"

"Guess so. You won't meet another man who has seen the inside of this book."

"Open her up then."

"Lean in and take a look," Francis said.

Liesl stepped back from the men and their mating. Percy preferred his conquests in ill-fitting blouses, but all attention gave him a hard-on. A powerful ego responded to stroking. The Peshawar was an international treasure, a clue in the development of modern mathematics, into the complexity of thought and writing carried out by people about whom scarcely any documentary history existed in the West. It was being treated as some Indian curiosity. Percy Pickens was a collection of sweaty chins and family money. He was being treated as remarkable, rousing. She walked backward toward the door. Cardboard ripped, someone opened a new case of wine. A roar of laughter. Someone had had one too many. The suits in the room were expensive, but one of these posh people was sure to ejaculate in the stairwell before the event was over. Nothing in the library was as it seemed.

3

I

She sat staring at the screen, listening to the library go quiet around her as the voices retreated one by one into the elevator and back onto the street. First the clinking Sancerre glasses at the donor event ceased, then readers went quiet, then the rumble of book trucks as materials were packed away, and finally the voices of the staff went dim and Liesl was left alone in the darkened building with only the hum of the air conditioner to keep her company.

Liesl savored the stillness. Her once-blond hair was blown shiny, and the blues of her eyes were even lined with mascara for the day, but it was a costume; a convincing disguise for a woman who preferred to be wallpaper and liked to describe her sense of responsibility as her most attractive trait. Dan had cleared the scattered volumes from around the office in her absence, so there were not even books to keep her company. Her solitude was absolute. Her cell phone lit up — her husband, John. She didn't move to answer it. She didn't call back. She hadn't answered a single one of the emails that blinked before her. She stared at the screen, wondering what to do next, until the ringing of Christopher's office phone startled her out of her meditation.

"Christopher Wolfe's office," Liesl answered.

"I'm sorry. I expected voicemail."

"Can I help you with something?"

"Sorry, how rude of me. My name is Rhonda Washington; I'm with the math department. Are you Mr. Wolfe's assistant? Can I leave a message with you?"

"He's on sick leave, I'm afraid. I'm his replacement, not his secretary. Can I help?"

"Gosh," the woman on the phone said. "I'm making a real mess of things, aren't I?"

"It's no problem, really. How can I help?"

"I'm new to the university, and I'm told you might have some materials in your collection that are of value to my research."

"What's your area of research?"

"I study the zero."

"How odd."

"That I study the zero?"

29

"No. Well, yes, it's a bit odd to me that someone would choose to study a single digit, but what do I know; I studied literature. You must know about the Peshawar?"

"Of course. I've read a lot about it."

"We happened to have it out today. That's what was odd."

"Can I come see it now?"

On the desk, Liesl's cell phone was ringing again. Her husband. No doubt wondering why she hadn't made her way home yet, even as the skies were darkening. If he was looking for her, it meant he was up, it meant it was a good day. Even still, she pressed End on the call.

"Well," Liesl said. "The library is closed for the night."

Liesl glanced down at the sheet of paper where she had written the woman's name so she wouldn't forget it: Rhonda Washington. Liesl wondered about this new breed of academics, who were so accustomed to getting what they wanted when they wanted it that they wouldn't even think to make an appointment to see a manuscript like the Peshawar. She opened the drawer of the desk to find a pencil sharpener and found instead a half-full bottle of whiskey and a couple of tumblers. She shut the drawer.

"Of course," Rhonda said. "I just thought

if you still had it out."

"You can make an appointment to come work here."

"My research need is a bit unusual."

Liesl kept the phone propped under her chin as she stood and began to gather her belongings. She switched the computer off without having done anything with it and stretched the phone cord as long as it would go so she could get her coat, hanging on the rack in the far corner of the office. She had heard thousands of researchers expound, all in the exact same way, about the unique character of their research. There was a catalog for an upcoming books-and-papers auction in the corner of Christopher's desk, and Liesl began to flip through it as the woman talked.

"Unusual how?"

"I'm less interested in the content of the manuscript than in the object itself."

"The study of manuscripts and bindings isn't uncommon."

"Yes. But I'd like to take a more . . . scientific approach."

Liesl was standing in her coat now, ready to get off the call and out of the library. She was suddenly starving. A good day meant John might have cooked something.

"I look forward to hearing about it when

we have a chance to meet."

"So you're open to the idea?"

"To what idea?"

Liesl had had few opportunities to be the decision-maker about the use of the library's collections herself — unless one counted the dozen or so times that Christopher had agreed to the loan of materials to other institutions without bothering to arrange shipping or insurance and Liesl was left in the position of stopping the materials before they left the building. After four decades working with Christopher, she had risen to the rank of his assistant director, a title with a pleasing ring but a day-to-day reality of tasks that Christopher didn't find especially interesting. When she approved expense reports or commissioned the creation of a website or found money in the budget for an interesting acquisition, she did so with the contented feeling of one who had done better than their peers, and it was only now, on this phone call, that she was coming to realize how seldom choice, real choice, had been a part of her work life.

"The Peshawar has been said to note the first use of the zero in mathematics," Rhonda continued, "but no one really knows how old the Peshawar is."

"Well, we have an idea based on the style

of writing, the language. There's a community of scholars who specialize in dating books."

The catalog was for a collection of books and manuscripts from the collection of a prominent Iranian scholar. She doubted that Christopher was planning to bid.

"So you have a best guess."

"A confident estimate."

"We could know for certain."

"How's that?"

"I'm proposing we carbon-date the Peshawar."

Liesl felt out of her depths and hungry. Neither state was conducive to a productive conversation. She knew little about how the manuscript had originally been dated, she knew nothing about carbon dating, and she was thinking of the macarons she had passed up earlier in the evening. "Let's set a meeting and discuss further."

"Wonderful," Rhonda said. "I'll email you to set it up. Liesl Weiss, is that you?"

What were the features of Lot 37 in the catalog that made it unique, lifted it out of the other ninety-nine? Liesl had the gold calligraphy on blue vellum burned into her retinas from the moment she saw it, estimated at £100,000, begging her to acquire it for the collection. But when this was all over, Christopher would be back or someone like him in his place and £100,000 would be desired for more appropriate purchases and Liesl would be back to settling invoices or strategizing to fundraise for what others felt was worthwhile. It was just that she had hoped that before the clouds parted and Garber or Christopher or the donors had time to question it, she would have the chance to do *all* of Christopher's job, not just the miserable bits. To hunt down the treasure and to raise the auction paddle and to bring Lot 37 home to rest with the other treasures. She took a last look — gold calligraphy on blue vellum — and closed the catalog.

Liesl had set the alarm and locked the door and was halfway to the subway before she realized that she had never given the woman her name. She supposed it was easy enough to figure out by looking at the library's website or the university's staff directory, but she was unnerved that Rhonda had been researching her during their conversation. She smoothed her hair against the humidity as if she were being watched at that very moment, and with a last look behind her, she walked down the steps to the subway.

II

"Now don't be upset," John said when she walked through the front door. "But I'm afraid I've got something to tell you."

"Telling me not to get upset almost assures that I will indeed get upset. You haven't gone off your medication?"

"There is no reason to. And no. Of course, no."

She walked past him, squeezing through the hallway that was narrowed, as were all their hallways, by canvases in various states of completion stacked against the walls. In the kitchen she poured herself a glass of wine and leaned against the counter to hear his news. "Is it about the commission?"

He looked back out into the hallway. When they had first moved into this house fifteen years ago, she took hold of the idea that the shabby streets could be brightened into an appropriate neighborhood for rearing a family through fertilizer and forsythias. Now, in the swell of late summer, when her garden was still in bloom and young couples walked labradoodles on the sidewalk past her front door, she could believe that the dirt under her fingernails had manifested the improved property values for the whole neighborhood. But after nearly a decade and a half here, even with friendly yellow flowers peeking up from a window box under her kitchen window, she had to concede that the interior of the house failed to match the picture of the open and uncluttered family home that she had conjured in that same imagination.

"Tell me what happened then."

"I knew I shouldn't have taken it," he said.

"It was such a terribly generous lot of money," she said. With understanding, not with regret. Something about John's face — sturdy, bearded, blue-eyed — conjured for Liesl a sense of warmth in the very bottom of her belly, a warmth like good whiskey or strings of white lights at Christmas that made disappointments devilishly hard to cling to.

Liesl had a healthy pension waiting for her, but she worried about having a cushion were something to go wrong, as John had no retirement money of his own. A couple of portrait commissions would have gone a long way in easing her concerns about finally retiring, and steady work gave John a reason to get out of bed every morning. If he kept turning them down, she would have to get him a dog, and she wasn't fond of animals.

John continued, "We don't even really need the money. And I had a bad feeling."

"You've said that about every commission you've ever received," she said and took a long drink of wine to try to stoke that warmth in her belly.

True, the job was a bit tacky. Someone John had met through a donors' function at the library wanted his new wife's perfect, unlined face preserved in oil paints and hung on his mantel.

"Indeed. But I don't believe my bad feelings manifested the demise of this particular deal," John said.

"Why not?"

"The subject of the portrait was found to be, shall we say, less than faithful to my patron." He took the glass from her hand and took a drink.

"Oh dear. How do you know? How did he know?" Liesl clasped a hand over her mouth as if she were the one who had something to be ashamed of, but John's face was twisted into a smirk.

"I believe he was an eyewitness," John said. "And he's not shy about telling me or anyone who will listen."

"No!"

"So he won't be wanting a picture of her face for his study," said John. He had finished her wine, so he moved to refill it. He wasn't supposed to drink. Not really.

But he was out of bed and smiling, and the loss of the commission really didn't seem to be his fault, so she said nothing.

"No, no more. I should get some work done," she said. She opened the refrigerator to find something she might put together for dinner.

"I've left some spaghetti warming in the oven for you," John said.

"My hero."

"You've been my real patron all these years. The least I can do is dinner."

There it was. That warmth again.

"Thank goodness for you."

"Have you had a bit of a day? Do you want to talk about it?"

"I have, and I don't."

She ate the pasta standing over the kitchen counter.

"Come on," John said. "At least sit down for a cup of coffee before you go back to your work."

Liesl shook her head and wandered down another crowded hallway to her small office. Her desk was scattered with materials for the book she was meant to be writing on her leave. Printouts about ancient landscaping practices, titles about floral crops. She pushed it all off to the side and switched on her computer.

"Mom?" She heard her daughter calling from somewhere in the house.

Hannah was about to complete her last year at the university but still treated her childhood home as a laundry and pantry, to Liesl's delight.

"Dad said you were in here working," Hannah said, poking her head into the office. The room got brighter when Hannah entered it, as though even the halogen bulbs were happy to see her. It was hard to be objective about her own child. About her sandy-blond hair that glowed like Liesl's own happy childhood. About the improbable brown eyes that kept Hannah from looking too flighty, so much more respectable and serious than blue might have been. Hannah was a whole person with bad habits and acne scars. But Liesl would be damned if she couldn't see any of that for all the light that shone off the girl.

"I'm trying to get ready for tomorrow. I feel a bit behind," Liesl said.

"It's nearly nine o'clock," Hannah said.

"Tell me about the first day of classes," Liesl asked.

"No classes," Hannah said. "I just had a meeting with my thesis advisor."

"And did you like him? Because if there is someone you would prefer to work with, I'll see what I can do. Your thesis advisor is the most important relationship you'll have during your academic career. He'll steer your research, provide you guidance on graduate schools, and his reference and introductions can really make or break your chances."

"She, not he," Hannah said.

"I wasn't assuming; I thought you told me it was a man," Liesl said.

"Right," said Hannah. "Dad told you about the commission?"

"I don't want to talk about that," Liesl said, glancing back at the computer. "It's terribly bad luck, but I'm really proud of your father for taking the job in the first place."

"So you're not mad then? Dad was worried you'd be upset with him."

"Hannah, baby," Liesl said, and she fixed her face as she said it, to look as un-angry as a person could look. "How could I possibly be annoyed with your father because some twenty-eight-year-old cheated on her septuagenarian husband?"

"I told him it was silly," Hannah said. "But he was worried."

Hannah had come and sat on the edge of the desk, the way she had been doing since she was a small child. She was as much a fixture in the room as the bookshelves.

"Now tell me about this thesis advisor. What's she like?"

"Nothing to tell yet. You tell me about this fancy new job. I'm so proud of you, Mom."

"Now you're the one being silly."

"Silly how! You've secretly been doing all of Chris's work for years."

"That's not true. The collection that Christopher has built . . ."

"If the dude had to have a stroke for you to finally get the job title you deserve, I'll take it."

Liesl shooed her daughter out of the office. "Don't ever say things like that where people can hear you."

Liesl drank a lot more wine once John wasn't there to see her pour it. She would have liked to go to bed but knew what her marriage needed was for John to go to sleep before she came up so she wouldn't have to reassure him over and over that she wasn't mad.

She heard the floorboards creaking above her. He was still awake. They didn't need this big old house, spread over three narrow stories that increasingly made her knees ache when she came down to get coffee in the morning. Hannah rarely spent the night and had no real attachment to her childhood room, which was now mostly used to

41

store canvases. John loved his attic studio and its dancing morning light, but Liesl would be happier if he rented a studio space and moved his operation there. She had once considered it romantic being married to a painter. But romance stories never detailed how much *stuff* came along with the profession. Blank canvases, abandoned canvases, completed canvases, oil paint, latex paint, paint remover, brushes, jars for brushes, scrapers, easels of every size. It was suffocating.

"I can't even list it until you get rid of all this stuff," a real estate agent had told her a couple of years ago when she had first begun to consider retirement and hoped to downsize to a smaller, easier home. The problem was that to John it wasn't *stuff*. It was evidence of his work, the output of his heart, the proof of his talent and worthiness. He wasn't suffocated by it; he was nourished by it. Liesl was awoken from her procrastination by the phone ringing.

"Hello," Liesl said to the empty office to see how it would sound. She overpronounced the *L*. She held the *O* too long. She sounded drunk.

A second ring. Liesl glanced at the display. Marie Wolfe. Christopher's wife, Marie Wolfe. Christopher's wife, Marie Wolfe, who

Liesl had not yet spoken to since his stroke. Christopher's wife, Marie Wolfe, who Liesl would not speak to for the first time after all that Chablis.

Liesl clicked the red button on the phone to reject the call and went back to her work, building a rudimentary understanding of carbon dating so she could sound halfway intelligent denying the young professor's request in the morning.

Mostly drunk and alone in one's office is not a good way to build an understanding of carbon dating. "How do you get a book in a test tube?" Liesl asked herself. There was no one listening, of course, but she was embarrassed for having even thought it.

She sent an email to Rhonda that she could come see the book the next day and that they would discuss the rest then. It was time to go to bed.

III

Seven in the morning and Liesl had a headache. Not enough food, not enough water, more wine than was wise. She'd need to be more careful. She got to the library early enough that she was the one to switch off the alarm that she'd set the night before. She walked through reading rooms and work areas and row after row of cages and stacks in the basement, flipping on light switches. She would have liked to linger longer, but she wanted to feel more prepared than she had the day before. She wrote a note for Dan, asking him to pull the Peshawar back up and to bring it into her office. She checked her email to be sure that President Garber wasn't springing another donor visit on her, and then she sat and processed invoices for recent acquisitions. The headache was nearly enough to convince her to break the rules about food and beverages near the books and risk a coffee stain on a medieval manuscript, but Liesl was ultimately a rule-follower, and throughout the morning the headache faded, even without the coffee she so craved.

The library was open. The staff had all arrived. Liesl walked out to the workroom. Dan was sitting at his desk wearing headphones plugged into the Discman and frowning. She tapped him on the shoulder and their dance — she attempting to exert authority and he rejecting it — began anew. He looked at her. He found the pause button. He pressed it. He took the headphones off and laid them neatly on the music player. Everyone in the workroom was watching.

"Good morning, Liesl," he said. "Here to

mingle with the commoners?"

"I need the Peshawar again this morning."

"The Peshawar?"

Francis with his summer tan and his slicked-back hair was seated at the desk closest to Dan's. He was pretending to read a bookseller's catalog.

"I left a note on your desk this morning," Liesl said.

"Right."

"For you to bring up the Peshawar when you got in."

"Right."

"And you haven't."

"Right."

Dan was the union representative for library workers. So if she fired him to exert some control or acquiesced to his bullying and burst into tears, there were sure to be consequences.

"Well, you're in now. So I'm hoping you can fetch the Peshawar."

"Christopher had a policy about pulling the Peshawar out for faculty," he said. "It's very fragile."

Liesl found that she had knit her hands together and was clenching them tightly. She dropped them to her sides. "We had it out just yesterday."

"For donors," he said. "It was an extraordinary circumstance, you'll admit."

"Of course it was an extraordinary circumstance," Liesl said. She immediately wished she hadn't conceded this point, even though it was an obvious one.

"President Garber himself requested it," he said.

"Well, no," Liesl said. "I did. As I am again today."

Francis looked up from his catalog. "Come on, Dan," he said. "Quit being lazy and giving Liesl a hard time. Just fetch the Peshawar if she says she needs the Peshawar. She's Christopher's proxy now."

"The white-collar man accusing the working man of laziness. What a cliché."

Liesl cut in.

"Francis didn't mean that."

"I bloody well did," Francis mumbled into the catalog.

"Francis, can you tell me of a single time Christopher pulled the Peshawar out for researchers?" Dan asked. "We had the thing photographed for a reason."

Liesl looked over at Francis, waiting for him to take her side even if it was just to prove Dan wrong. She waited and waited until the prolonged silence became uncomfortable for all parties. Help wasn't coming. Dan put his headphones back on, pushed the sleeves of his plaid shirt higher up his forearms, and looked at his computer screen.

Liesl was in an impossible position. She would look like a fool and an amateur in front of Rhonda Washington, who had been promised a visit with the Peshawar, or she would look like a fool and an amateur in front of a workroom of her staff who all knew of Christopher's policy that she was trying to violate. She needed the staff to respect her. She could handle Rhonda by email.

"The photographs are very good," Francis called as she walked away.

"Are they? I'll let her know."

"I'll get Dan to pull up the prints so she doesn't have to work at a screen." He had followed her out of the workroom.

"That's thoughtful of you."

"It's just so fragile, you know," he said.

She nodded. "I'm happy to defer to your expertise. I'm sure the photos will be fine."

They were huddled in the hallway now, out of earshot of the others.

"They're better than fine," Francis said.

"Is that what I'm meant to tell her?" Liesl asked.

"Yes. The photographs were made before that terrible binding. The mica sheets have caused the birch bark to darken."

He was probably just placating her. "It did look quite dark to me yesterday."

Francis nodded. "The photos were done before decades' worth of deterioration. She'll have a hell of an easier time."

"You'll take care of Dan then?" Liesl asked.

"As best I can," Francis said. "Within the confines of the law." He winked one of those impenetrable brown eyes at her, and for that moment she felt as though someone was on her side.

"Marie called me last night," she said to Francis.

"I'm glad. I told her about the fuss with the safe. She had the combination then?"

Liesl tried not to think of the security implications of Christopher sharing the safe's combination with anyone, even his wife.

"You told her?" she said. "You didn't tell me you were speaking with her."

"Keeping in touch. Seems right."

"I guess."

"So did she find it then? The combination?"

"Will you excuse me?" She left him without answering. When she returned to the office, she should have called Marie immediately, but her mind went to Rhonda instead. She had to email to call off the meeting or rearrange the terms of the meeting or somehow gently explain that the woman would have to do her work from photographs, yet that was easier than the long-overdue call to the wife at the sickbed.

The Plantin, she thought, could wait a few more minutes while she thought of the right thing to say. But the wife at the sickbed had other plans.

"Marie's here to see you," Dan said from the doorway of her office when she'd scarcely hit Send on her email to Rhonda.

"Thanks, Dan." Liesl put her palms on her desktop to steady herself. "I'll be right there."

"No hard feelings?"

"Should there be?"

"No."

"Well then."

"Christopher was so particular."

"And you owe him respect. But I'm owed it too."

"So I should have ignored his policy?"

"So you should have come to see me if there was a question about policy. Instead of defying instructions with no comment at all."

She went to meet Marie in the lobby and,

unable to find words for comfort, words for apology, she greeted her with a hug. Then, with an arm around her, Liesl guided Marie into the office. She was surprised that Marie hadn't just come to the back the way she would almost daily when Christopher was working. Her white hair looked whiter. Her small frame looked smaller. Liesl supposed that she wouldn't have come on back either, being in Marie's place.

"I called you yesterday," Marie said.

Liesl nodded. "I know. I'm sorry. It was an overwhelming day. Christopher's shoes . . ."

"Don't apologize. I should apologize." Marie was looking around the familiar room. "You didn't have what you needed to be successful."

Liesl looked back at the tiny woman, wanted to hug her again.

"It's hardly your fault, Marie."

"I'm sorry all the same. If this created an embarrassment for you," Marie said.

"You've had much more important matters to worry about," Liesl said. "Tell me, how is he?"

"The same," Marie said.

Liesl closed the door to the office. She thought the stale smell that bothered her so was probably giving Marie comfort. She was sorry now that she had reshelved Christopher's volumes so quickly. Marie might have liked to know what he was working on, what he was reading.

"You do have the combination then?"

"Shall we try it right away?" Marie said.

"We can sit a bit if you like."

"I should get back to the hospital."

"I hate that I dragged you all the way down here."

"You did no such thing. I came myself. I needed a bit of a break."

"You could stay, and we could have lunch?"

"He might wake up."

The way she said it, Liesl understood for the first time the severity. The truth.

That he would probably never wake up.

"Well," Liesl said. "Let's get you back to him then."

Liesl crouched on the floor by the safe, ready to enter the combination as Marie read it to her. Marie reached into her handbag — brown, sensible — and retrieved a small datebook. "Are you ready?" she asked.

"Whenever you are."

Liesl spun the dial right, then left, then right again, and when she got to the last digit, the safe gave an almost imperceptible click that indicated the right combination had been entered. Liesl closed her eyes with relief. She stood and jotted the numbers down on a pad before she could forget them. She'd have to change the combination. Marie was hardly a risk, but policy was policy, and having the numbers out there wasn't secure. She lifted the handle with her foot and crouched back down to the safe.

"It's empty. Marie. Marie, the safe is empty," Liesl said.

FOURTEEN YEARS EARLIER

Stumbling over a two-inch heel, Miriam fell into the messy kitchen with much less grace than she had intended.

"Oh no. Is that what you're going to wear?" Vivek asked, looking up at her.

"Yes. No. Why? What's the matter with it?" Miriam smoothed her gray blazer, her only blazer.

"I'm joking. Oh my gosh, I promise I'm joking. You look great. Professional. Beautiful."

"Please don't make jokes like that, I'm nervous enough."

He took her face between his hands and gave her a kiss. "There isn't anything to be nervous about. I've told Liesl all about you, and you met Christopher at the interview. They'll love you."

"They're all so smart."

"They're kind. If I ever do get this PhD, it should be Liesl's name on it, not mine.

Every time I go in there, she's dug out a new thing for me to read that I otherwise never would have heard of."

"That's what I mean; they're so smart. Am I supposed to be able to do that?"

"Miriam. They've all been there for a million years. Once you're there for a million years you'll be able to do that, but no one expects it on the first day."

"Christopher seemed a bit scary in the interview. I'll bet he expects it."

Vivek handed her a piece of toast. "He seems pretty intense, yeah. But in a good way. A bunch of the undergrads in my seminar section think he's hot. And there are rumors he's a bit of a tomcat."

Crumbs rained down on Miriam's blazer as she chewed her toast. "You know, I was so petrified during my interview that I don't even remember what he looks like. If you paid me money right now, I couldn't describe him. In my memory, he's a terrifying blob wearing a very nice suit."

"All the better that you don't remember him as handsome. The last thing I need is you running off with Indiana Gutenberg."

Miriam turned her head to hide her blush, her loose curls brushing against the collar of the big gray blazer. "I'm not the type that type goes for. Does he really have a reputation?" She buttoned the blazer and then unbuttoned it. Vivek walked up to her, wrapped his arms all the way around her, and whispered in her ear.

"You're totally the type who would have gone in for an affair with a professor, aren't you?"

Miriam swatted him away and went back to fussing over her clothes. Sighing at the uselessness of trying to look attractive, she only hoped she wouldn't look embarrassing. She took a last bite of toast and a deep breath as she turned to leave.

"You really think they're going to like me?"

"They're going to love you. How could they not?"

4

Liesl gathered them in the large reading room for a cross-examination — everyone who had seen or touched the Plantin Bible since it had been in the library's possession. The room was soundproof when the doors were closed, well suited for events when the donors overdid it with the Chablis. And perfect for an interrogation.

The campus buildings were scattered across a parcel of land in Toronto, just north of downtown on the dividing line between a neighborhood where the Korean noodle shops were celebrating their fiftieth year in business and where the owners of Victorian mansions wrote strongly worded letters to the city council to ensure that nothing so tacky as a condominium could be built in their neighborhood. The coffee shops had literary names where baristas with unironic mustaches shared their artistic ambitions as they made perfect pour-over coffee. Until about ten years ago, the students had their pick of spacious flats above the noodle shops, but all at once the streets had come to be lined with shiny Subarus instead of rusted Hondas. Days, young mothers pushed their strollers down well-swept sidewalks. Nights, the students vomited four-dollar dim sum into alleyways. And it was the university, the bricks and the books and the brilliance, that tied those two Torontos together.

Francis sat by the door across the room from Maximilian Hubbard, the head of religious acquisitions, and Miriam Peters, the head of the modern manuscripts division. Light streamed across their faces through the window, the city peeking in. The library stacks rose up above the room in an octagon over six stories, a cathedral of dark volumes barely illuminated by yellow lights lining the walls. It gave the space the feeling of a panopticon, but it was the people in the room who were being watched by the silent books.

Dan might emerge on one of the catwalks along the walls to retrieve a volume, but it was unlikely. These books had been chosen for their aesthetic beauty, to lend the space a sense of grandeur. They were rarely read.

The real collections were on book trucks in the small reading room or in the layers of basements beneath the building. Liesl pressed her lips together as she prepared to address the group.

"The Plantin Polyglot Bible," she said. "The volumes are not in the safe as they should be. The book is missing."

"Where is it?" Francis asked.

"Can I look myself?" Max said.

"Oh dear," Miriam said.

"My understanding is that each of you saw the Plantin after it arrived here."

"What are you accusing us of?" Max asked.

"Of seeing the Plantin after it arrived here. Of being able to help find where it was mislaid."

Max was a small man who got his thinning hair cut every Friday afternoon, and he had never come to work without his pressed white shirt buttoned to the chin. At a library where not much interesting ever happened, there was gossip any time Max opted for a sweater vest instead of a sport coat. Liesl tried to sound open-minded when leveling the question at Max, but there was no softening him; he was all angles.

"She's right that we all saw it, and she's

right that we might be able to help," Miriam said.

Miriam had her arms crossed and her legs crossed and her voice was just above a whisper. She looked in Liesl's eyes while the men, who had both risen from their chairs, were pacing around the room. As the only two women at the library, Liesl and Miriam had often found themselves bound together, and Liesl appreciated her support now. She just wished that support wasn't quite so hushed.

"You managed shipping and receiving, didn't you, Miriam?" Liesl asked.

"Well, yes," she said. "But only because Christopher asked me to."

"Why would he have asked you?" Francis asked. Against the September heat he'd left the top three buttons of his shirt open, which was really too many buttons. With his hands on his hips, the dark fabric stretched and showed quite a lot of chest.

"Liesl was away, I guess?" Miriam said. "I handle all the shipping for my own division, so I know the paperwork."

"So you just did the paperwork?" Francis said.

"That's enough, Francis. No one has asked you to conduct an interrogation," Liesl said.

Francis was still standing and Miriam was still sitting, and Liesl felt like she was losing control of the situation. She turned the attention off Miriam.

"When did you see it, Francis? Had it been placed in the safe yet?"

"The Plantin isn't a set of house keys," Max muttered. "You don't just mislay a priceless religious artifact."

"I'm trying to think of the simplest solutions first, Max."

"No, I mean *you* shouldn't have mislaid it."

"It was meant to be in the safe before I ever arrived." He wasn't looking at her; he was running a thumb over the razor's-edge crease ironed into his trousers. "I would like to take a systematic approach and understand where the book went in the building after it arrived. I'd like your help doing so."

"Well," Max said. "I'd like a leader who shows some regard for the sanctity of that book and the reputation of this library."

Liesl looked to Francis. Over the years they had joked about Max's self-importance, his irrationality. She waited for Francis to jump to her defense, to acknowledge that Max was being irrational now. He didn't.

"You always handle shipping," Max said.

"For an acquisition this significant, our most significant in maybe a decade? You couldn't have come back for one day to handle shipping?"

"You saw it after it arrived?" Her voice was flat as she said it.

"Christopher is a brilliant man. He raised hundreds of thousands of dollars for the thing. You couldn't have handled the shipping?"

She ignored the question, pushed the implication that she was good for FedEx paperwork and little else into storage, to be examined later.

"I need to know," she said, "what happened after it arrived here."

"We all have our responsibilities here. You failed at yours," Max said.

"There are hundreds of thousands of volumes here," Francis said. "If it was shelved in error somehow, the volumes separated, mixed in with the general collection . . ."

"Then we will find it, in time," Liesl said.

"At what cost to our reputation?" Max asked, so agitated that he ran the risk of a wrinkle in his button-down.

The room fell back into silence. Liesl thought of the volumes that had been scattered around Christopher's office, thought if the Plantin volumes could have been among them, but she didn't say anything. From the other side of the door she could hear the rumble of book trucks, the grind of the pencil sharpener, bursts of footsteps as they crossed from carpet to tile. She didn't have instructions or actions or a way forward. She'd hoped one of them might have volunteered an idea, might have been good for more than panic. But no. She thanked them and ended the meeting with instructions to prepare for the next day's reception for new university faculty and to keep their eyes peeled for the Plantin. Dan and his combat boots were waiting for Liesl at the door to the reading room.

"You had a call," he said.

"You could have just left it at my desk." He followed her as she walked to her office.

"It was a Rhonda Washington." Dan said. "She said she called your office line first before calling the main line." Liesl nodded, her face neutral. She took the message slip from Dan. "She said it was important to speak with you and wanted to make sure you got the message. Everything all right at the landowner's meeting?"

"Everything's great."

"Well I'm back to the fields then."

II

They didn't find the Plantin that first day. Eventually Liesl had to go home. She had emailed President Garber early in the day, asking him to call her. Her muscles were exhausted from bracing for the impact of his reply all day. He never called. When she got home, she threw her purse on the floor by the front door, inadvertently hitting a stack of canvases with it. She stood, sweating from the walk in the mid-September heat that didn't show any sign of waning, not moving to see if she had done any damage.

"The woman warrior," John called from the kitchen. He sounded good. She should have been relieved. "Get you a drink?"

"Mind if we eat out tonight?" She was all of a sudden feeling claustrophobic just being indoors. "You haven't cooked, have you?"

"Nothing that won't keep," he said. His beard, his blue eyes, and all the rest of him appeared in the hallway to greet her.

"Noodles then?" she said.

"It's a bit hot for noodles, but if that's what you want." If he noticed her purse resting against his canvases, he didn't flinch.

"It's what I want," she said.

"You all right? You seem tense. Even for

someone with a tense new job," John said, jogging to catch up with her after he'd paused to lock their front door.

"Fine. Fine, fine," Liesl said.

"No one fine has ever answered the question that way," he said as they walked. "You don't have to tell me, but you know I have to ask."

"We've had an incident," said Liesl. "I'm a bit over my head."

Their favorite noodle shop was on the corner of their street. They hadn't closed their patio yet for the season, so Liesl sat at an outdoor table.

"The great outdoors," John said. "These backless stools are for a younger man." He might have been asking for a move to a seat better suited to his large and aging frame, but Liesl pretended not to notice, to read it as an observation and not an ask so she could mark a win in her column for the day.

"We've lost the Plantin Bible."

"The book that Christopher was fundraising for while you were away? What do you mean you lost it? It's hardly a set of house keys, is it?"

"Why does everyone immediately go to that metaphor? It's a multivolume set, not just a book."

"Was it stolen then? Imagine walking

around with half a million dollars in your backpack. Good God, Liesl, I'm so sorry."

The idea of theft had hardly crossed her mind, and now that it had, she didn't like it in there. She pulled a strand of gray hair toward her lips and chewed on it while she waited for John to settle on his stool.

"No," she said, pushing the hair away from her mouth. "It wasn't stolen. We've misplaced it somehow."

"Come on, my girl. Imagine misplacing half a million dollars." He signaled to the server.

"Christopher didn't put it in the safe, and I accidentally had it shelved in an effort to tidy up. I think."

"Have you not called the police then?"

"It wasn't stolen," she said, and she believed that. Hardly anyone had access to the thing. Certainly no one who would want to steal it. "It couldn't have been."

They ordered their usual spicy garlic ramen bowls and sat in silence while the server fussed over their table, pouring water, arranging napkins, chopsticks, chili sauce. "I'll take a pint of lager too," Liesl said.

"You have to call the police, darling."

She waited to answer while her lager arrived. "You don't understand this," she said, once the server had gone.

"Explain then," he said. "The gist I'm getting is that you're failing to report the loss of something more valuable than our house."

Liesl shook her head. Arguing with John would require drawing a detailed picture of the intricacies of academic reputation management. She didn't have the energy for the art project. "I can fix this myself."

"And if you can't?"

"I can."

John reached over and cleared a small bit of foam that was clinging to Liesl's upper lip.

"That library," he said. "That collection. It's your responsibility now."

"Exactly. A responsibility that no one thinks I'm capable of as it is."

"You can't think this is your fault."

"It's my responsibility." She put her hand over her face, skimming where he had just touched her lip.

"You never even saw the thing," he said.

"I might have," she said. "If I had paid more attention to what was on Christopher's desk."

"You don't know that it was ever there."

"I don't want to talk about this anymore."

Liesl saw something cross John's face that suggested he did still want to talk about it, and she knew that he could build a blue period out of scraps of conversation. Their daughter, Hannah, called it scrapyarding. She said it mostly jokingly, but it was true that sometimes John couldn't see the whole car, only the rusted-out hubcaps and a bent antenna. And those things could convince him that there was no driving forward. Liesl was ready to assuage him, to play down the seriousness, if he looked to be heading in that direction, but he ended it first, the discussion about the police.

"Drink your beer then," said John, and their noodles arrived, and that was that.

III

Liesl walked to work in the early-morning hours. She'd abandoned the blow-dryer after that first day, letting her gray hair go wiry in exchange for the gift of an extra thirty minutes to herself before sunrise. It was easy to forget how quickly the summers ended — how quickly the dawn moved later and later and later — when one didn't spend a lot of time outside this early in the day. The noodle shop where they had eaten dinner the night before was darkened, and through its windows she could just make out the outlines of chairs turned upside down and stacked on tables. The Starbucks across the street had opened, and she could hear its John Mayer soundtrack leaking onto the street as the door swung open and closed, but the coffee shop she preferred, the one with the blue awning and the small ginger cookies, would not be open for another hour. There was another noodle shop and another and then a pharmacy. Closed, closed, closed. She felt she had more privacy here than even in her bedroom. The library was less than thirty minutes away on foot. Often she took the subway, and after she did, she always beat herself up a little. For forgoing this little bit of exercise on top of everything else.

Once inside the library building, she ignored the administrative tasks that beckoned from the office. Invoices sat unpaid, the faculty reception details remained unconfirmed. The basements drew her downstairs. The collections that were shelved in the upper stacks, the ones that were so often photographed by building visitors, were beautiful, true. But Liesl had always loved the basements. There was no intellectual arrangement of materials here; the books were shelved by size so that shelf space could be used to its maximum capacity and so the fragile old volumes could act as supports to their neighbors. The result was that Darwin might sit next to Shakespeare, and in Liesl's imagination they might convene and brew new ideas that would be impossible under the limits of the Library of Congress classification system. Each stack sat on a roller so it could be pushed flush with its neighbor, leaving the books alone to their secrets once a visitor pushed them aside to view the next bookshelf and then the next. Like everything else in the basements, the rollers were for space. They could fit twice as many stacks if they stored them right against each other, but in truth, the tall, heavy bookshelves on their flimsy rollers had always turned Liesl's stomach. It was inevitable, wasn't it, that one of these shelves would one day tip over onto a person?

The public, the donors, even university faculty — they weren't allowed down into these basements. They would see the books all scrunched together, they would see the Darwin right next to the Shakespeare, and they wouldn't understand. The basements were only for the ones who knew. From inside each book popped a tiny flag on acid-free card stock where someone had typed each book's call number. No title, nothing about the book itself. Just a number. Of course, there were computers and databases now, all sorts of things to tie it together, but it was all dependent on keeping the right little flag inside the right big book and putting the book in the exact right place next to its similarly sized neighbors. It seemed inevitable that something would go wrong eventually. It seemed impossible that nothing had gone seriously wrong up until that point. Someone sticks the wrong flag into the wrong book, or someone breaks up a six-volume set or slides a book next to the wrong neighbor, and it might be years before someone realized the mistake. They might never realize.

Liesl's head hurt again. The old headaches. She thought she should try to drink more water. She thought she should try to drink less lager. She walked through the fire door from one section of the basement to another, flipping the light switches as she went. There were four such fireproof chambers on this floor and two other levels of basement below her. There were books in the collection that she had never seen before, and she had always loved that, loved that she might discover something entirely new that no one had touched in one hundred years in these stacks. Now she was terrified by it. There were books in these stacks that hadn't been touched in one hundred years. How could they ever expect to find the Plantin volumes among all this? She pulled the book closest to her hand out of the stacks. A 1683 treatise by a religious dissenter from the library of an Italian priest. Not the Plantin. She pulled out its nearest neighbor. A 2018 book by a Polish comic artist working out of Montreal. Not the Plantin. Next to it, an 1832 Hebrew dictionary. Not the Plantin.

Liesl looked at her watch. Checking those three books had taken forty-five seconds. She tried to do the math, but there were so many variables. Some books, the modern ones especially, would be easy to rule out on sight. Others were shelved in boxes and would need to be totally unboxed before they could be ruled out. That could add almost a full minute per book. They might find one volume or two or three but not the others. That had to be considered when thinking about time, but this way, she thought, it wasn't impossible. What was impossible was the idea that they would find the book before the donors found out they'd lost it.

She kept pulling and reshelving books. It became meditative. She could have been there five minutes, she could have been there an hour; she became lost in it. All she knew was that the library wasn't yet open. The basement lights always gave a small flicker when the sign by the front door was turned on. She had been down here enough times to know that. And the lights hadn't yet flickered. Which is why she was surprised, knowing that the library was not yet open, to realize that she wasn't alone in the basement. She stopped pulling books. She stopped breathing.

It was the chain that gave it away. The sound came from behind the fire door, and if the culprit had only been pulling books, Liesl never would have heard it. But the chain. The monks who made illuminated manuscripts used to attach chains to the spines to keep them from getting stolen, and there were two in the library's collection that still had their chains attached. She heard the heavy chain against the metal shelf. There was no event planned that required one of those manuscripts, and a researcher request to view one would have had to be cleared by the library director. By Liesl. There was no reason for anyone to be touching that chain on that morning.

"Who is it? Who's there?" she called as she burst through the fire door.

"Liesl? Is that you?"

"What's going on, Max? It's barely seven

thirty. Why do you have that manuscript out?"

Liesl waited for him to answer, wondering if the hair curling near her ears from the humidity of the morning or the skin creasing in the corner of her eyes from the severity of her headache was undermining her authority. He'd had the manuscript laid open on a book truck, but he closed it, spine creaking, chain rattling, before he replied.

"I am responsible for religious collections here, am I not?" He stood impossibly straight. His attire impossibly smooth. His neck, what she could see of it, was impossibly free from sweat.

Liesl badly wanted some coffee and water. She should have stopped at that Starbucks. "It's a tense time," she said. "I'd be irresponsible if I didn't have questions."

"Yes. That's what would make you irresponsible."

"You haven't answered my question. What are you doing with that book?"

She glanced at her watch. The coffee shop in the adjoining building would be open in fifteen minutes. "What, do you think I was going to steal it?" he said. "I don't like being accused of things. I won't let myself be accused of things."

"That is not what I asked. I wasn't making accusations." She would splurge for an Americano, not just a regular coffee.

"The alarm was off," Max said. "The lights were on. Do you think I didn't know someone else was down here? Do you think everyone pays so little attention?"

"So little attention?"

"The rest of us are paying attention, Liesl. I'm paying attention. You're here to what, protect our reputation while we wait for Christopher to return? It took you a single day to fail at that."

If his shirt collar hadn't been the perfect size, his Adam's apple would have strained against the top button. But Max would never have allowed for such a thing.

Liesl turned to leave.

"Christopher would have wanted me. If he had to be away, if he was going to be ill, I'm the one who is best able to stand in for him. He knew that. I know he did. And you know it."

She kept her back turned, not wanting to give him the satisfaction of seeing her face. She could not be certain about the validity of Max's claim that he was best-equipped to stand in as interim director. But as for Christopher's preference for Max as his proxy over Liesl? They both knew that was true.

"Don't think I don't know about the Peshawar either. Dan told me you were about to let just anyone work with it."

"A respected faculty member."

"So respected that she's never been in here. We've never heard of her. Don't you care at all about these collections?"

"I've worked here longer than you have, Max."

"It's hardly about tenure, is it? I know these books in my bones. The way Christopher does. It's my calling. The library isn't just somewhere I've worked a long time."

"I didn't volunteer for this."

"No, I suppose you didn't. But you didn't say no either. You didn't think of what Christopher would want. What the library would need."

Liesl shook her head.

"Christopher will be back and well soon, I'm sure," she said. "Until then, we have to find a way to work together."

"Are you asking me to put on appearances?" Max said. "Well, I won't. You've lost a piece of religious history. Of world history. I won't put on appearances that everything is fine until that is resolved. Nor should anyone else around here."

She turned back around to face him, finally. "I don't understand, Max," she said.

"The Plantin never made it into the safe. Christopher didn't put it into the safe. Why are you so insistent that I'm to blame?"

"Why not?"

"You need a more compelling reason than that."

"Because you are the only one who doesn't seem certain that it wasn't their fault. I can see it in your eyes, the doubt."

"That's your imagination, I'm afraid."

"Are you down here, going through book by book, because you think it was on Christopher's desk and was mis-shelved? Is that my imagination?"

"Please make sure you sign out that manuscript if you're to use it," Liesl said. "Or put it right back."

She finally walked out the door, finally went to the elevator, finally got into the office, finally closed the door, and finally let herself cry, but only a little. She looked around the office and tried to imagine where the books had been before she'd had them removed. Three on the desk? Four? A stack on the filing cabinet. The Plantin was bound in the eighteenth century, in a red morocco binding. She checked her copy of the invoice. Six volumes. Could she have missed that? Could Dan? She had heard the binding was beautiful. The deep-red goatskin, the gilt edges. Could she have missed that? She walked back to the door of the office and stood facing the room as she had when she first entered on Monday. No, she didn't think she had missed anything. She was almost certain now. The Plantin hadn't been taken out of the office and mislaid. It had never been there in the first place.

5

I

The students interfered greatly with Liesl's enjoyment of the campus. The breeze rustling the old oaks, the September crispness nudging out the August humidity. It was a perfect time in a perfect place to remove one's shoes and read Jane Austen, but, Liesl thought, how could one go barefoot and not risk having one's toes crushed beneath all these undergraduates? There were students coming from every direction, heading toward the large lecture hall that was attached to the administration building. Liesl was a river rock, and they were the water that rushed around her.

There were serious types, wearing the leather bombers that branded them as engineering students, despite the warm weather. There were flighty types, in cutoff shorts and flip-flops, nothing in their backpacks or their heads. And the bicycles.

Screaming by with no regard for traffic laws or personal safety. As she waited for a pack of them to pass, Liesl tried to see if Garber was among them, tried to make out the recognizable shape of his calves, but the cyclists all passed her far too quickly.

She hoped she might run into Hannah on this walk, or that she might see the back of her daughter's blond head from afar and glimpse what her student life was like, but that was improbable. This group, heading into the giant lecture hall in their shower shoes or showy bombers, was almost certainly in their first year. She stepped aside to let the traffic flow uninterrupted and then stood off on the grass and watched for a moment so she wouldn't be too early for her meeting with President Garber. It was terrifying to finally be telling him about the Plantin. It was a relief to finally be telling him about the Plantin. She walked into the administration building.

Outside his office, Liesl was greeted by his secretary, offered coffee and a newspaper, and asked to wait. She declined the coffee because she didn't want to have foul breath, and she declined the newspaper because she was past the age where she could read newsprint without getting a headache. Her empty hands gave her plenty of time to check her watch. President Garber was late. The secretary made calls and clattered at her keyboard, typing emails or making herself look busy. Liesl did not ask how much longer it would be, but she wondered in silence how much longer he would make her wait. The secretary said nothing. It had been nearly an hour. The secretary had spent the last several minutes on the phone.

"Dr. Weiss?" she said. "I'm terribly sorry to interrupt." Liesl sat with her back straight and her empty hands in her lap.

"Mrs. Weiss. Not doctor."

"Mrs. Weiss, that was President Garber. On the phone."

"I thought he was just in his office, running late?"

"Did I say that?" the secretary said. "I'm sorry if you got that impression. He hasn't been in the office yet today."

"And he won't be making our meeting?" Liesl asked.

"Well, no," she said. "He sends sincere apologies. He said that the cancellation could not have been avoided. He's training for an Ironman, as I'm sure you know, and he has a calf strain that needed to be seen to immediately."

"Is it you that I reschedule with?" Liesl

asked. "It's terribly important that I see him as soon as possible."

"There is an opening next Thursday between his sports massage and the Icelandic ambassador. Could you come next Thursday morning?"

"You have to find something sooner than that."

"President Garber is extremely busy."

II

Liesl banged at her keyboard when she got back to her office. *Extremely important,* she wrote, *that we meet right away.*

She wiped an anxious bead of sweat from her hairline, looked around the empty shelves in Christopher's office, looked at the picture of the Plantin's brilliant-red binding in the auction catalog open in front of her. She typed the word *stolen,* then deleted it. Typed *stolen* again.

"How are you getting on then?" Francis poked his head into the office. "Did Garber melt into the floor when you told him?"

She deleted the word *stolen* again, hit Send on the email, and stood up.

"Are we prepared, Francis?" she said. "Did Dan pull all the titles on the list?"

"Nothing else is missing, if that's what you're asking."

"It's not. I'd like this event to go well."

Francis fiddled with his open shirt collar and looked bored. Despite being in the research business, Christopher had demonstrated a disdain for early-career researchers that many of the others on staff had inherited. The derision for the annual new-faculty reception was a symptom. Christopher and the lot had little use for the pretenure crowd. The university's administration loved the library building, though — the soaring ceilings, the sense of seriousness conferred on the event by all those books.

Francis waved his hand as he led her into the reading room. "It's a few new faculty members, not the pope."

"Exactly right."

He looked at her, waiting for an explanation. She opened a first-edition *Alice in Wonderland* to look at the frontispiece. "We're here to serve the faculty. I'd like to impress them."

"Christopher never gave this event much bother."

"Bully for him."

She walked out of the reading room, and Francis followed her. "What about Garber then?"

"I didn't see Garber. He had something

extremely urgent come up."

In the workroom, Miriam was the only one seated at her desk. She was wrapped in a big burgundy cardigan that Liesl could swear used to hang on a hook in Christopher's office. Her monitor had gone to sleep, black from having been left unattended. She sat, her hands poised over her keyboard as if about to type. Not noticing there was nothing there.

Miriam had been an odd duck since she came to them at the library nearly fifteen years ago, teenager-skinny with an early-bird-special fashion sense. In the last couple of years her husband, Vivek, had been doing a postdoc in London, and solitude could make a person loopy, but Liesl didn't think it fair to blame this strangeness on Vivek's absence. Miriam had made evasive maneuvers against Liesl's attempts at friendship and took weeks to even work her way up to a blushing "good morning" until Liesl cornered her in the basement one day, where she sat cross-legged on the dusty floor, inventorying a delivery of manuscript materials from a prominent Italian academic and author.

"I want to have dinner," Liesl had said. "You and Vivek and John and I should have dinner."

"Oh. Why?" When Liesl thought back to that afternoon, she had a perfect memory of Miriam's knit eyebrows creating a pattern of lines on her forehead that Liesl had read to understand that Miriam thought the dinner was some sort of punishment. Liesl had not allowed herself to be dissuaded.

"To eat the food we all need to keep ourselves alive, for one thing." She smiled when she said it, tried to make it clear that was a joke.

"But all together?"

"All together." Liesl kept the smile fixed on her face, hoping that social norms, if nothing else, would force Miriam to reciprocate.

"Okay. Thank you."

"I wanted to welcome you. Properly, to the library."

"Christopher already has."

"Christopher has? Welcomed you?" Liesl stepped back a second and was about to ask the meaning, but Miriam jumped to her feet and dusted off her trousers, making it clear she was looking to leave. Liesl stepped to the right to block her before she could go. "Saturday then?"

Miriam dropped her eyes to the floor, clutched her clipboard to her chest, flushed a spectacular crimson, and near-whispered her assent. "Saturday then," she said, as though Liesl had suggested that the four-some go drown kittens together. Surprised at the resistance to a simple meal, Liesl put a hand on Miriam's shoulder. She glanced behind her to make sure that no one else had come down to the basement who would be able to hear them. "I'll stay down here and help you with this inventory. This shipment will take ages to document if you're doing it yourself. I'd like to help you." She took the clipboard from Miriam. "Get into the habit of asking me for help. I'm never going to say no."

"It's all right, really. I'm halfway done."

Liesl didn't answer, but she didn't return the clipboard either. Refusing to be put off, she took the pencil that Miriam had tucked into the top of the board and crouched down beside the skid of file boxes.

"It's not always like that, you know," Miriam said. She didn't crouch down next to Liesl, not yet, but she had uncrossed her arms and her forehead was less severe. In remembering, Liesl remembered the forehead. When the crosshatch on the forehead faded, she knew she'd made progress. "When there's only a couple of women." Miriam stopped and chewed on her upper lip and thought about how to phrase the next part. "Someone told me once that you shouldn't trust them, the women you work with."

The statement was so odd that Liesl didn't question it. But she had disproved it by sitting there on the floor with Miriam and helping to inventory the Italian's papers in half the time it would have taken Miriam herself.

Miriam never got less odd, but she became a fraction less closed off over the years, thanks in part to Vivek, who insisted on accepting Liesl's invitations and who brought out a humor in his wife that was often absent when he wasn't at hand. This Miriam, though, poised in front of a dark computer, was so much like the Miriam in the basement all those years ago, clutching her clipboard and refusing to come to dinner.

"Does Miriam seem all right to you?" Liesl asked Francis.

"Garber still doesn't know?" Francis turned his back to Miriam. Liesl knit her hands. She wasn't holding a book, but she wanted to be. She wanted something to grasp, something to hold her steady.

"I don't think we can wait any longer," she said.

"Wait for what? Garber? I agree."

"Wait to involve the police." Liesl wondered who at the Toronto Police Service to even call. It wasn't as though she could dial 911 to report a missing book.

"Are you out of your bloody mind?" Francis took her shoulder and sat her down at his own desk. "You'd go to the police before Garber?"

"I've been trying to go to Garber, but too much time is passing."

"The thing has been misplaced."

"And if it hasn't?" she asked. She thumbed through the papers on his desk. An expense report from an annual conference in Boston that he should have filed a month ago. They had first met at that very conference years ago, Liesl and Francis had, and they'd reencountered each other there every year, getting acquainted over too many post-lecture whiskeys, ages before Francis had come to work at the library.

"Liesl."

"Well," she said. "We have to consider the possibility."

"You can consider whatever you like. But if you involve the police before the university president? That'll be the end of you."

"For doing my job?"

"Your job? Your job is to manage this library. The people and the collection."

Francis's voice had a slight rise to it that she didn't want on display for the rest of the staff.

Liesl glanced again at Miriam, then grabbed the expense report off the desk and pulled Francis back toward her office.

"Reporting a theft is part of that responsibility," she said as they walked.

"You think you'll be reporting to the police?" He put his palm on her doorjamb and shook his head. "What you're really doing is reporting to the donors. There's no way to keep it quiet once you start with police sniffing around."

"Why are the donors everyone's primary concern?"

"Don't be daft." She looked for humor in his familiar brown eyes but saw only censure.

"I'll remind you that you're speaking to a colleague." She went to her desk, waiting for him to follow. She wanted to be out of the hallway, away from other ears. "Not a friend from the pub."

"Apologies."

"Obviously I understand the importance of the donors," Liesl said. "But not at the expense of everything else."

"The donors enable everything else. I'm begging you not to go ahead with this."

"What if I tell Garber and he asks why I haven't gone to the police yet?"

"That won't happen," Francis said. "It's all a moot point anyway because we'll find the volumes before it comes to it."

"Because we've had such good luck up until this point?" She threw the expense report on her desk, onto a pile of other things that needed her overstretched attention.

"It'll start now," Francis said. The anxiety of the day had him running his hands over his slicked-back hair so often that he'd loosened whatever pomade kept it in place and it was beginning to flop boyishly onto his face.

"You lose half a million dollars, you go to the police. How is this even a question?"

"Liesl," Francis said, sitting in one of the chairs in front of her desk. "You have to listen to me. You know I'm on your side here. Just wait to talk to Garber."

"Why does it matter to you so much?"

Her instinct was to go over and smooth the hair back out of his face, but of course she was trying to emulate Christopher, and Christopher would never do such a thing.

"I'm trying to protect you," Francis said.

"What protection do I need in all this?" Liesl stayed standing, to try to retain some power, but her face went saggy.

"Your reputation needs plenty. Or it will if people find out we lost the Plantin on your watch."

"That seems inevitable now," she said.

"It doesn't have to be. Wait for Garber."

"What does that even accomplish? He calls the police and not me? What's the difference?"

"Well," Francis said. "He can give us the resources to search properly."

"I don't believe it was mislaid." She shook her head while she said it, but she had turned her back to him so he wouldn't see how undirected she looked, how firmly she was biting the inside of her cheek to stay in control.

"And I don't believe it was stolen. Wait for Garber."

"One more day."

"It's the right choice, Liesl." He had risen from his seat and was standing behind her. She still didn't turn, but he put a hand on her shoulder, and it was a comfort.

"If I can't get through to him tomorrow," she said, with more resolve. "I'm going to the police."

III

That evening, John was standing at the front door to greet her. Their front walk was visible from their kitchen, and she'd lingered there, crouching by her chrysanthemums, picking yellow leaves off sunny centers, the tips of her shoes lodged in the soil. John, who was usually still in his studio at this time of day, must have been watching her from the kitchen window, might have waved at her even as he stood over the sink and poured a glass of water or rinsed brushes and waited for his wife to run into the house and greet him.

They'd planted those chrysanthemums together, an idea of Liesl's to extend the feeling of summer with a fall bloom. She usually smiled when she saw those flowers and thought of that hot afternoon when, after hours of work in the garden, she'd gone inside to find a streak of dirt across her left cheek, and John had confessed it had been there all day, but he'd found it so fetching that he hadn't wanted to tell her for fear she'd wipe it off.

Liesl had tried Garber's direct line again as she walked home; she had the crisp tones of his outgoing voicemail message memorized and was reciting it to herself over the flowers when John opened the front door and called out to her.

"Wine?" John said. "I have a Riesling chilling."

Liesl pulled her hand back from the flower petals.

"I'm not sure I should."

"Oh? Are you well?" He walked out in his stocking feet to join her on the front walk, his big frame casting a John-shaped shadow over Liesl and the chrysanthemums in the slanting late-afternoon light.

"Heavy day at work."

"All the more reason for the Riesling," John said, wrapping an arm around her shoulder and leading her into the house.

"The misplaced Plantin," Liesl said, throwing down her purse where she stood. "I'm beginning to think it was stolen. I'm going to have to call the police in tomorrow."

"The police? Lord. Is that what the administration recommended?"

"It's the right thing to do," she said. "Rather than bury my head in the sand."

Liesl followed John into the cool kitchen and didn't protest again as he poured her that glass of Riesling. She had wanted to keep her head clear, but he seemed to be doing so well that she didn't want to disrupt the equilibrium by being argumentative, by disrupting the picture he'd painted of the two of them, sharing slow drinks and gossip as night fell outside their kitchen window.

"Shouldn't it be up to administration when to involve the police, darling?"

John wasn't tangled enough in the details of the case to recognize the flicker across Liesl's face when he asked her that question, but her desire to avoid argument evaporated immediately.

"Not you too. They don't know or care about the collection. I do."

"I know it," John said. "But they know and care plenty about the university's reputation."

She couldn't believe what she was hearing. "A reputation that will be damaged if it gets out that we failed to alert police to a major theft."

"It's not your call to make, my dear."

"Have your decades spent in the workforce convinced you of that?"

She regretted it as soon as she said it. Later that evening, when things had cooled down, she went up to his studio where he was working late and offered her apologies. He put his cool palm on her hot cheek and forgave her. Of course he forgave her. She went to bed before he did, knowing for certain that she would contact the police the next day, no matter what anyone said.

6

One of the pink-faced young men approached Liesl and shook her hand with vigor. He was waving a croissant closer to the library's copy of Shakespeare's First Folio than she would have liked, but she didn't snatch it from him and she didn't steer him away. She nodded. She introduced herself. She answered his questions. He was from the English department. Young men from the English department always treated Liesl like she was their mother. That is, when they noticed her at all. Young men from the English department were often the favorite great-grandsons of oil barons. She looked up at the rows and rows of books above her. There were buildings on campus that were architecturally more impressive than this library, but there was nothing as beautiful. Christopher once said that he wished the building were less beautiful, that people would take it more seriously if it were. Liesl disagreed. She had never been beautiful. She knew that a lack of aesthetic appeal was no way to get yourself taken seriously.

The new young English professor, his head on a swivel, stopped pretending to listen to the woman who reminded him of his mother. President Garber walked into the library reading room. Liesl stopped pretending to act as though the young English professor were listening to her. She broke off midsentence to approach Garber. Before she could get there, before she could walk fifteen feet across the room, she was interrupted by a familiar man. A familiar man who had bags under his eyes and who needed a shave.

"Vivek," said Liesl. "Miriam didn't tell me I would see you here."

"It's nice to see you, Liesl."

"Are you in town visiting your wife?"

"Visiting Miriam? You haven't spoken with her then?"

"About what?"

"It's not a visit. I've been offered a tenure-track position in the history department."

"So you're moving back from London?"

"I've moved back from London."

"Vivek, I'm so very happy for you both."

"It's nice to be back in the land of coffee

drinkers, that's for certain."

"This accounts for some of Miriam's strangeness of late. No wonder she's been distracted."

He glanced around as though looking for his wife, who wasn't in the room.

"Miriam's been acting strange? How so?"

"It's probably nothing. Distracted."

"Can you tell me anyway?"

Liesl described Miriam's spaciness. Vivek seemed concerned, which made Liesl concerned. She hedged and insisted that she had only been back from her sabbatical for a few days and had spent barely any time with Miriam.

"Can you try to?"

"Try to what? Spend time with her?" Liesl paused. "Is something going on, Vivek? I've always liked Miriam a great deal; would you like me to speak with her about something?"

He looked into his coffee cup.

"Just make yourself available to her."

"Of course."

"Thank you. Miriam will appreciate that."

"She's just in the workroom if you want to pop in."

"Best not for the moment."

"Going to do your best new-faculty-member mingling instead? The action is usually around the baked goods. You better get to the knishes before the adjunct professors stuff them all in their coat pockets."

They were interrupted by a tall, striking woman wearing a yellow hair wrap and a giant smile who parked herself in front of Liesl and looked as though she expected to be recognized.

"You must be Liesl Weiss."

"I am. Have we met?"

"We've spoken. I'm Rhonda Washington."

"Professor Washington. It's wonderful to put a face to a name. I'm terribly sorry to be rude, but I have to grab President Garber," Liesl said, trying to slide away. "Can you give me just one moment?"

"He looks busy."

"I'm not trying to brush you off," Liesl said. "I promise. But I've been trying to get in front of him for days and it's vital that I do so now."

"Administration giving the library the slip?" Rhonda said. "Imagine that."

"You can relate then?"

"I have a past life as a librarian," Rhonda said. "It was my first graduate degree before mathematics called me back."

"Well," Liesl said. She looked back at Rhonda, curious, and then again at Garber across the room. "That's unusual."

"I didn't know any mathematicians. But I

knew Black women who were librarians," Rhonda said. Liesl forgot about Garber for a moment and put out her hand to shake Rhonda's.

"It's a real pleasure to meet you."

"You as well," Rhonda said. "I'm hoping I can pressure you into letting me work with the Peshawar now that we've met in person and you can tell how charming and responsible I am."

Liesl laughed, louder than she'd intended.

"That's a good try," said Liesl. Garber was still in conversation across the room.

"Tell me what you know about it," Rhonda said.

"About the Peshawar?" Liesl said. She glanced over at Garber. He was in a crowd by the pastry table, frowning at the refined sugar and simple carbohydrates. "I'm not the expert," Liesl continued. "But it's said to note the first use of the zero in mathematics. You know that much, I'm sure. I'm really not an expert."

"How do you know?" Rhonda said, her smile conspiratorial.

"About the zero? There's never been an earlier document found."

"That's what we think. But really we can't know how old the manuscript is. We can only guess unless we properly date it."

"It's not a guess. We're using the long-established methods in our field."

"I know that," Rhonda said, putting up a hand to indicate she wasn't making accusations. "And I'm proposing we use more precise methods established by other fields."

Another glance at Garber. He was chatting with a man whose attire could only make him an environmental scientist.

"I've done a little reading on the method you proposed. You'd destroy half the manuscript if you tried it."

"I wouldn't put it at risk," Rhonda said. "I'm interested in the intersection between my science and your art. Not in destroying an artifact for science's sake."

"I misjudged you," Liesl said. "If I'm being honest, I assumed you were a new assistant professor looking to bolster her CV with a big discovery."

"I'm a mathematician," Rhonda said, deploying that easy smile again. "I was over the hill when I didn't have my big breakthrough by twenty-five."

Liesl laughed. "Is that so? I didn't know mathematicians were so ageist."

"I didn't even start my doctoral work until my midtwenties. I never stood a chance."

"It seems as though the math department is lucky to have you. Whether you're past your prime or not."

"Wouldn't they be luckier still if we could do some exciting work with the Peshawar?"

Liesl smiled in spite of herself but then stopped and maintained her resistance to the idea.

"Professor Washington," Liesl said. "I'm not sure if you've heard, but I'm only filling in as the director of this department."

"So you said," she said. "I'm not sure what that has to do with my request."

"What you're asking," Liesl said, "would be a departure from established policy. I think that is a decision better made by the department's real director when he returns from his sick leave."

Rhonda's claims about her own charm were proven when Liesl totally missed the approach of President Garber.

"Professor Washington," Garber said. "I see you've met the acting director of our great library." He was suddenly between the women, clutching a small container of trail mix that he had presumably brought from home.

"I have," she said. "Liesl and I were just talking about some of the treasures in the library's collection."

"It grows every year," Garber said. "We have an extremely passionate network of donors."

"I'm sure they keep you very busy."

"Indeed. Liesl, Professor Washington has come to the university to hold the chair of the professor of the public understanding of science. You might recognize her from television or know of her books."

The last chair had been a white-haired Irish Nobel Prize winner who had held the position for thirty years. Rhonda had severely undersold herself. In a room full of men who were acting as though the paper they had once published in an academic journal read by exactly seventeen people made them groundbreaking. The woman was quietly a mathematician, a librarian, and the holder of one of the university's most important and public research positions.

Liesl had known that she would have very little understanding of Rhonda's work, but she had never thought that Rhonda would know so much about her own work. Rhonda, smile still big, hand on her hip, talked rapidly to Garber about her plans for her first year. She had a girlish sort of cheerfulness that belied the confidence with which she was dominating the conversation with the most intimidating person in the room. Amid the gray and blue suits, she wore her yellow hair wrap and a blue cotton A-line skirt. She demanded attention. And why shouldn't she when what she had to say was so interesting. Liesl wasn't angry at having her time with Garber interrupted. This woman, this mathematician, this important public figure for the university who had never bothered to mention how important or how public she was. Liesl had never stood a chance.

Rhonda placed her hand on Garber's trail mix–bearing arm, turned to Liesl, and smiled her big smile.

"You'll have to excuse me," she said. "There's someone else I should introduce myself to."

"Where is it, Liesl?" Garber whispered once Rhonda had gone.

"You mean you know?" Liesl said.

"Know what?" Garber glanced over his shoulder to make sure no one was listening. "That you seem to be hiding an extremely important donation?"

"You don't know," Liesl said.

A man in his thirties wearing a page from the Brooks Brothers catalog was walking toward them. Liesl turned her back to him, making it clear that they weren't to be interrupted.

"I've also been thinking, and it matters

less with this younger crop, but I think we should play up the woman thing."

"The woman thing?"

He took a handful of trail mix in his mouth, and they were silent as he chewed. Trail mix is not a thing one can just swallow. "It's important that I get enough protein while I'm training," he said. "With the donors, I mean. Make the best of a bad situation."

"How's that?"

"A lot of these men, they have wives. If we play up the woman thing maybe we can appeal to them, get them out to more events, get them spending."

"So you think I should . . ."

"Keep reminding them you're a woman. Now. Where's the book?"

"We don't have it," Liesl said.

Any last trace of Garber's public-facing smile died. He looked at Liesl like she was a preschooler who had just wet her pants in front of him. "It's your second week," he said. "How, in two weeks, have you not managed to even get a safe open?" He picked a bit of sunflower seed out of a space between his teeth with the nail of his little finger.

Liesl took a breath to buy time. She wished this event had been scheduled in the evening so she'd have had access to wine. "I opened it last week. The Plantin wasn't inside the safe," she said.

"Where the hell is it if it's not inside the safe?" Garber shoved the trail mix into the pocket of his suit jacket. It bulged. "Somewhere else in Chris's office then."

She shook her head. "We have to contact the police. Today."

"Let me understand this," Garber said. "Chris would have put the Plantin in the safe while he waited for the insurance appraisal. You've opened the safe, no Plantin. It's been two weeks, maybe more since it's been seen. You haven't actually called the police yet, have you?"

"Well, no."

Across the room, a man wearing a blazer with suede elbow patches that someone at some point must have told him looked professorial was waving excitedly at Garber. Garber gave a sharp nod in his direction and huddled more closely to Liesl.

"Good, good. That's very good." He spoke mostly to himself. "It could be in the library or it could have been stolen, but if it was stolen, then it would have to be by someone in the library. Were you alone in the office when you opened the safe?"

"Pardon me?" Liesl had never considered

herself on any list of suspects.

"I take that back. Has anything like this ever happened before?"

"At other libraries. Never here," Liesl said.

"I wish you had told me this earlier."

Liesl said nothing. She couldn't remember how many times she had tried to gain access to Garber in the preceding days, but technology being what it was, she was certain she could have someone take a look at phone records and create a tally.

"Look, Liesl. I know you've been trying to get a meeting with me, but there are some instances where you bang down the door. Wouldn't you agree this is one of those instances?"

Liesl looked up to see that Miriam, cocooned again in that big burgundy sweater, had entered the reading room and was barreling toward them, her face red.

"What's the matter, Miriam?"

"Can I speak with you?" she said, staring at Liesl as if Garber weren't even there. "It's important that I speak with you."

"Not right now, miss," Garber said.

Garber went to take Liesl's arm and pull her to another part of the room to continue their conversation, but Miriam's features, shaped by their wild indignation, gave Liesl pause.

"Miriam, President Garber needs me for a few minutes. We've been trying to connect for days. Can I come find you when we've finished?"

It was fading back to pink, Miriam's face, as her anger faded to embarrassment and then to a kind of sadness that expressed that even when she was demanding of attention, she didn't warrant it.

"When you've finished?" she asked in a little-girl voice.

"You'll be in the workroom, is that right? I'll come and find you as soon as I can."

Garber and Liesl stood in silence while they waited for Miriam to get out of earshot.

"Miriam Peters, isn't that right?" Garber said. "Didn't you say that she was the receiver for the Plantin when it arrived here? I don't think I know much about her. Francis and Max and you, I've worked with all of you in the past, but why don't I remember her?"

Liesl said nothing.

"We have to be honest here, Liesl. If there's an odor, we have to say it stinks. That woman, that panicked-looking woman who just came to see you as you were reporting the possible theft of the Plantin to me . . . She did or she did not have physical access to it?"

"She did."

"She did. So let's have an honest conversation about that woman. Let's look into that woman a little further. Let's think about everyone who might have had access to the Plantin, and let's create a little plan, and let's do our due diligence. Then when Chris wakes up he can have a good chuckle at our panic, and he can tell us exactly where the Plantin has been all along, or we can have a good chuckle and tell him how we lost sight of it but only for a moment."

"What about the police?" Liesl didn't sound as sure about the police as she had when the conversation began. She'd been warned that Garber wouldn't want them called, but now that the warning was coming to pass, she didn't know what to do with it.

"We're not there yet. There is no way to involve the police without further undermining our credibility with our donors."

She took off her glasses and rubbed her eyes. "Will it not undermine us further if they find out that we knew the Plantin was missing and didn't call?"

"How would they find out?"

"All right. Putting that aside for a moment, I'm not sure how you'd like us to proceed. If the goal is to recover the Plantin before anyone suspects it is missing, but we can't use the police to help us recover the Plantin, what's the next step?"

She didn't have to put on her glasses to tell he was glaring, and she was embarrassed for having asked because it was clear that she was supposed to be in possession of the answer herself.

"You look for it. You ask intelligent questions, like why does the woman who arranged shipping and receiving of the Plantin all of a sudden look so panicked? You take initiative."

"I understand."

"Do you? Do you understand what this does to the reputation of not just the library but the university?"

"I do," Liesl said. As the people in the room had crept closer to the private zone that Liesl and Garber had established around themselves, the volume of their conversation had dropped lower and lower, and the volume of the "I do" was almost imperceptible.

"To my reputation, Liesl." He dropped all pretense of looking cheerful in front of the crowd. "We are in the middle of a billion-dollar fundraising campaign."

Liesl pictured Christopher's office; the doubt crept in. When she imagined the office now, the red volumes were there. Stacked up on the filing cabinet. Mixed with others on his desk. On the other hand, she had already convinced herself that the Plantin was stolen. Liesl thought of the odds that she and Dan could have looked right past it. Unlikely. But impossible? She thought of all the empty wine bottles in her recycling bin.

"We'll begin to systematically go through the stacks today. Today."

"You will, Liesl. Because a loss of this magnitude doesn't just impact our ability to buy fancy old bibles. It impacts our ability to find money for telescopes, for lab facilities. It's all the same money."

"No one will know. Not from me."

They turned to open themselves up to the room once again. The turnout for the event was good, the suits delighted by their proximity to historical artifacts.

"Who else would have had access?" Garber asked. "Who would have touched it?"

"As a bible, it falls within Max's collection area."

"Max is a good man, but he's a man with secrets," Garber said.

"His secrets aren't secret anymore. He lives with his partner openly now."

"You don't know everything," Garber

said, his eyes still scanning to make sure they weren't being overheard. "And you don't have to defend the character of everyone we discuss. We're taking an inventory."

"Francis, too, then," she said, showing that she too could remove emotion from their discussion.

"If it's in Max's area of collection, and Chris arranged the purchase, and that Miriam woman was the one who shipped the thing, then where does Francis fit in? Why would he have touched it?"

One of the suits waved at Garber from across the room. Garber smiled back at him.

"The text has Syriac and Aramaic. Francis has a reading knowledge of those languages and Max doesn't, so it's likely Francis would have taken a look at some point."

She felt like she was testifying before Joseph McCarthy. Listing the names of her friends and colleagues and thinking about all the ways they could have stolen the book, all the reasons they would have stolen the book. Garber was putting every accusation in his mental ledger. She wanted to stop, but she couldn't. Because if they weren't guilty, then she might be.

"Remind me if you were alone when you opened the safe," Garber said.

"I wasn't alone." She shook her head, a

little girl indignant at being accused of dipping into the cookie jar, and then she regretted the break in composure and began to answer more slowly and purposefully. "Marie was with me. She called me at home when she heard that we couldn't get the safe open. When she couldn't reach me, she just came in." She looked at him. His mouth half-open with the question that she answered before he could ask it.

"Embarrassed, I think that Christopher had shared the combination with her. I think she was overly helpful because she was embarrassed on Christopher's behalf at the break of policy. Useful though it was. So she came in and gave me the combination and was standing behind me when I opened the safe and saw it was empty. Marie can attest to all that."

Garber looked past Liesl's head, and she turned to see that Max was standing behind them.

"Sorry to interrupt, President Garber," Max said with his quiet, buttered-up energy. "It's almost time for your speech, sir. I wanted to make sure you had time for a sip of water and to look over your notes before things got started."

"No notes, but thanks all the same, Max."

"I'm happy to help," he said. "It sounds

like you and Liesl are discussing the Plantin. Terrible, isn't it? That such an important artifact in our church's history would be misplaced. Once we recover it, it will really be a cornerstone of our collection. I predict that it will attract donations of other religious publications from the same period."

Liesl stood, half in and half out of their circle of conversation, her core engaged to try to mimic the rigidity of Max's posture, her hands suddenly moved to cover the few inches of exposed skin at her throat. *Misplaced?* she thought. Misplaced. Max wasn't just brownnosing; he was taking Garber's temperature about the missing Plantin.

"We'll have to recover it first," Garber said. "I trust that you and the rest of the team are providing whatever support Liesl needs in that regard. We are in a defining moment for our institution, and the people here will be remembered by how they weather it."

"As soon as Liesl provides direction about how she'd like to proceed, the team and I will provide whatever support she needs." Max's hand tapped his collar as he spoke, a tic from a previous life. "While acting with great discretion of course. It's 9:59, sir. You said you wanted to speak promptly at 10:00."

Garber bared his teeth at Liesl. She gave him a nod, indicating that there weren't any trail-mix scraps caught behind an incisor. He took his place at a microphone that had been set up at the front of the space. The room fell quiet immediately.

"A very warm welcome to you all, and thanks to Liesl Weiss and the team at the Department of Rare Books and Special Collections who are generous enough to host new faculty for this welcome reception every year in this wonderful space. I hope you'll see that we're showing off a bit, introducing you to the wealth of resources you'll have during your career here." He gestured at the beautiful books, as he did every year at that part of the speech. The humanists looked up in awe. The scientists looked down at their muffins. "Tremendous opportunities await you here, where the best students, faculty, staff, and alumni are embracing innovation, teaching, learning, and research. If this is your first faculty appointment, welcome to the academy. If you are joining us from another institution, from government, from business, or from the nonprofit world, we are grateful that you have brought your experience here. We will offer you the tools to be exceptional. We will offer you state-of-the-art laboratories, we will offer you cutting-edge technology, we will offer you administrative support that year after year attracts over one billion dollars in research funding, and we will offer you unrivaled library collections that you will use to teach and discover.

"Today, our university is a success story with a distinct identity. That identity is excellence. That should be daunting, and it should be exhilarating. Because now that you are part of our community, we expect that excellence from you. We are giving you the tools: the labs, the tech, the administration, the library. But we want something in return. From every single member of our community we expect excellence because that is this university's reputation, and we will not compromise it. I will not compromise it. My job as president is to give you an unimpeded path to excellence. And your job as faculty is to not let me down. I want to thank you for joining the university. Thank you for your commitment to discovery, to collaboration, to teaching, to excellence. You have my best wishes as president, and as your colleague."

"Been taking oration lessons from Churchill, hasn't he?"

Liesl hadn't seen Francis enter the room or take up a spot behind her. She shared his sentiments about the fervor of the speech, although she might have drawn a parallel to another early-twentieth-century European orator.

By eleven that morning the pastries were gone, as were the attendees. Liesl was fielding phone calls about late invoices and scheduling appraisals of new collections and finding herself interrupted every time she tried to step out to go to the bathroom. Then she blinked and it was six o'clock and she was alone in the library again, typing the code into the alarm panel. Liesl had broken her promise and had failed to speak with Miriam at all that day. In the coming days and weeks and months, Liesl would reflect on that broken promise. But that evening, Miriam was the furthest thing from her mind.

Ten Years Earlier

Miriam snuck downstairs at the first sign that Dan was alone in the basement. She wanted to speak with him without anyone else around, without Christopher around, to see if she could make an appeal on her own behalf that would stick with him.

"I hope, Dan," Miriam whispered as she came up behind him in the stacks, "I hope this can be it. And that we never have to talk about what you saw again."

"It's Miriam, right? Miriam, you're putting me in an unreasonable position. It was wrong. You know it was wrong, and you know that I should report it."

A pipe clanged overhead, indicating that the heat was switching on. Miriam and Dan stood facing each another by the oversized map books, fifteen feet from where Dan had walked in on Miriam's secret a month earlier while he was bringing in a skid of author papers that had just come through the shipping department.

"It happened once," Miriam said. "It didn't hurt anyone."

He stopped stacking books onto his book truck, wriggled his toes inside the tip of his combat boot. He was still dressed like he belonged in shipping and receiving. He hadn't seen anything to make him eager to fit in with this new crowd. How could he know whether it was true, whether anyone had been hurt by what he saw?

"I could lose my job," she said.

Dan cleared his throat and looked at his shoes. He almost told Miriam that he was a new father, that he had a daughter, because he thought it would make her trust him more, but then he didn't say it because what he mostly wanted was to remain uninvolved in Miriam's mess.

"Maybe someone should lose their job," he said, looking up at her with golden retriever eyes and hoping she would understand his meaning.

"I love working here. You're new, but you'll see, we're so lucky to work here. I don't want to have to leave." She didn't understand his meaning. Or she did, but she understood the world better, because she was right that if responsibility were being apportioned, she would probably be the one sent somewhere else.

"I liked working in shipping and receiving," Dan said. "I get that I'm supposed to view the transfer to rare books as a favor, as some sort of promotion, but it's all the same shit to me. Buying my silence with this ever-so-slightly fancier job? I'm delivering books instead of packages." He tapped his pen against his clipboard. "It's all the same shit," he repeated.

It brought Dan no pleasure, none that Miriam could see, to make his new coworker so miserable. She sat on a step stool next to him and wrapped her arms around her body. He could feel she was waiting for reassurance that her secret wouldn't become public, but he was in no position to offer her that. He wished her no malice, but that was perhaps the best reason of all to tell someone what he'd seen.

"You know," Dan said, "everyone always says that the time they were caught doing something was the first time they ever did it."

Dan scratched a book title off his list with a pencil. He looked only at the call numbers on the flags that poked out of the books, and not at the titles. He didn't have any interest in the titles, in the books that some upmarket surname working on their second

PhD would pore over for weeks.

"I promise this is a really good job," said Miriam. "I know that it pays the same as the job in shipping, I know that, but it's not all skids and loading docks. It's beautiful books and brilliant minds. If you stick around, if you get to know the place and the people, you might be softened by the work. Inspired by it even. I was trying to do a good thing, bringing you here."

"Listen. You seem nice. I have no quarrel with you. I've seen plenty of what I needed to see of the people to make my judgments," Dan said. "And as for being inspired by work, you and I must come from different worlds. I don't need to be inspired by my work. I need to be paid for it, and for it to not interfere with the rest of my life."

7

Liesl completed the check of stack 538 as she had done with stack 537 and stack 536 before it. She scratched the row off her list and did some mental math that identified some day, approximately six months in the future, as the estimated date of completion for the current effort.

"Stack 540 is done," Francis called. "Can you cross it off the list?"

"Should I start in another area?"

"No, keep going. I like the idea of us meeting in the middle. Very unlike us, wouldn't you say?"

"The things that unite us, Francis."

"I don't know. More like reunite us." They were both poking their heads out of their stacks and looking at each other down the aisle. "Can I be honest? For a long time I thought that once we got old, when the past was far behind us, we'd be friends again."

"Francis. You didn't have to wait until we got old. I'd have been friends all along."

"Well, you know. There were the old complications. And my wife didn't very much like you."

"Nor you, in the end."

"Indeed. I think I'd have stayed with her, though, if I'd been given the choice."

"Would you have?"

"Yes, I think so. She was never very nice, but there's a lot to be said for not having to be alone as you enter your Metamucil years."

The old librarian, before he'd become old or a librarian, had served in the Foreign Service in some mysterious capacity. His facility with languages and the quick analysis of texts was an asset from the period, but the total lack of interpersonal relationships from that period of his life was a liability. The gregarious, intelligent, well-brought-up man with the mysterious brown eyes had spent his formative years learning to be alone. The lesson had stuck.

"And she doesn't mind being alone? Or is she with someone now? You've never told me."

"She's done with all that. Who needs a lover when you have a terrible grandchild to dote on? Perhaps if I didn't find the little bugger so hateful I'd have an easier time of it all."

Liesl walked around the corner and got started on stack 539, wondering now about what the lack of Christopher might mean to a man like Francis. She had stopped talking and so had he, but they were within each other's body heat now — him checking the books at one end of the stack and her at the other until eventually they would meet in the middle. He was pulling a book gently by its spine; she was opening an unmarked box.

"I think it's lonely," said Liesl. "No matter what. It's just a thing about getting older."

"Come on. That's just the feeling of lovely Hannah growing up. Not the same thing."

There was a long-unspoken rule that they didn't talk about Hannah. Certainly not when they were alone. She should have chided him for it, but to do so would mean breaking the rule herself so she let it pass quietly.

"That's part of it, I'm sure. But not all."

"John-O still having his troubles?"

"Nothing like that," she said. "I just think people retreat in on themselves as they age. So even if you're not alone it can get a bit lonely."

"I don't know," Francis studied the colophon of a book that was clearly not one of the Plantin volumes. "I think it's the fact that our friends keep dying on us." He reshelved the book and pulled out its nearest neighbor.

"Well, yes. That certainly doesn't help."

"I think I know what you're saying, though, about the loneliness that arrives in your sixties. I can't imagine it gets better as time goes on."

"Married or not, it creeps in."

"Still. Must be nice to have someone around to shag," Francis said with a grin.

"It's nice to have someone to have dinner with every night, absolutely." She shot him a wink. The giddiness of a good flirt got rarer with age, but it didn't get less potent.

"Don't play coy with me," he said. "You marry a man like that, it's not for his money. It's got to be something else."

"It is wild to me that your mind still goes there."

"It's wild to me that yours doesn't."

"We're not young," she said.

"Some might even call us old. But we weren't always."

"Living in the past," Liesl said. "Now there's a thing that will make you lonely."

"It's not living in the past."

"No?" she said. "Then what would you call it?"

"We were what, in our thirties when we met? You'll always be that girl to me."

They had reached the end of their work on stack 539 and stood arm to arm now. It was easy to imagine them as they had been. Francis with his flop of brown hair and enigmatic European past, her all legs and glasses and wit. If those two people had been standing this close, this alone. Well. The books in front of them might have burst into flames.

"Is that it then? Why you're so certain I don't know what I'm doing?"

They had been almost touching, but now Francis stepped back.

"What are you talking about?"

"I'm still that girl to you," she said. "And so you can't trust my judgment about the Plantin."

"Not this again."

"It's time to bring in the police."

She resettled her weight against the shelving unit, and it shifted, just a little, on its track.

"We can't have outsiders sniffing around this," Francis said.

"Not outsiders. The police."

Francis shook his head at her.

"You won't be able to keep it quiet once you involve them. Remember what my mates at Oxford went through back when that fellow was pinching books? They brought in Scotland Yard and wound up in the *Spectator.* Do you fancy a write-up in the *Spectator*?"

They had taken their argument out of stack 539, and Liesl would have to remember to note later that it had been checked. She followed Francis toward the elevator. His evocation of Oxford put her on the back foot. She didn't have mates. At Oxford, at Cambridge, anywhere really, who would know what to do. Christopher would have. Some friend he had roomed with at nineteen who would know just what the next move was to be.

"We have been looking for days," she said, trying to get Francis to turn to face her.

"And what good will police do?" He jabbed at the elevator button. It was old and unhurried.

"What a bizarre question. They'll investigate."

He turned to her. " 'Rogues and Ne'er-Do-Wells.' That was the *Spectator* headline. I remember it like yesterday. Will the police come down here and search the stacks with us?"

"Of course not."

"Access some network of rare-book dealers we don't know about? That's what my mate said, by the way. If they'd have just gone to their dealers before the police, they'd have solved the whole thing and prevented the 'rogues and ne'er-do-wells' business."

The elevator door rumbled open, and he took a step forward to enter it, to exit the conversation on a clever line, but politeness got the best of him, and he swept his arm to the side, indicating she should go first.

"They'll do the things police do," Liesl said. And even to her, it sounded like a thing a child would say. "See if there was a crime and then solve it."

She could feel the wave of frustration that washed over him when the elevator door closed before she had immediately agreed that he was in the right.

"You're being daft," Francis said, pushing the button for the ground floor. "Our entire job is finding information."

"Not like this."

"You think some suburbanite with a community-college education is going to help you find a priceless artifact?"

"Why are you so resistant to the idea that I try this?" She'd turned her back to the

127

elevator door, cornering him in the tiny space.

"Because of rogues and ne'er-do-wells. And because you've been told not to. Go ahead if you like. But I care about the library, and I care about you, and I know that the police would be a mistake."

"Is that all?"

"What else would it be? Am I the thief now? Keeping the police away for self-preservation?"

"I said no such thing." She turned away, stepping back from him and turning to face the lit buttons at the top of the elevators the way a good citizen should. She didn't want a quarrel. She wanted him to be on her side.

"Let's stop this now," Francis said. "Talking is a waste. You know very well what I think."

"And I value that opinion."

"Doesn't seem like it." He glanced in her direction when he said it but still stood in the very corner of the elevator, leaning against the wall with his arms crossed.

"I'm in an impossible position."

"You are doing all the right things."

"Am I?" She slumped against the wall then, too, the tiny bit of reassurance melting like a lump of sugar on her tongue.

"You are."

"What would Christopher do?" she asked.

"Chris? I have no idea. But it would be a hell of a thing to watch."

"We never agreed," Liesl said as the elevator chimed at their destination.

"You and Chris? Everyone knows that."

"Of course they do," she said. "And they probably think I want to bring the police in because it's the opposite of how Christopher would have handled it."

The elevator door opened into the library's reference area where all 130 pounds of Max was standing by the desk, arms crossed, red-faced, neck veins throbbing against the tightly buttoned collar of his impeccably pressed shirt.

"Max, what's going on?" Liesl asked.

"Did you forget to tell me something this morning? Fail to deliver a message?"

"A message?"

"Yes. Is there anything you've failed to tell me?"

"I have no idea. Can you tell me why you're upset?"

"I see. Maybe you don't know. Perhaps you haven't even checked your messages today. I'm not sure which is worse."

Francis had extricated himself from the conversation. The traitor. The only one in the library who absolutely had to listen to

Max when he was this obstinate was Liesl.

"I checked my messages right before the library opened," she said.

"So where the hell is Miriam?" Max was nearly shouting. "She was supposed to work the first reference-desk shift today." He gesticulated toward the desk, to make sure Liesl could see that there was no one there. "I had planned work to do this morning. I can't just rearrange my whole day on a whim because the acting director forgets to tell me about a sick call."

"Did she leave a message on the reference-desk phone?" Liesl asked.

"No, Liesl. And she didn't send a telegram or a carrier pigeon either."

"Perhaps she's just late," said Liesl. "I'll call her."

"I've already called her," said Max. "Home and mobile. No answer."

"Did she mention yesterday that she wasn't planning to be in today?" said Liesl, inwardly scrambling together the blurry jigsaw image of Miriam, eyes wide, brushing past Garber and begging for attention at the new-faculty reception. But that couldn't have been about something so mundane as a vacation day.

"Why would she mention it?" Max flung himself into the chair behind the reference desk. "Why would she warn me that she's planning to ruin my morning?"

"What I'm saying is that she's probably not sick at all," Liesl said.

"She just decided not to show up to work?"

"Or she asked Christopher for a vacation day. And he didn't get a chance to pass the message along." There was a creeping ache, just strong enough to make Liesl bite her own tongue, that she never had found Miriam to speak with her as she'd promised.

"And she wouldn't have checked the desk schedule," Max said, following Liesl's line of reasoning, "if she thought she had the day off."

Max was interrupted from his pout by the ding signaling the arrival of the elevator. Max and Liesl both swung their heads toward the door. It was not Miriam.

"President Garber," Liesl said. "What a surprise."

Max adjusted his slumped posture in the chair, and then he changed his mind and stood up. Garber nodded at him, then turned his full attention to Liesl. "Do you have a few minutes to talk?" he asked.

"Of course I do."

"Good. Let's go to your office." He turned to Max. "Nice to see you as always, Max."

"Do you mind," Liesl said to Max, "covering for the first hour until I can figure something out?"

"You know I'm always happy to help," said Max.

"Is there some other problem I should know about?" asked Garber.

She considered deflecting by asking about the rehabilitation of his calf strain but decided it would be impossible to feign genuine interest. "No. A staff member, Miriam, is unexpectedly away." She followed Garber into Christopher's office and closed the door. "Nothing out of the ordinary."

"Good," he said. "Listen, I've just come from seeing Chris."

He placed his bicycle helmet on the chair that Liesl had pulled out for him and stayed standing. As he spoke, he performed some sort of stretch focused on the lower portion of his legs.

"I met Marie there this morning," said Garber. "I was hoping to have a chance to speak with Chris."

Liesl, who had taken a seat behind Christopher's desk, slowly stood up. "Is he awake? That's brilliant. I had no idea."

"No. What a pity."

"Oh," said Liesl. "Then why did you think you'd have a chance to speak with him?"

"An awful lot of time has passed."

"He had a stroke." She walked back around the desk and tried to decide what to do with her hands. "That can be a slow recovery."

"It can," said Garber. "But not what I expected from Chris. The plan was for him to be back at work in a month."

"Whose plan?" said Liesl. "You can hardly plan for something like a medical emergency. We can only be patient."

"I'll make sure to get that embroidered on a throw pillow."

"I'm not sure what to say."

"That was rude of me. This situation with my injury is bringing out the worst in me."

Liesl thought the situation was bringing out his authentic self, not his worst one, but she didn't say so.

"You came to see me this morning, President Garber," said Liesl, kneading her temples. She was suddenly exhausted. "Tell me how I can help you."

Garber put the bicycle helmet on the floor and sat, which made Liesl feel as though she had to sit too.

"The Plantin," he said. "Tell me where we are."

"We're looking. Systematically searching the stacks."

He nodded as if she'd just told him something new. "You had mentioned that was the plan," Garber said. "What have you found so far?"

The dust in the room looked like snowfall in the morning sun. It was distracting. "We thought the Plantin might have been misshelved when we were trying to clean this office."

"If that's something that can happen, then it sounds like a good lead to pursue."

"It's one possibility. We haven't found anything yet. I think enough time has passed that we should start to explore other possibilities." When she said it, her fatigue grew deeper. She knew how the conversation would end.

"Of course. I agree. You should explore every possible inroad."

"Including the police," Liesl looked at the dust, not at Garber. "Including the possibility that the book was stolen."

"Not this again," Garber said.

"President Garber." Liesl tried to sit on the edge of the desk. "Do you really not think a theft is a possibility?"

He leaned over. She thought he was going to put his head in his hands, but he stretched out and touched his toes. "I never said I didn't think it could be a thief. I said it was up to us to solve this internally." He gave a quiet grunt as he leaned into the stretch. "We are trying to raise a billion dollars for this university."

"I'm aware. The library is a big part of the effort."

The sun had moved behind a cloud, and the dust had disappeared from view.

"It is my full-time job," Garber said. "And no one will ever give us another penny if they learn we can't be trusted with their money."

He picked up the helmet.

"I didn't ask for this job," Liesl said.

That was true. But she'd taken it hungrily when offered. She'd sat in the chair and marked up auction catalogs and fantasized about gold calligraphy on blue vellum arriving to join the library's collection because she had willed it to be so. She hadn't come right out and asked, true.

"But you accepted it," said Garber. "And now you're bound by its expectations."

Liesl turned away from him and his helmet, back to the window and the slowly falling dust, biting her tongue to fight tears. Expectations. Liesl didn't want to hear about expectations. But then it figured that President Garber would assume she wouldn't understand what was required of the big job, just as he assumed that she only ever wanted to work in the background of the big job.

"I'm trying my best."

"Chris has been the figurehead of this library for decades." Garber put the helmet on and clipped it under his chin. "We owe this to him. To protect his library while he recuperates. You owe this to him."

"Christopher and I always worked as a team."

"Of course you did."

"President Garber," she said, walking with him toward the door. "I've done much more than just work with books in the years that I've been here. I hope you know that."

"I wouldn't have asked you to fill in for Chris if I didn't."

To fill in. Garber knew Liesl as the one who could be trusted to sign invoices or arrange caterers, but invoice signers and caterer wranglers had no business in the business of leadership. She heard it all in the words *fill in.*

"I'm sorry to get emotional. I really am trying my best."

"You already said that," said Garber. "You were Chris's right hand. Everyone knows that."

"I'm sorry to have kept you. I'll keep you

posted on news about the Plantin."

"And I with news about Chris's health," Garber said. "We'll be in touch."

He opened the office door and closed it behind him. Liesl sat again. It was hard to believe that she could be made to feel so small by a grown man in a bicycle helmet.

"That went well then?" Francis strode in without knocking, as Liesl's hands were busy dabbing the corners of her eyes dry.

"Francis. Were you waiting outside my door?"

"News on Chris?"

Liesl spun back and forth in Christopher's chair.

"The news is that there's no news," she said. "I'm not sure if that's good or bad."

Francis nodded, distracted. Sat down in the chair across from her without being asked. Even in his distraction his dark hair stayed slicked, perfect, while Liesl was sure her grays were standing on end.

"He'll not leave us without finishing his work. Not the Chris I know."

"Was he working on something?" asked Liesl. "I don't think I knew that."

"We were working on a book together." Francis was looking down at his feet, frowning at the left knee that wouldn't stop bouncing.

"Not like Christopher to share credit," Liesl said. "How'd you talk him into that?"

The statement made Francis tense, made him look up from his feet.

"Don't be unkind. Not about a man who can't speak in his own defense."

"You're right. I'm sorry." Liesl's mouth got smaller, her head looser. She shrunk with the apology. And the shrinking seemed to satisfy Francis that Liesl hadn't meant any real disrespect.

"*El presidente* didn't seem happy as he was leaving," Francis clucked as he pulled the Christie's catalog off the desk and flipped to the first marked page. If he saw anything special in Lot 37, he didn't show it. Flipped right past it. "Did you bring up the idea of the police with him again?"

"Yes, of course I did."

"Of course you did," said Francis, sounding scolding in his artificial disinterest. "And he told you that it was a brilliant idea and to go ahead."

"And he forbade me from involving them," Liesl said.

"As I told you he would."

"As you told me he would."

"Chin up," said Francis. He paused to dog-ear a page in the catalog, then he looked up at her. "I was proven right, so we can all feel good about that."

"What am I supposed to do here?" she asked, overwhelmed with fatigue.

"What you've been doing. And I'll help you."

"It's not your responsibility."

"I'll meet you back here at five, and we'll get back to searching." He tossed the catalog back onto the desk and heaved himself out of the chair, his face fixed with a hero's resolve. "It'll mean giving up my evening with the grandchild again, but I reckon my heart will recover."

II

Liesl stood in the cigar-scented office, hands full of unanswered telephone messages, considering a request from Percy Pickens to come and cast an eye on the Plantin he had purchased but had yet to see, when the clock struck five. She shoved the stack of papers, Percy's message among them, into her appointment book to be dealt with at some better time.

"Shall we head down?" she said when Francis arrived at her door. They were the only people left in the library. The others had sensed something in the air and gone home promptly at five.

"Not so fast," Francis said. "Our souls are

in need of spirit and strength."

He pulled open the bottom drawer of the filing cabinet in the corner of the office.

"Spirit and strength. Dewar's Scotch whiskey," he said. He pulled the bottle out of the cabinet and a couple of glasses from the same hiding spot. "Chris and I did plenty of working late in this office."

The smooth hair, the dark shirt, the Scotch bottle held by the neck. Liesl reckoned he did look a little bit like a spy.

"I'd have thought his tastes would be more refined than Dewar's," she said.

"You mean the bottle in his desk? That was for his private consumption," Francis said. "The filing cabinet whiskey was for when he entertained. When Chris was paying, it was Dewar's."

"To Christopher's health," she said, glass in the air.

"To his health."

"Let's bring it downstairs and get to this."

"Bringing liquids down to the stacks," said Francis. "Maybe I'm the one who should call the police."

"I recently lived with a teenager," she said. "So I know if you're going to break the rules, best to do it all the way." Liesl had eyes on the bottle now and a hand came to her mouth, an immediate self-rebuke at having brought up Hannah.

"I won't tell John you said that," said Francis, brushing past the mention for both their sakes.

"We should get started." She was blushing.

"Yes, Boss."

"You start at 541, and I'll go over to 560?"

"Meet in the middle again?"

"Meet in the middle."

"Good. I'll see you there. Somewhere in the middle."

"Call them out when you're done. I'll hold the list and write them down."

"Yes, Boss."

"Please stop calling me that."

He went over to his stack and she to hers. Though they weren't standing close to one another, they could each hear the other breathe. Liesl was aware of it. She inhaled and exhaled with intention so that nothing could be read into the quickness of her pulse. When he came over to fill her glass, she didn't say no.

"Makes the work go quicker," he said.

"Someone once told me it gives you spirit and strength."

"That's right."

He liked that. She could tell by the length of the look he gave her when she said it. He liked that she remembered.

"Back to work then," Liesl said. "Or we'll be here all night."

They were very nearly there all night. There was work to do and whiskey to drink. And eventually they gave up on the work but not the whiskey. If they had been younger, they would have sat cross-legged on the cement floor, but old bones being what they are, they perched on rolling library stools until the bottle was empty.

"Let me walk you home," Francis said.

He watched Liesl as she punched in the alarm. There was nary a squirrel nor a security guard that could see them at this hour.

"I can take care of myself, Francis. You should get home too."

"I can't very well send a woman off alone into the dark. My mother would kill me."

"Your mother's dead."

"So let her rest in peace," he said. "And let me walk you home."

"I'm an old woman," Liesl said. "I'm pretty well invisible when I walk down the street. It's excellent armor."

"You're not old."

"You keep saying that. Of course I am, Francis. You are too."

"It's hard for me to fathom."

"Really? I find it impossible to forget how old I am. My body is always reminding me."

"This stuff with Chris. That's when I remember."

"He's scarcely older than us. It's a selfish point of view, but I've thought about that a lot. That it could have been me."

"I haven't thought that at all," Francis said.

"How can you avoid it? Christopher's only five or so years older than us."

A sushi shop they were passing had its neon sign turned on. It cast a red glow on Francis's face, drawing shadows in every line and crevice that defined the topology of its surface. But then the shop was behind them, and his face went dark again.

"I've always looked up to Chris," he said. "So he's always seemed somehow older."

Her steps swayed down Harbord Street, loose and unselfconscious in her whiskey-aided gait. Every few feet she half turned her head at her companion, trying to catch sight of his intentions out of the corner of her eye.

"Luckily that's not an issue with your new boss," she said.

"I've told you already."

"You've told me what?" she said.

"I can't look at you and see anything but

the thirty-year-old Liesl I first met. So you'll never be old to me."

She tried to imagine being back in her thirty-year-old skin, sliding a slender arm against an almost unfamiliar body just to feel the electricity of it, but she couldn't get the picture of their current anatomy, of the lines and crevices, to go dark for long enough. The red light kept bringing them forward.

"Perhaps," she said, "that's a way of making sure that you never seem old to yourself."

"Maybe. Wouldn't I be clever if that were the case?"

"I think we're drunk," Liesl said, slipping an arm through his even if it wasn't slender and thirty years old. Touching him because the whiskey gave her an excuse and because she wanted to see what it felt like with *this* body.

"I know," he slurred. "It's great. What about you, Liesl? Where do you fix me in time?"

"Ask me tomorrow when my head is clearer."

"I'd prefer to know now when you're not thinking straight." He ran a hand across the knuckles that were holding onto his arm, and Liesl saw a flash of hunger register across his face, or maybe she saw a reflection of her own ravenousness. But only a flash, because the sight of her front door, of her chrysanthemums, shook her loose. She pulled her arm free of his.

"This is me." Liesl pointed at the third house on the street where they were standing. "Thank you for the walk home. And for the help."

"Come on. I'll walk you to your door," Francis said.

He stood next to her as she unlocked it. The city stretched around them, empty. But the doorstep was crowded, intimate.

"Good night then," Liesl said. "Get home safely."

III

Liesl had the feeling of swimming through gelatin when she arrived at work the next morning.

Dan, looking impossibly athletic in his too-tight jeans, looking like he and his combat boots could go chop down a tree or build a house at a moment's notice, caught Liesl and her saggy under-eye skin as soon as she came in. "No Miriam again today."

"It's not yet nine."

"She usually arrives by eight thirty."

"I know. But she doesn't have to arrive

until nine."

Dan shrugged and pushed an empty book truck, the constant prop, toward the elevator.

"Who's scheduled to work the desk this morning?"

She had a growing sense of anxiety about Miriam's absence. A heaviness that started in her stomach and rose through her throat like acid after a heavy meal.

Dan turned back around. Slowly, always slowly.

"How would I know?" he said. "I just shelve the books."

Then again, the heaviness in her stomach could have been all the Dewar's.

"You usually know," she said. The elevator dinged its arrival. Everything at the library moved at a crawl.

"Miriam has the first shift." He wheeled his prop into the elevator. "Makes it especially strange that she's not here yet. Given that we open in a few minutes."

Liesl decided she hated Dan. But that might have been the hangover.

"Thanks for alerting me," she said. "Like I told Max yesterday, I'm sure she requested vacation time from Christopher before his departure."

"None of my business. I just shelve the

books," Dan said.

He disappeared into the elevator, and she was glad to be rid of him. It was four minutes until nine. She opened the door to her old office. The office she had tidied and closed up before her sabbatical. There was a folder of photocopied notes and pages waiting neatly on her desk. She took it with her to the reference area. Fussing over some work during a quiet reference shift would be a gift, she decided.

"What are you doing up here?" Francis asked, appearing around the corner almost as soon as she sat down at the reference desk.

"Covering for Miriam."

"Gone again?"

"Looks like it," she said. "I thought you might take the morning off."

"I'd have called. I wouldn't leave you wondering about me like that." He walked behind the desk where she was sitting and looked over her shoulder. She could smell his laundry detergent. "What are you working on?" he asked.

She leaned back. Just a little. So that he could better see the research materials in front of her. That she was leaning into his chest was a side effect. "My book materials," she said. Francis reached across to the open folder, and in doing so, he briefly rested his hand on hers.

8

Nearly lunch, no Miriam, and Liesl's sweat still smelled like last night's whiskey. Her whiskey sweat and the rest of her were expected at a press conference. She swiveled back and forth in Christopher's desk chair, unable to focus her eyes or attention on a piece of work. The draft press release in her email said the university was kicking off a billion-dollar fundraising campaign. She'd have given a billion dollars to drag herself, whiskey sweat and all, back to bed. But she didn't have it.

She would have to see Percy Pickens at the press conference. She would have to see other donors whose phone calls she had been so deliberately failing to return.

"Is it important that you have library representation there?" she asked the impatient secretary who had called to remind her. "The library is such a small part of the university's overall fundraising."

It was important, she was told, that they have library representation. She sat at her desk, at Christopher's desk really, and opened her appointment book to look at the stack of unanswered messages but then closed it because unanswered messages are poison. She wished she had worn a nicer jacket. She wished she weren't hungover. Noon arrived, and she walked away from the library and crossed the campus once again to go to the administration building. The sidewalks full of students were suffocating, and she felt drenched by the smell of hot dog carts and young people's hormones. Liesl was a woman who loved the outdoors. She wanted nothing more than to retreat to Christopher's stale, dark office. Any of these students could grow up to be a millionaire who donated money to the university and got to push Liesl around. Any of these students, all of these students, could one day be an unread phone message. She had worked at the university for decades; she had a pension. Liesl wanted her pension. And an aspirin.

There were press vans parked in front of the administration building. Local news. It was a big university, a big part of the city, talking about raising a big chunk of money.

Talking about asking people to donate big chunks of their money that the university would then be responsible for.

"Liesl." Garber spotted her as she checked in with his secretary. "You look terrible."

"Percy Pickens," she said. "He's been trying to call me."

"Have you spoken with him?"

"Not yet. We have to get on the same page about what we're telling him."

"The man himself!" Garber said, his face blooming into a strained smile. Liesl turned around to see Percy approaching them.

"Liesl. Have you been ill?"

Liesl paused to let the sensation of her pounding heart in her throat settle down. It didn't.

"Good afternoon, Percy. Yes, a little under the weather today."

Percy shook President Garber's hand while he looked at Liesl. "You should ask Lawrence here to make you one of his revolting smoothies. Explains why my calls are going unanswered, anyway."

"My apologies for that," she said. Liesl swayed and looked around for something to grab onto. She rested her fingertips on a wall.

"Figured I'd be certain to see you here, though."

"Yes, we're very excited about the campaign." She waited for Percy to ask if she was going to faint. He didn't.

"There's always lots of communication when you're asking for my money."

"Now, Percy," President Garber interrupted, breaking up the duo.

"Harmless joke. Is there wine?"

"Not in front of the press," Garber said with a cluck. "At the reception after."

"Good man. Liesl, can I come see my book this afternoon?"

"Terrible delays with insurance," Garber said.

"You really don't look well," Percy said. "Lawrence, does Liesl look right to you? Your skin is the color of one of Lawrence's smoothies."

Liesl, using the wall to stay upright, barely breathing as the intensity of her own pulse choked her, managed the only reply Percy wanted. "I'm fine."

"I don't think you are, Liesl," Garber said. "Percy's right. Why don't you pop back into my office and have a seat. I'll send my assistant back there to check on you in just a minute. Get your legs back. If you're feeling better, come out and join us, but stay there otherwise. Maybe it's best to give someone else at the library a call to come fill in. Max?

I'll have someone call Max, and you go on and have a seat."

"My apologies."

"None needed, Liesl. I'll give you a call later about making my date to see the Plantin."

Liesl held on to anything available as she stumbled back to Garber's office, stepping through a crowd that made way for her but didn't see her. Her head roared, her anxiety struggling to break free. She thought of the level of weakness she was displaying and only got more anxious thinking about it, and that rise in anxiety made her heart beat even harder.

Liesl crashed into Garber's office chair and waited for the dizziness to subside. This didn't feel like her. This felt like another woman. A woman who was casually lying to a billionaire. A woman who was ignoring her instincts to call the police. A woman who was expected to solve a half-million-dollar problem. A woman who had leaned back into a man who was not her husband. A woman who was hungover at work on a weekday. She waited for the dizziness to subside. She heard the crowd in the large meeting room next to Garber's office get louder and then hush as the proceedings began. She heard applause as he took the dais. She heard the click of cameras. She waited for the dizziness to subside. The dizziness didn't subside. She picked up Garber's phone. She dialed her home number.

"John speaking."

"John, it's Liesl. It's me, Liesl. Do you have a few minutes? Can you talk to me for just a few minutes?"

Back in the bad times, Liesl used to be able to push down the panic as a survival mechanism, to avoid Hannah having two parents with broken brains. Now that John had emerged from the fog, Liesl was more likely to descend into it herself occasionally. She had tried to calm the roaring with whiskey. That had worked to an extent, but it made parent-teacher conferences a bit of a mess, until one day John had noticed her peculiar shade of gray — he could recognize a fellow traveler — and began to try to calm her with his voice. The thing was, when you had spent all that time in therapy, you could get quite good at talking people off ledges.

"What's going on?" John asked.

"I think I'm having a panic attack," said Liesl. "And I hoped that you could talk to me in that way that makes me feel better when I get like this."

"My darling."

"It's fine, just talk to me."

The muffled speech through the office walls sped Liesl's breath, her heartbeat. She laid her head down on the desk and laid the phone receiver beside her.

"Did something happen today?"

"The same thing that's been happening."

"Breathe."

Garber's desk chair was wood and leather and impractical for everything besides making a man feel important. She was sweating wherever her body touched it.

"The missing book," Liesl said. "I was here half the night looking, and it seems like it's my responsibility but not my choice how I want to handle it."

He hadn't asked questions about how late she'd come in.

"Does it make you feel better to talk about it? Or does it make the panic worse?"

"Better," she said to his faint voice in the receiver. "When I'm not being blamed or told what to do."

"Then tell me about it," he said. "But first, how's your pulse?"

She closed her eyes a moment to listen to the rate of the pounding. "Slowing."

"Keep taking big breaths. Breathe like it's June and someone's just mown the grass."

"It was stolen, John." She sat up then, picked the phone back up off the desk. "I'm running around searching closets and book-shelves to keep myself busy. But it was stolen."

"How do you know?"

"Things don't disappear. I'm not stupid enough to have placed it in the wrong box or to have given it the wrong flier."

He waited for her to continue.

"Dan's not stupid enough to shelve a multivolume set incorrectly."

"When we last spoke, you said it had been misplaced. Everyone else says that too."

She began to sweat again, leaned forward so that less of the wretched chair was touching her body.

"I was wrong," she said. "Or I was saying what I hoped was true. But everyone is wrong. It was stolen."

He coached her through a few more breaths. She complied.

"Were you drinking last night?"

"I sipped at something while I was searching the stacks. Please don't lecture me. I called you because I was having a panic attack, because you're good at steadying my breathing."

"It smelled like more than a few sips when you came to bed."

"I didn't realize you were awake. And I don't know why we're talking about drinking and not the stolen book."

"Because you've said everyone is questioning your judgment."

"About the Plantin." She kneaded her temple with her hand. If the panic had subsided, then the headache, the hangover, were still in full force. "About the need to call in the police. No one except you is questioning my judgment around drinking."

"I had to ask."

"Splendid. You've asked. We drink wine in the same proportions every evening."

"How's your pulse?"

She had to put two fingers to her throat to check this time. A good sign, that she couldn't taste her pulse anymore.

"It's still elevated. My breathing is better. Arguing with you about my pinot noir consumption apparently has the effect of calming my panic attacks. They'll be finished soon; I should get ready to leave."

"Where are you?" he said. "This isn't your office number. Can I come get you?"

She turned the chair and glanced at the door as though she had to remind even herself where she was situated.

"I'm fine," said Liesl. "I'm going back to work."

"Come home early tonight."

The fatigue, the hangover, the guilt. None

of that was John's fault. But he was a place where she could put her anger.

"There's simply no way. I'm in Lawrence Garber's office. The university president. But he'll need it back now."

She hung up without saying thank you and stood to find the dizziness gone. She heard applause outside again and was sure she could sneak out of the room before she was pulled into a photo or some other obligation. There was a single knock on the door, and Garber walked into his office.

"Liesl," he said. "Not running off, I hope."

"I was," she said. "You're very busy."

"They're setting up for the photos."

Liesl smoothed her hair with her hands. "I'm in no state. I didn't dress for photos."

"You look better than you did twenty minutes ago."

"I'd have worn a suit."

"Chris is always in a suit, isn't he?"

"Noted. I'm not yet used to being the public face."

"Oh bother. That's not how I meant it. We need you in the photo."

"It will look strange to have me under-dressed."

"It will look stranger to not have the library represented."

"Max will get here soon enough if you've

158

called him."

She moved toward the door, but he didn't move away from it to let her through.

"I wanted to talk to you about something," Garber said. "I've had an idea."

"About the Plantin?"

He nodded. "What did it set us back?"

"It was 488,000 pounds. With some additional fees going to the auction house and for shipping."

"And you fundraised it all?"

"Most. We have a small discretionary fund for annual acquisitions."

"What if you didn't have to fundraise?"

"Fundraise for the Plantin?" she said. "But we already did."

"I have discretionary funds too," Garber said, leaning against his office door.

"I see," Liesl said. "But we've already paid for the Plantin."

"I'm saying we buy another."

In the mid-century modern office of a world-renowned academic, in the middle of the day, through a blistering hangover, Liesl wanted a drink.

"Well. Sir. That isn't possible."

"Wrong," he said. "Nothing is impossible if you're willing to pay for it. I have a million dollars I can put forward. For a million dollars you can make it possible."

She didn't want to insult him, but she wanted to laugh. "This is impossible," she said. "For us to buy a Plantin, one would have to be for sale."

"Let's find one for sale."

"There were only 1,200 ever printed. And that was in 1572."

"Twelve hundred is not a small number."

"I agree. But most of them were lost in a shipwreck en route to Spain shortly after they were printed."

"A shipwreck?"

"Indeed. There are only a handful in public collections around the world."

"What's a handful?" Garber asked.

Garber was bouncing on his toes, and Liesl felt her heart rate beginning to climb again.

"Twelve. There are twelve that we know of."

"So we'll have to pay a lot of money. We have a lot of money."

Liesl smiled at him. "That isn't how it works."

"That's just what you think," he said. "Anything can be bought."

"If a library holds a Plantin," Liesl said, "they can't just sell it off. It would be a public scandal."

"Libraries need money," he said. "We

quietly offer to overpay, and they wind up with an extra million dollars to fix a leaky roof or install new computers."

"Where on earth are you getting this million dollars?"

"That is up to me."

There was a polite knock on the door, but Garber yelled that he would need another minute.

"If we have a million dollars that we can quietly allocate to replace a stolen book, then why is the bulk of my time spent begging donors for money?"

"I'm certain a million dollars sounds like a lot to you, and I'm certain I sound crass, but while a million dollars is a public relations disaster, it's not a financial one. And the book was misplaced, not stolen." The knocker knocked again.

"Did Christopher know?" she asked. "About how much there was available in discretionary funds?"

"You said a library could never sell its Plantin."

"That's right," Liesl said. "We're not the only ones who are beholden to our donors. It would be a scandal."

"But they're not all held by libraries."

"What you're suggesting would never work."

The knocking on Garber's door became more rapid, louder.

"Didn't we just buy one of these books? And not from a library?"

"They're waiting for you."

Garber looked at Liesl, disappointed by her lack of imagination. Then he squared his shoulders, licked his teeth, and sent himself sailing out into the crowd without another word to her. She waited for him to get a proper head start so they wouldn't cross paths again on her way out and then went out as she had come, without being seen.

Liesl left the administration building without posing for any photos. The campus was especially crowded as students left their midday classes and headed toward libraries, dormitories, dining halls in swarms. Garber was right that the Plantin had most recently been in a private collection, but what good was that information? Could she conjure up some other distant descendant of Charles III of Spain who all of a sudden needed to pay gambling debts and was selling off family treasure?

"How was the event?" Max asked from the desk when she returned. "Did you outline our fundraising priorities to the press?" As ever, he had a hand to his collar, worrying the top button of his shirt.

Max had taken off his suit jacket and had put on a white lab coat to keep dust off of his clothes. It had never occurred to her before that like Christopher, Max wore a suit to work every day.

"There wasn't the opportunity," Liesl said to Max. "It's not a good time to be making ourselves available for questions."

"It's always a good time to let the public know what we need to complement our collections."

"I disagree."

II

Liesl hadn't come in early that morning, and she didn't stay late. She wanted only to ease out of the day without undue effort. She staggered through her front door at 5:20.

"I wasn't expecting you for a few more hours," John called down from the studio. "You said you couldn't get home early."

"Sorry to disappoint."

"Don't be silly. I'm thrilled you're home."

"Don't call me silly. That's not what I need today."

"Mom!"

Liesl took a step back at the warning, the reprimand laced through the familiar word.

She hadn't expected to see Hannah at the house and definitely hadn't expected to find herself called out for poor behavior by the girl. No matter. She was thrilled to see her daughter and pulled her into a hug as soon as she came into view.

"Oh, you beautiful thing."

"What's the matter?" Hannah asked.

Liesl took one of Hannah's hands and kissed her palm. The girl had all the best of Liesl. Her seriousness but not her reserve. Her big, open smile but not her crooked nose. When Liesl hugged her, it was like hugging a rose-scented blanket. She kissed Hannah's palm again. The girl brought her such comfort; the girl was her best evidence that she had done something right. It was a selfish way to think for a parent, so she never said it aloud, but on a day when she so needed comfort, she allowed herself a moment of relief in that blanket.

"What could be the matter," Liesl said, "when my beautiful girl is here?"

Hannah put her arm around her mother and walked her into the kitchen where the afternoon light was streaming through the big window over the sink. Liesl had come home needing to yell at someone after a long day of not being able to say how she felt, but Hannah was a balm. When John came into the kitchen and kissed the top of Liesl's head, she didn't flinch. She sat at the kitchen table and watched their backs, watched them preparing dinner together until the yellow afternoon light had passed and Hannah broke Liesl's spell, turning around to ask her mother to flip on a lamp.

III

Not for one minute had Liesl considered that Miriam would not be at work on Monday. Miriam's computer was set to sleep, not even logged all the way out. As if she had stepped away from it for a minute with a plan to return. There was a gray archival box on her desk and a series of acid-free folders containing manuscript pages from a semifamous Canadian writer stacked next to her keyboard. Resting next to the pages was a pencil in need of sharpening. Miriam's desk lamp had been left on this whole time. The lamp, the clutter, it had all escaped Liesl's notice until Monday morning when Miriam failed to arrive at work again.

"You haven't spoken with her?" Liesl asked.

"No," Francis said. "But I never do outside of work."

Francis was scheduled to work at the

reference desk, and Liesl was lingering beside him, looking for answers about Miriam. The rest of the library's staff had arrived for the day, and from the workroom she could hear laughing and clattering keyboards and squeaky book truck wheels. Behind the desk where Francis was sitting, someone had hung a giant red sign announcing an upcoming exhibition of Russian propaganda posters. The light bounced off it and made Francis look pink and healthy.

"What do you want to do?" Francis asked. "I thought you suspected she'd taken vacation days."

"I had."

Liesl had tried phoning Miriam on Friday, just as she had on Thursday. She'd tried again that very morning, and the only difference was that Miriam's voice mailbox was full so Liesl couldn't leave any additional messages.

Dan rolled a book truck through the reference area. He nodded hello, and the three stood in silence while he waited for the elevator.

"It was the most obvious explanation," she said once Dan had gone. "I never thought she'd just disappear."

"She hasn't disappeared."

"She has, though. An adult doesn't stop showing up for work on a whim. Not unless something has happened."

Liesl left Francis to his books. She had an idea for how she might reach Miriam that she was embarrassed hadn't occurred to her earlier.

She nodded as she walked to the office, thinking, *Daft woman, lousy leader, abysmal investigator, too wrapped up to grab the nearest rock and peer under it for answers.* She picked up the desk phone, began to dial, and then hung it up before she'd finished, walking instead to her purse and taking out her cell phone and, distracted by her task, taking it out to the loading dock where it would be loud, true, but loud with people who weren't interested in Liesl's business. She considered a seat on the concrete steps but wrote it off as too dusty, then she lightly tapped the numbers that she read off a card and dialed the person who she should have called immediately.

"It's so good to speak with you, Vivek," Liesl said when he answered the phone. "How are you settling into your new role?"

There was a pause as Vivek seemed to walk from a loud room to somewhere quieter.

"It's good, thank you," he said. "They

have me teaching three courses this term. I think it's a hazing ritual."

Liesl had viewed Vivek's profile page from the university directory to get his phone number. She pictured his staff photo as they spoke. He was handsome in a way she'd never noticed.

"Hazing indeed," she said as a heavy box of books landed on a squeaky dolly ten feet from her. "When I was in college the main method of hazing was servitude, so I guess a heavy course load isn't far off."

"I don't mind too much, to be honest."

"No. I'm sure it's a great way to get to know your students."

"Exactly," Vivek said. "I have a couple of papers that will be coming out this year, so I can take a bit of a research break."

She cleared her throat and turned her back to the noise. "Listen, Vivek. I actually have a sort of embarrassing reason to be calling."

"I'm sure it isn't embarrassing. Though I have to say I'm surprised to be hearing from you."

One of the shippers had lit a cigarette and the haze wafting over to Liesl reminded her of Christopher.

"I'm sure you are," she said.

"I mean no offense. I remember every dinner you ever bought me and Miriam while I was a grad student. I consider you a friend. But all things considered . . ." Vivek waited for Liesl to fill in the blank, but she didn't, so it was dead air between them.

She stretched her neck and took a long inhale of the downwind smoke, and it was only after she'd let it out in an equally long exhale that she broke the silence on the line.

"I don't know what things you mean."

"Maybe you should go first. Why are you calling, Liesl?"

"Miriam has been absent from work for a few days, and I'm getting worried."

Over on the loading dock, the back door of a delivery van closed with a satisfying rattle, and then there were no more people, just a skid of packaged books sitting all by itself.

"You mean she's been ill?" Vivek asked.

"It might be that. But she hasn't called to say so, and I can't get her on the phone."

"How long, Liesl? When did you last see her?" There was something in Vivek's voice that Liesl couldn't land on, a quality that made her want to, need to see his face to understand.

"She was last at work on Wednesday," Liesl said. "Has she been home sick?"

"I don't know," Vivek said. "I've been staying with my parents."

"I see."

"She didn't call at all?" Vivek said. "That isn't like her." The pitch of his voice was rising. "Why didn't you call sooner? How worried do you think I should be?"

Liesl held the phone against her shoulder, so she had her hands free to pick at a hangnail. "Things have been uncertain around here. I thought she might have taken the days as vacation."

"Is that possible? That she would have done that without you knowing?"

"It's possible, yes," Liesl said. "Christopher was never one for paperwork. She might have asked him for the days off." The timbre of Vivek's voice, the thing she couldn't see, had gotten all the way inside her and made her twitchy. She walked across the loading dock because she found she couldn't stand in one place any longer.

"And you have no reason to suspect anything different?" Vivek asked.

Liesl remembered it again. Miriam in front of her, desperate to talk. Brushed off, forgotten. Had it been about Vivek? Had she rushed to Liesl to confess their separation?

"Well, no. Unless you think I do?"

He mumbled a general no. "You'll let me

know when you hear from her?" Vivek asked.

Liesl agreed that she would. She had a lot of questions about the state of their marriage. How his move back to the city could bring them further apart rather than closer together. But it wasn't the time for those questions.

She hesitated before hanging up the phone, scratched at a loose label on one of the boxes, chemistry books from a German publisher for the science library. She didn't want to let him go yet, didn't think she should. "Maybe you and I can have lunch when things are more settled."

"Sure," Vivek said. "When things are more settled."

"She'll come back from her holiday and think we've been very silly for worrying," Liesl said.

"Well," Vivek said. "I don't think it's silly at all to worry."

9

I

The gilt-edged cards inviting the Friends of the Library to attend the annual Jackman Lecture didn't explicitly say that the Plantin would be the topic. The invitations had gone out months earlier, before the check cleared. But there was subtext. The Jackman Lecture existed to make the library's "friends" feel special. The university had more infrastructure to encourage donations than it had to keep the buildings standing.

There was condensation threatening the books in a small area on the northwest side of the building. But Liesl wasn't spending her time dealing with the water. She was spending her time planning the Jackman Lecture. Or not planning the Jackman Lecture but staring into the middle distance and fanning herself with one of the gilt-edged cards. The phone on Christopher's desk rang, scolding her for her lack of concentration. She reluctantly picked up the receiver, because the solution to her Jackman problem might be on the other end. It was a man from the university's IT department. Liesl did not ask him if he would be willing to deliver the Jackman Lecture. He asked if he could visit that day and change the passwords on Christopher's accounts so she could access them. This was such a sensible request that she was sure it had something to do with donations. She agreed. She put down the phone's receiver and, after a beat, tucked the card into her pocket, pulled on her coat, and left the office.

Visiting the computer science and mathematics building, Liesl came up with the beginnings of a plan. As she walked into the back stairwell, two undergrads were huddled in the corner. One of the kids had an orange prescription bottle, and he got so spooked that he jammed it into his pocket. By the time she understood the nature of the transaction she was halfway up the steps. By then, it was too late to tell the kids that prescription drugs weren't illegal, and acting as though they were was a great way to tip off a passerby that they were up to something.

Rhonda had a film crew outside her office. A couple of young men in black T-shirts were taking down an elaborate lighting setup. Rhonda was bent over in front of the camera on her laptop, wiping off makeup with a baby wipe.

"Is this a news crew or our internal people?" Liesl whispered as she greeted the woman. "There are some kids dealing Adderall in your stairwell. I don't want any of these guys getting the idea they're a journalist."

"Guys?" Rhonda looked up at the crew. "Can you make sure you take your stuff down through the service elevator? I know the stairs are faster, but they really don't want you interfering with students coming and going."

There were nods and mumbles of assent. Slowly, the crew and their lights cleared out.

"I wouldn't have guessed you as an expert in the collegiate drug trade," Rhonda said.

"I briefly sent my daughter to a private high school."

"But you're not here to bust local amphetamine entrepreneurs?" Rhonda knelt on the floor, picking at the edge of a masking-tape X, a lighting mark that the crew had forgotten to remove.

"I'm not." Liesl moved to help her but then stopped herself. "Was the crew here for the fundraising campaign launch?"

"Yes, they're going to run a series on our past Nobel winners. I was asked to speak for the dead ones." Rhonda managed to lift a corner and began to peel, but it immediately tore. She raised her eyes at Liesl in exasperation.

"I have a favor to ask," Liesl said. "Sorry to dive right in."

"Not at all," Rhonda said. "If you're interested in what I have to say about dead Nobel prize winners, you can tune into the local news tonight at 7:30."

"The library has an annual Jackman Memorial Lecture. For our donors. A major event. I was hoping you might come deliver the lecture this year."

"When is it?"

"It's a little tight to be honest. The lecture is scheduled for Friday." Liesl crouched, an unnatural position for a women of her vintage, but towering over someone as you were asking them to do you a favor felt wrong.

"Oh, I see," Rhonda said, still picking at bits of tape with the nail of her index finger. "I take it that I'm not the library's first choice. I'm not sure if my feelings should be hurt."

"I promise they shouldn't be."

"Don't console me too much; it only makes me more suspicious. What is it I'm to be lecturing about?" She crumpled the bits of tape she had managed to remove so far into a satisfying little ball.

"So you'll do it then?" Liesl asked, standing again before her knees failed her.

"It's my job to communicate with the public about the university's research."

"This is ultimately a fundraising venture."

"But isn't everything," Rhonda said, finally looking up from the tape, "when you look at it closely enough?"

"We were going to be unveiling a new acquisition," Liesl said.

"I see." She paused her work on the tape and put her hand to her cheek, likely feeling its soft coolness from the baby wipe. "Liesl, most of your work falls within the realm of the humanities and social sciences. I'm not sure how interesting I'd be to that crowd."

"You'd be perfect."

"I'll bet you said that to the first six people you asked too."

Liesl nodded, bit her thumbnail for a moment. She knew better than to flatter in this situation.

"There's been a hiccup, and instead of something new, I thought we might use the Peshawar as the subject of the lecture."

"Well. You have my attention."

Liesl really wished that Rhonda would get up off the floor, but she was sitting cross-legged now, craning her neck as though Liesl were a teacher with an acoustic guitar during circle time.

"You said the zero is your area of study . . ."

"So I can whip up a keynote presentation on seventy-two hours' notice."

"I shouldn't have asked," Liesl said.

"No, I'm saying I *can* whip up a keynote presentation on seventy-two hours' notice."

"So you'll do it?" Liesl said. She hadn't realized she'd been holding her breath, but it whooshed out with her relief. Finally, a problem solved. "I can hardly believe my luck."

"Luck has nothing to do with it," Rhonda said, going back to pick at the tape now that the matter was settled. "I'd love to lecture a bunch of moneyed humanists on the vitality of early mathematics."

"Well, yes. Though it is still a fundraiser."

"Liesl, you don't have to worry."

"I wasn't."

"It's my entire job. To make science sound interesting. I can handle this."

"I can't thank you enough," Liesl said. "I'm not sure what I would have done."

"You can thank me by allowing me some time to work with the manuscript to prepare. Seems a pity to meet for the first time on the wedding night. Is there a day this week I could come by?"

Liesl crossed her arms reflexively, not knowing how serious Rhonda's request was, not knowing its conditions.

"If it's no, will you still do it?" Liesl asked.

"Grudgingly, but I suppose I would."

Liesl thought of her calendar, of the pile of messages on her desk.

"It can't be this week."

"May I ask why?"

"Simple logistics," Liesl said. "I'm away at a book fair for most of the week."

There was no existing rule that the library director had to supervise the use of the highest-value collections. But Liesl wasn't taking chances.

"My office will be in touch to confirm the details for the lecture," Rhonda said.

"Thank you."

"Enjoy your book fair, Liesl," Rhonda said as she triumphantly pulled one full line of tape off the floor, dangling it in front of her like a scalp.

"Rhonda?" Liesl said.

"Yes?"

Liesl pressed her hands together in gratitude. "Really, though, thank you."

II

Liesl returned to the library at noon, shaking off the anxiety of a near disaster, and although he was meant to be presenting materials to a group of undergraduates, Francis was waiting at the door of her office when she returned. "You saw, then," he said. "No Miriam again today."

"I did."

"She was always a bit strange, that one."

"Why do you say that?" she asked.

"Always kind of quiet. I don't know."

"It's a library," Liesl said. "Everyone's quiet."

He came in and sat down.

"Probably run off with a lover."

"Don't say that," she said. "I'm getting quite worried about her."

He leaned back and put his feet on the desk.

"I'm wondering if I should report her missing," Liesl said. "Would you put your feet up like that if Christopher were here?"

"Suppose I wouldn't."

"Then please do me the courtesy."

The morning had passed in a blink, and with the day half-over, Liesl's anxiety about unfinished tasks came back around. Francis picked up on Liesl's disquiet and lowered his feet to the floor to keep from egging her on, as if a bit of dirt at the edge of the desk were the root of her consternation. Her face clouded with frustration.

"Chris's desk was always too cluttered with books to fit feet on it," Francis said. "If it wasn't, I might have done so."

"Do you think I should report Miriam?"

He leaned on his armrest and gave a weary sigh. "I don't."

"It's going to be a week soon."

"Liesl," he said. "What is it with you and wanting to go to the police?"

She looked over Francis's shoulder at her open office door, willing Miriam to walk through it. "What is it with you and telling me not to?"

"I'm saving you from your own worst inclinations."

"Wouldn't you want someone to call if you were missing?"

Francis was an old man who lived alone. It was an unfair question with unfair implications.

"Have you talked to Vivek?"

"Yes," Liesl said. "It sounds like they've separated or are having a big row."

He slapped his thigh. "Probably run off with a lover!"

With a little bit of guilt, but only a little, she rolled her eyes at him. "We're talking about Miriam here."

"I don't presume to make assumptions about librarians."

She put her hand to her cheek to conceal a blush that was creeping up from her neck. "You really don't think I should tell someone?"

"I don't. This is between her and Vivek. Don't embarrass her like this."

"Off with a lover?" she said, sounding more like an exasperated parent than a concerned manager. Rising from her seat, Liesl signaled to Francis that it was time to go.

"Don't be jealous now," he said with a wink.

He sprung from his chair and went toward the office door, where he had a book truck with a modern manuscript sitting on it, signaling to her that it was his intention to stay. He took the pages and laid them on the desk in front of Liesl. *The Department of Rare Books and Special Collections: Library Treasures Through the Ages,* the title read. By Christopher Wolfe and Francis Churchill. It was at least a couple hundred pages. Years of research must have gone into it.

She gently turned the first pages and

landed on the first chapter. It was about the Peshawar. She couldn't recognize the voice as fully belonging to Christopher or Francis. It was the best of both of them. A lively telling of how the manuscript had come to be in the library, written like a mystery, written to keep her turning pages.

"The real reason I came in to bother you."

"What is this?"

Francis walked around the desk and stood behind her, as if showing her how to swaddle his newborn baby.

"Chris and I," he said. "We've been doing this in the background for years. It's meant to be our masterpiece. To tell the story of the place through the books that live here."

"The Peshawar?" asked Liesl.

"A secret favorite of Chris's."

"It's wonderful," she said. "There's so much love in it."

She turned to see the other chapters. Next was on a groundbreaking work of human anatomy from the sixteenth century.

"The Vesalius," she said with a sigh. "Of course. I used to joke that I wanted to be loved by a man the way Christopher loved the Vesalius."

"Aren't you, though?" he said. She didn't reply.

"It'll be illustrated," Francis continued,

taking a seat again.

"It would need to be," said Liesl, "to show off how magnificent those anatomical drawings are."

"We were waiting for some funding to do the photographs properly."

"Can I see what's next?" Liesl said. "Is it the Shakespeare?"

"Indeed it is."

"I want to abandon my work and sit here and read every word. The writing is delightful, Francis."

"It's easy to do with Chris. The way he thinks about and talks about and writes about this collection. I really do think he considers the books to be like his children."

"There has to be more to the story, hasn't there?" Liesl said. "I know you two were great friends, but I never saw him as one to collaborate. His work always seemed so solitary."

"He's more collaborative than we think. Just private about it."

"Hard to be collaborative and private all at once."

"Maybe," he said. "It was his idea to keep our work quiet."

"Did he say why?"

"He wanted to work slowly. There will be such a great fuss once it's published."

"It will be great for your career, I'm sure you know."

"I can't say I haven't thought about it. He's generous in that way without showing it off. A good man. A damn good thing he's not dealing with the Plantin mess. It would have given him a stroke if he hadn't already had one."

"Are there more pages?" she asked.

Francis didn't immediately reply. Couldn't reply. He was weeping.

Liesl reached across the desk, hesitated a moment, and then covered his hand with hers, a comfort, a promise, a reminder. Francis turned his palm up. They sat and relived a shared and complicated history, theirs and Christopher's, as he stroked his thumb back and forth across her wrist.

"What a picture I am," he finally said. "But the man has meant so much in my life. And I'm scared he'll die. Almost as scared as I am he'll wake up to this."

"There's a third option," Liesl said. She pulled her hand back and passed him a tissue. She saw that the full weight of his emotion was wrapped in the possibility of his mentor's death. "He could come out of it and tell us all about the safe place where the Plantin has been all along, and we can all feel very silly and very relieved."

"Liesl," said Francis. "Do you believe that there's any chance at all of that happening?"

"I think there is very little chance. But not none."

"I'm scared he'll die."

"That might happen too. He's not a young man." She shot him a look of apology, but at her age she had learned it was easier to be honest about the proximity of death.

Francis rubbed his eyes with the heels of his hands.

"Is it daft if I say it feels like my father is dying?"

Liesl went over to the office door and closed it. She hated how it would look, sitting in here with Francis behind closed doors like coconspirators, but a man was owed a closed door for his tears. When the door clicked into place, Francis allowed himself permission to issue a great sob and then began to take deep breaths to try to stem the tears.

"There's nothing daft about it," Liesl said.

He nodded. "He's not that much older than I am."

"That's not what makes a father."

"He's taught me so bloody much."

It was too early for the bottle, but without the bottle she had no idea what to do about the tears.

"After my divorce," he said, "he taught me how to be excited about life again. The way he was excited by his books."

Liesl sat and listened as Francis wept over the man she would never measure up to. On the desk was a stack of preview catalogs from booksellers who would be at the fair. Her eyes wandered over, and she calculated how late she would be at work that evening, marking them up, but then she chastened herself. Here was a man putting the contents of his heart on display.

"He loves these books like a man loves his bloody children," he said. His tone had changed.

"And he'll be back with them," Liesl said. "And you. When it's time for goodbye it will be on his terms."

"Except with the Plantin," he said. "He'll never get to count the Plantin as part of his collection."

"You don't know that," Liesl said.

"Bollocks we don't. The book is gone. And you know what else? What I can't stop my mind from thinking? The book disappears and then who goes right after it? Seems too tidy to be a coincidence."

"Don't say something you'll later regret," Liesl said. "You're the one who said that you thought she had taken a lover."

"I did," he said. "And you said that was impossible."

Mousy Miriam. Maudlin Miriam. Mawkish Miriam. Thoroughly Medium Miriam. Malevolent Miriam? It was the only solution that was more ridiculous than Mistress Miriam.

"Isn't that all the more reason to report Miriam missing to the police?" Liesl asked. "If she's some brilliant bandit?"

"They'd learn of the theft, and then the donors would. Can't do it."

"You're going to get yourself committed with this line of thinking," Liesl said. Francis looked hurt.

She in her light-blue coat and he in his tears, she took him by the arm and swept him out of her office and out of the library. Past the yellow falafel truck and the stoic anti-abortion protesters they found an empty bench in the shade of the library building. Inside the library his tears were conspicuous, but out here, amid all this youth, they could be invisible.

"Don't tell me you haven't thought it," he said.

"Not for a moment. Not Miriam."

"I want to fix this for Chris."

"I know you do."

They sat on the bench under the tree close enough for their thighs to touch. There was no time for this sitting. Later that night, Liesl would think about the hour they spent, mostly in silence, and she would think of the pressure of his left thigh against her right. She thought about it as the sun set and as the streetlamps came on and as John called the office to see when she was coming home and she told him not for a while because she was poring over catalogs and planning for the book fair. She didn't regret the hour. Students followed by students followed by students walked by them, mothers pushing strollers on walks through the leafy campus, administrators in suits, and faculty members in brown blazers, but no one noticed them, and no one asked why they were sitting so close that their thighs touched. So they kept sitting.

"I'm moved that you shared the manuscript with me," she said.

"I knew you would understand. I hoped you would."

"Maybe you can show me the rest of the chapters later," she said.

They finally loped inside with the almost-limp of almost-old people who had been sitting on a hard surface for too long. At the revolving door he motioned for her to go ahead, and just for a moment, he placed his hand on the small of her back to guide her through.

But in the library there was a man, a man they had never seen before, and their guards went back up, and their hands stayed close to their own bodies.

"Hello, Liesl. I've been waiting for you."

"For me?" she said. "Is this about Miriam?"

"Who's Miriam?"

"Who are you?"

"I'm from IT," the man said. "Here to change the passwords." He was wearing a short-sleeved button-down shirt, fastened to the neck, tucked into oversized Dockers. There was no way he could be anything but a representative from the IT department.

"Come on back to the office. I'm sorry to keep you waiting."

She led him into Christopher's office. Her purse hung on the coatrack. Her papers and catalogs were stacked neatly on the table. The room was even beginning to smell like her shampoo. He sat down at the computer right away and clacked at the keys for only a moment before inviting her to sit down.

"It's unlocked for you," he said. "You'll be prompted to change the password right away. Once you do, you'll have access to his email, calendars, documents, to his full identity. I did a quick inventory, and it doesn't look like he ever accessed additional drives, so it will all be straightforward. Have any questions?"

She indicated that she didn't, and he left with a polite wave. She sat in front of the computer and, with the stroke of a few keys, slipped into Christopher's identity. She opened the documents folder. There was nothing in it. She clicked to open his email. There was an error message saying it had never been set up. She clicked through folder after folder after folder. Nothing. Christopher Wolfe was a digital ghost.

10

The book fair was in the big convention center, the one by the airport. It was not a good part of town. Liesl drove past the strip clubs advertising chicken-wing specials and past the Ramada and the Hilton and the Delta and the Best Western and past the motels that didn't have brand names and didn't care whether their guest stayed the whole night. The neighborhood couldn't decide whether it wanted to facilitate business or bad behavior.

She had left home not knowing if she would make it to the fair in time, but she found herself in the parking lot twenty minutes early, so she sat in the driver's seat and read her catalogs while hunger and anxiety turned her stomach. The engine ran so she could keep the windshield wipers running, and every five seconds they swished away the water and cleared her view.

When the doors to the fair were unlocked,

the windshield wipers were off and Liesl was out of the car, waiting. A man named Steve who didn't know that the book fair was a test of Liesl and her ability to do her job well scanned her badge and remarked about the weather.

The aisles of glass and wood bookshelves forming pretend bookshops had been laid over a deep-red carpet that stretched across the full conference center. Had the red carpet been here in previous years? Liesl couldn't remember, but she hated it. Her shoes were damp from the rain, and it felt as though blood were squelching up between her toes every time she took a step. The biggest vendors with the biggest shops had set up along the central aisle. They looked more like an outpost of Tiffany's than a dusty old book room, these big shops with their glass display cases, twinkling lights, and Hugo Boss–suited sales staff. They weren't for Liesl, these big shops.

They were after the big-fish private collectors who were looking for something to brag about at their next tennis game. Liesl would let those customers overpay, hold on to their treasures for ten years, and then donate their finds to the library when they decided they'd rather have a tax receipt than a signed first edition of *Goodbye, Columbus.*

She started at the edges of the show. Christopher had taught her that the first year. The stalls were smaller, the shelves were borrowed from someone's basement, and there were treasures. The inner aisles were where you went to shake hands; the outer aisles were where you went to make deals. She saw it all without making it look like she was too interested. She allowed her eyes to linger on some lovely eighteenth-century horticultural books, and she looked back over her shoulder, trying to mark their location in her memory. Maybe if there was money left at the end of the day, or maybe if she could convincingly call them science books and pay for them with the science fund, or maybe she would just buy them for herself and take them home so they could watch her work from her own bookshelf.

An exhibitor who knew how the game worked displayed some materials of regional interest on a folding card table. Turn-of-the-century ephemera advertising the railway, a Polish translation in a handsome dust jacket from a local author. The collection was a smattering with no melody tying it all together, but Liesl didn't mind. She liked the hunt. She didn't want arrows telling her where the pearls would be.

She left the quiet outer edge. The next

aisle over had mostly wood shelving, not plastic, but the exhibitors were in rumpled Oxford shirts, not Italian suits. A memorial pamphlet for a Chinese female revolutionary published in Shanghai in 1907. She paused. The bookseller explained that Qiu Jin had been an advocate of female education and women's rights before she was beheaded in 1907. The bookseller had failed to fasten one of the buttons on the collar of his button-down shirt. Liesl was hungry. She thought an $18,000 acquisition might satisfy her appetite. She asked the exhibitor to hold the pamphlet pending a call back to the university.

Two booths over and still tingling, she saw a familiar face.

Dressed like a history professor who had been on a two-day bender, Don Lake grabbed Liesl into a hug when he saw her. The bookseller had been operating D. E. Lake Books in the city since Liesl was a student. He was on the periphery of the show; business wasn't booming, but he looked nothing but pleased to see her.

Liesl looked at his table, second editions and minor works, until she caught sight of something that made her bite the inside of her cheek so hard it bled.

"What is that doing here?" she asked.

"It's been in my collection for years."

Don Lake put his hands on it. Don Lake wasn't a thief, but he would have to be if her eyes weren't deceiving her. She ran her hands over the familiar black binding of the Peshawar manuscript on his table.

"It's a facsimile, of course," he added.

She hadn't wet herself in decades. It would have been a terrible day to break the streak.

"Can't imagine it's of any interest for your collections; you already have one."

"Of course," she said. "It's so convincing."

She wanted to go collect herself, but now Don Lake wanted to talk about the facsimile. The early-twentieth-century printer had thought himself clever and printed onto birch bark, same as the original, and the effect was that the facsimiles had been darkening at more or less the same rate as the original. Liesl flexed her toes in her wet shoes as a way to offload her discomfort. It was like meeting her twin sister for the first time. The card stock that held the birch leaves in place was the same ridged beige, the album cover the same weathered black. Only the frontispiece, which gave the identity of the creator and indicated that 165 of these reproductions had been made, gave away that it was a facsimile.

The library held many of these facsimiles. They could be collector's items. But it was the first time that Liesl had stood in front of a facsimile of a book when she knew the original so well. It changed the shape of what she understood. It was an impostor, and she didn't like that it was allowed to exist.

She squeezed Don Lake's forearm and, legs stiff, limped toward the next booth. He called back to her, tried to draw her attention to a map that he thought would be a nice complement to the library's collection on the settlement of the American West, but she declined, promising to send her map expert to the bookshop to take a look if the item remained unsold by the close of the show. She crossed into the next aisle to get away from him, the time and the proximity to the center of the show meaning that the crowds were thickening now, and she could get lost in them.

This close to the heart, the treasures were in glass display cases rather than on plastic folding tables, and they had printed labels rather than hand-drawn pricing signs.

It went faster now. The sellers were busy; the materials couldn't be picked up and inspected. Liesl wanted to ask about a mid-century *Anne of Green Gables* in a dust jacket she hadn't ever seen before. But it would have to come later. At the appointed time, she was back at the front of the show, waiting.

It was uncharitable to think that Max had been lurking in a corner so that he and his sweater vest could stride out just as the second hand was striking, but his ability to arrive neither a second early nor late left little alternate explanation. At Max's suggestion, he and his sweater vest and Liesl and her wet feet started down the middle aisle.

The place was lousy with bibles. Printers loved printing bibles, and Max loved acquiring them, studying them, talking about them. The New Testaments were coming at her from every direction. Max would fall in love with a binding, a frontispiece, a printing error and would sing in her ear about the need to invest, the need to win the rare-books-library bible arms race. To Liesl, Max was the right choice over Francis to accompany her to the fair. There were never, wouldn't ever be rumors about her and Max. So she had to keep her mouth shut, nod in the right places, and wait for raised eyebrows to make their ways south.

There was a twelfth-century illuminated

leaf from the book of Joshua that Max insisted she had to see. Her mind wandered back to the gold calligraphy on blue vellum and to her wish to hold that piece in her hands. She could see that the book of Joshua leaf was special; she was skeptical but not blind to the winged creature inked in blue dividing the columns of text. She let Max haggle, knowing that with a starting cost of $5,900, there was no amount of bargaining that would reduce the fee to something reasonable for a single sheet.

"Well," she said when they walked off empty-handed. "There will be others."

"What a thing to think. You don't believe that?"

"Won't there?" she said. "Hundreds of exhibitors here would disagree."

"That piece is singular," he said.

"Of course I understand that," Liesl said.

He let it hang there. She knew he didn't think she understood at all.

"Somewhere in France, eight hundred years ago, a Dominican monk labored over that piece," Max said. To avoid a lecture about Dominican monks, she was willing to write him a check for the $5,900 from her own bank account.

"We're responsible for the pieces that are singular," he said, his hand back at his collar, always at that collar.

"Like the Plantin?" she asked. A lecture about the Plantin would still be a lecture, but it might be of use to her.

"Like the Plantin," he agreed.

"How are you taking the loss? It must be a blow."

"All right," he said. "I feel powerless, but I'm a Catholic, so it's a familiar feeling."

"That's funny," Liesl said in a tone that made clear that it wasn't, not really. "What were your plans for the Plantin? Exhibition? Digitization? Research?"

"You have a lot of questions," he said.

A map seller in a newsboy cap pulled Max into a hug as they walked by. He expressed his sorrow at Christopher's condition. He didn't acknowledge Liesl. They walked on.

"I had no plans yet," Max said when they were out of the map seller's earshot. "I just wanted a chance to see it."

"But you had a chance, didn't you? During the acquisition? I'm certain that you and I talked about it when it first went missing. You inspected it before the purchase?"

Max crossed his arms over his chest.

"I did no such thing."

"You're responsible for religion collections."

"Christopher didn't ask me to weigh in,"

Max said. "He went to the auction alone, and he handled the acquisition alone."

"Why didn't you say that? In our meeting, when I first asked?"

"I didn't realize I was under investigation."

She wondered about Max, and then she felt guilty for wondering about Max, but there was nothing she could do to keep from wondering. She wished she could remove the thought from her mind, but the truth was that Max was a man who had made certain promises to the church and had failed to keep them. She didn't know the details, but the broad strokes were enough to make an impression.

"Better to offer all the information you have from the outset, though, isn't it?"

"I've found that isn't always the case," he said. She wondered if a man who broke those big promises would not violate other types of trust.

They stopped for a coffee at the stand on the far end of the exhibition hall. It was watery and served in maroon paper cups. The aisles of the fair were properly full now. The professional collectors and cultural institutions already halfway through their days, the moneyed private collectors resting their elbows on glass cases as far as the eye

could see, and the spaces in between occupied by the garage-sale set in their cargo
shorts, looking for a treasure for less than
the cost of a tank of gas and oblivious to
how much the book dealers disdained them.
They were all so old, Liesl thought. Was she
that old?

"There wasn't any point where you saw
or handled or were alone with the Plantin?"

"No. There wasn't any point. You can ask
Dan if you like, since it's obvious that this
is an investigation. Just make it clear that
you're looking to humiliate me, not exoner-
ate me. He can confirm that I never got the
chance to help with the Plantin, because he
was delighted by the idea of my exclusion."

Liesl slid in closer, rested her fingers on
her pursed lips, thinking that this disclosure
that he was embarrassed to have been
excluded was as open as Max had ever been
with her. Max was ramrod straight, eyes on
his empty cup instead of her, but Liesl
wanted to believe that she'd be able to tell
if he was lying. And she didn't think he was.

"Would you like another coffee?" she
asked.

They were both at the end of their cups of
tepid brown water.

"Why not?"

"I'll get it," she said. "Maybe a biscuit too.

To help it go down easier." She went to stand in the line.

The first time she'd ever seen Max, he had still been wearing the collar of his chosen profession. He removed it for the last time shortly thereafter. But he still had posture like a priest. The sweater vest and shirt buttoned to its very top button, this was a man you could tell your sins to. Perched at the edge of his chair, he didn't notice that Liesl was watching him, because he was watching the room. That Liesl could see, there were three tiers of people in Max's eyes. Those at the convention who, upon sight, warranted a light nod. Those who warranted a wave and a hello, and in very special cases, those who got Max out of his chair for a handshake and a conversation with heads tilted toward each other. She wondered about these hushed conversations. She reached the front of the line and ordered more coffee and two biscuits. She crossed back to the table with the purchases, interrupting one of Max's tilted-head conversations.

He didn't offer the identity of his guest, and she didn't ask. He might have thought that she wasn't interested. He might have thought that he was entitled to his secrets. He oohed over the cookies, saying he rarely gave in to temptation. That brought about an awkward pause. They had been off the floor for forty-five minutes, which was too long. There were still hundreds of people in need of a nod, a wave, or a handshake.

When they returned to the show floor, Liesl looked at Max for signs of nervousness. If he was lying about the Plantin, the fair would be a place for him to meet a potential seller or to cross paths with an accomplice. Max's perpetually perfect posture made him undecipherable.

There was a display of Lutheran ephemera. A collector, to whom Max said hello, was writing a check for $25,000. The exhibitor noted the amount on a scratch pad and pocketed the check. The rules of modern commerce did not apply here.

"What if the check doesn't clear?" Liesl said. They were walking away from the Lutheran.

"No one here is a stranger," Max said.

Liesl nodded to an exhibitor who had once sold her a *Gatsby* with a perfect dust jacket.

"Don't want to go say hello?"

"No."

"You sometimes act as though you're new to this, or outside this somehow," Max said. "The book world is a small world."

"We take care of our own, is that right?"

Liesl said. "And that's why I shouldn't go to the police about the Plantin? I've heard it already."

"That isn't at all what I was talking about," Max said. "And if it were, I'd tell you that I think you should go to the police about the Plantin."

"What are you talking about?" she said. "All I've been hearing is that I shouldn't do that."

"You haven't been hearing that from me," Max said.

Liesl pulled him away from the table, away from where others could hear. "What do you mean?"

"That I agree you should go to the police."

For a long moment Liesl considered throwing her arms around Max, who still looked as warm as a light pole as he expressed solidarity with her. Liesl thought she finally had a partner, but then gradually she calmed and led him to the corner of the exhibition floor where there were two chairs set up at an empty table, a vacant booth that had been set aside for an Italian seller who had canceled due to a bout of the flu. Liesl waited until they were seated and private, her tongue clenched between her teeth all the while.

"The book world is an insular place," she

finally said, using his own words against him. She was arguing against her own position.

"The Plantin was stolen. I'm sure of it now," he said. "Whoever did this has broken the rules of our community."

Why she had assumed he was the enemy she didn't know. Or she did, but the reason made her ashamed. It was a kind of prejudice that came with not understanding the choices that someone had made. But they were not competitors. She knew he assumed himself to be next in line after Christopher, and that in no way interfered with her plan to retire.

"Well," she said. "You ought to have told me that earlier. I've been the only one arguing this position."

A dealer of regional literature interrupted their private session. Shook hands, reminded them of the location of his booth and that there was good money to be spent there.

"It wouldn't make a difference," Max said when they were alone again.

"The more on the side of reporting the theft, the better."

"The other voices are louder," Max said. "Louder and more influential."

Liesl was waiting for a sign, hoping that

the question of the missing books would resolve itself in her mind, but with every day that passed, with every conversation she had, the knot got more tangled. Liesl was dismayed at how uncertain she still felt, about the police, about all of it, her opinions so unused to having weight that they were still just vapor. Liesl and Max left the imperfect privacy of the empty booth and took a walk to the outer ring, deciding they would spend some time digging through the disorganization.

The pair were up to their elbows for forty-five minutes, Liesl passionately digging, become more and more consumed with finding a treasure for the library and less consumed with the troubles of the library as the time went on. Meditating on how that library had the power to shake her and soothe her in the same moment, Liesl smiled at a thousand-page recipe book for marmalade from 1909 which wasn't appropriate for the library's collection but made her fingers tingle nonetheless. Max came up with a copy of *Der Eigene,* a German-language magazine said to be the first gay periodical. Liesl was having fun. Christopher's illness, the missing Plantin, the disappearing Miriam, it all receded when they shared congratulations on the addition to the library's collection.

"There will be questions at the reception tonight," Max said. "About Chris, about the Plantin."

And then it all came back.

"I hadn't intended to go. For that very reason."

"Won't look good."

"Neither will the answers to those questions. In this case, people's assumptions are less damaging than the truth."

"What truth is that?"

"Let me ask you, what do you think of the theory that it was Miriam who took the Plantin?" Liesl said.

"Our Miriam? In the ill-fitting sweaters?" he said. "Is that your theory or Francis's?"

"Why would you think it came from Francis?"

"You two have been talking a lot."

"We have. But why can't it be my theory?"

"Well. Is it?"

She was jumpy again; she was on the opposite side of the argument again.

"If I had to theorize," he said, "Miriam is not where my mind would go."

"Why, then, did she disappear into thin air?"

"How would I know?" said Max. "Perhaps she's taken a lover."

"Why do all men immediately leap to that?"

"Did Francis suggest that too?"

"He did at first, but he talked himself out of it." She began to explain but stopped herself from going deeper on Francis's theory. It felt like a betrayal of his confidence.

Max made a face like he was chewing on an especially sour lime. They had all worked together for decades, but it was the first time she sensed something broken between the two men.

"And this lover, is that why Francis told you not to report Miriam missing?" Max asked.

"You just said the same thing. That you think Miriam ran off with someone." She was getting too worked up defending Francis. "Are you now saying that you think I should report her missing? What are you saying?"

"It's nothing."

"It's not. You're trying to imply something."

"That I don't think it was Miriam."

The books Liesl was carrying were getting heavy. Max didn't offer to hold them.

"Yes, you've made that clear," Liesl said. "A meek woman in ill-fitting sweaters could never be a thief."

"Tell me," Max said, "but don't get upset. Have you wondered at all why Francis is so resistant to the idea of the police?"

"Because Christopher would be."

Max looked around, and when he was sure there was no one within earshot, he went on.

"He doesn't know what Christopher would do any more than you or I do. A piece of religious history is missing. A woman is missing. And Francis's daily focus is making sure you don't call the police." He picked at an invisible speck of dust on his immaculate sleeve.

"You can't suspect Francis."

"Oh, yes I can. I can if he can suspect Miriam. I can be suspicious of someone who is acting suspicious."

She waited before responding. Smiled at a woman who walked past, close enough to hear.

"He is not acting suspicious," Liesl said.

"He's impeding the investigation."

She laughed.

"Then so is President Garber," she said. "He insists, louder than anyone else, that we shouldn't call the police. Are they in cahoots?"

"It's interesting. That you'll brook no

discussion of Francis as a suspect."

She rested the stack, $30,000 worth of rare books, on the floor. Liesl waited for an opening, hoping the passersby would leave enough space between them that she could continue without having to drag Max off to some corner again.

"Those are heavy. It would be helpful if you could take a few."

"Tell me you don't find Francis's actions strange, and I'll drop it." Max was going now, his raised voice a signal that he didn't care who heard them.

"I protested just as much when Francis implied that Miriam was a suspect," Liesl whispered, moving closer to him in an effort to get him to lower his voice.

"That wasn't my question. You don't think it's Miriam. You don't think it's Francis. That doesn't leave very many suspects. Unless of course you think it's me?" He made no move to pick the books up off the floor. "Is Dan my accomplice? Have you plied me with watery coffee and stale biscuits to procure my confession?"

"Of course not."

"I don't believe you. All those questions this morning about how I felt about the Plantin and whether or not I had worked with the Plantin. You're transparent." He stepped even closer to her. Close enough that she was uncomfortable, but relieved at his lowered volume. "If you want to know whether I took it, just ask me."

She took a step backward. Christopher wouldn't have stepped backward. He would have stayed in the confrontation until they were nose to nose.

"You told me," she said. "You told me you never touched the book."

He shook his head at her.

"Have you asked Francis?" Max said. "In all of your hushed conversations and all of your time in the basements alone, have you asked him whether he was ever alone with it?"

"Of course I have."

"I don't believe you. You're a capable woman, Liesl."

"Capable," for a woman, was a test shot fired in the air indicating that a full-on assault was coming.

"You were a capable part of Christopher's team. But you're in over your head here. A person who believes everything they're told can't be responsible for finding the Plantin."

The missile hit its target. A direct hit. She'd had plenty of opportunity to build up defenses against such a strike, but her shields were down that day. Depleted, relaxed, hard to say. Without those shields, Max had full view of the success of his strike.

"That's enough," Liesl said in a little voice. "Please pick up those books. I'd like to go."

11

The refreshments were in miniature; the anxieties were oversized. Mini canapés, mini macarons, mini bubbles popping into sculptured noses from delicate glasses of champagne. The catering was not the source of anxiety. The donors would be happy so long as Liesl let them eat cake. But they would have questions. In between bites of miniature pastries and in between sips of tiny bubbles, their lips sticky with sugar, they would have questions that Liesl was not prepared to answer. It was giving her a stomachache. Liesl had called Hannah that morning and asked her what she should wear to the event. Hannah had recommended Liesl's collarless white blazer. Liesl smoothed it again and again with her hands.

At Liesl's request, a couple of display cases had been pulled down into the reading room so that a few new acquisitions could be shown. The Qiu Jin pamphlet that

Liesl had acquired at the book fair was prominently displayed. Garber had praised the choice as strategic, had asked if she had read his proposal to attract more Asian money. She'd lifted the phone to invite a Professor Mahmoud she'd been reading about, a faculty member from the religious studies department who might advise her on the blue vellum, but realizing she had little in their collection to woo him with, she'd hung up before dialing.

One young man in a cater-waiter uniform was standing, holding every glass at eye level and polishing away every spot before setting the glass on the bar. Liesl thought she might love him, this young man who looked to understand exactly how important this evening was.

After a couple more hours of polishing and preening, the guests started to arrive, and Liesl and her blazer went to the door to receive them. The early questions, to Liesl's relief, were largely about Christopher's health. The wives of one of their prominent donors noted that Christopher was a genius, and a man with such an overactive brain was more likely to have a stroke. Liesl did not step in to correct the science. She nodded.

"What is this all about?" the wife asked.

"The history of mathematics," Liesl whispered to her as the lights went down and Rhonda took the podium.

Rhonda, most recognizable to Liesl by the halo of curls or colorful hair wrap that usually surrounded her head, had had her hair straightened into a businesswoman's bob. She wore a gray sheath dress and heels. Rhonda had heard "donor event" and had understood exactly what the evening was all about. Liesl was saddened by that.

"Good evening," Rhonda said. "Thank you for having me."

Even in her disguise, Rhonda was the type of academic, the type of person, that the crowd respected in theory but rarely interacted with in practice. Certainly most of the people in the room had read Toni Morrison in college, and if they didn't invite people of color to these donor events, they would swear it had nothing to do with racism and then remind you of the time in college they read that Toni Morrison novel. Percy Pickens was smirking at the stage. Sipping at a red wine and smirking.

"The Peshawar," Rhonda began, "was discovered buried in a farmer's field over one hundred years ago." Percy was still smirking, but others in the room began to lean forward as Rhonda introduced the threads of the story she would tell that night. Stories of pages and pages of sums in the manuscript that suggested a complex understanding of mathematics that shaped the current world.

"But you don't care about math," Rhonda said. "Not really." So her focus shifted and she began to tell them the story of the life of the book as they knew it, for these were book people.

"The Peshawar, the way it was discovered, reaffirms our values, our commitment to exploration, to hold that sense of awe against the indifference that can creep in, to ensure future generations of discovery. And I say to you tonight, we have more to discover. Discoveries like the seventy leaves of birch bark dug up in a field by a farmer plowing around the remnants of a ruined palace and then having the wherewithal to preserve, rather than discard, the soil-stained pages that kept him from his work. Discoveries like the police inspector who, upon hearing what his tenant farmer had dug up, made arrangements to deliver the leaves to the Lahore Museum."

Liesl clasped her hands and listened. The air stank of wine and self-importance. The thousand-dollar suits, the collections of letters that followed every name, the important men and the second wives, she was immune to all of it as Rhonda spoke and Liesl listened.

Rhonda leaned forward across the podium and told them about the loose leaves, ink on birch bark, that the library had bought after an aggressive auction in the early twentieth century.

"Discoveries like that of the faculty member from this very university, someone just like so many of you. Upon reading the 1886 Proceedings of the Seventh Oriental Conference, he sought out the Peshawar from across two seas, began the work of bringing the leaves to our library."

Liesl knew enough about these minds, about these important men, to know they would like that bit. They who had their graduate students teach all their classes, they who played golf with the editors of the academic presses to ensure their lethargic manuscripts were accepted for publication, they who fancied themselves explorers, every last one of them.

"And the story," Rhonda said, "isn't only the story of the Peshawar itself."

The room full of suits and hair spray leaned further forward as she told them about the heroic efforts of a 1927 researcher, a mathematician who had studied the manuscript, decided upon the order of the seventy leaves, decided to photograph the book and make the photographs available for study.

"It was in 1927 that George Kaye, not a young man but still a protégé of the renowned Indologist Dr. R. Hoernlé, took over the manuscript and the work of his mentor in the wake of Hoernlé's death. Kaye didn't grieve. Kaye worked. He didn't know it, but he was approaching the end of his own life, and would die only two years after making his landmark study, his important photographs, available to the world."

Her speech took a mournful turn when she told them what had happened to the book after that. That the birch pages had been sealed in mica and bound into a handsome album. That the mica, the very thing that was meant to preserve the pages, was the thing that was destroying them. The pages were deteriorating. The pages could not be removed from the mica without crumbling. The pages were darkening and, one day very soon, would be illegible. Rhonda likened it to human history that had been written with a stick in the sand, and now, over a thousand years after it was written, someone was pouring buckets of water over it. As the suits looked stricken,

Rhonda readopted her hopeful tone. The researcher, the hero of her story, reappeared. Through his work, the contents of the manuscript were forever preserved. There were facsimiles on the market that had been made to look like the real thing, but more importantly, there were photographs of the pages that were available to all researchers. The contents of the Peshawar, the secrets of mathematical history, would be preserved, even if the book was not.

Rhonda rounded the curve into the vital part of the donor event: flattery.

"Tonight, if you feel the same sense of awe I do, have the same appetite for discovery as I do, the same gratitude to those who came before us as I do — if you are prepared to do what you must, then I have no doubt that this library, this university, will continue to be a leader in the preservation and discovery of our shared history. It is true that we in this room will be among the last to share a space with the Peshawar, this delicate object. We will be among the last to see it in person. But we will keep this library's promise, and as the light goes out on this artifact, on this piece of history that we have worked together to preserve, the sun will rise on the new histories that we will unearth together."

They liked that. Liesl saw them sit up straighter, saw them make eye contact with one another and give slight nods. Of course they should have access to this disintegrating object that was off-limits to the rest of the world. Given enough champagne, they might toss the fragments of birch bark up into the air and dance in the shards of human history like they were confetti. Rhonda continued.

She told the group that because the contents of the book were well preserved, but not the book itself, that the study of the book and not the contents was the next matter of great importance.

Liesl looked Rhonda in the eyes, and Rhonda gave her a little smile. Liesl should have been expecting the turn, but she'd gotten lost, as captivated as the rest of them by Rhonda's storytelling even as she was able to see exactly the ways in which Rhonda was working on the crowd. As it turned out, Rhonda had been expecting payment for her time that evening. She finished her story by revealing the book's greatest mystery: when it had actually been written. If the university was to claim evidence of the first use of zero in mathematics, should they not be able to say when a hand had written that character? There were nods throughout the room. Of course they should. Rhonda leaned all the way over the podium and asked the group if they should go on this journey of discovery together. If they wanted to tell the world for certain about the importance of the Peshawar by telling the world for certain when it was written. She had hypnotized them. There was no answer they could have given but yes.

The suits were generous with their applause. She had won them over. At the cocktail reception after the talk, they were fruit flies on a particularly juicy slice of pineapple. They wanted to know all about her research. They wanted to know all about her *background.* Liesl wanted to thank her but found Rhonda cornered by Percy, who had now decided that she warranted his attention, and two other suits who both had campus buildings named after them and were taking Rhonda's temperature as someone who might add a different flavor of prestige to their portfolios.

"Baltimore," Rhonda said as Liesl joined the group.

"I've been there," said Percy Pickens. "Rough town."

Rhonda smiled. She had met many Percies.

"Some parts."

"Your parts?"

Liesl frowned at Percy, he oblivious and flagging a server for a top-up of wine.

"My parents worked in government."

"What sort of work?"

"State Department."

Liesl found herself inching toward Rhonda. The group, the suits, the weight of their questions, all designed to make Rhonda a bit smaller, and Liesl imagined that by standing next to her, if they were really shoulder to shoulder, she could make Rhonda bigger than these men.

"They pushed you into maths?" Percy said. "Sensible choice."

Nodding from the suits.

"Not at all. I didn't fancy the subject much when I was in grade school."

"Tell me, Rhonda, what did you fancy?"

Rhonda took a glass of wine from the server who had come to wait on Percy. Smiled. Said thank you. And then returned to Percy's questioning in her own time.

"I was sure my mother was a spy, so I studied languages so I could be a spy too."

"Language?"

"Non-Roman alphabets," she said. "Eventually a teacher explained to me that my talent for those translated to figures."

He asked her to name the languages. Nodded when she said Greek. Frowned when she said Arabic. Changed the subject when she said Hindi.

"And then I became a librarian."

"A librarian? But you're at the university in the sciences."

"But I was a librarian first."

"All right," he said, nodding at the suits. "I can understand your popularity a bit more now that I know your story."

"Can you?" she asked, pausing for a long sip of cool wine. "How's that?"

"The history of math . . . It's all a bit fussy."

"The field of astrophysics might disagree," Rhonda said sweetly.

"Less useful than your Latin and your Greek."

"So you say." Rhonda gave Liesl, who was now right next to her, a playful nudge with her shoulder.

"So I say," he said. "It's for industry. It doesn't need public support in the same way."

Rhonda and Percy had an audience for their conversation. Rhonda turned to them, an orator facing her audience.

"I can only presume Mr. Pickens did poorly in math at school and has held a grudge against it ever since," Rhonda said.

Liesl dropped her head and bit her tongue to keep from laughing. How silly she had been to think Rhonda needed her help. Rhonda who was already so much bigger than these men.

"Latin and Greek and the bible. They underpin all of arts and humanities. They shape our understanding of ourselves," said Percy.

"Well," she said. "Mathematics underpins all of the sciences and technology that runs our lives."

He shook her hand to end the conversation. Liesl had been observing and allowed herself to breathe now that the adversaries were separated. Rhonda knew the importance of donors, knew what she had been asked here to do. But Rhonda would not let herself be disrespected, and if allowed to go on, the exchange was unlikely to end positively. Liesl took a drink to soothe her throat and turned to Rhonda to ask her about her study of Arabic, about her interest in advising on a possible acquisition. But Rhonda gave a quick smile and slipped away from Liesl.

A waiter appeared to refill Liesl's wine. It was hard to keep count when the glass was never allowed to empty. Percy and Rhonda were both in need of Liesl's handling. She took a swallow of Riesling that left her glass half-full. From across the room she saw that Max had reached Percy before she could. They had their backs to her. They were whispering. They were not like the pink-sweatshirted girls that Liesl had consoled Hannah about during middle school, promising the girl that in the long run their whispers wouldn't matter. If Max and Percy were conspiring in some way, there would be consequences.

Liesl looked around until she spotted Rhonda in the opposite corner of the room. She had stopped drinking after one glass of wine and was clutching a bottle of Perrier by its neck and nodding as an octogenarian with an unconvincing wig and a large inheritance from her recently departed husband talked at her. Liesl went over and put a hand on each of the women's shoulders to interrupt. The touching did not come naturally to her, but she had seen Christopher announce himself this way hundreds of times. The wig looked down at Liesl's hand. Liesl removed it.

"Wonderful lecture," Liesl said to Rhonda.

"Thank you."

"We were near halfway through when I realized we weren't talking about the Plantin," the old woman said.

"I'm sorry we weren't more clear," Liesl said.

"Not at all," the woman said. "It was delightful once I put it together."

"We're lucky to have Professor Washington," Liesl said.

Max and Percy were occasionally glancing over at Rhonda and Liesl. A waiter refilled Liesl's glass. The canapés were running low. Liesl needed a moment alone with Rhonda more than she needed the canapés to be refreshed. She took a sip of her wine and made a hand signal to one of the waiters, hoping he would understand to see to the food. Her glass was refilled again.

"Will the Plantin lecture be soon?" the wig asked.

Rhonda looked up at Liesl and waited for the answer. She would have heard about the acquisition, too, and as a student of languages, she might have personal interest in the object.

"It's not yet scheduled," Liesl said.

"A fine book, though?"

Liesl agreed that it was but explained that it was actually several books. That the Plantin was bound into multiple volumes.

"It's very educational," said the wig. "But I wish it were printed on something vegan."

"Printing on vellum was a standard practice of the time," Liesl said.

Rhonda put the Perrier up to her lips and kept it there for longer than was necessary to take a sip of water.

"The idea that sheep and ewes shed blood to print a bible just turns my stomach. My grandson and I are vegans. Do you know what that is?"

The head caterer came into the room and tapped Liesl on the shoulder. She placed her glass on the nearest surface, offered her apologies, and got as far away from the wig as possible. The caterer explained that the reason the canapés had not been refreshed was because there were no more canapés, which was a disaster at a donor event almost on par with the guest speaker getting into a row with an important donor. The suits were hungry. She instructed the catering team to more aggressively circulate with the wine. If their glasses were full, the donors wouldn't notice that their stomachs weren't.

Rhonda strolled back into sight, trying not to interrupt Liesl's discussion with the caterer but making it clear that she was next in line. Liesl waved her over, confident that the catering dilemma had been resolved the way they always were — by offering more wine. Looking down, Liesl saw the empty glass of wine in her hand and felt a twinge of embarrassment.

"I was hoping to speak with you before I left."

"Rhonda, I'm so glad you caught me."

Rhonda was still holding her sparkling water. Liesl gave the caterer a nod, and he left them.

"About Percy Pickens," Liesl said. "I'm sorry if you felt attacked by him."

"I can handle men like him."

"You shouldn't have to handle men like him."

"And here I thought you were going to admonish me for talking back."

The apology had been a lead up to that. Liesl had no talent for admonishing adults who had done no wrong.

"He's an important donor to the university," Liesl said.

"I know."

"Well," Liesl said. "There was no harm done."

They turned back toward the room. Percy and Max were still huddled together, but their limbs looked looser now. On account of the wine. The volume of the reading room was turned all the way up, the conversations of the suits floating up high to mingle with the several stories of books above their heads.

"I would have ended the conversation if he hadn't," Rhonda said. "I had an agenda in agreeing to do this for you."

The vegan in the wig interrupted them to say she was leaving. Both Liesl and Rhonda shook her hand and wished her a good night. Her wig had slipped slightly to the left. On account of the wine.

"The Peshawar should be carbon-dated," Rhonda said. "I can find us the resources to do it."

A waiter came by with more wine. Liesl covered her glass with her hand to refuse him.

"You'd ruin it," said Liesl. "We'd lose the book."

A weak argument. They were already losing the book.

"A lot of the money in this room is supportive of the idea. Don't say no out of fear of the unknown."

Liesl made Rhonda no promises. Walking home that night, she called and left a message. For Professor Mahmoud. Asking him about his interest in a leaf from a Quran; gold calligraphy on blue vellum.

Liesl stopped by the noodle shop on the corner on her way home and asked for an order of dumplings. It was only a minute or two between the noodle shop and her front door, but she ate the slippery dumplings with her fingers as she walked, plucking them from the tray and slurping them up in giant bites.

Nineteen Years Earlier

Max sweated under the fluorescent lobby lights, one of the first times he'd been out of the house at all since his secret stopped being a secret.

"You're not wearing the collar." Christopher walked a lap around Max when he greeted him in the library's lobby and found him in a suit that looked very much like his own. "Are we worried that the change will raise questions?"

Christopher was striding back toward his office. Max followed. Every person they passed on the way through the workroom was staring at him; he was sure of it. Max put his fingers up to his neck where the collar had been. Mourning its departure.

"It was in the newspaper. The questions are no longer sleeping." He pulled his tie tighter, wanting it to act as armor the way his collar always had.

"It's fine, I guess. They'll know you've left

the church . . ." Christopher's voice trailed off as he searched through stacks of papers on his desk, shoving piles from one side to the other.

"Wait, do they know I'm coming?" Max put his hands in his pockets, then crossed his arms in front of him, then clasped them behind his back. Without the armor of the collar, he wasn't even certain how to stand.

"I thought it best not to leave a lot of time in advance for questions. It'll be a nice surprise." He held a sheet of paper, finally retrieved from the piles, up in the air like a victor's flag.

Max thought it would have been better to be honest. To confess about the scandal. To be open about the stolen money. To tell them exactly why he had been asked to leave the church. He had been under the impression that Christopher agreed with him, but now it was clear that wasn't true, and he let Christopher take the lead. He knew this place and these people better, and besides, he was Max's boss now, and even outside of the church, it was in Max's nature to be an obedient servant.

Ever since he had left St. Peter's parish, he had been in a state of disorder, looking for a job, looking for a home, waiting for the police to come and disrupt it all. He might have checked himself into a hospital if not for Christopher. Christopher knew him well enough to invite him to deliver the Jackman Lecture a year earlier, to speak on the King James Bible. What did Christopher care about scandal when there was a great-books man who could be brought onto staff?

12

I

It was an aching and unpleasant morning, the kind that let an old woman know exactly how old she was: puffy face, sore knees, the fuzz on the tongue of a crone who had been using wine to help her sleep. John had left the bed without waking her; he was up in his attic studio alone. He raised his eyes when she came up to see him but didn't say anything. He could see she wasn't at her best.

They weren't at their best. But she needed his counsel. She sat on the stool in front of a blank canvas, but he told her she looked too serious for there to not be coffee, and he wouldn't let her tell him what was on her mind until they were dressed and out of the house at the coffee shop with the blue awning and the ginger cookies. He insisted on taking their coffee outside, walking with it.

Powerless, afraid to go to the library for another day, the library she was meant to be leading, Liesl kicked a stone on the sidewalk, lost in her disquiet and doubt, pulling from her memory stories and images about Miriam and testing theories and fears out on John so that he might tell her what to do. She couldn't remember Miriam ever arriving anywhere late or breaking any rule at all. Miriam had been comforting in her predictability. Liesl recalled the time she and Miriam were filling out the paperwork for a large donation of materials by a prominent Caribbean poet, maybe two years after Miriam had started at the library. They were sitting at Liesl's desk in front of a pastel sketch interpretation of one of the poems by the poet himself, trying to describe the depth of the shade of yellow and the feeling it conjured in an application for a tax receipt, and Miriam said, " 'Nature rarer uses yellow.' " Liesl looked at her, surprised, but Miriam found her voice and continued from memory, " 'Than another hue; Saves she all of that for sunsets, Prodigal of blue, Spending scarlet like a woman, Yellow she affords Only scantly and selectively, Like a lover's words.' "

Liesl had left her seat, walked across the office, and cleared the tears from her eyes with her fingertips as Miriam sat upright and still, the Dickinson poem having adequately expressed her emotion that the pastel sketch had conjured. Liesl asked her why she didn't work more closely with the literary donors, who would recognize in her a kindred spirit.

"That's Christopher's role, to work with the donors. It wouldn't be right for me to interfere." She said it so plainly, like Liesl had suggested she request a pop song from an orchestra conductor. And later, years later, when it was arranged for Miriam to meet with poets and novelists who were considering donating their papers, when Miriam impressed them, as she always did, Miriam would still come back to the library, signed donation agreement in hand, apologetic that she was breaking from the prescribed order, taking on a task that wasn't meant for her.

Miriam had always been that way, effective but effectual but self-effacing, with a rigid sense of responsibility to move through the world in a way that was sure to never disappoint anyone, with a look in her eye that made you want to ask her for a favor because you knew she would be happy to complete a task for you. And then at the reception when her eyes had turned pleading and she'd needed something from Liesl. What? To confess she'd stolen the library's Plantin? Impossible. That some harm had come to her was the only scenario that made sense.

Liesl told John all of the theories. About the maybe-lover. About invisible women who are allowed to vanish. Modest Miriam. He didn't believe the thing about a lover. He told her that she had to report Miriam missing; he told her what she had already talked herself into. And he sat next to her on a bench and held her coffee as she called the police and answered their questions.

II

"Do you know something I don't?" Liesl jerked her head up. Dan slammed her office door closed.

"Is it Miriam?"

"Miriam? I don't give a crack about Miriam. Miriam? It's the Vesalius."

Liesl sighed as Dan puffed up in his denim for what was sure to be a lecture about some perceived break in procedure.

"I haven't so much as thought of the Vesalius," she said. "Thought of, touched, referenced, requested, nothing."

With a mournful look that Liesl would have thought an impossible undertaking for his arrogant features, he nodded.

"I know. No one has. Until today. And it's gone."

"Absolutely not," she said. "It can't be missing."

"It was last used six weeks ago," Dan said. "I know for certain that it was returned to the right place."

He was combing his hands through his thick gray hair. Pulling at it.

"It wasn't me," he said. "I put it back. I returned it to the right place."

It had never occurred to her that it would be him. Only the librarians had alarm codes for the building and could come and go unsupervised. She didn't say it, but the status of his position, which Dan resented so much, saved him from her suspicion.

"You're certain it wasn't misshelved?" Liesl asked.

"It's gone. The Vesalius has been stolen."

"Why the Vesalius? It has nothing at all to do with the Plantin. A work of religion alongside a work of science. Why those two books?"

"It might be more than those two."

"What do you mean?" Liesl opened her office door and motioned to Dan to follow her. "Do you have reason to think that something else is missing?"

She unlocked the fire stairs to get down to the basements so she could be sure they would have privacy.

"No. Not yet."

She stopped on the stairs, waited for him to explain.

"We only know the Vesalius is missing because an instructor requested it for a class this week."

She leaned against the wall of the stairwell, letting the obvious sink in.

"So we won't know what else is missing until we go looking for it."

They walked down into the basements together, toward the Vesalius's permanent home. She did a mental inventory of the library's treasures: the Peshawar, the Vesalius, the Shakespeare First Folio. It made her uncomfortable how closely the list hewed to the table of contents of the book Francis had shown her. Like he had written a shopping list. She leaned against a shelf as if she was too sad to remain upright, her shoulders slumping in despair.

"You're sure it was reshelved after the last use?" Liesl asked.

"Stop asking that. I did it myself."

"And it couldn't have been used in between?"

"It couldn't," Dan said. "I haven't taken a

day off between then and now. I would know."

They came to the spot. Dan had pulled the large acid-free box that housed the Vesalius onto a book truck. The box was empty.

"They took it without the box," Liesl said. "They could damage it."

"The missing box would have tipped us off."

"Has anyone else been around here? Is there anything suspicious?"

The hole left by the Vesalius's box gaped like a missing tooth. Inside the box, the thief had left the cardboard flag that identified the book. This had been no mistake.

"It's been weeks."

"This is a nightmare," Liesl said. "Say something to make me feel better. Something about how collecting rare objects is a capitalist diversion that ultimately doesn't matter. That private property should be abolished, so it was never really ours."

"I could say that, but my heart is broken. I love the Vesalius."

"Do you?" said Liesl. She stood up straighter, taken aback. "Please don't choose this moment to get mad at me, but it's not the type of thing I picture you reading. Vesalius didn't talk much about the proletariat."

"It's the corrections."

She pictured the handwritten scrawls on the perimeter of the text.

"The annotations? I guess I see that. It's why it's so valuable."

The library's copy of the Vesalius was a first edition. The author's own copy where he had jotted in the margins the corrections and improvements he wanted for future editions.

"Oh hell," Dan said. He refastened the acid-free box with care and slid it, empty, to its home on the shelf. "It has nothing to do with value."

"What then?"

"The imperfection of genius. The man is understood to have founded the field of modern anatomy. There was a fortune spent at the time to print this grand pictorial work. But it wasn't good enough for him. He kept working at it. I find it inspiring."

"That's lovely," she said, running her fingers over the box, then fixing the flag, making sure it was perfectly upright. "I didn't know you felt that way."

"Yeah, well. I'm sure you and the other white collars would be surprised to learn the rest of us are even literate."

"You weren't going to do this now."

"Okay. Before it all goes into motion, before we tell the instructor that he can't have the book for his class, before we tell Garber that he has a serial thief, and before someone whispers it in Christopher's ear at his bedside and kills him, can we just sit here a minute and be sad about it all?"

She nodded, slow and stricken. He sat on a shelving stool and she sat down next to him.

They only took five minutes, and as they breathed their silent prayers for the book to the soundtrack of the humming fluorescent lights, ideas for what to do arose and then were dismissed before they were ever spoken. Liesl was alternately sure a solution would come to her and terrified it wouldn't.

"The police, a detective from the police." Out of breath, Max interrupted the séance. "I'm thrilled that you listened to me, but you can't call the police and then go hide in the basement. They're looking for you."

"When did you call the police?" Dan asked. "Did you already know?"

She had to get up, of course. But she wanted to refuse. To keep her basement vigil for what had been lost. Light candles, shed tears, say prayers. She rose to her feet instead.

"It's not for this," Liesl said. "We have so much bad news. So much bad news."

"What's he talking about?" Max asked.

"Why exactly are they here if not for the Plantin?"

"Don't say anything," Liesl said to Dan. "I've reported Miriam missing. The rest we'll talk about as a team later. Everyone needs to get back to work."

The detective was not in a uniform and looked neither like a gumshoe from the movies of her youth nor a bodybuilder from the crime movies Hannah watched.

"Professor Weiss," he said. "Detective Peter Yuan."

"It's not professor. Just Liesl is fine."

"Great," he said. "Let's talk in your office, and you can let me know what's been going on."

"You've spoken with Vivek?"

"Yes," he said. "He reported her missing before you did."

"Why didn't I know about that?" she asked.

"In all honesty, it seemed like a marital issue more than a missing person."

"Are you going to tell me you thought she ran off with a lover?" Liesl said. "But now that her boss has complained . . . ?"

"Something like that."

"What happens now?"

"Quite a bit already has. Professor Patel — Vivek — gave us credit card and cellular phone information for Miriam, and we have someone following up on that. We've been in her apartment this morning, but there isn't anything suspicious there. In any case, she's not at home, and it seems she has not been in a while. Her car is not in its parking spot, so the most likely solution is that she left for a trip of some sort." He stopped.

"Is this where you bring up the lover?"

"No," he said. "Do you have reason to think that's a possibility?"

"No," she said.

"But you brought it up."

The detective produced a leather notebook from the inside pocket of his too-big jacket. In that respect he was exactly like a gumshoe, asking Liesl questions to which he already knew the answers and scrawling her responses in tiny print into the notebook, which might hold the answers to Miriam's whereabouts. Liesl described Miriam: what she looked like, what she acted like, what she was working on, what time she had her morning coffee. On the wall, there was a framed photograph of James Joyce. At some point Detective Yuan stopped scrawling and started staring in the direction of the celebrated scribe.

They went on like that for a bit, but then he stopped asking questions, and she stopped offering information. He asked to see Miriam's desk. She agreed. The detective sat in her chair. The burgundy sweater that Liesl remembered her wearing that last day, the sweater she was now certain was Christopher's, hung off the back of the chair. Without touching anything, the detective began to write what he saw in his notebook.

The hackles in the room went up. Max looked up from his bible, and Francis laid down his pencil, and Dan pressed Pause on his Discman. They watched the detective.

Liesl was standing in silence, also watching. She was telling two lies. She didn't give the detective the full context surrounding Miriam's disappearance. And she didn't pick up the phone to tell Garber that another book was missing.

"Will you excuse me?" Liesl said.

The detective nodded. Having answered some rudimentary questions, she was already invisible to him. Dan and Max and Francis watched Liesl leave the workroom. She heard the scraping of a chair; someone was walking behind her. She quickened her pace, walked into the office, and closed the heavy door before her pursuer could confront her.

Garber had not explicitly told her to avoid

sending emails about the theft. Yet, without explicitly telling her, it had been made clear that there should be no paper trail, no evidence that the administration had known about a theft and failed to act. Liesl looked at the phone but didn't pick it up. She began to type an email.

"Did Garber tell you to invite the police in?" Francis blew through her office door without knocking. "Are they investigating Miriam for the Plantin?"

"I need a moment to do something."

"Are you not going to tell me what's going on? Don't I deserve to know?"

"Deserve to know. Do you deserve to know? I'm emailing President Garber to report the theft of the Vesalius as a courtesy before I report it to the police."

He crossed his arms over his chest, dropped his eyes to the floor, shrinking himself. Every feature that made him look like a spy could also make him look like a villain. It didn't mean he was guilty. The news of a second theft was shocking. The news of Liesl's disloyalty to Garber was shocking. It didn't mean he was guilty.

They were interrupted by the detective at the office door. He looked between them, the air full of accusation.

Francis backed out of the room, having

said nothing, and Detective Yuan reentered it, closing the door softly behind him.

"I haven't told you the whole story," Liesl said.

"I see that now." The air of accusation lingered. The detective could smell in the air that there was information that had been withheld from him.

"This isn't my office. I'm not the library director."

"Yes, that's obvious."

"That I'm not the director?"

"That this isn't your office. The upholstery smells like testosterone."

"The director had a stroke," she said. "And a situation has arisen while I've been filling in."

"A situation. Does it have to do with Miriam's disappearance?"

The phone on Christopher's desk rang.

"That's one theory."

"Okay. I'd prefer not to entertain theories. I like my information served straight."

It was a ridiculous line that only a movie detective would say. But it made her like him.

"Miriam," she said over the sound of the ringing phone. "Miriam disappeared at around the same time as two priceless manuscripts from our collection."

"All right," he said. Detective Yuan looked down at the phone and waited for her to answer it. The call display indicated that it was President Garber's office. It seemed that the busy university president did indeed check his emails right away.

III

Liesl followed the blue arrows on the floor toward the intensive care unit. There were purple arrows for obstetrics, red for emergency, yellow for palliative care. Door after door clicked open as she approached, and she got a tour of most of the white-walled sterile space before she came to the ICU and encountered the first door that did not open on command. She almost turned around to leave. No one had known she had come in the first place. But then a sturdy nurse opened the door to get through and Liesl stepped through behind her.

She did not find Christopher's room right away. In the first ICU suite she tried, a very handsome, very young man lay surrounded by tubes and computers while an equally young, equally attractive woman in her third trimester of pregnancy sat on the edge of his bed and wept.

While Liesl stared through the doorway at the dying man, Detective Yuan was moving, inhabiting her space and filling it with questions behind closed doors. She had left him to the library so she didn't have to watch it, didn't have to watch him draw conclusions and make assumptions about the people and the place. He knocked off interviews one by one, scrawling notes in his book while the assembly line deposited librarians and administrators and spouses and friends at the door of his makeshift interrogation room. They all looked so nice in their pressed shirts before they went behind the closed door to accuse their colleagues of major crimes and minor indiscretions.

From the ICU hallway Liesl could not hear nurses or doctors speaking or machines beeping. If she had encountered a person, she would have been too embarrassed to break the silence to ask for Christopher's room.

The others had been taking turns going to visit, armed with books he couldn't read and flowers he couldn't smell. In the weeks it had taken her to make her first trip to the hospital to see him, she hadn't been able to conjure any guilt. She was filling his chair; that would be more important to him than a visit. In those weeks, she hadn't felt the need to see him. But now there was a detective in the library, and dominoes were falling, and she would have been too embarrassed to admit it to anyone, but she wanted to go and stand beside the book man to see if there were any answers in his aura.

His room was the last one along the corridor, but then she got there and wasn't sure if she could go in. She had brought him a book, a collection of William Sydney Porter's letters, and though she knew he was unconscious and couldn't read, she thought that having the book in his room might have some sort of impact. That the smell of the paper and cardboard and glue would shake him awake.

"Christopher?" she whispered from the doorway. He looked one hundred years old. The skin on his face hung off his skull like a wet rag on a rock.

The hospital room was cut off from three others in an ICU cluster by a frosted-glass partition and a blue cotton sheet. A dozen floral arrangements in various states of decomposition were clustered on a side table, and Liesl didn't know where to look in the room that would keep her from having to watch something decay. She'd sat in many rooms with Christopher Wolfe, and no matter the setting, he'd always managed to make himself the center of the space, always managed to suck all the air out.

Here, with his bed in the very middle of the floor, with his breath drawing from a lightly beeping ventilator, he looked as unimportant as she'd ever seen him. She was filled with a sense of foreboding that she hadn't felt in her stomach since her own mother died. A sense that a source of answers, of steadiness, had been taken from her. It was John who had coached her through the dread, reminding her that her mother had suffered from dementia for at least the last ten years of her life, and that even if death lent the feeling of finality, her mother hadn't been a source of answers in a long, long time.

"Liesl. I didn't know you were coming."

Liesl gasped, audibly gasped, at the sound of Marie's voice behind her. Shocked that someone would dare interrupt her reverie, embarrassed that she'd been caught tiptoeing around the ICU. She stuck out the book and forced it on Marie like an offering on an altar.

"I'm intruding."

"You're not."

"Is there any news?"

"He's the same."

"I'm terribly sorry."

"The same isn't necessarily bad."

"Is there anything I can do?"

"Find the Plantin."

"The police are involved now."

"Yes."

"I'm intruding."

The book was in Marie's hands, and there was nothing else to say. Liesl was wet from sweat and followed the blue arrows back to the cold October air as fast as she could.

A cryptic call from a blocked number had reached Liesl's cell phone at some point between obstetrics and Marie, and while a call from a concealed number was not an uncommon occurrence, a call from a concealed number that was accompanied by a voicemail was unusual enough to catch Liesl's attention. So when Liesl exited the hospital, she didn't walk right for the Bathurst bus to get back to the library. She clicked the button to play the message because there was a chance the message was the detective or Miriam herself or some other sort of good or at least relieving news. Strange as it sounds, Liesl was convinced that a voicemail from a blocked number had to be a happy announcement, if only to even the odds.

President Garber, ignorant of Liesl's need for cheer, had used all 120 seconds allowable in a single voice message, intent on expressing his displeasure, intent on putting

Liesl in her place after she had dared, *dared* contact a prominent Quranic scholar to advocate for the purchase of some blue manuscript, a purchase that the scholar was now near-insisting the university make.

Delete. She deleted the 120-second berating about her place and responsibilities and "times like these" and then went to wait for the bus. She couldn't delete the words from her memory but she deleted them from her phone, and as the bus pulled up, she deleted the record of the call from the blocked number, just for good measure.

The door of the office was open when she returned to the library. Detective Yuan was seated at the desk. He was flipping through a Sotheby's catalog she had left by the computer. He looked up and waved her in when she came to the door.

"Are these really the prices?" he said. He turned the catalog over so she could see the page. "Someone is going to pay $35,000 for a children's book?"

"For a first edition of Harry Potter."

He turned the catalog back over and looked at the page again.

"It's ten dollars at the store down the street," he said.

"There were only five hundred printed in that edition," she said.

He shrugged and tossed the catalog aside. "It has a couple of typos. It's very rare."

"Would you like to get lunch?"

"Is this another interview?"

"I'm not planning an interrogation," the detective said. "Just an update. I thought you'd be interested."

"Do you think she's dead?"

"Miriam? Why would you ask that?"

"I don't know. Because it's the worst possible outcome."

Yuan pulled on his trench coat.

"It's unlikely," he said as he walked toward the elevator. Liesl hadn't agreed to lunch but didn't feel like there was a choice. "I also don't think she's taken a lover."

"Are people still proposing that as a theory?"

"Once or twice," he said, leading her out of the elevator. "You people love your gossip. But I agree that she doesn't seem the type for a lover."

"Do you suspect Vivek?"

Yuan shook his head and jogged through the cold October afternoon to the bright-yellow falafel truck that parked outside the library.

"I hope you're okay with falafel. I've had a hankering since I first saw this truck. Everything Professor Patel has told us has checked out."

"What then?"

Detective Yuan spoke Arabic to order their sandwiches. Liesl squinted at him.

"Languages are useful in my line of work." He handed her a bottle of water. "The missing books and the missing woman could be a coincidence. And sometimes there are coincidences. But rarely." He filled a tiny plastic ramekin with hot sauce as he waited for their meal. "It looks like she took your books. Maybe only temporarily. But the theft was discovered, and she probably ran off. Got spooked. Do you like hot sauce?"

"No," she said. "I'm fine with tahini."

He poured a second ramekin anyway.

"So what you're saying," Liesl said, "is that when you find her, you'll find the books."

"That's not what I'm saying," said Yuan. "The books aren't my concern."

Liesl cleared her throat, swallowing the saliva that had risen when she caught the scent of the vinegary hot sauce. She wished she'd asked for some, that she hadn't given in to her reflex of saying no to every question.

"But you said they were stolen."

"It looks that way," He glanced at the window of the truck but received a slight headshake from the proprietor. "But that's a property crime."

"It's a crime."

"The books are my concern only in that they relate to Miriam." Summoned by something inaudible to Liesl, he began to walk away from their conversation.

"I don't understand," Liesl said, taking hold of his arm in her frustration. "You just said you think she stole them."

"Lunch is ready," he said, removing his arm from her grasp and reaching up to the truck window to claim their sandwiches.

"Can you explain this?"

"Are you okay to sit outside?"

"I don't mind the cold," Liesl said. She followed him to a bench a few feet from the truck. "Can you be frank with me out here? Maybe I'm dense, but I'm missing something."

"The university hasn't filed a complaint about the books." He unwrapped the foil all the way to drench his sandwich in hot sauce, and she wanted to scold him that he would make a mess trying to eat it like that.

"They haven't?"

"This sandwich is dynamite," he said, licking hot sauce off his pinkie.

"Can I file the complaint?" She took a small bite, trying her best to ensure that nothing dripped into her lap. She had never thought to eat at this truck.

"No," he said with a full mouth.

"This doesn't make any sense."

"You really should try it with the hot sauce." He held the second ramekin out to her, but she shook her head and swallowed her bite.

"No, thank you," said Liesl. "I'm worried I'll spill some on my blouse. The rest of the sandwich is pretty beige, but the sauce is a risk."

"Your loss," he said, seasoning his next bite with an extra dab of the sauce. "You're not the property owner."

"The owner is the institution," Liesl said. "This isn't a purse snatching."

She always felt it was a good policy to remain calm, maybe to the point of stoicism, when anger or frustration were expected from her — holding back tears at funerals, speaking in a low tone when someone else was yelling — so she could never be categorized as hysterical. She had worked at it for years. But as she placed her sandwich down in her lap, it took all her energy to suppress a scream of aggravation.

"You have to take that up with President Garber," the detective said with a shrug.

"Have you spoken with him?"

"Briefly."

"And he didn't report the books stolen?" She looked at the sandwich in her lap, picked at a piece of lettuce, and took deep, calming breaths.

"He didn't file an official complaint."

"So, what now?"

Yuan had a mouthful of pita and falafel. He took a long time to chew and swallow.

"We're searching for her car."

"Okay," Liesl said. "How does that help me?"

He scrunched up the wax paper from his sandwich. Hers was only a quarter eaten.

"Well," Yuan said over his shoulder as he got up to throw away his trash. "She may have the books with her."

"And that's it?"

"That's all you can hope for."

"Why?"

"It's still only a missing person case." He hadn't sat back down, and she sensed that he was preparing to leave, that he had given her enough of his time.

"So you suspect she is missing because she committed a crime."

"Right," Yuan said. "Most logical explanation."

"Right," Liesl said. She stayed sitting as a form of protest, not wanting him to leave until she had some small bit of satisfaction, some answer that made sense. "But you won't investigate her for the commission of said crime."

"Right."

"Is all law enforcement this insane?" she asked.

"No. But in my experience, all academia is."

"What should I be doing now?"

"Eating your delicious sandwich," he said. He put his hands in the pockets of his trench coat.

"You know," she said, "I've never had more authority and less control in my life."

"That's funny."

"Not to me."

"Let President Garber deal with the theft, and let me deal with Miriam," he said. "You keep yourself sane by finding yourself something no one else can say no to."

IV

She asked Dan to clear some boxes out of the receiving room. He cited a clause from the collective bargaining agreement explaining why he wouldn't. She picked up the Christie's catalog, looking with longing at Lot 37. She ignored the stack of unpaid invoices on the desk. She took her half-eaten sandwich to the lunchroom and threw the sandwich and the wrapper in the general trash bin instead of the green bin. It didn't satisfy her. She went back to the office and picked up the phone.

"Rhonda," she said. "It's Liesl from the library."

"Is everything all right?"

"All right? Why wouldn't it be?"

She was drumming her fingers on the table and clenching her jaw. She might have sounded manic.

"I'm calling about the Peshawar."

Somewhere in a hospital bed, Christopher's eyelids fluttered.

"I'd love for you to take it for your research."

A team from the university's Radiocarbon Accelerator Unit came to the library the next day. All three wore eccentric designer glasses.

They came several times over the next few days. There were measurements and preparations and discussions about how to carry out sampling. Liesl did not ask Dan to bring out and put away the Peshawar every time it was needed for these meetings. She did it herself. In the evenings she called Vivek and Detective Yuan to check on progress, and she responded to President Garber's voicemails with curt emails. It began to get dark very early in the evenings, but Liesl did not let that deter her from walking home through the cold every night.

13

I

Liesl lay on rumpled linens, drool puddling on her pillow, one eye half-open and watching the clock so she could count every second that she had left to sleep, pretending not to notice the sour smell of night sweat paired with last night's gewürztraminer on her breath.

"Liesl, wake up." John came into the room smelling of shampoo. "You have to go to work."

He was washed and dressed. Gray beard, blue eyes, white teeth. The man she was married to had once spent fifteen consecutive days in bed, and now he looked like an advertisement for a retirement home for active seniors; she was stupefied by how much she resented it. She calculated that she had thirty minutes longer to sleep. She turned her back to him.

"You're in the newspaper. The library is."

He set a mug of coffee on her night table and then the newspaper on the opposite side of the bed so she could see the frowning photo of Miriam on the front page next to the cathedral of the library's inner stacks.

She sat up.

The rare books library thought it was just unlucky earlier this year when a rare Plantin Polyglot Bible, printed between 1568 and 1572, went missing.

"The Plantin Polyglot Bible closes the most notable gap in our collection of post-1500 bibles," said Maximilian Hubbard, a former Catholic priest and the library's religion collections coordinator, when the book was acquired.

He had no idea that the book would soon go missing, alongside one of the institution's librarians. Miriam Peters was reported missing two weeks ago. A source familiar with the case, speaking on background to reporters, said Peters is suspected of having made off with the Plantin Bible and at least one other work from the library's vast and valuable collection.

"Who else has seen this?" Liesl asked John.

"Liesl. It's the front page of the newspaper. We're not in the boom days of journalism, but it's the front page."

"If we leave now, can we buy them all before anyone else is awake?"

"You didn't tell me about Miriam."

"Of course I did. I told you she was missing."

"That she was missing. You didn't tell me that you suspected her of the theft."

"I don't suspect her. But she is suspected."

"Nice girl, that Miriam. I always assumed you quite liked her."

"Do I stink? Can I run in now without a shower?"

"You need a shower. Would you like to do some breathing exercises?"

"I don't think you understand what this news story means for me."

"I understand precisely. But this is about more than your work. Miriam is someone you care about."

Liesl threw the newspaper aside so she didn't have to look at the familiar wounded expression on Miriam's face as she contemplated what to do next.

Liesl felt nauseated with guilt; there was no way to tell John of his role in her quiet detachment from Miriam. Ashamed, embarrassed, disgusted with herself for looking the other direction when Miriam's demeanor began to look too much like John's and the weight of another John seemed too heavy.

"A coworker," she said, her voice creaking.

"Your protégé, I thought."

"I told you she was missing," Liesl said.

"You told me half the story."

In the early days of their marriage, the smell of toast in the kitchen meant John was up early to fix breakfast for her, and in the later days of their marriage it meant he couldn't get out of bed and that Hannah had cooked dinner for herself after school. He had put two slices in the toaster before going outside to get the paper. They were forgotten now, gone cold and stale. But the smell of toast lingered when she rushed down to the kitchen with wet hair and her blouse unbuttoned.

"It's going to look as though I leaked to the press."

He looked at her like she was a stranger. "That's your concern?"

"It's one of them."

He sat in a creaky chair at the creaky kitchen table. "Who cares what people think?"

She did not sit down beside him.

"Everyone — humans — care what people think," she said.

"A young woman has disappeared!" he said. "And her reputation is being ruined. She is being called a thief while she can't defend herself."

"I know that. Of course I know it's terrible."

"Then why are you thinking only of yourself?" he said. "Are you still not telling me the truth? Is it that you suspect Miriam too?"

"Her disappearance is suspicious," said Liesl. "Right as the thefts were discovered."

John got out of his chair and walked to the toaster, taking the cold bread out and handing it to her on a napkin.

"You should eat something," he said.

"I should go to work."

II

The glass towers of the business school sent darts of early morning light into Liesl's eyes. She dropped her head to stave off the sun and walked the rest of the way to the administration building looking at the scuff on the toe of her left shoe.

She didn't make it all the way inside before encountering Garber and his bicycle helmet. "I'm happy to not have to hunt you down today."

He held the door for her, and she, still

worried about that scuff, went into his office.

"It wasn't me," Liesl said.

"I know it wasn't you," he said. "That doesn't mean it's not your fault."

"I don't understand," she said. Garber hung his bicycle helmet on his coatrack.

"You called the police."

He stood right in front of her. She hadn't sat down, so he wouldn't either. His gray hair was slightly sweaty from the bike ride.

"To report a missing person," Liesl said, running her hands through her still-damp hair. "What choice did I have?"

"That's not the question," Garber said.

"Then what is the question?"

"Look," said Garber, "you asked why I considered you at fault." He reached into his briefcase and pulled out the paper.

It lay where he tossed it, on the coffee table in the office's seating area. The picture of Miriam was uglier than Liesl remembered. She put her hands on her hips to stare down at the photo. In doing so, she realized she had missed a belt loop on her trousers and her black leather belt was riding up slightly on her left hip.

"Without a police investigation, there's nothing for the press to write about."

"You don't think the police leaked it?" she asked.

The picture of the library was even nicer than Liesl remembered.

"I don't care who leaked it. The minute there was paper — official reports, emails — there was going to be a leak. Any sensible leader would know that. Christopher would have known that. And you should have too."

Liesl moved her left side away from him, fingers twitching at her hip, hoping to correct the belt before he noticed.

"I should get to the library. There will be questions."

"There will. And I'll thank you not to answer any." He insisted on standing face-to-face with her, thinking her half turn was a way of evading his authority.

"What would you like me to do?"

"Use the press office," said Garber.

"The press office?" Liesl said. She managed to hook her thumb around the belt, and she turned her body away from him again. "You think there will be more press?"

"The story is delicious. A rogue librarian." He stepped in front of her again.

"I don't think she did it," Liesl said.

Garber picked the paper up and looked at Miriam's picture. Her hair hung to her chin in limp curls, and her eyes looked like they were two different sizes. Liesl took his moment of distraction as an opportunity to give the belt a yank so at least it was level with her trousers. The loop would come later.

"So you say. But nothing matters less than the truth now that the press is involved."

There was a break in the conversation. A long enough break that Liesl thought she could leave. She was cold with defeat; she had been since the news of the article had woken her up that morning. The scolding was robbing her of the last of her strength, and she wanted to get back out into the air.

"There will be donor questions."

"I know," she said. "Would you like me to route those to your office as well?"

"Not unless you have to," Garber said. "Just try your best to reassure them. Can you manage that, at least?"

"What do you suggest?"

"Tell them that we called the police as soon as the thefts were detected, just a matter of time now until they have a suspect, et cetera." He threw the newspaper back down on the table. To her relief, he was too disgusted with it or with her to muster the energy to scold her about the blue manuscript. That, at least, could wait for another day. "Don't get too creative, and don't be more honest than you have to be."

Don't be more honest than you have to be. Liesl walked to the library in the sweater-weather cold, wondering if that advice was meant for today's donor inquiries or if Garber applied it to all his dealings. Whichever, it wasn't how Liesl operated. The library lights were on, and through the window at street level she could see the nervous rustling of bodies, like all the orange leaves in the October wind, clinging to the trees but threatening to drop. Liesl didn't want to go in and be their leader, didn't want to be the force that finally shook them loose, but she had scheduled a meeting, and for the sake of her sanity, she planned to keep it.

Rhonda was waiting by the elevator when Liesl arrived.

"I'm so sorry," Rhonda began.

"You're sorry?" Liesl said. "Why on earth are you sorry? Do you moonlight as a journalist? Did you write the story?"

Liesl was exasperated by the reactions to the story; she wanted help, not anger, not empty apologies. The mathematician's open face pinched into a wince, and that made Liesl want to apologize, but that seemed even worse, the idea of an endless cycle of expressions of regret. Rhonda's face reassembled — back to its familiar friendliness — and Liesl saw then that the woman knew something about finding oneself in the woods without a map. She would not judge Liesl for any lack of grace in handling impossible circumstances.

Max was sitting at the reference desk, watching them. His unconcealed fury at her gave Liesl a chill that no sweater could remedy.

"We can reschedule," Rhonda said.

"We're not going to reschedule." She said it loud enough for Max to hear.

"I'm sure this is an overwhelming day."

"It's an overwhelming year. But that's no one's business but my own. I made a commitment to you. To your research."

"I really don't mind coming back another day."

"There's no saying that things will be better on any other day. Come downstairs. Let's get the Peshawar."

"Am I allowed down here?" Rhonda stood just outside the elevator door looking like she might genuflect before the thousands of volumes that lined the aisles. "I don't need to be security-screened or baptized or disinfected or something?"

Liesl hallucinated the smell of flesh even though the animals that had donated their skins to cover the books had been dead for hundreds of years. She looked to see if Rhonda was wrinkling her nose, but she was agape, trailing her fingers over gilt on green spines and hand-scratched titles on vellum.

"Thank you for bringing me here," she said.

"It's where the book is kept."

"Liesl? Will you be all right?"

Liesl smiled as though she would be, although of course that wasn't true.

"The next few days will be long. Here it is."

"The Peshawar. Do I just carry it out?"

"We'll wrap it like we would for shipping. But then, yes."

"I'll keep it safe."

"Can I be honest with you?"

"You don't trust me with it, do you? Not fully."

Liesl shook her head. "I don't. It's not you," she said. "I have a feeling. Like the last blow hasn't yet been delivered."

"The lab has excellent security."

Liesl pulled the book off the shelf.

"So does the library."

III

Liesl stood in the moldy staff bathroom, eyes on herself in the spotted mirror, watching drops of water wind their way through the cracks in her face and drip back into the sink that was in need of a good bleaching. She left that way, water clinging to her earlobe, wanting to feel purified on the way to her dreaded next stop.

"I guess I should have expected you," Vivek said when he opened his office door.

"I called. All morning. There was no answer."

"Right." Vivek wasn't polite about it. "Not the day to be answering my phone."

He sat down in the Vivek-shaped divot on his office couch.

"Have people been harassing you?"

"About my missing wife, the master thief?"

It was clear he had been crying all morning. Perhaps he had been crying since Miriam disappeared. Liesl had no way of knowing whether or not that was true. But the bloat of the face and the lines around the eyes and the tint of the nose didn't lie. Vivek had been crying all morning. Back on his tearstained couch, he resumed his business. Liesl was not embarrassed for him that he was crying in front of her; she was embarrassed for herself that she could not comfort him. She did not sit down on the couch beside him. She did not move from her spot by the door. She stood there and waited while a grown man cried.

The office had a 1950s stink. Vivek had been dumped among the dusty deceased houseplants and dog-eared academic journals of his predecessor. Scuffed, ink-stained, wobbly furniture that had been used by the generation before Vivek and would be used decades after he was gone. In this case, it fit. Vivek's despair would have been out of place had the room been furnished by IKEA.

Behind the couch, closer to the heavy wooden desk, was a red duffel bag. Liesl didn't think that Vivek had been taking breaks from his bouts of weeping to go swim some laps. A blue shirt, similar to the blue shirt Vivek was already wearing, peeked out of the red bag.

Liesl waited for a break in the crying so she could ask Vivek why he was living out of his office.

"Well," he said, "I have no home to go to."

"I thought you had been staying with your parents."

"I broke them when I married a white lady."

"I thought they loved Miriam."

"Can you imagine proving them right?"

"But your apartment? Why not stay there while Miriam isn't there?"

274

"Would you?" Those red-rimmed eyes looked up at her, and she had to acknowledge that in his position, no, she wouldn't.

"What was going on?" she said. "You two had separated before she went missing; you told me that yourself. Was it before you moved back from London? Could it explain why she's disappeared?"

"You must have noticed?"

"No. I don't know what you mean."

"Miriam could be a difficult woman."

"Most people are difficult at one time or another."

"Miriam's difficulty had to do with illness."

"Her illness was difficult to deal with, or her illness made her difficult?"

"Miriam was depressed."

He was absorbed by the crying again. She helplessly looked around the office for a box of tissues or a tranquilizer. There were none. Men never had tissues. She waited again for the crying to stop.

Liesl adjusted the damp collar of her shirt and tried to decide how much of this revelation was a revelation at all. Not long before Liesl's book leave, Miriam had moved her desk in the work space. Liesl had come to work one day to find that Miriam had relocated from the center desk where she had sat for years to a corner desk where she faced the wall.

"Your desk?" She had stood in front of Miriam's new work space, talking to Miriam's back, which was the only way to address her in the new configuration. "You moved your desk?"

Miriam had turned around. Not before completing the sentence she was typing and adjusting the collar of her blouse. "Is it a problem?"

"Was the other one?" Liesl asked. "A problem, I mean. You'd been in that desk since you started working here."

"And now I've moved," Miriam said.

Liesl tapped her fingernails on the filing cabinet that was being used as a divider. Miriam's eyes were pocketed in dark circles.

"Is it a problem?" Miriam repeated the question, and her voice quavered like a violin string that was pulled too tight. Liesl decided that an office move wasn't worth making someone upset, so she shook her head, indicating that no, it wasn't a problem. She decided not to ask if the tears that were welling were really about the desk. She wouldn't have framed it that way at the time, but stasis is a decision too. No one ever said anything to her about it again. The corner desk had been empty. Miriam took a lot of sick days — that was true too — but in an office full of elderly people, that didn't stand out. Even though Miriam was not herself elderly.

"To call her a thief," Vivek whispered.

Liesl was ashamed. She shouldn't have entertained the possibility for even a minute. She shouldn't have let the police entertain the possibility.

"You should get up and have a drink of water."

"She was too sick to be a thief," he said.

Pacing the office like it was a prison cell, Liesl tried to conjure Miriam in her mind. The only picture that came to her was that of the back of Miriam's head, the familiar posture at the desk pushed in the corner, begging for privacy, begging for help.

"What do you mean, too sick?" Liesl said.

"Being a thief takes work," Vivek said. "She could barely get up and shower most days."

"That isn't true." She thought of John. In bed for two weeks at a time. Hannah eating dry toast for dinner when there was no one around to cook her soup.

"You weren't paying attention."

"Maybe not," Liesl said. "But I think I'd have noticed if it were that bad."

"It was that bad. You didn't notice." He

lay on his side on the couch. Curled in on himself. His despair didn't allow him the energy to sit upright any longer.

"I'm sure she was sad," Liesl said. "But people have ways of hiding that."

"Depressed isn't sad."

"Of course, I know that," Liesl said. "But it's part of it."

"Some days she would sit on our bed and stare at the wall for hours. Not move. Not cry. Just stare. That isn't sad."

Liesl sensed his need for comfort and stopped her pacing. She dropped to a squat on the floor in front of the couch. Put her hand on his head like he was a feverish child.

"Did you tell the police?" Liesl said. "Maybe refer them to her doctor?"

"I'm her husband," Vivek said. "You think the police are going to believe me when I say she couldn't have stolen those books?"

"Her doctor then?"

"That's just it, Liesl," Vivek said, sitting up again, pushing her hand away.

"Will her doctor not share information?"

"There is no doctor," Vivek said. "That's why I left her. It got too hard, and she wouldn't get help. So I asked for a divorce."

Back in those dark days with John, Liesl had tried an ultimatum. She'd packed a bag — a suitcase, not a duffel bag — rested it by their bedroom door, and tried to bargain with the monsters in John's head. It was all for show. They both knew that she wouldn't leave without Hannah and wouldn't deprive John of her either.

Liesl stayed in place despite Vivek's agitation. She would not allow him to carry the blame for this. She knew that the weight of it could break a person. She put her hands on him, lightly touching his knee so that he would look at her.

"Vivek. This isn't your fault."

"Of course it is," Vivek said.

"You tried to get her help. It sounds like you really tried."

"In sickness and in health. All that shit."

"People have asked for divorces for worse reasons."

"Have they?" He tried to pull his knee away. She didn't let him.

"People have affairs. People have midlife crises. This is harder."

"I put her in danger."

"How?"

"By asking her to make a choice when she was in no position to make one."

"Vivek, this isn't your fault."

"I wanted to do something radical to get her to act. To get her to admit that she was really sick. But it was more than that, Liesl.

I couldn't bear to live with her like that. I couldn't bear to live like that. She'd had bouts before, and she would get through them, but it was never this bad, it was never this long. And she wouldn't go see a therapist, she wouldn't consider antidepressants. She thought that would make people say she was crazy. But she was fine to sit and stare at the wall for six hours or cry for three days straight or bite at her hangnails until each of her fingers was bleeding. Like none of that is crazy? I was so excited when I got this job, I was so excited to be with my wife again, to really begin to build our lives. But it only took, I don't know, a week? Before I felt sick at the idea of coming home to her every night. I thought if I threatened to leave, she would finally get help. But I also just wanted to get out of that apartment."

He stopped and waited for Liesl to reply.

"Maybe she's gone to get help?" She finally withdrew her hand. Put it to her face. Conceding that she was just as helpless as he was.

"Were that true, how do you think this news will fit in?"

"It's a misunderstanding," said Liesl. "We can explain."

Neither one of them believed that.

"It wouldn't matter," he said.

"Why wouldn't it matter?"

"It's not as though she's doing art therapy at a sanatorium somewhere," Vivek said. He had stopped crying. That was somehow worse. "I made an awful threat, a selfish threat, and now something has happened to her. Or she's done something to herself."

"You don't mean it," Liesl said. "Has she ever tried that before?"

"I don't know. But it's the next step in all this, isn't it?" Vivek said. "When I was in London, I used to panic if she took longer than an hour to answer a text message. Do you know how many times I sent my mom or my sister over to our apartment, certain that they would find her drowned in the bathtub?"

"But you said she never talked about it," Liesl said.

"They called her a thief," Vivek went on, but the display of emotion had sapped him. He lay down again. "My sweet wife."

"We can fix it."

"My sweet wife," said Vivek. "Other people's opinions made her so anxious. She would have an upset stomach for days if she thought she said the wrong thing to someone."

"And now she's on the front page of the newspaper," Liesl said.

"The front page of the newspaper," Vivek said. "Being called a thief."

"I'm so sorry," Liesl said. She fought a swell of tears that threatened to accompany the apology, but he could hear it in her voice. "If I hadn't called the police."

"I called them first," Vivek said. "I didn't know about the missing books and all that, but what could we do but report her missing?"

"The police might find her safe," Liesl said.

"They won't," Vivek said, fixing his eyes on some blank spot on the wall behind Liesl. "Tell the police to focus on finding the books. If we can't save her, we can save her reputation."

IV

Another moldy bathroom, this time in the history department. Liesl locked the door and yanked paper towels out of the dispenser an arm's length at a time. She pulled and pulled and pulled until she had a pillow's worth, and then she balled it up and buried her face in it and screamed.

On the way back to the library, she walked on the shady side of the street, under the ginkgo trees that shielded the campus from the sun in the summer but shed their fruit and stunk like vomit through the autumn. The sidewalks were littered with the rotting yellow berries, and she smashed them with her shoes as she walked. It was midterm season, so the students didn't gather in clusters by the food trucks anymore. They walked from class to class with their heads down, their backpacks full.

"What are we supposed to do?" Max said when she walked in, looking at the ringing phone on the reference desk like it was a bomb.

Liesl shook her head. "Proactively contact the Plantin donors, hold their hands, stroke their heads, feed them warm milk, all while not giving them too much information about what's actually going on."

As she approached him, he stuck out his hand, holding a stack of messages. It was too late to contact the Plantin donors proactively. She wanted to stick the stack in the trash and run away. The authority she had entered with evaporated in an audible puff.

She didn't have a full list of the Plantin donors. She didn't tell Max that part. Christopher hadn't saved anything on his computer, so it could be anywhere on one of the thousands of sheets of loose paper in his office. Max was already panicking, so she didn't tell him that part. He was the type who still received the morning paper. Liesl imagined him wearing a dressing gown. Not a robe, but a dressing gown. His husband becoming increasingly concerned as he watched the horror spread over Max's face as he read the article, letting his coffee get cold. Or maybe there had been no horror at all. Maybe he was the one who leaked to the press.

She clutched the stack of messages with her sweaty hands. She was panicking too.

"We can split them up," he said.

"They're going to want to hear from me," Liesl said.

"All they want is to have their call returned."

She didn't argue because she didn't want to. She wanted someone to offer to help her, and he had. If he had an agenda, she didn't care. Max had a talent for soothing donors.

"Should I handle Percy?" Max asked.

The right answer was no. Percy was their most important donor, Percy had fronted most of the money for the Plantin, Percy would be among the angriest of the donors because Percy was often angry anyway. Liesl nodded. Percy would prefer to hear from the one of them who came to work in a tie. He pulled Percy's message slip from the pile.

"Don't be more honest than you have to," Liesl said.

The phone was ringing again, the bomb ticking again. He reached for it, but she shook her head. If the reference desk phone went unanswered, the call would be re-routed to an open line in the workroom. Right now they were doing triage. Someone inside could deal with new messages.

She handed Max his pile of messages. His skin drooped against his eye sockets and his tie had skewed to the left, but he didn't look like he was panicking anymore. He was a man who knew about secrets. He had done this before.

"We tell the truth," Liesl said. She placed a message from a retired faculty member and good friend on top of her pile.

"But not too much of it?"

"The Plantin disappeared. With Christopher's illness, there was a delay in reporting." She paused. "We believe it will be recovered."

"What about Miriam?"

"I went and saw Vivek this morning."

A flinch. A blow making it past his armor. He had imagination enough to think of what the conversation must have been like. The elevator door opened, and Liesl crushed the pile of messages in her fists. A young man, a graduate student, walked out into the artificial light. The university marched forward. He had requested the use of the papers of a prominent songwriter and poet. There were dozens of gray archive boxes in the main reading room waiting for him.

"Can I have your student card?" Max asked. His hands weren't shaking; his fists weren't clenched. He had done this before. He noted the young man's details, directed him to his papers. They stayed quiet until he was through the door.

"Where does Vivek think she is?" Max said.

"Nowhere good," she said. "He asked her for a divorce."

"Goodness. When?"

The graduate student — buzz-cut brown hair, Labrador grin — came back out front. He had only brought a pen to take notes. He didn't know the rules. He'd been sent out to the reference area in search of a pencil. Liesl opened the top drawer of the desk and rooted around for a sharpened pencil. She handed it to him, and instead of looking grateful, he looked amused. He likely hadn't used a pencil since grade school. No matter. He trotted back into the reading room, tail wagging as he went.

She unclenched her fists and smoothed the messages. Impossible to know how much she should tell Max, how much she should trust him. In the end, trust didn't matter. It was a grim morning. She needed to talk to someone, and Max was there.

The reading room door swung open again. The graduate student came back out into the reference area, holding up the pencil, its tip snapped. She motioned to the pencil sharpener.

Liesl and Max watched him make his way over, insert the pencil into the old steel sharpener bolted to the long desk, and begin to turn the hand crank. It roared. He smiled to himself, the graduate student, at the noise he was making.

Finally, they were alone.

"He said that Miriam was mentally ill," Liesl said. Vivek had not asked her to keep it a secret.

"Depression, or something else?" Max asked. "My father was a depressive. Terrible thing."

"Could you tell?" she said. "The way that Vivek described it, I should have been able to tell."

"In hindsight, I guess," Max said. "But a depressive can be like an alcoholic. Masters of disguise."

"He said there's no way she could be the thief. That she wasn't functional enough to do something like that. But she was functional enough to fake being well?"

"Not the same," Max said. "And she wasn't faking being well. If we were paying attention, we'd have seen it."

"She got her work done. She functioned enough to get her work done."

He straightened his tie. He was almost totally Max again.

"If you still suspect her, then go ahead and suspect her. You read the paper; you're not the only one."

"She stopped joining us in the staff room when we would stop for tea. I shouldn't have let her do that. It was obvious she was ill, wasn't it?"

"Quite obvious. But it's an ugly thing, mental illness. No one will fault you for not asking."

"Having a suspect would be a comfort."

"Liesl. Try and show a little sense. You have a suspect. It's not the same suspect who has an unflattering photo on the front page of today's newspaper, but if we are playing Sherlock Holmes, then there is some bloody suspicious behavior you seem desperate to ignore."

"What suspect?" Liesl said. The phone

was ringing again. "Ignore it."

"Don't act as though we haven't had this conversation before, as if I haven't brought this up before. When you act this way, it makes me feel as though I'm grasping at something, as if I'm seeing something that isn't there. But I'm not. I know suspicious behavior. And insisting, against all good judgment, that the police should not be called when it is clear that a crime has been committed. That is suspicious behavior."

"You mean Francis."

"Of course I mean Francis. Of course I mean Christopher's protégé who even Christopher must have suspected of some sort of wrongdoing. Why do you think you were promoted to Christopher's deputy when you and Francis have both been here for so long? Christopher must have suspected something shifty. He's just not awake to point a finger."

"Because I was better. I was promoted over Francis because I'm better than him at schedules and budgets and tax fillings and all the things that the leader of this place has to do but Christopher didn't want to bother with. Can you not believe that?"

"How many languages do you speak then," Max said. "More than he does?"

"There's more to it," Liesl said.

"Your education then. Better than his?"

If she asked him to stop, she knew he would. But she didn't.

"Tell me," Max said. "Tell me that I'm wrong."

She didn't tell him he was wrong, because their conversation ended. They were no longer alone. Francis walked into the reference area. There was no way to know if he had heard them.

"A fine morning for the library, wouldn't you say?" Francis said. "The reference desk calls have been coming to my desk." He held a pile of messages.

Did he look smug? Did he look suspicious? He just looked like Francis.

"Thank you for answering them," Liesl said.

"Two were really reference questions," Francis said.

"What a treat," Liesl said.

"One was researching armorial bindings."

"How are the donor calls?" Max asked.

"Plentiful," Francis said. "Bit surprising, isn't it, how many people still read the morning paper? Makes you think those doom-and-gloom stories about the death of print are overstated."

"I'll take the messages," Liesl said.

"I suppose I should say I told you so,"

Francis said. "Liesl, I warned you against calling the police, didn't I?"

"Indeed you did."

"Nothing to do about it now. The story named a suspect, which is helpful to us, I'd say."

"I disagree," Liesl said. "How is it helpful that the donors and everyone else think Miriam is a suspect in the theft?"

"Looks better than us twiddling our thumbs," Francis said.

"It's a woman's reputation," Liesl said. "I'd prefer to look bad."

"The police suspect her," Francis said. "That's the simple truth."

"We should know better."

"Why are you all of a sudden so adamant?"

"Maybe I'm in receipt of new information. Maybe I'm thinking straight."

"I'm not sure what's going on," Francis said. "It's a stressful day, Liesl. Here are the messages. Let me know if I can help."

A moment later, after Francis had made a statement with his exit, spinning on a heel as he delivered his last statement, Max and Liesl found themselves locking eyes. They were again alone; the graduate student's pencil was sharp. He was hunched over a desk behind a glass door, tip of his tongue sticking through his lips in concentration.

Max adjusted his already-perfect tie and watched Liesl in silence as the memory of Francis receded from the space. When she said nothing, Max raised his eyebrows at her; she was standing with her arms crossed.

"So you believe me then?" Max said.

"I didn't say that."

"You didn't have to, Liesl. You behaved like it."

"No," she said, looking off in the direction where Francis had disappeared. "I spoke in defense of Miriam."

"Right, Liesl. But if Miriam isn't the thief, then someone else is."

"Someone. Not Francis."

Max gave her a steady look, then spun the chair around and faced the computer screen. After a few moments of silence, he gave a slight shake of the head.

"Right," he said. "You two are close, so this is hard for you."

Liesl refused to accept that. She changed direction.

"You've offered no evidence."

"Haven't I?"

"He was against the police, Max. That's all."

Liesl was surprised that Max seemed so fixed on the idea of Francis as the culprit.

The men had a long relationship, no history of coldness between them that she knew.

"It might be all," Max said. "Or it might be the first piece of something bigger."

Max waved a hand as to if signal the conversation was over, but Liesl felt determined to continue. She pulled a chair over directly next to Max and sat herself in it. Refused to accept his back to her any longer. This time she took the accusing tone.

"You sound paranoid," Liesl said. "Francis is your colleague."

"I know," he said. This time he was the one who glanced over to make sure Francis was not returning. "But we won't find who did it without asking questions."

"Christopher would know," Liesl said, thinking of the confident Christopher holding court in his office, the one who didn't exist anymore, not the near-corpse in the ICU. "I'm sure he would just know."

"He's as good with people as he is with books," Max said.

"That's why he's so good at this job."

"It's hard," Max said, "to think of someone replacing him."

"Not satisfied with my performance?" Liesl said.

"That's not fair. You're only interim."

"It's all right. My feelings aren't hurt,"

Liesl said. "I'm good with books, not people."

With Liesl sitting next to him, Max struggled to hide his unease, but didn't conceal his meaning. Some other man might have paid her a compliment, thought of ways in which she was appropriate for the leadership position. Max was not that man.

"The fundraising is an awfully important part of the job," he said.

"Yes. I'm learning that it's difficult to be successful without a membership to the right golf club or wine club or cigar club. I don't even know the right kind of club."

The phone rang again. Max was waiting for Liesl to say that he could be the one. That he had the talent for books and the talent for people. She wouldn't offer him that kindness.

The call was rerouted, and it went quiet again.

"You should call Percy first," Liesl said.

"Yes. He'll be waiting."

"When you do, make sure he knows you're calling him first."

"Bit late to be sucking up."

"Not with Percy. Let's do what we can to keep him feeling important."

"I'll do my best."

They both stood up. Liesl waited for him

to realize that he had to stay at the reference desk, that it was his shift. He didn't.

"The desk," Liesl said.

"There's no one else?"

"You were scheduled."

"Well, yes," Max said. "But I thought that with everything going on . . ."

"If staffing weren't so tight. The absences. You understand."

"I'll call Percy from here."

She nodded, prepared to leave, and then stopped herself, catching on something that he had said earlier. She tapped a finger on the desk, wondering if her question was out of line and finally deciding they were past the point of niceties.

"What happened with your father," she said, "in the end?"

"How do you mean?"

"Your father. You said he was a depressive, that he suffered from it throughout his life. Did he ever get better?"

"Are you asking if my father killed himself?"

"Not at all. I'm sorry. None of my business."

"It's fine. It's been a long time."

"So he did, then?"

"Alas, no. He drank himself to death. His liver killed him before his hand could."

"I'm terribly sorry. I shouldn't have asked."

"Yes. I'm going to get to these calls."

"Thank you."

Faint and frail, Liesl began to make phone calls, and after a prolonged explanation to the first call recipient, she learned that rich people love gossip more than rich people love old books and that she shouldn't have been worried at all. She had sat in the cigar stink of Christopher's office and prepared a script about open communication and about the police investigation and about the expected recovery of the books. None of the old wankers cared a lick. They wanted color for their upcoming cocktail parties. They asked about how the theft had been discovered, they asked if the investigating detective was handsome, they asked if there was a ransom note for the books, and when she said there was not, they said there must be and she just had not discovered it yet. Rich people loved gossip almost as much as they loved money.

The gossip was currency. They took ages, the calls did, because of all that back-and-forth about ransom notes. At three in the afternoon, sitting in Christopher's office, she poured herself a drink and found that made the calls easier still. They were nice people, these donors, she decided after her third tumbler. They just wanted a good story.

14

I

The library basement. Waterproof, fireproof, soundproof, down a rumbling elevator or a locked staircase. No one went down there to hide, exactly, but people who went down there couldn't easily be found.

Liesl had suggested installing a phone line once, years ago. They'd never gotten around to it. Miriam's front-page picture had been lining hamster cages for days now, and Liesl was back in the basement, not exactly hiding.

The only way to reach her was to walk, stack by stack, through the repository until you caught a glimpse of something human. She heard the door click, heard Francis's throat clear, and wondered if he would stand in place and summon her like a dog. He didn't. She heard his dragging feet, step by step until they were in sight of each other's tired eyes. She would learn later that he had been in possession of the bad news for nearly twenty minutes by the time he spotted her in the appraiser's area. He could have just yelled her name and gotten it over with, but she was grateful he decided that she and the news deserved more respect.

She knew it as soon as she saw his basset hound eyes. She knew that Christopher was alive. She knew that the building wasn't on fire. She knew that Miriam's body had been found.

There's this myth that dogs go away to be alone when it's time for them to die so that they can spare the pack the sadness of their death. It isn't true. If a dog goes into hiding when it becomes ill, it does so to avoid becoming a target for other animals when it can't protect itself. A dying dog doesn't hide out of compassion. It does so out of fear.

Liesl had been prepared for bad news. The bad news had been coming and coming and coming. No reason to think it would suddenly get better. That wasn't the way of the world. When a bad thing happens, it is usually the signal that more bad things are about to happen. Earthquakes have aftershocks and all that. In early September, Liesl had been working on a book about gardening, in her house with her husband, getting ready to retire. Nothing good had happened since. Still, when Francis gave her the news, she was worried she would fall down from the shock of it. She took his arm and then let go of it and sat alone on the dusty concrete floor.

Liesl wanted to work on her book. She didn't know what to do with any of this situation. The dying man, the dead woman, the criminal working somewhere close to her. She wanted to go and tell Garber that she was leaving, going home to work on her book of flowers.

She wished she didn't need Francis's comfort to bear the news. She wished she wasn't glad that Francis was there. He took her hand and pulled her up off the floor. This was practical, not romantic. They were old, and sitting on a concrete floor could lead to days of aches. Liesl and Francis and the whole library staff had braced for a death for weeks, but not for Miriam's death. Preparation for one did not mean they were prepared for the other. Francis took her to some shelving stools. They might have been the same stools that the two had sat on in weeks past.

Liesl shuddered and pressed her hands together to keep them from shaking. The news made her think of the time Miriam had spontaneously recited the Dickinson poem, made her think of a woman full of poetry, a woman moved to recite by the sight of a rich yellow hue, and it made her wonder if the thoughtful poet could be the same soul as the self-slaughterer. The news made her think of Miriam at the new-faculty reception. Begging for attention and, it seemed, finally begging for help.

Liesl had never known anyone who had taken their own life. Francis had. This history did not lend him additional perspective. It was just a fact about him. Because they were not young, they had dealt with a lot of death, but Liesl did not know if a suicide should be treated like any other death. Usually she would bring a lasagna from the Harbord Bakery. She wondered if it was appropriate to bring Vivek a lasagna. She didn't ask Francis. Men never knew the answers to these sorts of things.

After about thirty minutes, they went upstairs. Liesl gathered the staff who were working that day. They sat in the reading room that wasn't really a reading room, and in that beautiful space, in that cathedral of books, she told them Miriam was dead. Francis stood at the back of the room and nodded with encouragement. Liesl was not encouraged. One of their own was dead, and one of them was a thief.

II

Miriam had been discovered by a couple of teenagers who went to the woods to get high. They had stolen the pot from an elder brother's T-shirt drawer. This information came tumbling out of one of the boys without prompting from the police. Minor crimes were not crimes at all when there was a body under discussion. The woods weren't really wild forest; that scarcely exists close to a city anymore. Rather, in the trees ninety minutes from the campus was a campground. The type of place where teenagers in packs or families with small children congregate on long weekends. With flattened patches of dirt to pitch a tent and poles with water and electricity at the far end of each campsite so one can be in nature but not forgo a cell phone charger or a French press. In high summer the place was not like the woods at all; it rang with music and laughter, the sounds of beer cans being cracked open and the smell of marshmallows charring over a fire.

Come Labor Day, the crowds disappeared. The type of person who goes camping in the cold is not the type of person who comes to such a place. There was a park ranger stationed by the gate, but the teen boys, and presumably Miriam, knew that there were ways to sneak in. The boys had been driving a twenty-seven-year-old aquamarine Dodge Shadow that made a high whistling sound as it ran, so they ditched it by the gate and decided they would get high on foot. They were nervous. Scared of what the sensation would be like, scared they would get caught. Neither had ever done drugs, not even marijuana, before. They were good kids.

The park had been well cleaned at the end of the season, but there were still clues to be found. A fire pit containing the charred spine of a John Grisham novel. The outlines in the grass of so many tents and coolers and cars. If they hadn't been so nervous about the weed, the boys probably wouldn't have walked so far into the campsite, and if they hadn't been so nervous about being caught, they probably wouldn't have been looking so closely for other signs of life.

They were teenagers. They didn't read the newspaper. If they had, they might have known to be on the lookout for a navy Toyota sedan. In their whispered conversation, they were sure that there were people having sex in the back seat of the car, and they were delighted that they might get to see the act in person.

Miriam had been dead for a long time

when the boys snuck over to her car to peek at her. The pills she had taken had caused her to vomit bile and foam all over herself, all over her maroon blouse, but that had long since dried and crusted over. The boys were not looking at her blouse. *Law & Order* had not prepared them for what her skin would look like. Miriam was blue and black and bloated, and the contours of her nose and mouth were only discernible from the white mold that grew around them. The car doors were closed. The boys did not try to open them, which was a mercy because as much as they were unprepared for the sight, they might not have survived the smell. Like all teenagers they had cell phones, but they were too far from a tower to get any signal, so they wept and shook and tried to call for help but eventually had to stagger all the way back to the Dodge Shadow and drive to the main road before they could call their parents and then the police. They never did smoke the weed.

A police officer who was among the first on the scene found the baggie in the mud. He wasn't sure if it had belonged to the victim, so he entered it into evidence. The coroner later confirmed that Miriam had been dead for several weeks, likely since the first day she had failed to come to work.

The police found no evidence of the books in her car or in her apartment.

If there was solace to be found, it was that Miriam never knew that she stood accused of the thefts.

FORTY YEARS EARLIER

The Department of Rare Books and Special Collections: fourteen men and Liesl Weiss in a shiny new building attached to the humanities and social sciences library tasked with developing a collection that would bring the British Library to a curtsy. Liesl was on the sidewalk out front, terrified to go in.

"It was a mistake," she said.

She'd been changing her mind for the twenty-six blocks they'd been walking — twice while waiting at a crosswalk, once while John had stopped to tie his shoe, and every time they'd passed a baby carriage.

A tweed jacket with elbow patches got out of a taxi in front of where they were standing. The wearer flicked a cigarette past the curb and took the library steps two at a time.

"That's him," Liesl said.

"He's very tall," John said.

They'd done the mental math the whole

way there, adding to one column and subtracting from another while they passed all those baby carriages: a full-time salary, health insurance, leadership opportunities, the challenge of doing something brand new, her lack of knowledge of rare books, being the only woman, the challenge of doing something brand new. And then finally, as Christopher Wolfe dashed past them up the stairs, an argument with potential.

"It's not forever." John held her arm and took a step toward the stairs. "Just until the baby."

"Don't say that too loud," Liesl said.

"No one's listening. And it's not as though you're knocked up now. But you have an out. If it's not where you think you should be."

"That's it, is it? You want me barefoot and pregnant. I should have known."

"My secret plan. There's a check for the blue canvases coming. We could be okay."

"The two of us, maybe. But if we had to buy diapers?"

"And then there were three, and then there were three, how sweet it would be . . ." John stopped singing and read her face. "Do you want it to be forever?"

"Forever? I don't know. But it's a good opportunity, working for a man like that.

Getting in at the ground floor. Might get to lead the whole thing one day instead of being a glorified secretary somewhere else."

John smiled. "My wife, the library director."

"It's silly," she said, straightening her shoulders, experiencing a small rush of excitement. She pictured herself haggling with book dealers, filling the shelves with volumes on horticulture, imagined the treasures she might bring to the university. John continued to hold her as they stared up at the building, but Liesl had forgotten all about him, lost in her imaginings. The picture of a rare books collection built of something more than just old bibles. John studied his wife's determined face so he could sketch it later, and when he was sure he'd memorized it, leaned over to kiss her smooth cheek.

"I'm ready. I'm going in," she said as she abruptly let go of his arm, losing her slouch and taking the stairs two at a time, waving at John but not looking back at him, not even once, before she pushed her way through the heavy door for her first day at work at the new rare books library.

15

I

The first time Liesl saw the Peshawar laid out on the slab, she realized that she knew little, so very little, about the lives of her books. Just that morning a student had been asking her a question like she was some sort of expert — she bloviated on the printing device of Immanuel Benveniste — but the feeling that she was an impostor crept over her shoulders and wrapped itself around her neck.

Liesl followed Rhonda to her workstation: a laptop and a can of Diet Coke on a stainless-steel table.

That morning Liesl had walked through the little Jewish cemetery hidden behind a courtyard in her neighborhood. She'd paid respect at the end of the lives of many Jewish friends, laid a stone on top of a grave to weigh the spirit down and keep it longer in this world as custom dictated. No one had been buried there in at least a hundred years, and from the street, passersby could see only a tall stone wall topped with threatening wire and a permanently locked blue door. There were few loved ones left to leave stones on these graves. If you knew how to wrap your way through the courtyard, there was an entrance into the garden of headstones.

Vivek had decided that there would be no service for Miriam, religious or otherwise. It was what Miriam would have wanted, he said, and Liesl agreed, but for her own sake, not for Miriam's, she wished that she had been given a venue to mourn, a grave on which to rest her hand. She had left a small rock on one of the headstones here. She hoped it would be clear to the spirits, whatever or wherever they were, that it was Miriam's soul that Liesl wanted to keep in this world for just a bit longer.

"We're taking good care of your book," Rhonda said, bringing Liesl to the table with the manuscript.

"I don't doubt it," Liesl said.

"Don't lie. You doubt it a little."

There would have to be some disassembly before the testing could be done. The bindings were from the twentieth century, and the manuscript leaves inside the bindings had begun to disintegrate. The mica covers that had been used as sleeves for each manuscript page had caused the destruction of something that had survived in the dirt for over a thousand years, but the same mica was now the only thing holding each leaf together. If they tried to remove the pages from the binding, they would disintegrate into dust. Someone — a graduate student? An artist? — had been assigned the task of taking the book apart. The threads had been delicately removed with tweezers and a steady hand, the glue had been melted with a solvent, and the leaves lay spread out in the order that they had been bound, one next to the other, so that this area of the lab looked like it hosted an art exhibition and the pages of figures and equations were works on display. The order of the pages had been determined by the scholar who wrote the seminal work on the Peshawar, who had made those famous photographs. By keeping the pages in order, the lab was preserving the work of a twentieth-century scholar, not an eighth-century one, but they did it all the same, showing respect for every hand that had ever touched the book.

"We'll be sampling from three separate pages," Rhonda said. "But only slivers."

How would they decide on the sacrifices? Liesl looked at the laid-out leaves and thought about how she might determine which of them should have a piece removed.

Have you completed your lab notes? read a sign posted on the wall above the table.

"We'll be losing three pages then?" Liesl asked.

"No, of course not," Rhonda said.

The lab door swung open, and a young woman walked in and nodded hello. She pulled a computer from her backpack and began to work at one of the bare tables.

"But you're removing samples from them," Liesl asked.

"Slivers, small slivers," Rhonda said.

"So we won't be able to tell there's anything missing?"

Having overheard, the young woman looked up from her computer. She walked over and introduced herself, and Liesl felt embarrassed for having interrupted her work. She was the manager in charge of the lab. She talked about the nature of the sampling, and Liesl didn't listen as she was busy trying to calculate the girl's age.

There was something about choosing samples from three pages that had slightly different coloration. The girl's straight black hair was pulled back into a ponytail, and though the frames of her glasses obscured her eyes a little, it didn't look like they hid any lines or sagging. She had worn a backpack. Not a briefcase. Not a purse. A backpack. A full professor. It was maroon with oversized gold zippers. Once the pages had been sorted by color, the girl explained, they had looked for pages where they thought they could remove a good-sized sliver while doing the least harm to the rest of the material.

Liesl nodded, made an effort to look convinced, but grieved for those pages and the tiny pieces of them that would be taken forever.

Others began to filter into the lab. No one wore a lab coat. Liesl wasn't sure if they were supposed to. She never wore white gloves when handling books, and everyone assumed librarians did that, so maybe lab coats were one of those things. More for TV than for life.

She didn't want to ask; it seemed like such a stupid question, the way the questions about the gloves always did. The girl asked if Liesl wanted to see the machine, and Rhonda looked delighted, as did the rest of the staff who were now in the lab. Liesl cared nothing for machines, but they all looked so pleased to show her that of course she agreed. She was led to another room, and there it was, the monstrosity of a thing. White cylinders of various sizes were linked together by silver pipes, but from every surface sprung wires and tubes. It was a science experiment that had been dreamed up by an eleven-year-old boy in his bedroom. They were looking at her, Rhonda and the rest of them, waiting to hear that she was impressed. She tried to think of something nice to say about the thing.

"There certainly are a lot of pieces," Liesl finally said.

"There are a lot of steps required," Rhonda said, "when it comes to revealing secrets."

II

Liesl noticed Hannah's haircut, half of her head buzzed nearly bald, before Hannah noticed Liesl outside the noodle shop. The half-bald head moved back and forth, back and forth, back and forth, as Hannah swiveled on her stool at the counter. It was strange that Hannah had a haircut that Liesl hadn't known about. That she could have passed her daughter on the street and not known her.

When she came up behind Hannah, Liesl ran her hand over the buzzed side of her head, and Hannah turned to her with a big grin. When her daughter's face came into view, Liesl nearly wept with relief; the sight of Hannah was always the best balm. They sat together, laughing for a minute at Liesl's betrayal at being the last to know of such a big event in a young woman's life as a haircut and Liesl recovering almost immediately from any hurt feeling she may have harbored.

Though Liesl wished they could talk only of haircuts and lunch dates and other whimsical things, they moved, of course, to sadder matters. Hannah asked about Miriam. A crowd of students, their denim coats covered in layers of scarves against the mean November, came into the noodle shop, bringing their noise and the cold in with them. They packed a table at the far end of the shop. John had told Hannah about Miriam. Liesl hadn't wanted to speak about it. She still didn't want to. Their noodle bowls arrived. Had Hannah cut her hair before or after the news about Miriam? Liesl wanted to ask but didn't.

The steam smelled like chile and ginger. The students were having pitchers of Sapporo brought to their table. They poured it out in glasses and raised them in a toast; they were celebrating. Liesl was sweating,

not unpleasantly, from the heat of the noodles.

"They've made it spicier, I think."

"It's been exactly the same since I was
ten. Why won't you answer me about Miriam? Have you seen Vivek?"

Liesl took a big mouthful of noodles, taking her time to chew.

"Have you ever seen a machine for carbon
dating?"

"When would I have seen that?"

Another bite of noodles.

"You're a student. You took sciences
classes all through high school."

"You think that radiocarbon dating is a
standard part of a high-school science cur-
riculum?"

The group of students toasted again,
sloshing some beer on the table as they did.

"Maybe," Liesl said. "We paid for that
fancy private school that one year."

They slurped and sweated over their bowls
of noodles. The shop got darker, louder,
more crowded. Liesl considered ordering
herself a beer to cool the tingling of her
tongue, but she knew that Hannah would
notice. As they'd tended to John over the
long years, Hannah had more than once
pulled Liesl's empty wine bottles out of the
bin, called to attention that their numbers

expanded when the family was in moments of tension. And Liesl could feel her counter-argument boiling up; it never interfered with her life, it never rose to the point of a *problem,* it relaxed her, and she cut it back when she was less in need of relaxation. But then Hannah would point to the arguments, to the type of person who might have arguments about the level of their alcohol consumption always at the ready.

So Liesl sipped water. Hannah reached over into Liesl's bowl with her chopsticks and plucked out a piece of pork belly. If John had done that, it would have made Liesl mad. When Hannah did it, it was charming. She didn't like not knowing about what Hannah was doing, about her haircuts, about what the girl ate all week. She took another piece of pork belly out of her bowl and placed it in Hannah's.

"I won't say no," Hannah said with a shrug.

Liesl leaned back from the table and dabbed at her hairline with a napkin. Hannah grinned at her mother, who had never had the same stomach for spice as her husband or daughter but who had always insisted she did. From across the restaurant, one of the students gave a laugh that was like a roar, fueled by belly and beer.

"Maybe you should study science," Liesl said. "Seeing all of those women in the lab. Young women like you. You'd fit in there. They'd probably even like this haircut."

Hannah had just crammed a tangle of noodles into her mouth and took a moment to slurp before responding.

"Those are serious scientists, Mom," she said through half-chewed food. "It would take more than a haircut."

"They're young like you." She wished Hannah wouldn't talk with her mouth full.

"Okay," she said. "But they are serious about science."

Liesl took a deep drink of her water and signaled to her server for more. She drained the new glass as soon as it was poured.

The buzzing and laughter from the table of students meant she and Hannah had to raise their voices to hear each other.

"Do you know that all of the people in charge are women?" Liesl said.

"I didn't," Hannah said. "But that's hardly unusual anymore."

"The head of your department is a man," Liesl said.

"That's one example," Hannah said. "And it doesn't matter anyway. I'm not a scientist."

"Christopher is a man."

"But you're not," Hannah said. "And you're in charge. Doesn't that disprove your point?"

"It might."

"It might?"

"If I were really in charge," Liesl said. "Then I agree it would disprove my point."

"Mom," Hannah said. "You know I'm not all of a sudden going to become a scientist just because you met some cool lady scientists. Right?"

Liesl thought of her daughter being made to feel unimportant. It made her stomach hurt.

"No," Liesl said. "Of course not."

"It's nice that you were so inspired."

The server dropped off the bill. Liesl hadn't seen Hannah signal for it. Hannah's bowl was empty, but Liesl wasn't ready to go.

"More jealous than inspired, I think."

"That's fair," Hannah said. "Though I always wondered what would have happened if you had put your name forward to be in a leadership position."

"Didn't I?"

"You kept your head down and did the work. It's not the same."

"I guess not," Liesl said. She recognized the line of conversation from lectures she'd given Hannah through the years, about naming your goals and pushing toward them; an illusion dispelled for Liesl by the disappointments of participating in society for sixty years.

"You might have been the type of leader that you always said you wanted."

Hannah wiped her mouth with a paper napkin and stood to leave.

"Thanks for the noodles, Mom."

III

Liesl couldn't get control of the paper in Christopher's office. She'd been reading it and filing it and shredding it, but every time she opened another box, another drawer, another cupboard, there was more paper. The man had loved to print things. Essential things like the full donor list for the Plantin that she still hadn't managed to find and trivial things like movie listings from the week of March 15, 2000. Every time she thought she had carved out some cleanliness, there was more aging paper.

"Call for you," Francis said, poking his head through the door. "Percy on line two."

Francis played with the buttons on what looked like a new cardigan. Too cozy-looking to fit with his image. She pictured him at the store, trying it on, wondering if it looked nice. She didn't say anything about it.

"I'll take it in here," she said.

"I'll close the door then." And he did.

"How can I help you, Mr. Pickens?" Liesl said.

"I think you know, Liesl."

"It's been a hard month, Percy. Tell me, what can I do for you?"

"A hard month for me too," Percy said. "My accountant is getting nervous."

Liesl stood and stretched her back. She knew what he was after. She knew she couldn't get it for him.

"A nervous accountant," Liesl said. "That sounds ominous."

"It's November," Percy said. "November is almost the end of the year."

There were jokes she could have made, of course, about having learned the order of the months in kindergarten. She refrained.

"I need a tax receipt for the Plantin by the end of the year."

"I'd like to give it to you," Liesl said. "But I can't do anything until it's recovered."

"Yes," said Percy. "So my accountant tells me."

"So how can I help?"

"You can recover the Plantin manuscript, or you can tell President Garber that the university has lost my funding support."

In the library's collection, there were a lot of bookplates with Percy Pickens's name on them. Like most rich people, he loved writing his name on things. Hospital departments, university buildings, ancient texts. That's what she was thinking about as Percy hung up on her. What the campus might look like if everything in it tagged with the name Pickens were to simply disappear.

It was raining outside, and Liesl decided to go for a walk in it. Her breath came easier as soon as she left the cluttered library and stepped into the rain under her purple umbrella. The sidewalks were her own as students hid under awnings or stayed inside buildings waiting for the rain to pass. No one else was willing to get wet.

The St. James Hotel was only a nine-minute walk from the library. Closer than the subway, so it only made sense to go in and get dry, and once she was inside, it only made sense to take a seat in a corner booth, and once she was seated, it only made sense to order herself a bottle of sparkling water, and once the water was ordered, it only made sense to ask for a whiskey, neat, as though it were an afterthought. Liesl hadn't been sleeping. Miriam was making it impossible. Liesl was afraid that if she dozed off she'd be flooded with that image of the back of Miriam's head, alone in the corner of the workroom, and in doing so she'd be immersed in her complicity in Miriam's death, that she'd wake up drenched in sweat and guilt, bringing down the straw house built of the notion that Miriam's death had been unavoidable. And now this, this threat from Percy and the knowledge that Liesl was going to undo what Christopher had spent decades building, and that when he woke up, if he woke up, he would be so disappointed.

The St. James Hotel had undergone a recent renovation, and the lobby bar banquettes were now upholstered with aquamarine velvet. Hideous. When she was younger, when Hannah was in preschool and Liesl would stay after work to have a drink rather than go home to an itinerant toddler, the room was mauve, and bartenders got your order right and weren't judgmental. Liesl fished an ice cube out of the whiskey with her fingertips and cracked it with her teeth.

She left a twenty-dollar bill on the table and left the hotel. The rain had stopped. She walked across the street to the subway station and almost bought gum but then realized that the smell of whiskey and gum was more telling than the smell of just whiskey. So she bought peanut M&M's and popped them in her mouth, one by one, as she walked back to the library. She had barely been gone thirty minutes. But her hands weren't shaking anymore.

She didn't say anything to anyone as she went back to her desk.

"Detective Yuan speaking." He answered on the first ring.

"It's Liesl. Liesl Weiss."

"Hello, Liesl Weiss."

"I'm a librarian? We met when you were investigating the disappearance of one of my staff?"

"Not a thing I would forget."

"Right. Sorry. I was hoping we might speak again. Do you have time?"

"Nah, people keep getting murdered."

"Oh my goodness. I'm so sorry. I'll let you go."

"I'm mostly joking, Liesl."

"It's about the missing books."

"Have you had lunch?" he said.

"Lunch? I guess it's almost lunch," Liesl said. "No, not yet."

"That great falafel truck still parked out front?"

She looked out the window at the yellow truck.

"It's still there."

"You had to check and see, didn't you? How you can walk by such a thing every day and miss it, I'll never know."

"You'd like to meet there?"

"Sure thing. Thirty minutes?"

"Thirty minutes."

She didn't like waiting; it made her feel visible. She thought she would feel less awkward if she were a person waiting for food and not a person just waiting. She wasn't hungry but ordered herself a sandwich anyway. A line was forming behind her, the area around the yellow truck all of a sudden swarming with students. The sun was out now. It might be one of the last days of the year where it was warm enough to stand and eat a sandwich in the street.

She looked up and down the sidewalk for Yuan. Anxious that if the sandwiches arrived before he did, she would once again be standing anxiously. Two sandwiches getting cold in her hands while everyone around her chewed. The one bench near where the truck parked was available, and she inched toward it, knowing full well that even if she got the seat, she would have to give it up once the sandwiches were ready. She heard her name called and looked up at the truck but saw that it was Detective Yuan, striding toward her with a grin.

"Did you already order? Liesl Weiss, I could swear you're beginning to like me," he said.

"I didn't know how much time you'd have." She glanced up at the truck as their order was called.

"I'll grab the sandwiches," he said. "No hot sauce for you, right?" He didn't wait for her to answer. "I suppose you haven't brought me here to inquire after the health of my family, but before you start your grilling, I have to remind you that I don't work in the property crime unit, and I can't help with your missing books."

"I don't understand," Liesl said. "If you can't help, then why did you agree to meet me?"

He signaled for her to wait, heading to the truck window. He came back with hands full of the foil-wrapped sandwiches, balancing the ramekins of hot sauce on top.

"This is great falafel. I agreed to have lunch with you and to talk. I was assigned to a missing persons case, and that case is now closed." He reshuffled and held her sandwich out to her. She kept her arms crossed.

"I need your help," Liesl said. "As a police officer."

"I really prefer detective," Yuan said.

"Every time you get my rank wrong, my mother is reminded that I didn't go to medical school."

"I can't tell if you're joking or if you're serious," Liesl said, finally taking the sandwich. "You didn't come down here just to eat lunch?"

"I mostly did. But we can talk," Yuan said.

They walked back to the bench that was somehow still empty.

"I'm with you," Yuan said. "I don't know how these kids do all of their eating standing up. It's a recipe for a soiled shirt."

"Can we talk about something besides the sandwiches?" she said, though he had just taken a ravenous first bite.

"Sure. It's not as good today anyway."

"Sorry you're disappointed," she said.

"I ordered in Arabic last time," he said through a full mouth. "He must have made it special."

Liesl had yet to tear open her wax paper.

"Come on," Yuan said. "Your lunch is going to get cold."

"It's fine," she said. "I'm all of a sudden not hungry."

He crumpled his empty paper, stained with grease and hot sauce.

"I'll eat it," he said. "If you're not going to."

She stared at the sandwich in her lap and wanted to cry. The sky had clouded over again; the weather refused to make its mind up. Detective Yuan stood and left her and her uneaten sandwich. He walked to a nearby trash bin and tossed his crumpled wax paper into it with a perfect jump shot. When the wax paper cleared the rim, he threw his arms up into the air in silent celebration, as if an arena full of spectators was cheering him on. She waited for him to come back to the bench, but he didn't. He strode back over to the yellow truck and greeted the man taking orders as if the two had gone to summer camp together. Money changed hands and then something in a brown paper bag, and Liesl wondered if the man ever stopped eating.

"Baklava, if you're not hungry for falafel," he said, handing her the bag.

"I'm just not hungry," she said, shaking her head.

"You've been drinking. You should eat." He held the bag out until she took it from him.

She thanked him. Didn't ask how he knew about the whiskey. She ate her baklava instead, setting the still-wrapped sandwich on the bench beside her. It was good, the baklava. Smelling of rosewater and dripping with honey.

"Not much of a market for stolen rare books is my understanding," he said.

"You're looking into the thefts?" she said.

"I've asked some colleagues to weigh in on the thefts," he said. "Out of personal interest. I like books. Though I'm more of a Grisham man myself."

"Thank you," she said, turning away so the degree of relief on her face couldn't be read.

"The reason for the theft wouldn't have been money," Detective Yuan said. He handed her a napkin just as she needed one, and she did her best to clean the honey from the tips of her fingers. He went on talking about noncommercial reasons for theft. Told her about stamp and coin thefts committed by prominent collectors, about manuscript thefts committed by workers as revenge when they felt wronged by their employers, told her about an art theft committed just for the thrill of it that sounded suspiciously like the plot of *The Thomas Crown Affair.*

Several times during his explanation, as he laid out what sounded like an awful lot of research, she thought to ask him why he was helping her, and each time stopped herself for fear of making him think too deeply about it.

"I'm sorry, by the way, about Miriam," he said, standing to leave. "It must be very difficult for you."

"Thank you," Liesl said. "We were close once."

He nodded.

"I'm going to go ahead and take this sandwich."

IV

Liesl tried to work as Detective Yuan's suggestion stumbled around in her brain. For spite, for a thrill, for passion. No one hated them enough to steal from them; they were a library. No one would steal for the thrill of it; they were librarians. That left only passion.

She pulled out a stack of invoices and began the work of reconciling them against her purchase orders. She made tiny check marks with a well-sharpened pencil, checked exchange rates and tax rates. She liked this work where right and wrong were laid out so clearly. The manuscript that Francis had brought her to read was still stacked on the corner of her desk. She put the invoices aside and flipped the manuscript back open to the chapter about the Vesalius. Francis had said they were waiting to add illustrations until they found funding to have new photographs taken. They'd have to work from low-quality file photographs now that the manuscript was gone, she thought.

She was going to reread the Vesalius chapter, but she was still stuck on what Yuan had said. There would be no concentrating that afternoon. She put the manuscript aside and picked up the phone.

"It's a surprise to hear from you," Marie said when she answered the telephone, after Liesl had waited through five rings, fussing all the while to make sure the materials on her desk were perfectly perpendicular.

"How's Christopher?"

"Same as ever," Marie said, a telltale background beeping suggesting that she was right by his side. "His strength is keeping him in the fight. It's mine that's fading."

"I'm sure he can feel you there."

Liesl drummed her fingers against the desktop. Pulled the manuscript back toward her and opened it back up to the description of the Vesalius. On the other end of the phone, Marie murmured about heart rates, rehabilitation schedules. Liesl muttered occasionally to indicate that she was listening as she waited for a way into the conversation.

"I'd like to do something for Christopher," Liesl said.

Marie paused, waited to hear more.

"I'd like to find the books for him," Liesl said.

She tried to flip back to the table of contents without taking her hand off the telephone receiver. She succeeded in giving herself a paper cut on her way to the listing.

"Goodness," Marie said. "We'd all like that."

"I think I know how," Liesl said. "But I'll need your help."

"I'm at the hospital full-time now," Marie said. "I don't know how I can be of use."

"I didn't realize you were spending so much time there." The cut was bleeding, threatening to streak red onto the white pages.

"I don't want him to have to be alone."

"What about taking care of yourself?"

"That can come after. For now, I'm taking care of Chris."

"If he wakes up, he'll need your strength," Liesl said, looking for something that wasn't her light-gray trousers that she could use to stem the bleeding.

"When he wakes up."

"Of course," Liesl said. "When he wakes up."

"When he wakes up, someone should be here for him," Marie said. "So I'll be there until that happens."

"He's lucky to have you."

"I'm lucky to be able to do this for him."

"I think, Marie," Liesl said, "that I might know who stole his books."

She looked around the empty office and, certain she wouldn't be caught, stuck her bleeding finger into her mouth. She had always kind of liked it, the faint metallic tinge of one's own blood.

"How can you know?" Marie said.

"I don't yet for certain," said Liesl.

Marie laughed.

"We're going in circles, Detective Liesl."

"I have a suspicion," Liesl said, looking down at the manuscript's table of contents, at the listing of magnificent publications. "And a good reason for it."

"I see," Marie said. "And I'm to be your Watson?"

"Marie, the theft is upsetting. But the identity of the thief might be even more so."

"I'm sitting in a hospital next to my comatose husband, Liesl. I'm shockproof at this point."

Liesl made the consideration and, torn between need for Marie's help and the consequences of expressing the accusation aloud, decided it best to go all the way in.

"I have reason to suspect Francis."

"Francis Churchill?" Marie expressed something between a laugh and a cough. "Francis from the library?"

"Well, yes," Liesl said, tracing the names of other entries in the manuscript with her finger. "Francis Churchill from the library."

"You and Francis are great friends," Marie said. "I've heard rumors that you and Francis are *more* than great friends."

"I'm not even sure what that means," Liesl said.

"What a time for silly rumors. I'm sorry," Marie said. "Why in the world do you suspect Francis?"

"Something the police said."

"The police?" said Marie.

"A detective became involved with us after Miriam's disappearance."

In her distraction, Liesl had forgotten about the bleeding. She looked down to see that the manuscript had been marked, her blood underlining the name "Vesalius."

"Terrible tragedy, that," Marie said.

In the background of the call, Liesl could hear the sound of serious medical professionals talking.

"Did you know Miriam well?" Liesl asked.

"Hardly at all." Marie seemed eager to move on from the subject of the suicide. Liesl figured she was steeped enough in her own misfortune. "I can't recall ever speaking with her."

"Well, yes. Miriam could be very quiet," Liesl said.

"You were going to tell me about Francis," Marie said.

"A police detective advised me. And based on that advice, I think Francis might be a suspect."

"It's all very vague," Marie said. "Did the police say that they're investigating him?"

"He and Christopher were writing together," Liesl said.

"Yes, I remember," Marie said.

"What they wrote might be a clue," Liesl said, dog-earing the corners of the manuscript pages on her desk.

"Francis has the manuscript, I think," Marie said. "I'd have noticed a giant stack of pages."

"Not the manuscript," Liesl said. "Just a final chapter or two. I have most of it. I need the ending."

"I don't know about my appetite for sleuthing right now, Liesl."

"Imagine solving this for Christopher," Liesl said, pushing the pages away from her finally, before she could do further damage to them.

"I'll look around when I'm back at the house. But for now, I have to go."

16

I

Insolvent and anxious, the remnants of the library's senior team were sitting around and strategizing with Liesl in Christopher's office about how to pay for a collection of letters from the War of 1812 without any new donor money when the news came. Dan rapped at the door and summoned Liesl to take a phone call, shifting back and forth in his big boots as he waited for her to follow him out. A phone call in the middle of a meeting, a phone call to the front desk rather than one of their private lines. There was every reason to dismiss it and keep at the business of the war letters. Still, she walked with Dan to go answer it because the money conversation wasn't going any-where, and at least the phone call would give her a break from feeling desperate.

There was a researcher at the reference desk waiting for service. An elderly man with curly gray hair tied into a low ponytail who was there to view videos from their Holocaust oral history collection. He was waiting for someone to set up the filmstrip machine for him in a private viewing room. It was an instinct, when she heard the news, to turn her back on the waiting man. It was rude, but she didn't do it to be rude.

She nodded at the phone, though the caller couldn't see her nodding, the useless action of a helpless woman. Only the old man, who was looking at her back, and Dan, who was looking at her face with a growing sense of understanding. When she hung up, feeling like she had just stepped off the ledge of something and was dangling in midair, she asked Dan to gather the staff in the large reading room, the one that was not used for reading. Francis and Max were still sitting in Liesl's office, or Christopher's really, trying to solve the payment-for-letters problem. There were a dozen or so people in the workroom, doing cataloging work, doing preservation work, standing at the paper cutter and slicing bookplates down to size on acid-free paper. It would require choreography to get it right. They would close early. Against the rules, but appropriate given the circumstances.

She wanted to give them privacy. To lock

the doors before she said the words aloud so that no one was interrupted to go find a pencil sharpener as the grief — and there would certainly be grief — set in. Liesl pushed through her unmoored sensation, moving with plan and purpose toward that simple goal of privacy. When she returned to her office, it had already emptied. Dan had been there before her to herd Francis and Max. She made a simple sign to hang on the library door explaining the early closure. Should a student or faculty member or member of the public come by to use the library, they would hear the news before the staff did. When she walked back through the workroom with her sign, it was already empty. Dan was fast. She poked her head into the reading room, the one that was actually used for reading, and saw that it too was empty. That made it easier, no one to hustle out. She hung the sign on the door, flipped the lock, and headed downstairs to face the staff.

"Has something terrible happened?" Francis asked when she entered the room.

"Haven't you been paying attention?" Max said.

"If you don't think things can get worse," Francis said, "it shows what a soft life you've lived."

"In grade school they used to call me soft too," Max said, hand immediately going to his collar as he spoke in his own defense. "But I didn't have a human resources department to turn to in grade school."

"My goodness, will you stop?" Liesl said.

"No, Liesl, please let them continue," Dan said. "I love learning from those who outrank me."

"That's enough from everybody."

"Go on then, Liesl. Tell us whatever it is you've brought us in here to tell us," Francis said.

"We're going to be closing early today."

"Oh no," Max said. "Christopher has a policy about that. If someone comes to use the library and you're closed even a few minutes before your posted hours, they'll never come back. They'll feel as if they can't count on you."

"Is it Christopher?" Dan asked.

"We've had some news," Liesl said. She almost gagged on the dread, the anxiety of having to be the one to tell them.

Anyone who had been standing sat down. Anyone who had been having a side conversation fell silent. They waited. Turned to her like sunflowers, their quiet faces open for the news that had long been coming. Above their heads, the panopticon of books, the building itself seemed to tense for the blow.

"Christopher passed away this morning."

"Not really," Francis said. He had been sitting in a chair, but slid out of it to sit on the floor. Dan moved toward him as if he had fallen, but Francis waved him away. Liesl briefly caught Dan's eyes, gave a sad half smile, and looked away immediately to stem the unexpected wave of sadness that little bit of eye contact wrought. Ignoring the others, Max was pacing back and forth across the room. He walked to the bust of Shakespeare in the far corner, tapped the head, and then turned around and walked to the door before doing it all over again. Each time he came back to old Will he gave him another tap. With perfect posture he kept at it, back and forth across the room, drawing not a single look from the others until, satisfied with his penance, he dropped into a chair in the back of the room and slouched over to look at his feet. Liesl stared at the unlikely army, amazed at the consistency of their emotion, at how each of them was processing the news as a deep and personal loss.

"Should I go lock the doors?" Dan asked. "I can make a sign."

"It's already done," Liesl said.

After a long silence they walked, one by

one, back into the workroom. The old man with the ponytail, clutching an armful of film reels, stood in the center of the empty room, bewildered as to why he had been left all alone.

II

On the second Monday in November, it was raining. The sidewalks were slick with damp leaves. The navy flags with the school crest that hung from the pillars on Convocation Hall dangled limp and dripping. Liesl walked to the illustrious lecture hall under a giant black umbrella. A rumble of thunder in the distance promised more rain.

The steps of the hall were clustered with black umbrellas that covered smart black coats; the army of black-clad soldiers was reflected up to Liesl in the puddles, but the umbrellas hid their faces and hers, so she slid into the lecture hall without having to shake hands, without having to give or to accept condolences. Despite the rain, the crowds lingered outside.

Over the next thirty minutes, the wet mourners would filter in, occupying the creaking wood seats, filling the domed roof with their hushed conversation and their subtle perfume until, at exactly eleven o'clock, they would fall silent as a solo violin played a mournful Mahler piece to signal the start of the proceedings. The crowd, their wet coats hung over the backs of their chairs, their dripping umbrellas creating puddles at their feet, would be moved, or they would act as though they were, for here was the funeral of a great man, a literary man. The booksellers who had benefitted from his acquisition budget came, the writers who had donated their manuscript materials, the writers who hoped they might be important enough one day to be asked for theirs, they came too.

Liesl watched the crowd from the wings, waiting for her turn to speak. She felt herself being watched and turned to see President Garber who, mercifully, was not wearing his bicycle helmet.

"Nice turnout," he said.

She nodded. Watched the crowd.

"You heard the religious studies department is canvassing their alumni to raise moncy for that manuscript?" He bounced on his toes.

"I hadn't."

He kept on bouncing. "You must be so pleased with yourself."

There wasn't a good response so she didn't offer one, but of course she was pleased. In the third row a very old man was using his very big hand to very slowly scratch what must have been very itchy genitals. Liesl had been watching him all along. He just kept scratching.

"The press is here," he said.

"I saw."

"Sad event," he said. "But still nice that we'll get in the culture pages."

"It's an opportunity, isn't it?" she asked.

"Press coverage always shakes a few donors loose."

She looked back at him. He had on a placid smile.

"No," she said. "I meant an opportunity to set the record straight about Miriam."

"What?" he said. "Set what record straight?"

"To say she wasn't the thief."

"No," he said. "I don't think it's the time for that at all."

"There will be interview requests," Liesl said, "to accompany the coverage of the funeral." Garber pulled a tissue from his pocket and fiddled with it.

"Liesl," he said. "Now's not the time."

"The press is paying attention to us. It's the only opportunity we'll have to clear her name."

He finally put the tissue to his nose and cleared his sinuses with an aggressive honk.

She stood there, embarrassed for him.

"Look," he said. "You're not thinking of all the implications of such an announcement. Right now, the world believes we found the thief, if not the books themselves."

"Yes," she said, "but we know Miriam wasn't the thief."

"If Miriam wasn't the thief, then we have nothing. No books. No thief. No justice. It's hard for our community to hand us any of their trust in that case, isn't it?"

Garber had tiny flecks of tissue stuck to the stubble under his nose.

"It's an innocent woman's reputation," Liesl said.

"She's not using it at the moment."

"Pardon me?"

Garber looked pleased with himself.

"That was crass, I'll admit," he said. "It's the wrong time for this conversation."

"When is the right time?"

"Look," said Garber. "We aren't saying that Miriam was the thief. But we aren't saying she wasn't. A news report — a news report I'll remind you I was angry about — called her the thief. Now Miriam has sadly passed, and I don't see the harm in leaving this alone."

"Leaving it alone?" Liesl said.

"Yes, leaving it alone."

"She has a family," Liesl said. "For whom a proclamation of her innocence might mean some peace."

"And they'll get it. Once we know who was really guilty."

"That isn't fair," Liesl said. "Letting people believe in her guilt isn't fair to Miriam."

"And having this conversation right now isn't fair to Christopher."

"Fine," Liesl said. "If not right now, then tell me when we can have it."

"Clean up the mess at the library," said Garber. "When I no longer have angry donors calling my office and academic departments going rogue to fundraise for themselves, you can issue whatever press release you want."

"It's your turn to speak," she said.

"Indeed it is," said Garber. "Wish me luck." He went out in front of the crowd. The room was too large for the assembled mourners to see the tiny flecks of tissue that clung to his face. But Liesl knew they were there. Glancing back at the third row, she saw the scratcher still scratching with abandon.

She walked back out to the atrium, knowing that Garber would go past his allotted time, knowing that she had some time before she was expected onstage. One of the doors had been propped open to allow cool air to flow in. It was still raining. She turned a corner and ran right into John and Hannah. Hannah was wearing an orange dress that rang like an alarm.

It made Liesl happy that the girl hadn't worn black. John was appropriately attired, his teddy-bear air made serious in dark slacks and a charcoal sport coat, but not their daughter. Hannah smiled, a happy girl in an orange dress, when she saw her mother.

"We were waiting to meet you after you did your bit," Hannah said. "Have you decided to make a break for it instead?"

Liesl wanted so much to hug her daughter. So she did.

"Just getting some air," she said.

"Mom?" Hannah said from inside the hug. "Is everything okay?"

Before they could untangle, Francis poked his head around a corner, his hair even smoother and his eyes puffier than normal.

"They're looking for you, Liesl," he said. So she left her family behind.

Liesl was drinking water. She didn't want to be red-mouthed or slow-tongued for her portion of the program. In the very first row of attendees, there was a Nobel Prize winner. She had her head tilted down, inspecting the program, every time Liesl glanced over at her, but Liesl was sure that any stumbles would be noticed and, even worse, would find their way into the woman's fiction. In the row behind there were prominent local philanthropists. As well as handpicking the speakers, Christopher had left behind suggestions for the types of people he would like invited to a memorial service, should the university choose to host such an event in his honor.

"Many years ago when he was neither ill nor particularly old, I received in the mail a letter in which Christopher, ever the captain of his own ship, outlined the instructions for his memorial service," Garber told the assembled mourners.

The line got a laugh, and Garber looked pleased about it. Liesl wondered if the use of that specific line, if that joke that was sure to draw a laugh because it called to mind just how controlling Christopher was, had itself been a part of the instructions. Her own portion of the program was a small one. Christopher hadn't mentioned her by name in his instructions, but the poet that she would be introducing had been specifically requested. It was Garber who had suggested that Liesl should be involved in the event. Garber who thought always of continuity and the way things might appear to those who were paying attention.

The readings that Christopher had requested were from *The Death of Ivan Ilych* and *The Brothers Karamazov.* As if Christopher had been Russian. During the preparations, Liesl had joked that they should use the Auden poem "Funeral Blues" that Christopher thought was forever sullied through its use in a film. The suggestion had been received as appalling. Liesl quite liked Auden, quite liked the poem, quite liked the scene in *Four Weddings and a Funeral* when it had been read. No matter. The readings were from heavily bearded Russian novelists, just as Christopher had requested. *A rhyming scheme is nice!* Liesl wanted to yell from the podium.

"Beautiful service, wasn't it, Liesl?" Percy asked afterward. "Very moving."

"Yes," she lied. She had hoped the umbrella would keep her concealed while she walked back to the library where the reception was being held. But Percy had found her.

"Did I hear old Chris designed the program himself?"

"You did."

"Not a bad idea, that," he said. "Maybe I'll ask my assistant to do the same. The queen's funeral is all planned and ready, did you know that?" He stayed on the sidewalk beside her.

He was not embarrassed to be comparing himself to the queen. As they walked, his umbrella bumped against hers, moving it over enough that the rain fell on the shoulder of her coat.

"I should go check on the catering," she said when they arrived at the library. "Christopher left instructions for that too."

Seeing that others had begun to arrive, he'd already lost interest in her, and she wandered off to leave her coat in her office. John and Hannah were waiting there for her.

"Hey, you," Hannah said.

"Hope you don't mind," John said. "You seemed as though you might need some moral support."

"The crowd is a bit much." She hung her coat on the rack. The shoulder of her blouse was damp.

Hannah looked at her mother with her wide-open face and serious dark eyes, waiting to be asked to stay.

"How many are coming back to the library, Mom?"

"Only about a hundred, chickadee," she said.

"Just the really fancy ones, huh?"

Liesl straightened her blouse.

"None as fancy as you."

"Let us help," John said. "No one does small talk quite like your daughter."

"It's true," said Hannah. "And if nothing else, they'll be distracted by my haircut."

"I'll be worried you're bored or annoyed," said Liesl.

"Never," said Hannah.

"Go get yourself some noodles. I'll be home as soon as I can," Liesl said.

"Noodles without our third musketeer?" said John. He pulled Liesl into a hug. "Imagine that level of betrayal."

"Dad," Hannah said. "Mom and I get noodles without you all the time."

"Well, that's it," said John. "Now I'm definitely leaving. It's like I don't know either of you anymore."

"Come on, Mom," said Hannah. "I know you hate this stuff. Let us stay here so you have a friendly face."

"I'm fine," Liesl said. "And I'll be even better when I know you're fed."

"We can eat tiny canapés."

"And very expensive cookies," John added.

Liesl stepped away from them toward the door.

"Noodles," she said. "And I'll be home soon."

"She can tell you all about Stockholm," President Garber said. He had not stopped pulling her by the arm to introduce her to fancy people. She took a glass of chardonnay from a passing member of the wait staff. The Nobel winner was already surrounded by five celebrants.

Liesl was introduced, and they gave her a nod. She sipped the chardonnay. She hated chardonnay. Hated the vanilla, hated the oakiness. Chardonnay had been in Christopher's instructions.

"Tell her what you think of her writing," Garber said. "No need to be shy. The library has all of your first editions."

The Nobel winner nodded. Liesl finished her chardonnay.

"Go on. Tell her," Garber said.

The Nobel winner shook her head and smiled.

"Christopher," she said. "We're here to celebrate him, not me."

Liesl's estimation of the woman grew. "A toast to Christopher," she said, flagging a waiter for a refill.

"This library is his monument," the writer said, looking at President Garber. "Lawrence, don't you think this library is his monument?"

"Built in his image," one of the onlookers said.

Liesl rolled her eyes without meaning to, but it didn't matter as she had gone invisible in this group of important and moneyed people.

"Really," the writer said. "Imagine this place without Christopher. Without his constant arm-twisting to part us from our papers and our books."

"And our money!"

"Percy, don't be crass."

Predictably, Percy Pickens had joined their circle.

"Don't misunderstand me," Percy shouted, slurring slightly, attracting attention from the rest of the room.

"Was there more, Percy?" Liesl asked.

The important heads all turned in unison to her. Her invisibility cloak had slipped a bit.

"What's that, Liesl?" Percy said.

"Percy," Liesl said. "You said 'Don't misunderstand me' but then never finished your thought."

"Indeed I did!" he said.

"Well?"

She was sure he wouldn't regain his train of thought, but she was wrong.

"I loved giving old Chris my money."

"You've been very generous, Percy," she said.

"I don't regret a penny I gave Chris. What I regret is this terrible business with the thief."

During this proclamation, President Garber had managed to slide his way out of the circle. He was well on his way to the other side of the room where he could act oblivious.

Liesl drained her glass.

"Terrible business, that woman," Percy said.

"Percy, it's not the time for this," the Nobel winner said.

"They'll show up on some black market years from now, the books will," Percy said. "You mark my words. Of course, we'll all be dead by then."

Liesl smiled at the writer, thankful for her help. "Let's not spoil this," Liesl said.

Enter Marie. Marie, who had declined to speak at the memorial service as Christopher must have known she would. Marie, who was left out of his instructions. Marie, who was clutching a bottle of water. Marie, who nodded at Liesl but didn't come over.

Marie attracted her own circle of sycophants. Liesl tried to make eye contact across the room to give a supportive smile but couldn't quite capture Marie's attention and then reckoned it was for the best. Max was by her side in a moment proposing a toast, and the circle that had been assembled was immediately busy, filling glasses, raising glasses, clinking glasses. Marie let the group make their toast, but she didn't take a glass. She clung to her bottle of water. Max held her arm like she was a valuable possession. She let him. It kept her upright. The tragedy of Christopher was all the more tragic with Marie in the room.

"It's the perfect time," Percy said. "This business. What that woman did. It breaks my heart."

Liesl tensed at his tone, at his accusation. She waited for one of the important heads to chide him, to steer him away from the topic of Miriam. None did.

"It breaks my heart for Chris too," the writer said. "But she was a sick woman. Wasn't she sick? That's what I understand of the mess."

"She offed herself. Is that what you mean?"

"What a terrible way to put it, Percy." She

355

swatted his arm. Playfully, it looked to Liesl. As if it were a playful thing. "She was a troubled person, and it's terrible for the library, of course. But what can you do? She was clearly having a difficult time, and that is how it manifested. A grasp for money. A cry for help."

"A scream for help," one of the group chimed in.

"So you're all saying I should feel sorry for that woman? After what she did?"

"Have a little compassion, Percy."

"Call me uncompassionate." Percy wiped the back of his hand against a slightly sweating forehead. "But I don't have a lick of sympathy for that woman. After what she did. I think the thefts, everything that was going on, I think that's what killed Christopher. Don't you think she killed Christopher?"

Liesl shut her eyes and reflexively bit her lip to keep from speaking up, as she'd been conditioned to keep from speaking up against people with money who she might have to ask for favors.

Percy waited for the group to agree.

"What she did to him," Percy said. "It breaks my heart."

"Percy, Christopher has been unconscious through all of this," Liesl said. Not an admonishment. A reminder.

"Oh, Liesl," Percy said. "A great man like that. You don't think he could feel all this in his bones?"

"Can I borrow Liesl for a moment, folks?" Francis said, appearing in the circle. His eyes were puffy from wine and tears. It was perfect stage makeup. It added depth and character. It made Liesl want to stroke his face. She was on her fourth chardonnay. She nodded to the group and let Francis lead her away.

"What is it?" Liesl said. Her muscles became looser the further she walked from Percy. "Do the caterers need something?" She froze for a moment. "We're not out of wine, are we?"

"You just looked like you needed a rescue," said Francis.

"Oh, God bless you." Liesl looked around the crowded room. President Garber had his back to her. Percy was waving his hands and proselytizing. If she was going to slither out, now was the time.

She grabbed a bottle of wine by the neck. "Fancy some fresh air?" she said. "It would do us both some good."

"Fresh air," said Francis, "is exactly what we need."

They slipped out of the reading room. It

was immediately cooler, but she kept leading him. In one of the private study carrels she saw a donor she recognized, a pharmaceutical executive in her forties, with her back pressed against the glass and her skirt pulled up around her stomach, some unseen suitor presumably under the desk. Funerals were a funny thing.

In the corridor that connected her old office with Christopher's, she stuck a key into the lock of the emergency exit, deactivating the alarm. They stepped into evening and at the last moment, Liesl took off her shoe to leave the door propped open. The rain had stopped falling. They sat on the top step of the small staircase that led from the fire escape to the library's loading dock. They could hear nothing of the roaring conversation inside. Liesl stretched her one bare foot out down the steps, hoping the rough cement wouldn't ruin her pantyhose.

She handed Francis the bottle, and he yanked the cork out with his teeth. That made them both laugh, as did the realization that they hadn't brought glasses and had no choice but to drink the chardonnay straight from the bottle. Francis handed it to Liesl to allow her the first swig. A gentleman. Her neck was rubber and her vision was blurry and the air was cool, but Francis's shoulder against hers was warm. Somewhere, John and Hannah were eating noodles and talking about Hannah's thesis.

"You don't even like chardonnay," Francis said.

"Just for tonight, I love chardonnay," Liesl said.

"Did you see Max? Snogging with the fellow from the philosophy department in the stairway."

"The philosophy department?" Liesl said. "Max was always a passionate supporter of the humanities."

A gust of wind found its way into the loading dock, and she shivered.

"I'm going to more funerals these days. I'm sure you are too," Francis said. "And I reckon there's far more licentiousness at funerals then I ever saw at weddings."

"Same amount of wine, twice the reminders of one's impending doom," Liesl said.

"Think Max's husband will find out?" Francis said. "About the philosopher?"

"Maybe," said Liesl. "Might not matter. People's marital arrangements can surprise you."

"John couldn't stay tonight?" Francis said.

"Let's not talk about John," Liesl said.

The wind came in again, and again Liesl shivered. This time, Francis noticed. He kicked off his own shoe and placed his sock-clad foot over Liesl's pantyhosed one.

"No one likes cold feet," he said.

The chardonnay was half-spent, resting on the step to the right of Francis. Liesl wasn't cold anymore. She was wearing a purple silk shirt tucked into a black skirt. Control-top pantyhose under the skirt. She had looped her arm through his. She didn't remember doing it, but their arms were linked together. That was a fact.

"It's raining again," Francis said. At the end of the loading dock they could hear it, and they could see just enough of the pavement beyond it to see that the pavement was shining. The rain was falling. Their heads were swimming. Francis leaned in to kiss her.

"What are you doing?" Liesl said. She had leaned in to meet him but pulled up short. Well oiled though she was, she had the sense to stop from leaning all the way in.

"We're both doing it."

"I've had too much to drink," Liesl said. "We both have. Let's not get carried away and do something we regret. Not again."

"It's not just the wine, Liesl," Francis said. "This got started before the chardonnay."

"Maybe," Liesl said. "But it was a mistake."

"We've known each other a long time," Francis said. "You know me, and you knew what was happening. What mistake?"

"I wasn't thinking," Liesl said, and she got to her feet to make sure that if she stopped thinking again, her lips were a safe distance from trouble.

"Tell me the truth," Francis said, looking up at her. She stood, balancing with her one bare foot rested on her other shoe. "Is it that you suspect me?"

"Don't do this now, Francis."

"I thought I felt something thawing between us. After a long, long winter. Until Miriam, and all of a sudden I'm in a hailstorm. So tell me what's happened."

"Miriam, then," Liesl said. "The awfulness with Miriam."

"Is it?" Francis said. "Or is it what Max has been putting in your head since Miriam and the books disappeared? Go on and tell me, Liesl."

Marie had never brought Liesl the manuscript pages that might have given her a definitive answer. Liesl was uneasy. He could feel her uneasiness. Had been feeling it all this time.

"I don't know what you mean about Max," she said.

"Bollocks you don't," Francis said, hunching over his knees.

"I don't," Liesl said. "You've had too much to drink, and so have I. We almost made a mistake, and then we didn't."

"You're lying," Francis said. "When you call this a mistake, I know you're lying."

"You don't know a lick about what I'm thinking. If I say this is a mistake, then it is."

"Then why haven't you brought up your husband," Francis said. "Such a mistake, you and I, but your marriage is nowhere on your mind."

Liesl helped herself to a long breath before responding. Tried to be as serious as a woman balancing on one foot could be.

"You don't know what's in my head."

"Of course I do. I've been in a marriage."

"You haven't been in mine."

"You're not worried about adultery all of a sudden. You're worried about proximity to a criminal." Francis's face went dark and disappointed.

"You're calling yourself a criminal now?"

"No. You are. Or you may as well be. This suspicion is typical coming from Max, but I expected better from you."

"That's not fair."

Wine-woozy, Liesl watched Francis go slack, saw the anger slide right from his body and the sadness, cold and low, come in to fill the cracks that were left.

"There was something happening between us, I know there was," Francis said. "You're right; this isn't fair. It isn't fair to me."

"Max and his suspicions have nothing to do with me."

"There it is. You admit he suspects me."

"He's a rare-books librarian, not Hercule Poirot," she said. "What do you care if he suspects you?"

"I do if it's changed the way you think of me." Francis reached up for her.

"I'm thinking of my marriage," Liesl said, pulling her hand away from him.

"Darling," he said, looking at the space where her hand should have been. "I don't believe you."

"All right. It's not my concern if you do."

"Hannah is out of the house. You're about to retire. People around you are dying, for Christ's sake."

"Stop it, Francis." She pulled her arms around herself by reflex, a flash of anger that he had invoked Hannah in the heat of the argument. Hannah was out of bounds.

"You're not thinking of life changes, of opportunities? Darling, I don't believe you."

"Francis," she said, thawed now that he had moved away from talk of her daughter.

"We've had so very much to drink."

"Don't I know it. But not enough to make you shake off your suspicions of me."

Francis was miserable, and Liesl was cold. She looked at the door, at her shoe propping open the door, and wanted terribly to go home.

"We should go home, Francis."

"No, darling. We should keep drinking."

He took another gulp from the chardonnay and held it out to her. She didn't take it.

"People our age shouldn't drink like this," Liesl said. "Bad for the heart."

He was still holding the bottle, and finally she took it from him and placed it on the stair.

"Come on," said Liesl, and she finally extended the hand that he'd been looking to grasp earlier and helped to pull him to his feet.

They went inside through the fire exit. At the end of the corridor, Max was leaving the restroom, straightening his tie.

"I should kill him," Francis said.

"He's as protective of the library as you are."

"He's a liar."

"Enough of this now. Enough of the name-calling and accusations."

"I only called him a liar," Francis said with a slur. "But that liar called me a thief."

IV

Liesl walked home through the rain, her umbrella forgotten on the coatrack in her office. The rain was a mist now, and though it clung to her hair and to the threads of her coat, she let it cover her since it was doing the work of turning the cells in her neck from rubber back to flesh and bone. She took her shoes off on the doormat outside the front door so she wouldn't wake anyone with her footsteps.

"It ran quite late," John said. Didn't ask, but said it as a fact.

"You're awake?"

John stood in the cluttered hallway. There were canvases resting against the baseboards on either side of him, and he couldn't lean against the wall without disturbing them. So he just stood in the center of the hall. Fully dressed in the middle of the night. Watching his rain-soaked, barefoot wife.

"I thought you'd want a chat," he said.

"It's been a day," Liesl said. "Chat tomorrow?"

He didn't move from the center of the hallway. Nor did he turn on any lights. The canvases guarded the hallway like little soldiers. John approached her, and she tensed. He pulled the wet coat off her shoulders, kissed the top of her head, and hung the damp garment off the closet door to dry. He turned and walked toward the kitchen. She followed him.

"I'll make you some tea."

"There's really no need."

"You're soaked through, darling."

He had called her *darling* through all their years of marriage, but on that night the word only conjured Francis. Francis who had used it last. Francis who had begged her to return the sentiment.

"A tea would be lovely, John."

"Good," he said.

"Did Hannah stay?" Liesl asked.

"No."

"What a pity. I would have liked to have breakfast with her in the morning."

Liesl made her way to the kitchen table and sat herself down, the night's chardonnay sloshing around in her belly.

"She had schoolwork to attend to."

"Of course. Did the two of you have a nice dinner?" She fought off a vibratory yawn.

"It was nice. You had quite a bit to drink?"

"Not so very much."

"Didn't you? You're speaking in that strange way you do."

366

The kettle began to whistle.

"I'm mostly just tired."

"Would you like a glass of wine then?"

"No, John. Just the tea is fine. The tea is perfect."

Her foot was hot where Francis's had touched it. Her head was swimming where the chardonnay was slipping between her neurons. John studied her and could see every bit of it. She was sure of it.

"Good," he said.

"I'll have to go in for a bit tomorrow, but the library will be closed, so I'll be around during the day."

"Your decision? To close it?"

"President Garber's. I don't mind. There will be work to catch up on, but it seems the respectful thing to do."

"Right."

"Gives us all a chance to sleep it off, anyway."

"Right."

"Did you and Hannah have a nice dinner together? Pity I couldn't come."

"Yes."

"I asked that already. It's been such a long day, and there really was quite a bit of wine."

"Milk in your tea?"

"Please," she said. "And just a touch of sugar."

He brought the two cups of tea over to the kitchen table and sat down next to her. He drank from a large orange mug, she from a cream-colored teacup. She hated the types of homes that had dozens of mismatched mugs, but she let him keep the one because Hannah had bought it for him with money from her first paper route.

Each took a first sip of the hot tea. She was still wearing her damp clothing, but he hadn't suggested that she go change, so she didn't. She crossed her legs, and her knee began to bounce with anxiety. He looked down at her bouncing foot.

John looked at his wine-weary wife, down at the bouncing foot. Signaled to her that whatever was happening, he wasn't blind to it.

"Your stockings are shredded."

"I saw," she nodded and nodded, too long. Looked at her foot instead of at him. "I'll have to throw them out."

He kept watching her face, taking a long sip of tea as he watched, waiting for the eye contact that wouldn't come.

"Did something happen, darling?"

"Two deaths. A funeral," she said. A subdued shrug, but still she didn't look at him.

"Something tonight, I meant."

"What could have happened?"

"Why won't you talk to me?"

He refused to look away from her. He knew there was something there, and finally when she believed she had composed herself, she lifted her head and met his gaze.

"John," she said.

"Liesl," he said. "It's the middle of the night. You're drunk. You're upset. Talk to me."

"I have to go to bed."

He reached across the table and took her hand. She smiled at him, or she tried to. His eyes were big and watery and a little bit bloodshot because he was tired too. In the kitchen, over tea, she almost told him all of her secrets. All of the secrets of a forty-year marriage.

"Stay a little longer," he said.

"I promise everything is fine," she said. She got up from the table, took her mostly full cup of tea to the sink, and poured it down the drain. John stayed drinking his. He had let go of her hand; he didn't get up to try and follow her.

"I don't believe you," he said.

"Well, I can't help that."

Liesl and her secrets went to bed.

V

She had worn jeans and an Oxford shirt. The jeans made Liesl look younger. Looking younger undermined her authority. The white shirt collar made her skin look pinker. She wouldn't have worn it if she thought she needed her authority on that day, but the library was closed. Rhonda rang and asked if she could come by.

In her jeans and white button-down, Liesl was too impatient to sit and wait for Rhonda. She had tried the humanities building, the religious studies library, the coffee shop, and the garden behind the music building where faculty liked to go to think. The class schedule was an afterthought but one that was rewarded because the class schedule answered for Liesl the question of where Professor Mahmoud was at that exact moment and where he would remain for the next ninety minutes. It was only days from the auction, so no matter how strange it was to go visit Professor Mahmoud in a lecture hall, Liesl was carried by her loafers and her determination to Lecture Hall LL 104 in the Sid Smith Building.

This late in the term, the classroom was full. Liesl had to head for a standing spot, leaning against the back wall, to step over a toppled blue backpack and balance herself over two sets of outstretched legs before she reached the bare patch of wall located, happily, next to the other adult in the room, a man as tall as he was skinny, crooked into a question mark against the too-low wall, pulling laconically on his chin as he listened to an adolescent with a spectacular beard deliver the lecture.

"Is that Professor Mahmoud?" Liesl whispered.

"Speaking down there?" the man next to her said with a grin.

"Well, yes."

"Please, ma'am. Though I've heard Professor Mahmoud described as impossibly youthful and dynamic, I think the young man at the podium still has spots."

At the podium the presenter paused his speech. He had a graphic that was meant to be animated on his slide and the failure of the animation, a failure that his facial expression suggested he interpreted as a failure of his entire presentation and perhaps academic career, was a paralyzing force.

Professor Mahmoud smiled at Liesl. "I tell them that relying on such sparkles takes away one's power as a speaker, but they never listen. People like you and I, we'll be the last to revere oration. These kids all want a PowerPoint presentation."

He waved his arms, straightening into an exclamation point and offering a smile and a keep-it-moving motion with his hand to break the paralysis.

"Mahmoud? You're Professor Mahmoud?" Liesl asked.

Satisfied that the lecture was continuing, he greeted her with an exaggerated bow. "In the flesh. Have you paid to be in this class, young lady?"

Liesl extended her hand, disarmed by his vivacity. "I'm Liesl Weiss. We've spoken."

"The librarian. Lovely to meet you. Can you wait for just a moment?" He held up a finger to pause her and raised his voice so three hundred students could hear. "Please disregard the last thing Samer said. Al-Hallaj's ashes were thrown in the Tigris, not consumed by a tiger."

"The auction is next week," Liesl said.

"I'm afraid I've disappointed you, Liesl. I've been doing my research — great fun, by the way — and the inventory of the Great Mosque of Kairouan mentions a manuscript which I think is the lot for sale. If that's true, it'll be worth at least half a million. We've only managed to raise about fifty grand."

Liesl nodded. Leaned into Professor

Mahmoud like a coconspirator. "Did you find that published somewhere, or did you put together the pieces yourself?"

"Well," said Professor Mahmoud. "Research is my whole job, isn't it?"

Liesl gave the professor a bemused shrug, and they both turned back to the speaker.

The poor student giving the presentation was still projecting a giant image of a tiger onto all five screens in the lecture hall.

"The library hasn't expressed any intent, officially." Liesl gazed at the tiger. A Siberian, she thought. The poor boy could have at least displayed a geographically appropriate tiger. "There's no reason to think the lot will reach its estimated price."

"Will you go bid?" Professor Mahmoud asked at the same moment he kicked the back of the chair of a student in the back row who had switched his laptop screen to a YouTube video.

"You will," she said.

The scheme was set. Taking the suggestion of the acting director of the Department of Rare Books and Special Collections, Professor Mahmoud, feeling like a secret operative, resolved to arrive at the auction as an interested layman, not a representative of the university. Giving no prewarning of the library's interest or his own suspicions about the piece's value, he would cautiously raise his paddle and hope to bring the blue Quran home for no more than the $50,000 he had raised, a tenth of its suspected value.

In those blue jeans and that white Oxford, energized by her scheme, made even more youthful by her scheme, Liesl returned to the library just in time for Rhonda's arrival.

"There's no one here," Rhonda said.

"No," Liesl said. "We closed for the day in Christopher's honor. Did you hear?"

"No," Rhonda said. "Has he died?"

Liesl nodded.

"My condolences." They stood by the elevator, Rhonda holding a report and Liesl holding her own elbows, offering Christopher a moment of silence.

"Liesl," Rhonda said. "It's probably for the best there's no one here."

There was warning in Rhonda's tone, but Liesl was so caught up in the grief and anxiety of a thousand other problems and in her excitement about the blue Quran that she didn't think to listen for it.

"Let's go sit," Liesl said. "Shall we?"

"Sure. Good idea." She allowed Liesl to lead her to the small reading room, the one used for reading. "Not as grand as the other one, is it?" She stood, waiting for instruction. Holding on tight to that report. Liesl pulled two chairs up to a table for them.

"I had put the work with the Peshawar totally out of my head," Liesl said. "Had just about forgotten it. Isn't that awful?"

Rhonda nodded. She placed her stack of papers on the reading table. Smoothed the smooth pages.

"It's not good news, Liesl," Rhonda said. She turned over the first page as if the papers themselves would speak the words for her.

"It never is," Liesl said with a laugh. "But tell me all the same." She leaned forward and whispered, "It's not the oldest zero, is it?"

"It's not," Rhonda said. "But I don't think you understand the seriousness of this."

"Tell me. Will we have to remove this particular claim from the library's Wikipedia page?"

"I'm going to try my best to explain."

"Please do," Liesl said. "I imagine I'll have to explain to the marketing department why they need to update the library's brochures."

Liesl leaned back in her chair. Crossed her legs at the ankles. Rhonda remained upright, hands folded on the report.

"Liesl. My high-school calculus textbook used the zero before the manuscript we tested did."

The stone that Liesl had been carrying around in her stomach since September was back. She let her head roll backward so she was looking at the ceiling. There was a light bulb out.

"It's a fake?" she asked.

"Yes," Rhonda said. "Now I know mathematics, and I know libraries, but I'm not a physicist. But I'll try to explain what the physicists found." She slid the report across the table.

"There's always been some variation in the estimates," Liesl said. "It could be eleventh century." Her response was perfectly rational. Her behavior, perfectly rational, but she could feel her pulse beating in her throat, and her muscles and bones and tendons were begging her to get out of that chair, out of the library, and run as fast as she could from this stack of problems.

"Yes," Rhonda said. "That's what we thought at first. So the lab redid the testing when the first result was so confusing."

"And?" said Liesl.

"Again, I'm not a physicist. But there's something called the bomb peak."

"Sounds ominous."

"In the 1950s and 1960s, the frequent testing of nuclear weapons caused large variations in radiocarbon concentration."

"So the 'bomb' is a nuclear bomb?"

Liesl was looking through the pages of the report. There were charts and graphs and lists of numbers she didn't know the significance of.

"It roughly doubled the radiocarbon concentration in the atmosphere." Rhonda reached over and closed the report. "It allows physicists to tell with a great deal of accuracy when something was created in the second half of the twentieth century or later."

"It's been in the university's collection for over a hundred years," Liesl said.

"No."

"No?"

"Not the manuscript we sampled."

Liesl covered her mouth with her hands.

"So you're not saying we acquired a forgery a hundred years ago," Liesl said.

"Liesl. You know I can't speculate."

"Right. But you can confirm that even if we acquired a forgery a hundred years ago, this isn't it?"

"Yes. I suppose I can confirm that."

Liesl stood up and then Rhonda did.

"How long?" Liesl said. "How long do I have until the lab submits the results for publication and this goes public?"

Rhonda picked up the loose pages of the report. She knew exactly what Liesl was asking of her. Her answer confirmed that yes, she knew.

"They'll wait," Rhonda said. "No one at the lab will report anything until you have told us we can do so."

Liesl led Rhonda back to the elevator. They said a quiet goodbye. Liesl walked back through to the larger reading room. It had been cleaned from the night before; there was no trace of the drinking or the mourning that had taken place under the eyes of the books. Liesl stretched out, resting her feet on a table and looking up to the shining books and the one burned-out light bulb, hoping the answer of what to do would suddenly come to her.

NINE YEARS EARLIER

The sixty-one-year-old chief librarian of the Department of Rare Books and Special Collections was forty-five minutes late for his meeting with the brand-new university president, Lawrence Garber. By the time the librarian arrived, the university's youngest-ever president was scheduled to leave for his next meeting with the dean of the medical school. Garber wanted to leave on general principle, but as an economist, he subscribed to the idea of sunk cost and knew that the time already spent waiting could not be recovered. The board of regents at the university had advised of the importance of the rare books library as a major source of donors, and Garber knew that leaving now would only mean another wasted forty-five minutes as a result of another power play by a man who didn't like answering to someone ten years his junior.

"Mr. Garber," Christopher said with a warm handshake when he finally appeared. He made no apologies for his tardiness.

"You have a beautiful library here," Garber said, not too proud to flatter. "Opened in '69, I understand?"

"We got our own building then, yes."

"And you've been the chief since then? Since 1969?"

"Why?"

Garber took a seat without being asked. The room had swung back in his favor. "Thirty-one years is an awfully long time. I'm interested in planning for the future."

Christopher paused before answering. And then, slowly, his weathered face spread into a smile. Here was a worthy adversary. "Not even niceties to ease me into it, eh?"

"No. I had reserved the first forty-five minutes for niceties."

Christopher knew he had to say something else to rebalance the room. "So, who'd you have in mind to take my job?"

"Your job?" Garber said. "Well, for a future chief librarian, I've heard Max Hubbard has impressive credentials."

"Pity he's a queer, though," Christopher said. "And that nasty business about how he left the church. I agree he would be ideal, but if the donors ever learned about it, it would be a scandal."

This time it was Garber who took a long pause. He considered telling Christopher that he himself was gay, considered admonishing him for his dated language. But showing offense was showing weakness, and there was no room for that in this first meeting. "What's this about the church?"

"You don't know?"

"Pretend I don't."

"He had a parish here in town. As well as being a well-known scholar, he led a congregation. He was popular. Busy church. Brought in a lot of donations. And he was caught stealing fifty thousand dollars."

"Fifty thousand dollars?" Garber said. "What the hell is he doing working for us?"

"Well, he's a talented books man, Mr. Garber. That can't be understated. And as it turned out, the fifty thousand dollars was to pay off a parishioner who had learned that the beloved father was a flamer and was blackmailing him. Ugly business."

"And the church learned of this?" Garber shook his head. "Of the blackmail, I mean?"

Christopher interrupted to answer the incomplete question. "They didn't press charges. Against either party. Max was asked to quietly give up the collar. In the end, they cared more about the queer thing than the money thing."

"And you gave him a position?"

"Yes! A great books man was available."

"Is it common knowledge that . . ."

"That a thief was invited to work with our precious collections? He's a great books man, but some things, to some people, would be unforgivable. The only way to keep Max's secret safe is to keep his name out of the press, and the only way to do that is to keep Max exactly where he is. Wouldn't you agree?"

17

Liesl stood at one of the tall, dusty windows that lined the south side of Christopher's office and watched the two old men in charcoal suits on the stairs outside exhibit the copulatory behavior of the educated upper classes vis-à-vis compliments on each other's wristwatches and marathon times. Their pointless patter snuck in through the slightly open window, and she braced herself for a tiresome meeting.

Liesl gave up a morning of solitary anxiety about the loss of one precious text via theft and the capture of another via auction when an early-morning email from President Garber summoned her to her office at exactly nine without further explanation. She had taken this to mean it would be a morning of public anxiety.

At nine exactly, having exhausted all their compliments and other formalities while still outdoors, the suits had made their way to her office door. Punctual.

"I'd like you to meet Professor Langdon Sibley," Garber said.

"Call me Sib," the man said. "I hear 'Langdon,' and I start looking for my father."

"I've heard a lot about you, Sib," Liesl said. "Welcome to our library."

Garber was grinning from ear to ear.

"Heard of each other?" he said. "Brilliant. Shared friends?"

"Not that I know of," Liesl said. "Mr. Sibley's reputation precedes him."

"A famous librarian?" Garber said. "Brilliant."

"Not at all," Sibley said. "I've sat on some committees, authored some papers. Nothing more."

"Of course," Garber said. "You'll have heard then, Liesl, that Sib was planning on moving on from his role in Boston."

"I hadn't," Liesl said. "I'm sure they'll be sorry to lose you."

"They'll never replace him," Garber said. "Sib's is the name I hear most when I ask about great libraries. He was considering the private sector for his next stage." The dollar-bill sound of *private sector* hung in the air.

"Nothing's decided," Sibley said. "And President Garber was kind enough to invite me for a tour of your beautiful campus."

"That *was* kind of him," Liesl said. "Did you know Christopher?"

"Socially, of course. He once sent me a John Grisham paperback for my birthday. As a kind of joke."

Garber's smile was so wide. He didn't get the joke at all.

"You have plans to write, Liesl? About gardens?"

"About gardening books," Liesl said. "A study of knowledge sharing about plant cultivation."

"Very interesting," Sibley said. "My wife is a great horticulturalist; she'd find that fascinating."

"Your wife," Liesl said. "Is she an academic too?"

"She's the brains in our family," said Sibley. "But no, she chose to work in our home, taking care of our children."

"Sib wanted to see some highlights from the collection," Garber said.

"What did you have in mind?" Liesl asked.

"Well, I was hoping you might have suggestions."

"I'd love to see the Peshawar," Sibley said.

"It's not here, I'm afraid. We're having it

carbon-dated," Liesl said.

"The Peshawar manuscript is out of the library?" Garber said.

"Rhonda Washington suggested it as a research project," Liesl said.

"She's the chair for the communication of science," Garber explained.

"You're doing some innovative work here," Sibley said.

"Apparently we are," Garber said. "Who knew?"

"If your researchers aren't one step ahead of you, you're not doing it right," Sibley said. Liesl got up to lead them out of the office and down into the stacks so they could stroke some prize horses.

"I'd be interested to hear the results of this carbon dating when it comes back, Liesl. I imagine Professor Washington is planning a public rollout?"

"That's the idea," Liesl said. "It's sure to be quite a grand reveal."

Before they'd even left her office, she'd forgotten about them. Liesl wasn't worried about the charcoal suit brought in to replace her or about the other charcoal suit who had been making her miserable for months. Liesl turned her attention to the manila envelope, the yellow paper parcel addressed by Marie's hand, which had landed on her desk with the morning mail only moments before Garber and Sibley had walked in to make their introductions.

There had been something physically overpowering about the sensation of tearing the envelope open, something so decisive and exciting that, in a way, it reduced Liesl to an observer of her own actions. As an observer, rather than a participant, in the envelope opening, she never got to experience that moment of perfect clarity. She would put it together later, would narrow her eyes with understanding as she began to come out of her stupor, but as she leafed through the contents of the envelope, which were immediately recognizable as the final chapters of Francis and Christopher's book, she was struck with a certain blindness rather than a perfect lucidity. Liesl's vision would clear; the desk, the phone, the computer, the open office door, and finally the pages would come back into focus, not as a snap but as a gradual turning of the lens until she understood who had done what and that it was up to her — not because she had the smarts or the title, but because there would be no one else willing to do the hard thing, and that if objective truth and consequences for actions mattered at all, it would be up to her to find confirmation for her suspicions.

She had gone over to one of the bookshelves where she had left Christopher's yellowing Rolodex months earlier. She flicked her fingers past handwritten index cards until she found the one she was seeking and plucked it out. Before she entered the number, she cleared her throat and put on a smile. Then she dialed the number for D. E. Lake Books and asked him to call her back on Christopher's office line at his earliest convenience.

II

She was just opening a plastic clamshell of questionable cafeteria sushi when President Garber walked back into her office.

"Have a moment?" he asked.

"I was just about to eat some lunch."

"Terrible levels of mercury in tuna, you know."

"I went for salmon."

"Good, good."

"You've lost your shadow?"

He took a seat across from her. He would not be leaving her to finish her lunch alone.

"Max will be disappointed," Liesl said. "I think he expected the appointment."

"Maximilian Hubbard as director?"

"He did his doctoral work in Leuven."

"It's not all education."

"He's decent with donors."

"We need more than decent, Liesl."

"He has a good relationship with Percy."

"Percy?" Garber shook his head. "I think we both know that this library is going to have to expand the donor base beyond Percy Pickens."

"I did know that, yes."

"He comes with baggage," Garber said.

"Baggage? That's not baggage anymore," Liesl said with a mouthful of salmon and rice.

He shook his head. "You'd be surprised." And then he reached over and plucked a piece of salmon roll from the plastic tray. Liesl nearly swatted his hand away. She nearly fell off her chair. He chewed, and she gaped at him chewing. She slid the rest of the tray over to him. He nodded with thanks. Took another piece with his fingers.

"You're all right if I finish this?" he said. "If you're not going to?"

"By all means."

"You're familiar with what Sibley did in Boston?" Garber asked. "You must be if you've heard of him."

"Well, yes," Liesl said. "I've heard he's been extremely effective for the library. For the school."

Garber held up a finger as he chewed a piece of her sushi. "Effective!" he said. "A stop sign is effective."

Liesl picked up the empty plastic tray and tossed it in the trash.

"He's a good fundraiser then," Liesl said. "Is that what you mean?"

"During the university's last capital campaign," Garber said, "he came in so far over his target that they had to tear down a perfectly good library and build a new one."

"Why wouldn't they have just spent the money on collections?" Liesl said. "Or held it for when it was needed?"

"Liesl," he said.

"Of course," Liesl said. "Because people like buildings with their names on them."

"They buy books too, of course," Garber said. "Boston has a Gutenberg. Maybe he could get us a Gutenberg."

She looked at her phone. Willed it to ring with news of the auction, news from D. E. Lake, with any break from Garber's conversation.

"That's been in Boston's collection for 150 years," Liesl said. "No one, not even Langdon Sibley, is going to get us a Gutenberg."

"Something else then."

"You know," Liesl said, "the way you

describe him, he sounds a lot like Christopher."

"Exactly right," Garber said. "Good with the books, good with the donors. A face to represent the library."

"Right."

"Christopher led this place admirably," Garber said. "If I can find someone who wears the same-sized shoes . . ."

"Then why go out and buy a new pair," Liesl said. She was compassionate to fear of the unknown. Her single academic term in a position of authority was overflowing with the unknown. And she wasn't surprised by Garber's predictable choice. The last months had been erratic, uncertain. Heroes into villains, opportunities into disappointments, friends into corpses. But the path of academic administration would always run directly down the road of men in charcoal suits. She wasn't dashed by Garber's choice; she was satisfied that someone was at last behaving as expected.

"The donors will love him," Garber said. "Can you imagine how the donors will love him?"

"Is he even interested?" Liesl said.

He stood up and rubbed his hands together, like he was piecing together a difficult riddle.

"He's ready to leave Boston," Garber said.

"To go and do the exact same thing somewhere else?" Liesl said.

"Well. There would be a few differences."

"Right," Liesl said. "Your discretionary funds."

She reached for the purse hanging on the back of her chair. There was an apple buried in there somewhere. She rooted around until she felt the smooth apple skin on her fingers, but she hesitated. Would he take the apple from her too?

She pulled a lip balm in a small yellow pot from her purse so he wouldn't wonder what she was doing. When she turned around to replace the purse on its perch, she saw that it had begun to snow. Seeing the campus covered in snow was a surprise every year. In her imagination, the campus was always flooded with yellow light filtered through green leaves, and the snow made it look like another planet. Garber was still speaking, but Liesl turned fully around to watch the fat flakes land on the old buildings and the young students. It was so clean.

Garber's voice rang in the back of her head as if she were wearing headphones that didn't quite block out external sound. If she were to strain, she could hear him, but she didn't strain. She watched the snow. She remembered then that she hadn't planted tulips. Every fall she replanted tulips in her garden. Not content with the sparse second-year blooms that sprouted from her bulbs, she tilled and washed and dug and fertilized to guarantee the annual show of purple and red and yellow in her giant garden bed. But she'd forgotten. And now the snow was here, and she wouldn't get the opportunity.

"Listen," he said. "If I thought you would do it, I'd certainly factor that in."

"It would save you some money."

"Easy now. We're looking for someone to agree to a seven-year term."

She wanted to rush home and plant her tulips before the ground froze.

"You're right that I couldn't agree to that."

"I know you better than you think. You'll retire at the end of the next academic year . . ."

"Or when Langdon Sibley or whoever else is hired," she said.

"After an acceptable transition period," Garber said. "He can hardly be expected to pick up and leave Boston midway through the year."

"I see," she said. Delaying her departure would leave Langdon Sibley free from the stink of the stolen manuscripts, in Garber's plan. The thefts would be Liesl's legacy.

"So it will be Sibley?"

"If he'll have us."

"It sounds like you'll make it difficult to say no."

He walked around her desk and stood behind her. She tensed with him so close to her, not sure what to expect. But he was looking out the window at the snow.

"I shouldn't have ridden my bike today."

"Have you told Sibley about the thefts?"

He kept his back to her, kept looking at the snow. If she expected her question to startle him, she was disappointed. There was no reason to think he was worried about anything except cycling through the snow.

"No need to bother with all that yet," he said.

Liesl's phone was ringing. As a small act of rebellion as payback for the sushi, she answered it, cutting off Garber. John's voice on the other end came as a great relief. She was happier to hear from him than she had been in a long time. She listened to the familiar voice asking if she had time for an unscheduled lunch, and she knew she didn't; she told him to come anyway. Each act, each choice she made for herself since taking this job, even if it was just deciding to spare an hour for a lunch break, salvaged some small part of that long-forgotten Liesl, the one who'd vowed to be no man's secretary.

"I thought you weren't hungry," Garber said when she got off the phone.

"I'm suddenly starving."

"Have you got anything for lunch tomorrow?"

She searched for an excuse. Didn't find one quickly enough.

"Good," he said. "You can join me and Langdon."

"I'm sure you two have plenty to discuss on your own."

"And yet I expect you to be there."

"I'd only be in the way."

He didn't care. He wanted her help with the wooing.

"You'll be in the exact right place," he said. "I'll see you at noon."

John was prompt but Liesl wasn't. The ringing phone pulled her back to her desk at 11:59, just as she was trying to leave it, and Professor Mahmoud's name on the display intrigued her enough to answer.

"Forty-three thousand dollars," he said instead of *hello.*

"You've won it?" She grinned like she had personally won the lottery.

"They're asking about shipping and insurance. I didn't prep for this part. No one else even bid."

Christopher entered auctions with a bang, flashing donors about to scare off other bidders. This plan had been all Liesl's.

"Give them my contact information and I'll arrange it all," she said. And then they offered each other congratulations and Liesl ended the call with an unbelieving shake of the head.

John was waiting for her by the elevator. He had on a white button-down shirt. He had ironed it.

"Do you have a hot date after this?" Liesl asked.

He looked so very happy to see her.

"A hot date with a librarian," he said. "Can you believe my luck? I'm meant to meet her right here at the entrance to this library. I'm told she has sea-blue eyes and that she blushes to the most delightful shade of pink when she's embarrassed. Have you seen her?"

And she was happy to see him.

"It snowed," she said. "We'll have to go somewhere close by."

"I've packed you some mittens. So not so terribly close by."

"Well," she said. "You've thought of everything."

"You run and grab your coat," he said.

"And we'll be on your way."

"I haven't brought a coat."

"Oh dear. I haven't thought of everything after all."

"My fault," she said. "I should have mentioned on the phone."

"I won't be put off. Why don't we do something wild and take a taxi to lunch?"

"Deal," she said. "I'm just hungry enough to agree to that."

He handed her the mittens, which she pulled on with her pants suit.

"Perfect," she said. "Did you paint today?"

"Just sketched."

He held her hand through her woolen mitten, letting go only to open the door for her.

"Blocked?" she said. "Is this lunch a way to shake loose ideas?"

"This lunch is an excuse to see my wife."

"You see me every day," she said.

He motioned for her to walk through first.

"You seemed as though you could use a break in routine."

"Yes," she said. "I haven't been myself."

The snow imbued them with magical powers. As soon as they got down to the curb and Liesl raised her arm, a taxi pulled up in front of them. They barely had time to get snow in their eyelashes. The radio was playing Gershwin. What kind of taxi plays Gershwin in the middle of the day? John turned to Liesl and smiled a smile that glowed. He was so very happy to see her.

She left it to him to select the restaurant, and though she was surprised when he said Paris, a place with white tablecloths and fresh-baked rolls served with little silver tongs, she didn't complain. It was only a few blocks from the library, which made the whole situation with the taxi seem even more luxurious. Imagine taking a taxi in the middle of the day to go only a few blocks! When the taxi pulled in front of the restaurant's pink facade, John jumped out and ran around to hold her door open for her. He looped his arm through hers and walked her to the restaurant door, both of them tiptoeing through the now-ankle-deep snow.

"You're acting as though we're celebrating."

"Aren't we? I've accepted a commission."

She held his arm tighter. They were greeted by a white shirt and black apron. The restaurant smelled like butter and money.

John had decided to forsake their budget that afternoon, not to celebrate his new commission, but because of the snow. For some perplexing reason he had come to regard the snow as a breakpoint in which their anxieties were covered like furniture protected from dust by drop cloths.

True, the place was fit for new beginnings — the water glasses were crystal. Liesl's eyes fell to the wall behind the bar. John saw it at the same time as she did. The twenty-foot wall behind the bar had been lined with bookshelves and filled with books. Thousands of them. And each of the thousands of books had its cover torn off, exposing its cream-colored paper and subtle stitching. Liesl asked the white shirt about it, waved her hand at the wall. The white shirt grinned. Said the designer had removed the book covers in order to create a more restful atmosphere. Wasn't it delightful, he wanted to know. They left behind the crystal water glasses and went to a noodle shop down the street instead.

Seated, warm, and waiting for lunch, John pulled a brush pen out of his pocket. He took the thick paper napkin from under his glass of water and turned it over to the dry side. He began to sketch. He pursed his lips when he was doing it, the way he had pursed his lips while sketching for decades. He had sketched her hundreds of times in their lives together. She didn't much like being looked at, but she had never minded being sketched. Their noodles arrived, and she stirred a clump of garlic through the hot broth. Her glasses fogged up, and the snow was still falling, and she felt like finally something good was about to happen.

He lay the completed sketch in front of her. Liesl Weiss. Black ink on paper. He took a bite of his noodles and immediately had broth splattered on his chin, on his nose. In John's sketches, Liesl always looked so much like Hannah, and vice versa. The high cheekbones. The bemused half smile. In an ink sketch there was no telling that one had gray hair and the other had brown eyes. As if fearing that no one would ever see her looking fresh-faced and unflappable the way her husband did, Liesl always kept these sketches as proof. She quickly slid this one into her purse.

"Tell me about the commission."

"Corporate portrait. I met the subject today, seems a nice fellow."

"Corporate?"

"Here." He reached across the table with a clean napkin and dabbed a spot of broth from her lapel. If someone else had done it, she might have been embarrassed, but he meant well. She could be a messy eater, and he knew it. As he knew everything about her. John didn't love the idea of her, he loved the reality of her.

"I phoned my agent," he said. "Told him I was looking to take on some work."

The server came back to top up their water. John beamed a smile at the young man who was filling his glass, and once it was full, he picked it up and took a satisfied drink.

"I didn't know you still had an agent," she said. She put her chopsticks down and adjusted her tone to make sure it was clear she was being playful, not accusatory. "He was happy to hear from you, I'm sure."

"A bit surprised."

"He works with artists. He's used to temperament."

"I told him I wanted to work, but I'd prefer to paint people who are, you know, nice people. I haven't been pulling my weight, I don't think. I didn't tell him that part. But it's true."

The table seated next to them had an order of gyoza delivered, and they looked so plump and delicious that Liesl immediately regretted not having ordered some. John read her mind.

"Gyoza?" he called to the server.

The server disappeared into the kitchen. The couple next to them ate their gyoza. Liesl and John were left to regard each other.

"We're hardly starving," she said. "I don't want you to take work that you're unhappy about."

"I'm not unhappy."

Liesl had been deafened by the chorus of voices in her head for so long. The daughter, the husband, the ex-lover who had been pulling her in one direction and then another for decades. She imagined the next phase of her life if she answered the call of those deafening voices: going to Francis to try and start something she had decided against twenty years ago, standing rigid and self-conscious in Hannah's student apartment to deliver an old secret that might ruin them, closing the door on John when he was finally well, finally happy. At that table, in that restaurant with the soft snow falling out the window, a sketch of her own untroubled face in her purse and hot gyoza on their way out from the kitchen, the voices finally went quiet enough for Liesl to hear her own thoughts, to decide what she wanted.

"Good," Liesl said. "I'm not unhappy either."

III

Long after lunch, during that slow day of reassessment, she heard her first news of

Vivek since just after Miriam's death. It came from a history professor who was visiting the library to view a collection of nineteenth-century feminist periodicals that she wanted to use in her teaching. She was grumbling that she had been asked to take on the winter-term course at the very last minute, that another faculty member had been assigned to teach it, and wasn't it always the way with this younger generation, that they couldn't be counted on.

Liesl asked how the other instructor had weaseled his way out of teaching the course, and the woman had launched into a series of complaints about a man being assigned to teach a course on feminist history in the first place, and eventually she mentioned that the man's wife had died, and he was leaving the university. Liesl turned the page of delicate newsprint to show the woman an editorial about a protest that had been staged at parliament. Liesl had prepared a printout from a digital edition of the paper of record covering the same event so that the woman could offer the contrast in how the event was discussed in her class. She was delighted by the idea, delighted that Liesl had so well understood her needs. The course was usually assigned to new faculty, she explained, and she hadn't taught it in years and didn't like the idea of being un-derprepared.

They went back over to the reference desk and wrote out order slips for the material. The professor remarked that a woman who had secured a tenure-track position at a prestigious university would never give up that position, no matter her personal cir-cumstances. She tapped her fingernails atop the stack of brittle newsprint while Liesl filled out the course details, the professor's name, in pencil in her neat penmanship. A suicide is an awful thing, the professor continued. But a professorship is a rare thing that any woman would know should be gripped onto.

Back in the workroom, Liesl explained to Max which papers would be needed for the course. She rarely presented materials to undergraduate students anymore, though she had loved it when it was a larger part of her role. She offered to send him the link to the digital version of the paper she had used, and he recoiled, aghast at the idea of providing a digital alternative to something that was held in their collections. The fight wasn't in her. She left as he was still lectur-ing her and walked back to her office, think-ing of Vivek. Her jaw was sore from holding it closed tight. She began to type an email

404

to Vivek but stopped. She picked up her phone and dialed instead. He deserved more than an email. He deserved to stay at the university. At the very least he deserved a phone call.

"Vivek. What are you doing?"

He didn't say he was happy to hear from her. He didn't say anything.

"I'm leaving," he said finally. "I'm leaving."

Liesl shook her head, though he couldn't see her. Vivek leaving the university where he had tried for years to find a position. Liesl felt that she personally had failed Miriam by not preventing this from happening.

"It's not what Miriam would have wanted," Liesl said. "For you to leave what you've worked for."

"Don't you dare," Vivek said. "You don't know what Miriam did or did not want any more than I do. The only thing we can be sure she wanted was to die."

Liesl's bottom lip was trembling now, making her go for a long pause, a deep breath, and a change in tactic. She couldn't think about Miriam and her last wishes. Not without thinking about Miriam and her last days and her own blindness to her old friend's desperation. Liesl had spent weeks now with the image of Miriam waiting to speak with her on repeat. At moments she'd believed that Miriam had wanted to talk about Vivek, at times she wasn't proud of she was almost convinced that Miriam wanted to confess the thefts, but she'd finally come to rest on the real answer. Help. Miriam had been reaching for a life preserver, and Liesl had never thrown it in the water.

"Why are you leaving?"

"Why would I stay?" he said. "What is there for me here?"

"A job you were excited about," Liesl said. "Stability. The stability you need to rebuild your life after going through something terrible."

"After causing something terrible, I don't deserve anything," Vivek said.

"You know that isn't true."

"I know I killed her," Vivek said.

"The medical examiner would say otherwise."

"If I bought a gun, loaded it, and put it in her mouth, but she pulled the trigger? Who's the killer?"

"Miriam was an ill woman. A mentally ill woman," Liesl said.

"And I abandoned her," Vivek said. "They should arrest me. The police who were so focused on arresting a thief? They should arrest me. I'm a murderer."

"They weren't that interested, in the end," Liesl said.

"They called her a thief."

"Do you think you would feel better if there was a service for her?" Liesl said.

"Who would even come?" Vivek said. "People think she's a criminal. People think she's a coward."

"Let me come see you," Liesl said.

"I'm packing to move. It's not convenient."

"I'll sit on a box. I'll sit on the floor."

"I don't want to."

"Vivek. Do it anyway. Let me come see you."

"Not at the apartment," Vivek said.

"Fine, I'll meet you anywhere you like," Liesl said. "Can I buy you a meal?"

"I'm not a child, Liesl. I've been feeding myself," Vivek said.

"Then where?" Liesl said. "Where and when?"

"I was going to go to the library later," Vivek said.

"Our library?"

Vivek laughed. "I would never come there."

"Then where?" Liesl said. "One of the other university libraries? I didn't know you were still spending time on campus. If I'd known, I would have come to see you earlier. I can be at any one of those libraries in ten minutes."

"The public library," he said. "The big one downtown. I'll meet you up in the fourth-floor reading area."

IV

Liesl pushed through the revolving door, padded across burgundy carpet and up three flights of curved stairs. Vivek was on the fourth floor as promised, head down on a big wooden table, wrapped in his winter coat. When she greeted him, he took a good long time before acknowledging her.

"I haven't been to this library since Hannah was a child," she said.

"I'll bet it looks exactly the same," Vivek said.

"Back then we used to come here three times a week." Vivek finally lifted his head. Liesl pulled out a chair and sat at the table across from him.

"Not anymore?" Vivek said.

"Hannah would still come here with her friends during high school, but I would just send library holds to the branch closest to the house."

"No time to browse the stacks?"

"No time to browse the stacks."

"Miriam loved this library," Vivek said.

"I didn't know that. Is that why you've come here? It makes you feel close to her? I'm glad you've found a place you can come. I hope it gives you some peace."

He ran his fingers over a metal nameplate screwed to the center of the table.

"I bought this table for her."

"What do you mean?"

"A stupid thing. A named gift. The library lets you do that."

"The nameplate says anonymous donor," Liesl said.

"She would have hated having her name on it. It would have made her embarrassed. But the donation would have made her happy."

Liesl heard the woodenness in his voice. Tears, screaming, those would have been easier for her than this bareness.

"All the more reason to stay here. Now that you've made this place."

"Is it? I think it's just a table. I come here because I can't think of where else I'm supposed to go and because my therapist insists that I'm not allowed to stay in my apartment all day. There are libraries in every city."

"I'm glad to hear you're seeing a therapist."

"Yes. The chair of my department all but insisted."

"Will you continue after you leave?"

"No. If the point of therapy is for me to feel better, then no. I don't deserve to feel better. Miriam didn't get to feel better, so why should I? Maybe I'll travel the world donating tables to libraries and feeling like absolute shit. I have a bunch of money now, did you hear? Not her life insurance; they don't pay that off if you . . . Well, there's no life insurance, but I was the beneficiary of her retirement accounts, and she must have planned to play a lot of golf because it's so much money I don't want that they insisted on giving me."

"It's good that you won't be worried about money."

"Why?" asked Vivek. "Don't I deserve to be worried?"

"This table is a beautiful gesture in Miriam's memory. It can be the first of many gestures in her memory. But you can't make those gestures if you disappear from here. I'm here because I want to talk to you about preserving Miriam's memory and restoring her reputation. A terrible thing happened to her, but I can fix it; I think I can fix it. You and I have always known that Miriam wasn't the thief, but I know now who was." Her voice cracked at the end and she tried to hold his despair-dulled eyes.

"The butler in the pantry with a candlestick?" Vivek said.

"Vivek, be serious. Do you think you're the only one who feels like they failed her? I worked with Miriam five days a week, and I should have known something was wrong, I should have done something, but I kept my head down. And I should have done something to prevent that story about her being printed. As soon as I heard a rumble about her being a suspect, I should have done everything in my power to end those suspicions."

"But you didn't do those things," Vivek said.

He didn't say it as an accusation. He didn't need to. She was working hard to punish herself. He could see it.

"I didn't. We can still fix this."

"Not me. Me and my shitty guilt money know it's too late."

A teenager at the next table over shushed them.

"The chair of your department cares enough about you to insist on therapy. I'm sure they would agree to a leave of absence."

"A leave isn't an option," Vivek said.

"I'm sure it is," Liesl said. "They stop people's tenure clock for maternity leave all the time; I'm certain an exception can be made in this case."

He rubbed the nameplate with the sleeve of his coat until it shone.

"A maternity leave is a legitimate claim. Bringing a life into the world. Who would argue with that?" He stopped rubbing, satisfied with the sheen of the nameplate. "Liesl, drop this. I'm not going to stay. I can't."

"Please," she said, veering close to a tone that begged. "I'm sure if you just asked for a leave."

Vivek started to get up. "They offered me a leave." He pulled his parka closed and turned to go.

"Take the offer!" Liesl said. It was unfair to him perhaps. Probably. But she felt she needed him near to complete her penance. "The idea of returning there must seem awful now, I know. But if you just give yourself some time to heal. And if you give me some time to fix all of this. I promise that I can fix this."

He kept walking.

"I don't have all the evidence yet, Vivek. I have to be responsible here. But I know it wasn't Miriam, and I think I understand the rest of the pieces, and once I'm certain we can make it public and maybe even get an apology, maybe we can get the university to do something in Miriam's name, something brilliant, so that she'll be remembered for her brilliant work and not for this awful thing."

He stopped at the top of the stairs.

"I don't need her to be valorized. What we owe her is peace."

"Justice for who did this, for the real thief, wouldn't that give her peace?" Liesl asked. "Wouldn't that give you peace?"

"It might. If I believed justice was at all possible."

He continued down the stairs. And she let him. Because she didn't have an argument that might convince him to stay.

18

I

After work she met Francis at a playground. It was packed despite the cold. Small children in bright parkas, shoving each other into snowbanks as they clamored to be next in line for the slide. There was a cluster of mothers in designer coats talking in a huddle. Liesl sat on a cold wooden bench next to Francis. The grandson he was babysitting was among the children. She didn't see him.

A small band of slightly older boys — Liesl was never very good at guessing the ages of children, but these were larger than the preschoolers who occupied most of the playground — had climbed to the top of a play structure and were pelting with snowballs anyone who tried to approach. One of the boys had his navy parka unzipped, and his brown hair had sprung loose from its ponytail so that it haloed his frost-pink face.

He let out a guttural scream that drew Francis's attention enough for him to whistle and wave the boy over.

"Robespierre! Here!" Francis yelled.

He marched in their direction, the child who had screamed, with his brows knit and his chest pushed forward. He was ready for a confrontation.

"Do you really call him that?" she asked. "Or is it just Robbie?"

"Never Robbie," Francis said as the boy approached. "He goes into a frenzy if you try Robbie."

"Robespierre it is."

"What is it, Grandpa?" the boy asked.

"The snowballs," Francis said. "And the screaming."

Freed by the absence of their tormentor, the small children had reoccupied the play structure. He looked back at it with regret.

"Is that all?" the boy asked.

"That's all," Francis said. The boy ran back in the direction of his kingdom, emitting another scream to let everyone know who was in charge.

"Sorry I didn't introduce you," Francis said.

"No. I'm quite glad you didn't."

"When they gave him a name like Robespierre," Francis said, "did they think for a moment he would be a normal kid?"

"I'm glad you invited me."

"Even though you're terrified of my grandson?"

"I wanted a chance to apologize." The playground was penance. Because Liesl had the soot of accusation on her and mere water couldn't get her hands clean. Instead, she had insisted on accompanying Francis somewhere on his turf, even if it really meant Robespierre's turf, to ask his forgiveness.

"There's nothing to it, Liesl. Whatever it is you want to say isn't worth dwelling on."

"I treated you badly."

"You believed something unbelievable about me."

"I think I did." Liesl said. It was hard to come to terms with the depth of her suspicion. Liesl had drawn a thorough picture to settle the case — Francis's skulking around with his manuscript-as-shopping-list, using old intelligence connections to sell the books on the black market — but once all the detail of the picture was filled in, it revealed itself as ridiculous. So there she was. A cold bench in a cold playground.

The detail that made Francis's innocence true to Liesl was the first bit of the picture Liesl had drawn: Francis rolling his manuscript into the office on a book truck. A stack of papers with the clue that the Vesalius was about to be found missing (if she had known then the depth of what would follow!) and asked her, begged her, to read his words, the words that his mentor had, until that point, asked him to keep a secret. This had been in September, but it took everything that came after for Liesl to understand it.

"What I need to know," Francis said, "is if you kept me close to, I don't know, crack the case?"

Liesl shook her head. "No, Francis. I just liked having you close."

"But you don't anymore?"

"I wasn't being fair," Liesl said. "To you or to John."

Robespierre came barreling back over to their bench. "Grandpa," he said. "Give me a stick."

"What's that?" Francis said.

"Give me a stick."

"Why on earth would I give you a stick?"

"*F-I-T-E.* Do you know what that spells?"

"What?"

"*F-I-T-E.* Do you know what word that spells?"

"That doesn't spell anything. *F-I-G-H-T* spells 'fight.' You want me to give you a stick so you can go fight?"

"Yes."

"Go away."

He hurtled himself back into the pack of children at the other end of the playground. Francis crossed his legs and, in doing so, turned his body away from Liesl.

"Did you really believe I could have done it?" Francis said. "That I would have done that to Chris, to the library, to you?"

She got up from the bench and stood over him, stomping her feet to keep them warm. On the street beyond the playground fence, a streetcar rumbled past. The sun was nearing the horizon, and one by one, the mothers and fathers who had been standing at the park's periphery were taking small mittened hands and walking them home for warm dinners.

"You haven't asked me," Liesl said. "Why I no longer suspect you."

Without the sun to warm them, the cold came quickly.

"I supposed you had come to your senses," Francis said. "It's getting cold."

"We'll leave in a minute."

"Should we just leave the boy here, do you think?"

"Are you going to ask me?"

"He's feral as it is. He'd survive out here."

Robespierre was alone now at the top of the play structure. Quiet and cross-legged.

"Ask me who the thief is, Francis."

Liesl was not surprised to discover that he wouldn't meet her eyes then. Gazing off, he confirmed for Liesl that he wasn't blind to what had been in front of him all along.

"I won't, Liesl. Knowing it for certain will break my heart."

II

Two minutes after its scheduled opening the next morning, she pushed open the heavy door of Don Lake's shop. The bookshop was dark. There were stacks of books and papers on every surface, covering every window and lighting fixture. She ran her fingers over the embossed cover of a Thomas Hardy novel that might have been valuable if Don could convince anyone to come into his dusty shop to buy it.

"Who's there?" Don said, poking his head around the corner. "Liesl Weiss. What a pleasure."

Don was wearing a dust-streaked shirt and carrying a mug of what Liesl hoped was only coffee but was probably something stronger.

"You've been avoiding my calls," Liesl said. "So I thought a field trip was in order."

419

She rested her elbow on a stack that wobbled perilously.

"I've been doing no such thing," Don said. "But I'm damn glad to see a friendly face."

"Has business been slow?" Liesl said. "I've been hearing that from some other sellers."

"These are not literary times we're living in."

"Maybe a freshen up of the shop?"

"And ruin the thrill of the hunt?"

"Indeed. No."

"What's this about ignoring your calls?" he said.

"I've left a couple of messages on your machine. Have you been getting them?"

"That bloody thing."

"No matter," Liesl said. "A trip in person is twice as nice. Do you have a minute now to chat?"

"The crowds will simply have to wait."

"Oh good," said Liesl. "I wanted to ask about something you said to me when I ran into you at the book fair."

It had been stuck in her brain like a splinter since they'd had the conversation. Not in deep enough to find some tweezers to remove it, but an irritant nonetheless. Something she could never quite forget about.

"Good turnout this year," Don said. "And they poured a lovely rioja at the reception."

"Do you remember we talked about the Peshawar facsimile?" Liesl said. She cleared a smear of dust off a book jacket with her thumb as she spoke.

"Still hasn't sold, I'm afraid. Would you like to see it?"

"No, thank you."

"Pity," said Don.

"You said I probably wouldn't be interested in it," Liesl said. She asked it without making eye contact, without looking up from the dust.

"Well, no. It's already in your collection."

"Right," Liesl said.

"Christopher bought another copy of that facsimile from me, was it five years ago now?"

"From the same printer?"

"From the very same print run," Don said. "He was amazed by the quality of the reproduction. I suppose you use it for teaching alongside the original?"

She'd thought the truth would be more violent, a confrontation with a savage stranger. But it was gentler than that. It was recognizing someone you were certain you'd seen before and then having their identity reveal itself in your memory.

"We do something like that," Liesl said. "Thanks so much for your time, Don."

III

Garber's office door looked like a fortified bank vault, protected by a twenty-six-year-old administrative assistant armed with hair spray and a pencil skirt.

Liesl watched Garber's door from the outer hallway and waited for the assistant to need to pee. At her desk, the woman sat with perfect posture, fingers flying over a keyboard that she never once looked at.

A woman like this, Liesl thought, might never abandon her post. She would rush the bank vault; it was the only way.

She walked right past the woman's desk to Garber's door. He was sitting in his office chair with his feet up on his desk. Across from him there was another man, another suit, another set of feet on the desk. The men were laughing. Until they saw that they had been interrupted, and then slowly, they were not laughing anymore.

"What is this, Liesl?" Garber said, rising from his desk.

"I'm here to cancel our lunch."

"My assistant handles my calendar."

The assistant was standing at the door, powerless despite her hair-spray-and-pencil-skirt armor.

"Fine. Would you like to know why I'm canceling?"

"You're not canceling. We're meeting Langdon Sibley."

"Make up your mind," Liesl said. "Do you handle your calendar or does your assistant?"

The other suit slowly swung his legs off the desk.

"Are you quite all right, Liesl?" Garber asked.

"Yes. I'm perfect. Better than I've long been."

"So good that you're barging in on my meeting. Canceling an important commitment?"

She turned her head to the suit. Gave him a long look and a raised eyebrow. He stood and left the room.

"We should go, President Garber," she said.

"Where?"

"To see the police."

"I have an appointment to have lunch with a prospective hire, and so do you."

"I have an appointment with a police detective."

"You are acting inappropriately."

She walked to the coat closet in the corner

of the room and retrieved his overcoat.

"You'll want to come to this," Liesl said.

"And what about Sibley?"

He pulled the coat over his suit jacket, but in his rush and confusion, the sleeve of his suit coat kept bunching and forcing him to take it off and try again.

"Talk to your assistant. She handles your calendar," Liesl said.

The taxi dropped them off in the middle of a puddle of slush in front of the police station. Uniformed officers were smoking cigarettes in the heat from a subway grate. They stopped to watch as first Liesl and then Garber maneuvered their way out of the cab and over the puddle. Liesl held the doorframe for leverage and swung her foot over to a solid-looking snowbank. Garber tried to leap and wound up in slush up to his ankle.

Garber had tried to ask her questions in the taxi, but she had refused him. The pink-stone brutalist police headquarters was busier than Liesl had expected. Detectives in ill-fitting suits streamed out the doors; witnesses clutching their subpoenas streamed in. A news van from a local broadcaster was parked outside, and an unmanned camera was set up pointing at the police station doors. Off to the side of the camera, a woman wearing heavy makeup, a purple blazer, and gray sweatpants was doing vocal exercises. Garber held the heavy glass door for Liesl to go through, and then found himself continuing to hold it for a boy who wasn't more than fifteen and his mother who wasn't impressed as they walked into the building sniping at each other.

"Imagine finding yourself in a place like this," Garber said. "We're very lucky, you and I, aren't we?"

"We have found ourselves in a place like this."

"Well, not really we haven't."

"We're not better than the other people here."

"No, of course," Garber said. "That wasn't what I was implying."

"Funny," Liesl said. "It sounded like that was exactly what you were implying."

By the elevator, Detective Yuan was waiting for them, just as Liesl had arranged. He shook President Garber's hand and reminded him that the men had met before, on more than one occasion. Garber began to ask what was going on, but Yuan stopped him and told him it was best that they had their discussion in private, with all of the relevant parties there. They stepped into the elevator together, and Garber crossed his arms tight, making himself as small as possible so that he would not accidentally touch anything.

"Let's do whatever it is we are here to do so I can get back to work."

Detective Yuan smiled at President Garber and led him into an office. Waiting inside was a man who looked like he had been lifted directly out of a network television drama. He was only about Liesl's height, but he was roped with muscle. His head was shaved and polished to a spectacular shine, but it was his outfit that stole the day. He wore immaculate jeans that hugged every curve of his body and a perfectly crisp, perfectly fitted, perfectly blue jean shirt, a slightly different shade of denim, tucked into those jeans. The garments had either been lovingly cleaned and ironed or had been procured from a store that very morning and would be discarded that evening when they were no longer fresh. Around his shoulders he wore a holster with a handgun tucked neatly under each arm. He was introduced as a detective from the property crimes unit. Liesl heard and immediately forgot his name — the tight jeans, the gun, it was all too overwhelming to be real, easier to leave him as an abstraction.

"Detective Yuan laid out some basic information about your case," Detective Denim said.

Detective Yuan was wearing a suit, as he had been wearing every time that Liesl had encountered him. She would have thought that a missing persons detective would have the need for guns and breathable fabrics and a property crimes detective would be the one in the suit, but very little up until this point had met her expectations about the city police. The room was set up as an office, not an interrogation room, but the lack of personalization and the convenient availability of four chairs and a bare table where evidence could be laid out made it clear that it was, in fact, an interrogation room, though perhaps one that was meant to make its occupants feel as though they were having off-the-record conversations. Garber took off his wool coat and looked around the room for a coatrack. Finding none, he gave a disappointed sigh, folded the coat neatly, and hung it from the back of his chair, being careful to make sure that it did not touch the floor or anything else that could transfer dirt or parasites from the room onto his body.

"Who'd like to start?" Lieutenant Levi said.

President Garber and both detectives turned to look at Liesl. She in turn looked at the floor. She was prepared, of course she was prepared, but she had expected some lubrication to get things started.

"If you're not going to say anything," Garber said, "then I won't sit here and have my time be wasted."

Liesl pulled Christopher's manuscript out of her bag.

President Garber didn't know what he was looking at. He waited for the detectives to tell him what to do. Liesl pushed the stack of papers over to Garber so he could read the title page. *The Department of Rare Books and Special Collections* by Christopher Wolfe and Francis Churchill. His eyes went wider, ever so slightly wider as he read the names. Detective Yuan got up from the table and poured two glasses of water. He handed one to Garber and one to Liesl. Garber licked his lips and began to smile. He tasted blood.

"I didn't think he had it in him," Garber said.

"Then you thought less of him than I believed."

"I've scarcely thought of him at all," Garber said.

"You're misreading," Liesl said. "I'm not

presenting this as evidence of a crime by Francis."

The first blow landed. Liesl felt the crunch. The case against Christopher could have been made without the final chapter of the manuscript, but its delivery from Marie earlier that week could leave no doubt for anyone.

After Christopher's death, Liesl had lost all hope of ever securing the last piece of evidence. Marie couldn't be blamed for a desire to protect her late husband's legacy. It had come as a parcel, not delivered by Marie herself. Typed pages in a yellow envelope, with Christopher's familiar script up and down the margins of the pages that were meant to be the final chapter of the book that he and Francis were writing together. Liesl would have recognized that handwriting anywhere. She had seen it thousands of times. Notes left on her desk, scribbled onto cocktail napkins, telling her of five-figure deals he had made over Laphroaig that she was to find the money for. Red ink over her own manuscripts that she gave him to edit and he returned, purportedly strengthened but really just transliterated into his own voice. She would have recognized the handwriting anywhere, so she recognized it immediately when she saw the notes he had left all over the chapter he had written about the Plantin Polyglot Bible.

Christopher was a talented writer and had done the book justice. He had written in depth about the feat of typesetting that was required to print the parallel texts in Hebrew, Greek, Syriac, and Aramaic alongside the translations and commentary in Latin. In the earlier part of the chapter, he had devoted some time to the scholarly significance of the work, for its contributions to philological and biblical scholarship and printing arts and the way that the Plantin would complement the library's existing collections. The chapter would have been incomplete if Christopher had not written about the enormous undertaking the book represented for the printer, the level of scholarship that was involved, the money that would have been required to make the project possible, not to mention the work the publisher did to negotiate the religious and political issues of Reformation Europe. It was a feat, and Christopher wrote about it beautifully. Beautifully and briefly. The chapter was not ultimately interested in the history of the book, or the scholarly significance of the book. It was interested in the beauty of the book. He called it sumptuous.

He wrote about the flirty serifs on the Greek characters. The woodcut signature of the scholar who oversaw the translations that ended every section. The shine of the gilt backstrip. Christopher had written about the beauty of the book in a way that only someone who had held it in his arms could have.

The Vesalius chapter had the same magic. From the moment the library had received the book on deposit, decades ago, the librarians had seen that there was something exceptional about the edition. There was scarcely a page that did not have handwritten annotations. The chapter about the Vesalius in Christopher's book detailed the notes which in many cases did not amount to changes to the meaning of the text but to changes in the style of writing. The annotations, it turned out, were Vesalius's own and influenced the changes he made to *De humani corporis fabrica* in subsequent editions. The loving way that Christopher wrote about the Vesalius, the attention he bestowed to each annotation, the way he identified that the annotator wrote in three slightly different styles, and the way he was able to argue that the different styles of annotation matched the letters and other manuscript material that Vesalius was creating at the time: It was masterful. And Christopher's chapter should have been masterful, because he had spent years with the Vesalius.

The discovery that the annotations were in Vesalius's own hand was one of Christopher's most notable contributions to the scholarship of medical history, of book history. The nature of the discovery was itself an argument for the vitality of rare book libraries, because it would have been impossible for him to discover such a thing had he not had access to the physical object of the Vesalius. Vesalius had lived five hundred years before Christopher studied his work, and yet the two men had known each other intimately. Had Christopher been working from facsimiles or from digital images, such a level of fraternity between the two men would have been impossible. Christopher wove fact and story and history in the way he wrote about the Vesalius; it was a beautiful thing to read. The problem that Liesl pointed out to the assembled group was that Christopher wrote with the same familiarity about the Plantin, a book that he should have no personal history with.

Christopher Wolfe was a great scholar. He had an encyclopedic knowledge of book history and had done extensive research about the Plantin Polyglot Bible when it became apparent that the library might find the money to acquire it. One could write about an artifact without possessing it. But that had not happened in this case. Christopher had felt the binding under his fingertips. He had turned the pages and smirked at the flirty serifs. Which should have been impossible, because the book had been delivered on a Friday afternoon and presumably locked in a safe at the university while Christopher was home for the weekend before having his stroke early on Monday.

President Garber's first reaction was disbelief. The two detectives did not share this sentiment. Men of the law know that the most obvious suspect in a crime is usually the ultimate culprit, and who could be more obvious than the man who had greatest access to the library's collections over the years? Garber stood and shouted. Liesl asked him to sit and be quiet. Detective Yuan provided more water. He knew that upset witnesses could often be calmed with water. Liesl began to talk about carbon dating. Garber drank his glass of water in one swallow and explained that he and Christopher had belonged to the same club, that they had dined together dozens of times. Liesl produced the carbon-dating report about the Peshawar. Garber argued against the validity of the science. Detective Yuan asked him if he was a scientist. Garber explained that he was an economist. Liesl offered to add Rhonda Washington to their quartet. Garber reminded everyone in the room that Rhonda was a mathematician, not a physicist.

President Garber had conducted interviews with dozens of outlets about the superiority of the university's laboratory facilities. He had personally fundraised for the radiocarbon accelerator. Liesl recounted her conversation with Don Lake. Garber continued to argue, though his volume dropped. Detective Yuan filled their glasses of water again. The quality of the facsimile in Lake's shop was exceptional, Liesl reported. No one was a fool for having been fooled. Garber held the glass of water like a security blanket. At the conclusion of Liesl's explanation, the four sat at the table in silence. Everyone's glass of water was empty, as was the pitcher that had been used to refill them. No one had anything left to offer.

Garber had been made a fool. To their credit, the detectives were largely silent during Liesl's presentation so that Garber could convince himself that he was being made a fool of in front of Liesl only. By his own telling, Garber had been friends with Christopher. They had dined together. And Christopher had made him a fool. If what Liesl was describing was true, then the scale of Garber's blindness, his ineptitude, was marvelous. And a man like Garber did not take kindly to being made a fool. So he doubled down on his denial.

"There isn't enough here to convince a judge," Garber said.

"I'm not in front of a judge," Liesl said. "My goal here is for you to understand what happened at the library. To understand what Christopher did."

"It's hardly fair to accuse a man who can't stand to defend himself."

"That's what we've done to Miriam."

"And why are the police here? Christopher is dead. He can't be prosecuted."

"That's true of the courts. But not of the press."

It's an ugly thing to watch people be so ugly with one another. Detective Yuan cleared his throat and stood, drawing the attention of the room over to him and away from Liesl's blackmail attempt, which was wholly reasonable but was nonetheless unwise to conduct in the presence of law enforcement. Garber was right that Christopher would not be posthumously prosecuted, but there was still the not-insignificant matter of trying to recover the library's property. Here Garber was stumped. The recovery of the books would allow him to issue tax receipts, reassure donors, and altogether save face. But the recovery of the books, if they were recovered from Christopher's home or office or wherever else he may have put them, would prove absolutely that Garber had been a fool. So he tried a last approach.

"Christopher's isn't the only name on the manuscript. If he can't be prosecuted, then it seems he has an accomplice who can be."

"The detectives here have indicated that they don't believe Francis was involved."

"But if he were? He would be humiliated. Or even worse."

"Professor Garber, I'm going to stop you right there," Detective Yuan said. "Mr. Churchill is the one who brought Christopher's writing, which we consider the key piece of evidence, to our attention. He shared the early chapters of the manuscript, chapters which were as incriminating to himself as they were to Mr. Wolfe, with Liesl shortly after the first theft was discovered. Mr. Lake has indicated that Christopher acted alone in the purchase of the Peshawar facsimile. Mr. Churchill is not under suspicion at this time."

IV

The property crimes unit secured a warrant to search Christopher and Marie's home, but they needn't have done so. Had they asked, Marie would have held the door wide open for them. When Detective Yuan recounted the scene to Liesl later, he described Marie as resigned, prepared for the detectives. Dressed in her layers of knit fabrics, she hadn't even glanced at the warrant when they held it for her inspection. She waved her hand to let them in and suggested they begin in Christopher's home office.

"She walked us to his office door," Detective Yuan said. "But she refused to go inside while we looked."

There was not a secret swinging bookcase that opened to reveal five hundred years of book-printing treasures. For all of his machinations to keep the thefts concealed, Christopher's hiding place for the books was rather inelegant. He kept a big, beige metal filing cabinet in his office. Liesl recognized it in the photo; he had brought it home from the office nearly ten years earlier when they had rearranged the space.

437

The library had less and less need for filing cabinets as record-keeping became a digital process, and for years they had struggled with what to do with the ugly old pieces of furniture. The old wooden card catalogs were snatched up, usually by an undergraduate library assistant to be used for wine storage, as soon as they were offered. But nobody wanted old metal filing cabinets. It was a relief, then, when Christopher had asked for one to be shipped to his house. In a room full of mahogany and chestnut-colored leather, the filing cabinet was an eyesore. It was one of the last places the police had looked. They had spent a lot of time trying to find the swinging bookcase.

"We checked the filing cabinet as an afterthought," Detective Yuan said.

The six volumes of the Plantin Bible had occupied the bottom drawer of the cabinet. The Vesalius and the Peshawar were in the middle, and in total there were nine other books recovered from the cabinet and taken to police headquarters for cataloging as evidence.

The rest of the books in the office were a complicating factor. The room was lined with bookshelves, none of which swung to reveal a secret passageway, but all of which were heavy with rare and valuable books of uncertain provenance.

"How did Marie handle that?" Liesl asked.

"That's where it fell apart," Yuan said. He took a bite of his noodles, for of course it was only over lunch that he was able to meet with Liesl. She had suggested the restaurant, and he had looked slightly disappointed when they sat down, reminding her that if he wanted spicy noodles he could just go to his mom's house.

Marie had objected to the removal of the books from the shelves. Christopher had been formed by those books, she argued, and they were all she had left of the man.

Her pleas were ignored, and the books were taken as evidence. They were kept separate from the books that had been recovered from the filing cabinet and under a separate agreement. The filing cabinet books were taken with the presumption they were stolen. If Marie could not prove legal ownership, they would not be returned. The bookshelf books would be sent back to her if no one came forward to claim them. As the books were boxed, Marie had stood in the office doorway and wept, issuing occasional instructions about how to pack a box full of books in a way that would not damage their bindings.

When they were finished with Christopher's office, all that remained on the shelves were a few hardback John Grisham novels that had been removed from their book jackets, probably so that no one would notice that they were John Grisham novels. If a man was defined by the contents of his bookshelves, then Christopher was nothing more than a few airplane books, trying to pass themselves off as something grander.

V

The Christmas tree was still up in the corner of the reading room. Before even taking off her coat, Liesl walked over and plugged in the string of lights so they could keep her company while she waited. She put her phone on the desk in front of her, so she wouldn't miss it when the detective called, and sat down to wait. Out the large window, the snow was falling in sheets over the empty campus. She craned her neck to look all the way down the street, and in the distance she could see an unmarked navy van making its way down the slippery road, just as she had been assured it would. At the stop sign before the library, the back wheels of the van slipped slightly, sending the van into a slow-motion fishtail that spun it halfway through the intersection. There was no reason to worry. There was nothing with which the van could collide. They had thought carefully about making the delivery to a totally empty campus. If she had asked, campus security would have opened the library's loading dock for Liesl; they were working even on Christmas Eve. But she hadn't asked. As per her instruction, the van slowly made its way over the curb and pulled up directly next to the fire exit of the reading room. Three times the van pulled forward and reversed, pulled forward and reversed, pulled forward and reversed until the van's back doors were perfectly aligned with the entrance that Liesl had propped open. Finally, the engine and the lights cut out, and Detective Yuan jumped out of the driver-side door.

Liesl greeted him with a hug. He motioned for her to wait and reached back into the van where he retrieved a large box of sweets marked with Arabic script. She pulled it open and selected a honey-soaked pastry.

"You're a terrible driver," Liesl said.

He couldn't immediately respond as his mouth was full of halvah. So he shrugged, indicating that he didn't necessarily disagree.

"I didn't think we could eat in here," he said when he had finally finished chewing. He was right. Eating was strictly forbidden in the library unless one was a donor attending a cocktail reception. But stealing millions of dollars' worth of rare books was also forbidden, and that had been allowed to go on for years, so she wasn't going to let herself sweat over some baklava on Christmas Eve. She offered him another piece, but he refused. He could tell she was stalling. He walked with her to the staff area so they could wash the honey off their hands, and then they returned to the van and popped the latch on the back doors, revealing the boxes of books inside.

Liesl had prepared several book trucks for the job. They were lined up by the fire exit. Detective Yuan hopped into the van and began to hand boxes down to Liesl. She didn't open them to see what was inside. That would come later. For now she loaded, truck after truck, until the van was empty and the reading room was lined with brown-paper packages waiting to be torn open and inventoried for insurance purposes. Detective Yuan slammed the van door closed, and the fire exit door behind it.

The boxes didn't need to be immediately opened. She could leave them on the book trucks in the basement and worry about the unpacking after the Christmas break. The empty campus was necessary for the delivery, but not for the unpacking. Even still, she could not help herself.

"Which one is the Plantin?" Liesl asked. "Do you remember?"

He remembered. The officer in the evidence room had asked for Detective Yuan to come down and help pack the boxes, even though Yuan insisted he had no idea how to properly pack a rare book. He was certainly less qualified than the officer who spent most of his days keeping guns and cocaine contained. But his colleague had insisted that Yuan would have a feel for it. He was right. The books were arranged snugly, the boxes labeled neatly.

"Isn't she beautiful?" Liesl said when she opened the box, the sumptuous red Spanish leather appearing to glow within its cardboard confines, the light dancing against the gilt on the spine that was so brilliantly preserved that it might have been applied that very morning. There were some scuffs on the bindings, a bit of a watermark in the gutter of one of the volumes. The little flaws only made the set more beautiful, a beauty mark on a perfectly proportioned cheek. She pulled one of the large volumes out, opened the creaking vellum pages so she could run a finger down the handsome columns of text, feel the slight raise of the intricate floral woodcut that marked the beginning of each section with the pad of her index finger. Yuan looked at her, unconvinced, as she looked at the pages. He shrugged.

"It's got nothing on the baklava."

VI

Christmas Eve, near sunset. Liesl arrived at the downtown television studio to find her suit, chosen with care and donned moments before her departure, looked shabby next to the tight and trim and tone of television people all around her. She was self-conscious, and she looked it.

"You look like such an authority," said Professor Mahmoud, rounding the corner to greet her.

Liesl was pliable, the emotion of the day making a compliment enough to set her straight, and she regained her footing. "Are you wearing makeup, Professor?"

He shrugged. "I didn't ask for it, but I'm not mad about how it looks. The producer wants to run through some details before we film."

"I'm ready when they are."

Professor Mahmoud led her to the makeup room where she was seated under bright lights, her face dabbed with powders as an obscenely young television producer confirmed details for the segment.

"So you suspected the blue Quran might be a hidden treasure?" he asked.

"I knew only that the catalog description speculated as to Tunisian origin and that Professor Mahmoud was a great scholar of the library of the Tunisian Great Mosque of Kairouan."

"You're being modest," the producer said.

"I only asked some good questions of some smart people."

"That's just it, though, isn't it? The key to treasure hunting? Know when to shut up and ask good questions?"

Contrary to Liesl's expectations, this was not taking shape as a fifteen-second feel-good clip on the local news. The producer was beguiled. He dug into their story, and while the money bit was important, the steal of a price at auction and subsequent valuation, he wanted to know about the history of the thing and about the nature of the discovery itself. How they knew what they knew and turned a paragraph-long description in an auction catalog into a treasure missing from the library that contained the oldest Arabic manuscripts in existence. He filled the room with the details of their discovery. Every bibliographical reference, every footnote in someone else's story, every clue that others had ignored.

The set Liesl and Professor Mahmoud were led to had a podium that had been built to tilt the blue page toward the camera.

The producer introduced them to the anchor who would be conducting the interview. And then the lights in the studio darkened and the lights on Liesl brightened, and she took a last glance at her feet to confirm she was standing on the masking tape X that was her mark, and then she tilted her face up to the camera and prepared to talk about her work.

VII

When she went to Marie's house, she went alone and with the television makeup scrubbed off. Knocking with one hand, clutching a rioja by the neck with the other. She knocked as Marie was washing a single dinner plate, and when Marie answered the door, she was still holding a dish towel, twisting it back and forth in that way people do when they're uneasy.

"Are you here caroling?"

Liesl didn't answer. She hadn't expected Marie to lead with a joke.

"Lighten up and come in," Marie said. "It's very charitable of you."

"I'm not here for charity, Marie," Liesl said. Her palms sweating, Liesl cast an agitated eye at Marie and followed her into the house. The door clunked closed behind them, but Marie didn't invite her further. She crossed her arms and waited for answers.

"Then why are you here?"

"To drink this wine." Liesl lifted the bottle. Proof of her good intentions.

"I had other invitations, you know."

"I don't doubt you did."

"People aren't so terrible as to leave a widow alone at Christmas." Softening a bit, Marie turned and led Liesl out of the foyer, into the quiet of the house.

"So why stay home?" Liesl asked.

"No one here to ask me any questions."

Liesl followed Marie into the kitchen to get a corkscrew. They passed the dining room. Candle still lit. Single place mat ready for tomorrow's breakfast.

"Would you like to see his office?" Marie asked.

Liesl didn't move from where she was leaning against the kitchen counter.

"Not at all," she said.

Liesl poured them each a glass. "To a Merry Christmas," she said, raising hers.

"Yes," Marie said, failing to return the

gesture and bringing the glass right to her lips instead. "What a festive year it is."

"You can't cut yourself off from all happiness."

"Can't I?" Marie said. "I'll accept that challenge."

"Would you like to talk about it?"

"It seems that you do."

"I'm not here for the gossip, Marie. I'm here to check if you're all right."

"But only now that I've helped you . . ." Marie said, drinking again.

"That isn't fair," Liesl said. "I would have come before."

Marie's glass was empty, and Liesl moved to refill it. She hadn't drunk a sip of her own.

"But you didn't."

"I wasn't sure if you wanted to see me."

"My husband had just died."

"I should have come."

"Ask me. That's why you're here, I know it is, so just ask me. Ask me why I sent you the pages. Ask me if I knew."

The cracks in Marie's lips were stained red from the wine. They must have been very dry to take on the color so quickly. Liesl had always thought of Marie as the type of woman who took very good care of her skin. But the cracks were showing.

"Did you know?" Liesl asked.

"No."

"I believe you. There's no reason for you to lie about it now."

Liesl set down her glass on the white marble counter. She'd never thought much about what Marie and Christopher's kitchen might look like, but she didn't expect it to be so sleek. So modern. She still hadn't had any of her wine.

"Except for the small matter of prosecution," Marie said.

"That would never happen," Liesl said, nonetheless conjuring a picture of tiny Marie in her twin set being led away in handcuffs.

"Wouldn't it? Isn't it what I deserve?"

"You just said you didn't know."

"But I should have. I can be prosecuted for being stupid."

She sprayed spit when she slurred the word *stupid*. The wine wasn't the first she'd had to drink that night. It couldn't have been.

"That's enough." Liesl reached across the counter and pulled a sheet of paper towel off the roll, handed it to Marie, and cast her eyes downward to give the woman a second of privacy to pat her mouth dry.

"There's a second part of the question,"

Marie said. "Ask me."

Marie was very drunk, and Liesl was very sober. They were not on even ground, and the right thing to do would have been to pour Marie a glass of water, put her to bed, and continue the conversation another day. Liesl refilled Marie's glass.

"Why?" Liesl said. "Why send me the chapter once you found out?"

Marie. Marie with the chapped lips, Marie with the finger-spotted wineglass pulled herself into a chair by the kitchen counter.

"I never went into his home office. Did you know that?" Marie set her glass down on the counter. Too hard. Liesl cringed, sure it would crack, but it held.

"No," Liesl said.

"We agreed. It was his private work space. A brilliant man can't be interrupted."

Feeling awkward about Marie's condition, Liesl tried to sound maternal.

"I'm surprised you agreed to that."

"The cleaning lady would go in," Marie said, her face breaking into a mean grin that put her stained gums on display. "So there was really no reason for me to ever enter."

"Until after." Liesl reached forward from where she was standing, and Marie pulled back as if Liesl were coming in for a hug, but she was reaching for Marie's glass, sliding it out of the way of the woman's hands that were waving the more agitated she became.

"He was so sure of my stupidity that he didn't even try to hide it."

"We've had too much wine," Liesl said. "Let's talk another day."

"You haven't had any wine."

"All the same," Liesl said. "Another day."

"It's Christmas," Marie said. "You won't leave a poor old widow alone on Christmas."

She swayed her way down from her stool and stumbled out of the kitchen. Liesl wasn't sure what to do, wasn't sure whether Marie was going to go to bed, was going to go vomit. But she didn't feel right leaving the woman alone, so she finally got up and went to follow her. She found her standing in the doorway to Christopher's office.

"He couldn't even respect me enough to try to hide it."

"He did, though," Liesl said. "They were in the filing cabinet."

Liesl walked into the room where uniformed officers had removed thousands of books from built-in shelves. They'd left only papers. Piles and piles of papers that Christopher had refused to read on a screen, had refused to save in a folder so that someone after him could make sense of them. Marie staggered forward and grabbed a pile of printouts from the desk, sloppily handing them to Liesl.

They were emails. They were emails from Miriam to Christopher. The old man had set up an email account after all.

"Right here on the desk," Marie said. "He left that woman's pleading letters to him right here on the desk under his manuscript."

Liesl glanced at the stack and almost immediately wanted to look away from the ugliness of what the messages exposed, but in the brief moments she laid eyes on the typed lines, she saw references to embraces held, to promises broken, to a heart shattered, to a mind that was fragmenting, and to a man who didn't care any longer.

"Marie, I'm so sorry," Liesl said.

"That poor girl killed herself, and that snake got to die quietly without ever taking any responsibility."

With that, Marie buckled over and vomited red wine all over the polished wooden floorboards in Christopher's office.

Twenty-One Years Earlier

The library basement, 3:30 p.m. Liesl had just about made it; ninety minutes and the workday would be over.

Francis was waiting for her by the elevator. "Hello, stranger."

Liesl pressed the elevator call button. "I have a list I have to pull for a class tomorrow. Head of the history department, he can be a real shark. Sorry to have missed you on your first day."

"Sorry to have missed me, or sorry to be avoiding me?"

He stepped toward her; she stepped back. "Christopher had a lot planned for you," Liesl said.

"And I have a lot planned for you, darling," Francis said, stepping closer still. "I've had a lot of time and a lot of miles to think about it."

"Francis. You can't call me darling."

"There isn't anyone down here to hear."

Liesl shook her head. "I mean not ever. Not ever again."

"Liesl, what is this? I haven't seen you since the Boston conference. You just about arranged this job for me . . ."

Liesl tucked her head down to recall their last meeting, a long embrace in a small hotel room. Liesl might be reserved, but she was too human to do away with the memories altogether, no matter the decisions she had made after. Those annual encounters, the afternoons in the small hotel room as rare-books scholars spoke in the ballroom downstairs; those afternoons lingered.

"I arranged the interview. Christopher loves you, and your credentials are good. You got the job yourself."

"Grand. And I admire Christopher, but he's a bloke, and I didn't pick up my life to shag him. Nice fellow and all, but I don't believe he's ever said he'd leave his wife for me."

Liesl put her hand on the wall to steady herself. "I didn't promise that. And if . . . I shouldn't have if I did. John doesn't deserve the things I said. Nor does your wife."

"What of the things we did? What of those?"

The elevator pinged. The door slid open; Christopher stepped out. He was curtained in shadow. Liesl caught a sway in his posture.

Christopher put his arm around Francis's neck. "Time to go, plebe. Whiskey and the world await us. If I'm to impart twenty years' worth of knowledge, we have to get started."

"Whiskey" spooked Liesl. Francis saw her go gray, saw her eyes change. "Will you be joining us then?" he asked her.

Christopher didn't laugh; he boomed. "She's in the family way."

There it was.

The elevator was about to close. "I'll grab this lift," Liesl said. "See you both in the morning."

Francis was silent, the long silence allowing him the time to count back months should he be so inclined. Christopher said, "You two know each other from the conference circuit. Better to let me get a look under Francis's covers myself. Spirit and strength to you, Liesl! Isn't that your standard toast, Francis?"

Liesl nodded as the elevator closed on her.

When he thought she was out of earshot, Christopher said, "I thought I was home free with the old bird and the baby business, but these career women can surprise you."

19

I

It was January, and it was all over. The books had been restored to their places on the shelves. The cardboard boxes marked "evidence" had been flattened and taken to the recycling station on the loading dock. Researchers came to do their research, and students came to do their studying, and the library ceased being a crime scene and resumed the role of library. Criminal charges would not be filed against a dead man, and the people outside of the library had long forgotten about any intrigue. It was as though nothing had ever happened.

Liesl leaned back in one of the reading room chairs. Working in Christopher's office had gone from uncomfortable to untenable, so she had taken to bringing her work out to the public areas of the library. Reading auction catalogs in the reference area, writing the schedule in a study carrel. It made the staff uncomfortable, her constant lurking, but she didn't care. She didn't like the feeling of Christopher's desk against her skin.

She was marking up a Christie's catalog with a fine-tipped mechanical pencil when President Garber's shadow fell over her. She recognized him by the chrome bicycle helmet dangling from his hand by its leather strap.

"Liesl," he said. "Why on earth are you working in here?"

"I'm reading," she said. "It's a reading room."

"You're responsible for this library, and no one can find you." He did not speak quietly, and it was a library. The reading room supervisor looked up, trying to catch Liesl's eye.

"Not so. The staff all know exactly where I am." She smiled when she said it.

"I expected you to be in your office."

"If I'd been expecting you, I would have told you otherwise."

"I didn't realize I was required to make an appointment."

The reading room supervisor and the handful of readers were trying their best to pretend to ignore the exchange — necks bent, pencils moving furiously — but the tension was out in the open for all to see.

"I'm responsible for this library. Wouldn't you hope that a person in my position is keeping busy?"

"I came to take you to lunch, not to suffer one of your moods."

"All right. Let's go to lunch."

John had made pizza the night before. It had sausage from their favorite butcher, rapini, chili oil, and a luscious dough that John made by hand. The leftovers were in the refrigerator of the lunchroom, and she'd been thinking about cold rapini-and-sausage pizza all morning. The day was cold and sunny, and Liesl glanced down at the bicycle helmet often as they made their way outside. It wasn't clear if she would be expected to jog alongside him while they made their way to the restaurant. It was just absurd enough to be possible. He led her right past the bike racks and around the corner past the zoological building, by which point she knew exactly where they were going. They gave their coats to the maître d' of the Faculty Club. Garber didn't wait to be seated. He made his way over to the corner table of the robin's-egg-blue room. Staff in black coats scurried to bring them warm rolls and cool water.

"Don't we need menus?" Liesl asked.

"I always get the same thing," Garber said. "Are you looking to try something new?"

"I'm not sure," Liesl said. "I don't often eat here."

"It's the Faculty Club. Where do you eat if not here?"

"The campus isn't lacking for lunch options," Liesl said.

A menu appeared before her. There was meat and more meat and a couple of half-hearted attempts at salads.

"Bring me the usual," Garber said.

"A Niçoise salad, please," Liesl said.

Garber tore open a roll and smeared it with butter. He ate loudly, like someone who felt entitled to take up a lot of space. Liesl's Niçoise salad had been listed at thirty-eight dollars on the menu, and it wasn't as though she couldn't afford a thirty-eight-dollar salad, but she objected to it on general principle. The whispered conversations of men in gray suits bounced around the high ceiling of the club.

Their plates were delivered only minutes after they ordered, no doubt a nod to her high-ranking dining companion. Garber's usual was plain steamed fish and vegetables. Liesl's salad included one small piece of potato and only a quarter of an egg. What did they do with the other seventy-five percent of the egg, she wondered.

"It's yours, Liesl," Garber said. "The library is yours."

"I'm sorry," Liesl said. "Mine in what sense?"

"I'm appointing you chief."

"I'm set to retire," Liesl said. "Those plans haven't changed."

Garber took a bite of his fish before continuing.

"Where do you take donors if not the Faculty Club? That will need to change once your term starts."

"I take them to a local restaurant," Liesl said.

"That's charming, but they don't write us checks so they can eat dinner next to an undergraduate."

"Did you hear when I said I was retiring?"

"I'm offering you a leadership position. The chance for more thrilling discoveries in auction catalogs and special presentations on the news all about how clever you are. Control of the acquisitions budget. You'd be the first woman in the library's history. Surely your knitting group can wait."

"I've never been much for knitting," Liesl said. "Despite what you've assumed about me."

"Well then, you have lots of free time.

You'll take the role."

"I have no desire for a leadership position," Liesl said. She was mostly telling the truth; she had spent plenty of time thinking about having the reins to the acquisitions budget and the ability to set new coordinates for the team and all the library's resources. She'd tried on the leader's clothes and found they fit, found that her instincts were sharp when she got to follow them.

"Fine. You don't want the role," Garber said. "But think of what the library needs." He smacked his lips and waited for her to respond. But Liesl, to her credit, wanted more for the library than someone who could be as good a leader as Christopher. She didn't want to get the leader's clothes pressed and ready for their next wear; she wanted to toss them in the bin and install someone who wore leadership as an altogether different color. At the same time, Liesl, here eating a thirty-eight-dollar salad with President Garber, planned on making one last move while the leader's clothes still hung on her body, while Garber sat across from her and saw how well they'd been tailored.

"The library needs a change," Liesl said. "A move into the twenty-first century and away from the old way of doing things."

"But before all that, it needs stability," he said.

"That sounds like the opposite of what I'm saying. Isn't it stability, the idea that everything was fine so long as it was the same, that got us into this mess?"

"It's a steady hand that will get us out," said Garber.

"Maybe. Or an honest reckoning with what was done. And how it was enabled."

"That can happen under your leadership," Garber said.

"So you'll allow for a formal inquiry? A public airing?"

"Well," Garber said. "If it happened in a way that it didn't spook the donors."

"It sounds to me," Liesl said, "as though you're proposing that nothing changes at all."

"That isn't what I said," said Garber. It was Liesl's turn to take a long chew at her lunch.

"If it were all to become public, though . . ." Liesl said.

"Let's not speculate on that. Publicity of our sins would be a messy business."

"Messy. It would be that. But it couldn't help but inspire change."

"I know you wouldn't do anything to put our reputation in jeopardy, Liesl."

"And I know that you would do anything to protect it."

II

In the reception area of the history department a half-dozen people were waiting, students mostly. Liesl worried briefly about whether she'd have the time to sit and wait but decided it was important enough.

"Is the chair in today?" Liesl said. "I don't have an appointment."

"He's busy, I'm afraid," the receptionist said.

"It's about Vivek Patel," she said.

"Can you take a seat?" the receptionist said. "I'll call back to his desk and see if he can take you in between appointments."

"Thank you."

"It's nothing. I'm just following instructions."

She waited less than two minutes. The receptionist waved her hand to get Liesl's attention and sent her to the end of the hallway where a big wooden door stood open and the chair of the history department stood in front of his desk, looking concerned.

"Has something happened to him?" he asked.

"No. I mean, I don't know."

"You're not here with news about Vivek?"

"I'm here to ask you about him. Is he missing?"

"No. Not exactly," the chair said. "I have a forwarding address. But he said he's listed the department as his emergency contact."

"Where has he gone?"

"I'm not to say."

"I have news about his wife. Or, I could have. I have news I think he'd want to hear."

"He was very specific, I'm afraid. He said that even if someone wanted to talk about Miriam, especially if they did, he wasn't to be contacted."

"And you think this is healthy?"

"I think this is what he wants and that I'm willing to try it."

Liesl shuffled back into the library, ignoring Dan as he spoke to her. A cure for Vivek's grief had been one of her last handholds. Without it, with him gone, she felt herself slipping. Her posture was more stooped, her eyes were sunk deeper than they had been just that summer. Squinting as she walked through the dark library, she let herself half believe that the news would find its way to Vivek somehow. That he would find some comfort somehow. The *somehow* had to be enough to hold on to. Francis was in the parcel room. Liesl went and stood beside him.

"Have you come to help unpack boxes?" he asked. His sweater was streaked with dust, and he was to his knees in packing material.

"What are we unpacking?"

"The loan for my exhibition. The shipment from Boston came today."

"You're making a register of it all?"

"And putting it straight in lockup."

"I've come from the history department."

"He's stayed then, Vivek has?" Francis said. "I'm happy to hear it."

Remarkable work in those boxes — the first volume that Liesl released from its cocoon of bubble wrap and dust was a later work from the Plantin Press. It was the artistry of the press that recommended it, the elaborate Rubens engravings, the flirty typography, and the small-format *Caesaris* made those talents manifest. She opened the cover and lay open the fold-out leaves in her hands to look at the printing details of the maps that were bound with the book. The quality of the type was lovely. It was so small, the book. So small that it could fit in the palm of her hand. So small that it could disappear into the pocket of the coat she was wearing. The idea made her lick her lips. She put the book down on the packing

465

table. A safe distance from her empty pocket.

At the next table, Francis was making notes in a paper register. She had once found it charming; she had recently found it charming, how old-fashioned the place was. Now it was all she could do to not yell that it was a waste of time to have an intern redo the work Francis was doing right now because he didn't know how to use a spreadsheet. She didn't yell. There was no use to it now, and there never had been. She was part of the fabric of what had kept the place stuck in the past. They were not going to change for her now just because she decided that she wanted to. There were wonderful books in these boxes and wonderful ideas in these books. That much remained true even if her devotion to the old ways of doing things did not. She dictated the details of the *Caesaris,* and Francis wrote them in the register.

"You didn't have any trouble getting the loans?" she asked.

"Not at all. Not after they heard that the missing books had been found in our stacks."

"Good. I'm glad."

She had come to Francis to talk about Vivek. To talk about Miriam. To talk about their role in preserving her memory, now that there were so few of them left who remembered her at all. Instead she handed Francis books, and he wrote their details in his tidy handwriting, with a mechanical pencil, in the paper registry. When they had unpacked it all, they rolled the two book trucks up to the exhibition area on the library's top floor. The display cases were empty and unlocked, an abandoned museum. The most recent exhibition, featuring the manuscripts and hand-drawn illustrations of a Nobel Prize–winning poet and playwright, had been emptied out to make way for the A. A. Milne exhibition that was coming next.

Francis was giddy among the open display cases. He handed Liesl volumes and took photos of how the pairings looked together and made copious notes in his little notebook with his mechanical pencil. It would be months before these works were mounted. There was research to be done, a catalog to write, a poster to design, invitations and press releases to be distributed. Now, at the beginning of this work, Francis was steeped in the pleasure of it. He was not exhausted by it, not spoiled by it. Standing now as he did, surrounded by books and empty display cases, he could tell himself with all sincerity that the best was yet to come. She envied his folly.

Excusing herself, she disappeared back into the bowels of the library. Her work was waiting for her, but she ignored it. She went to the bindery. There, the library's conservator was wearing a navy smock and working to bring life back to a 1498 collection of Aristotle's writing. She gently uncreased a sheet of paper with a polished whalebone tool the shape of a tongue depressor.

The bindery looked halfway between an apothecary shop and Gutenberg's workroom, and it was stacked high with books to be washed, books to be bound, books to be boxed, books to be repaired. The conservator never looked up at Liesl. Of her, too, Liesl was envious. For years she had slipped on her own smock and stood over books in this very room, looking over the conservator's shoulder, apportioning resources to the preservation of some objects and giving up on others, deciding how the lives of the most vital of the books could be saved, how they could be kept intact for the next generation of readers and scholars. On that day she wasn't moved to put on her smock. She could only watch.

She tiptoed out into the church-quiet workroom. There were mostly empty desks or desks that were only occupied by books. The room had an electric hum, reminding Liesl that things would be discovered here. Dan was the only one who was seated, and he didn't look up to acknowledge Liesl. He was used to her recent lurking. And he was immersed in the project that kept his hands busy in the in-between minutes.

Headphones plugged into his Discman, Dan was lovingly cataloging a leaflet from the library of the country's foremost Communist. There were 25,000 items that had come to the library in moldy boxes, and Dan wanted to touch every single one, wanted to preserve it, wanted to make sure that the socialists of the future could find it.

She came behind him and watched him work. He had a clear plastic ruler, like something Hannah might have used in primary school, and he measured the leaflet and noted the results on a scrap of paper by his side. Satisfied, he moved to counting pages, and again like a schoolchild, confident that he was all alone, he muttered the numbers under his breath as he counted. The next part was best. He knew it, and she did. He leaned back in his chair, and she caught the edge of his grin as he considered what he should title the thing that had come into their collection with no title. The pamphlet hadn't been printed so it could be an artifact in a library. It was made to provide union information for seamstresses. And here Dan was, deciding what it would be called in their shared history.

Liesl left the sanctuary of the workroom. If Dan had seen her come, or saw her go, he didn't indicate. The large reading room, stripped for the day of cocktail glasses and canapés, was hosting a group of undergraduates.

Max and his full suit were leading them through a collection of sacred texts. The fifteen or so undergraduates had all adopted the same posture: hands clasped behind their backs, leaning forward at the waist but not too far, afraid to breathe too heavily in the direction of the precious things laid out on low tables.

The objects on display consisted of a handful of Max's favorite volumes: bibles, hymnals, a thousand-year-old copy of the Gospels in Greek that Liesl recognized immediately. It made her smile, that book, its cover pockmarked where rats had gnawed at the leather over the centuries. It was no secret why Max chose that book for teaching.

He invited one of the students, a shy-looking one with brown hair falling into his eyes, to touch the book, to pick it up. The whole room held its breath as the lucky boy lifted the book by the tips of his fingers. One of the students asked about gloves — they always asked about gloves — and Max dispelled the myth, telling the boy, the class, that the book was safer when the holder had full use of his senses. Max invited the boy to lift the book, to feel it, to run his fingers over it and get to know it. When the boy lifted the book to his nose, and they always did — it was human nature to smell it — Max told him the thing about the rats.

He shot his arms forward, disgusted by the idea of centuries-old rats, and then he almost dropped the book and was horrified that he almost dropped the book, so he grasped it tighter, inviting bubonic plague, and then the whole group of undergraduates laughed and unclasped their hands from behind their backs and began to really see the treasures that Max had selected so lovingly.

It was already becoming dark outside; there were long shadows out the library window as she waited for the elevator. The elevator, the basement, her proximity to the work she was meant to be doing was getting colder, colder. She pressed the button for B2. In the holding cages, right outside the

471

elevator, a new donation had been unpacked by an army of graduate-student assistants earlier in the week. They were all editions of the works of Thomas Hardy. Thousands of them. First editions and foreign-language editions and illustrated editions. Editions that had been owned by other writers and editions that had been owned by heads of state and editions that had been owned by Hardy himself. They were bound with wood and cloth and leather and paper.

The man who sat cross-legged on the floor inspecting one of the volumes was the proprietor of a local rare-books shop who was often called in to do appraisal work for the library. His khaki trousers were covered in dust from perching on the floor. He held up an autograph on the title page of an edition of *Jude the Obscure* for Liesl to see.

"Look at this," he said. "Is this a convincing Emile Zola, or is my imagination running away with me? Do you have a Zola autograph on file?"

Liesl left him to his work with promises to send someone down with research about Zola's penmanship. He pulled another volume off the shelf as she stepped into the elevator.

When she returned to her table, the reading room supervisor asked if she'd like to have the catalogs tidied up and put away until the morning. Liesl shook her head. The room was quieter and dimmer now that the readers had left and the desk lamps had been switched off. It was exactly the way that she wanted to work. The supervisor wavered for a moment, unsure if she was meant to stay and supervise her boss or if she should leave as scheduled. Liesl assured her that she would lock up the room before leaving.

Once alone, she shrugged out of her cardigan and returned to her creaky wooden chair. She found it difficult to focus. There was a major collection going up through Christie's, and she had to decide whether she wanted anything for the library, and if so, how much she might be willing to spend. Turning the catalog pages, she saw only smears. There was a mechanical click as elsewhere in the building someone turned the main lights off. The rest of the staff, save for maybe Francis, had left. Liesl stood to stretch and wandered over to the book truck full of materials that were currently in use by readers. A first edition of the score of Mozart's *Don Giovanni.* John Nash's doctoral thesis. They were so small, most of them. Slender enough to fit into a laptop sleeve. She didn't especially want any of them; what would Liesl do with the score to *Don Giovanni*? But she could take it; that was the point. There was no one who could stop her.

She looked at those books for a long time. They looked so ordinary. After a while she turned back to her work and reopened the abandoned Christie's catalog. There was a fifteenth-century illuminated manuscript of Christine de Pizan's *Livre de paix* that would be coming up. A fifteenth-century woman who made her living as a writer. Liesl wanted it.

After she had scratched out some figures in the margins of the auction catalog, Liesl closed all her volumes. She ran her fingers along the spines of the lonely books in the reading room, and then she turned off the light and closed the door. Francis surprised her as she was putting her things away on Christopher's desk.

"I was certain I was the last one here," Francis said.

She set the auction catalogs and her notepad on the desk at a neat right angle. She could return to them in the morning.

Francis had his coat in his arms, a red knit cap already on his head. The red made him look more grandfatherly than she had ever seen him. He cocked his head at her, waiting for a reply.

"You weren't planning to rob the place, were you?" she asked.

"Not tonight," he said.

She tapped the neat pile of catalogs. She thought of the Pizan manuscript and its half-million-dollar price tag.

Francis still stood, waiting to be paid attention to.

"Fancy a drink somewhere before you head home?" he asked.

"I've been here since eight, Francis. I don't fancy anything except the idea of a cup of tea and my bed tonight."

"Can I say something then? It would be more easily said over a drink, but it should be said either way."

"If you want to," she said. "If you feel you have to." It was easier now. No more fear of the pending conversation. For twenty-one years they'd avoided the question of what-if, had avoided each other as much as was possible. For Liesl had feared learning she'd made the wrong decision. Wrong lover. Wrong father. Wrong type of life. But having opened themselves to the possibilities, examined them up close, held them in hand, Liesl understood now that the conversation had been nothing to fear. The choice young Liesl had made had been the right one.

"It's not that," he said, and Liesl was satisfied that Francis felt the same way as she did.

She nodded. Left space for him to say what he needed to say.

"Take Garber's job offer. Please." He took off his red knit cap and held it in his hands as he asked.

It was the last thing that she expected. He laid out his case. That without Liesl, the job would be filled in Christopher's image. By a man like Langdon Sibley. Or perhaps worse, in Francis's eyes, by a man like Max Hubbard.

She struggled to sleep that night. Despite the warm tea on her nightstand. Despite the twelve-hour workday that had left her mind so foggy. She watched John's big shoulder rising and falling beside her and was envious of him. She gave up finally and rose to go look out the window. At the snow-smeared backyard, at the outline of her garden underneath all that winter.

She would have liked to think that Francis believed she was the best person for the job. And not that he was worried it would go to his rival. The idea of being anyone's unthreatening choice was ghastly. It made her want to spend a half-million dollars on a manuscript on a whim. It made her want to dump armfuls of books into her purse or else to sit on the floor of the stacks in the basement and tear pages out of precious ancient texts one by one. Their old bed creaked as John turned to look for her. He sighed when he saw that she was looking at the garden, mumbled something about the thaw coming soon, and then rolled over and went right back to his easy sleep.

20

"Has it already started?" Liesl asked.

Dan turned at the sound of her voice.

"They waited six months for you," he said, "so I told them they could wait six more minutes."

She gave him a peck on the cheek and then rushed into the large reading room. A ten-foot-tall banner announcing the *Forgeries and Thieves* exhibition hung from the third-story railing.

"Thank goodness," Francis said. "I was beginning to think you had stood us up. After we got the place all dressed up for you."

"I wouldn't have missed it. The banner is lovely. Are we using a different graphic designer?"

"Yes. One that's more 'web-friendly,' " Francis said.

"Sounds like a smart move," Liesl said.

"Not a popular one."

"Puppies in the library would be a popular idea. Not a smart one, though."

"I bet that even puppies would give some of the regulars reason to grumble about the new comandante."

"How about you? Have you been grumbling?"

He motioned to the front of the room, to the star of the exhibition, to avoid answering the question.

A large glass display case had been assembled at the front of the room. In the corner of the case Liesl could see the red glint of a laser beam that would shriek if the case were to be pried open. Not that anyone would ever do such a thing. Liesl took Francis's cue and stepped toward the case to see the contents. The Peshawar manuscript. And next to it, the facsimile.

The explanatory plaque explained the details of the carbon-dating process that had been used to differentiate the two.

"Remarkable, isn't it," Liesl said. "How quickly the exhibition was pulled together."

"Remarkable indeed."

Francis's exhibition centering on the Plantin was next on the calendar. Still far from ready.

"The science bit," Francis said. "It's not really what we do."

"It is now, though, isn't it?" Liesl said.

"Should I get my Bunsen burner then?"

She stepped back from the case to admire the lighting setup. The room was filling. As she suspected, the beginning of the ceremonies had not been held up on her behalf. They were waiting for the money. And the money walked into the room and right toward her.

"My favorite librarian," Percy Pickens said.

No sooner had he greeted her than she spotted President Garber who was, with no discretion whatsoever, rushing across the room so that Liesl would not be left alone with the donor. He very nearly spilled his pinot noir.

"What a surprise that you made it to our celebration, Liesl."

"I RSVP'd."

"Of course. For the exhibition opening. It's very exciting."

"The turnout is rather good." She wandered to the next case, and he had to trail behind her. The blue and gold. It still took her breath away.

"It should be," Percy said. "You've invited Chris's family and lots of friends, haven't you?"

"You thought Chris's family and friends

would be especially interested in this exhibition, President Garber?" Liesl asked. She leaned closer to the case to read the plaque explaining the scholar's theories about the plundering of treasures from the Great Mosque, the centuries-long search for the blue Quran.

"The exhibition, sure," Percy said. "But the real draw is the presentation, isn't it? This wine is terrible."

"Oh?" Liesl said as she finally turned and looked back at the men.

"Acidic," Percy said. "Has the library changed caterers? Liesl, where were you sourcing your wine when you did all this? I think they must be using someone different now. Cheaper. Or new world."

"What's to be presented?" she asked.

"It's meant to be a surprise," Percy said. "Though I could enjoy a surprise better if I had something more appropriate to toast with."

"What's being presented?"

"Percy has made a generous donation," Garber said. Percy frowned at his wineglass. And Liesl noticed, for the first time, that there was a black drape covering something on the wall of the large reading room.

"Something for the collection?"

"You really don't know?" Garber asked.

"Perhaps we should leave it a secret after all."

"Best not to have secrets among friends," Liesl said.

"Oh, all right," Percy said. "President Garber recently informed me that the naming rights for this very reading room were available."

"The naming rights?" She managed a half smile. "So am I now standing in the Percy Pickens Reading Room?"

"That was my first thought, but no. I did one better. There are plenty of rooms in plenty of buildings that bear my name, but this will be the first named after a man of letters, a man who gave me plenty of laughs and plenty of tax receipts, a great man. Can you guess?"

"No."

"Oh, be serious now. It's the Christopher Wolfe Reading Room. A fitting honor for an honorable man."

Liesl's half smile was fixed in place. She bobbed her head to some unheard music and then reached her hand out, took Percy's glass of pinot noir, and downed the remnants in one mighty gulp.

His mouth opened and she could see the tip of his tongue, flexing to find words and failing spectacularly. She handed back the glass.

"He's right, you know," she said to Garber. "The wine is rubbish."

"She drank my wine," Percy said, to no one and everyone.

"We should let them get started," Liesl said.

Before Garber could snap his fingers to summon a fresh glass and an ice pack for Percy's ego, the new chief librarian walked into the reading room. The two women spoke often, but Liesl hadn't seen her since her retirement.

"Rhonda, congratulations on the exhibition," Liesl said. "What I've seen so far is thrilling."

"Hello, Professor Washington," Percy said.

"How nice to see you again, Percy." Rhonda kept her arm around Liesl's waist as she greeted the donor. "I see your wine is empty. Is someone bringing you another?"

He looked down at the empty vessel, betrayed by it.

"Now, I hate to be a gossip," Liesl said. "But what's this top-secret new research project I'm hearing about?"

Liesl stole a peek at Percy. He was frowning. A rich man doesn't appreciate being the last to know. Garber frowned because

Percy was frowning. Rhonda smiled even wider.

"Not a secret anymore," Rhonda said. "The grant funding just came through, so I can uncross my fingers."

Liesl knew about the grant funding. During the changeover, her email address hadn't been removed from the funder's notification system. One of a thousand little changes that had to be made, little mistakes that would be found over time. There had been a lot of zeroes on the grant notification.

"The press office has been in touch with me," Garber said. "For a grant this size they'd like to put out a release."

"We're going to be using MRI technology to look at the internal construction of books," Rhonda explained to the group.

"So that you can diagnose their herniated discs?" Percy said.

He waited for the appreciative rumble of laugher. There was none.

"A CT scan would do that more effectively," Rhonda said.

"Well, for what then?"

"We're looking at book construction technology in East Asia and Europe over a period of about five hundred years."

"Your thesis," Liesl said, "if I recall correctly, is that the development of European books was heavily influenced by East Asian technology. Isn't that right?"

The event coordinator walked over and whispered something in Rhonda's ear. She glanced at her watch and nodded. A moment later, the lights dimmed slightly.

"I need another drink," said Percy.

"There's some Scotch at the bar if we ask nicely," Rhonda said. "Shall I walk you over?"

"I asked earlier, and they said it was just wine."

"Well, I know the secret password."

Rhonda led Percy to the bar, leaving Liesl alone with President Garber. In the past she might have used a drink for armor, but now she was glad her hands were free. Across the room, Rhonda walked to the podium and tapped the microphone.

"A nice event," Liesl said. "You must be pleased."

"They're all nice events," said Garber.

"Interesting research attracts interesting people," she gestured to the full room. "Some of those people will be the moneyed sort. You must be happy about that."

"Six months in and donations are already down," Garber said. He looked at the same full room. Saw something different.

"She just won a million-dollar grant. Surely that offsets things."

"You can't form a warm and lasting relationship with a granting agency."

"So your concern is that she's not building relationships?"

"It's part of the job, Liesl," Garber said, whispering over Rhonda's speech.

Liesl tilted her head, questioning, and then turned to look at Rhonda, holding the room at attention as if she were a snake charmer.

"Many of the people in this room are here because of their relationships with Rhonda or her work."

"The wrong kinds of people," Garber said.

"The wrong kinds?"

"You know what I mean," Garber said, pursing his lips in frustration. "This has nothing to do with that, obviously. But we need people who will donate."

Liesl looked around the crowded room. Younger and with fewer charcoal suits than a year earlier. "And 'these people' won't?"

"They'll donate to community programs. Build basketball courts all day long. But donate to the university? I don't know. But I know that Percy's kind will."

"As long as he's served the right type of Scotch."

"And this business with the MRIs." Garber waved his hand to get a server's attention, mimed a bottle of water.

"You're objecting to research now?"

"I'm objecting to her planned takedown of European history."

"You mean her contribution to our understanding of book history?"

They both paused to turn and look again in Rhonda's direction as the assembled group applauded lightly. The two joined in, congratulating her or the university or someone for some accomplishment or other before they turned back to their conversation.

"Is this what you wanted?" Garber asked. "When you insisted upon her? The ruin of this place?"

"The rebuilding," Liesl said.

"To rebuild we'd have to knock it down first. Is that what you want to do?"

"That's what was already done." A server approached, handing Garber a small Perrier. Liesl smiled in thanks when Garber didn't.

"That's not my reading of what happened here," he said.

"It doesn't matter, though, does it?" Liesl asked, arms crossed. "What your reading is?"

"I'm confident you'll come around to my way of thinking, Liesl."

"You should get something stronger than water, Lawrence."

The bar was at the other end of the room, and the speeches were underway, and President Garber didn't think that they were done with their discussion.

"I just hope it's not too late when you realize how wrong you are," Garber said. He was up above a whisper, and the man closest to them turned to look.

"In two years," Liesl said, "or in ten years, or in thirty years, I'll be dead, Lawrence, and this library's secrets will be dead with me."

"But you're to keep threatening me until then?"

"I'm to keep our bargain until then."

At the conclusion to Rhonda's speech, the applause was vigorous. Old friends and colleagues clustered around Liesl, welcoming her back. She had a little Riesling that night. But not too much. Well before the last glass was poured, Liesl went home.

"How was the evening?" John asked. "Was the place just as you remember?"

"I've only been gone a few months!"

"Even still."

He handed her a glass of iced tea from

the refrigerator.

"They finally got rid of the typewriters from the workroom," she said.

"Gosh," he said. "I'm surprised we didn't read about the riots in the paper."

"I'll bet most folks didn't even notice."

"I don't know," he said. "There might have been one or two who were waiting for them to come back into fashion. Fancy a sit in the garden?"

"If I'm not taking you away from anything," Liesl said.

"You are," he said. "But I've accomplished enough today to have earned a break."

"Rhonda's doing well."

"You always knew she would," he said.

"In a sense. I knew she could manage to juggle both roles."

"Shall I get some lemon for the teas?" he said. He had a bowl of them presliced and squeezed half a lemon into his own glass. He licked the juice off his fingers.

"Cheers," she said. She raised her glass of cold tea and tapped it against his. He followed her out to the garden.

"Her work is so interesting," Liesl said. "She's pulling in research partners from all over the university."

"Does it make you a bit jealous?"

"Jealous?" Liesl said. "I couldn't have

dreamed up any of what she's done."

"Not of what she's doing," he said. "Of the others who are still there, doing the work with her?"

"I don't know," she said. "But I don't think so."

"Want me to strengthen that?" he said. "There's an open bottle of whiskey somewhere in there."

"Maybe later," Liesl said. "Seems a pity to get up now that we're so comfortable."

"Quite right."

The kitchen light left on behind them was enough to illuminate the small terrace. Liesl and John reclined in wooden chairs. Above their heads, Hannah had hung strings of bare bulbs that she promised were fashionable. Neither moved to turn them on. The extra light was nice when they had company around, but near-darkness suited the comfortable quiet between them. John pulled his chair closer to Liesl's. She rested her glass on the ground, on a patio stone, and leaned toward him. The humidity of high summer was gone, and the heat was comfortable. The moon slipped behind a cloud, and for a moment it was even darker.

"That library," John said. "It sounds as though it might finally be turning into something modern."

In the near distance a streetcar rumbled past, as it would every six minutes all night long.

"Yes," Liesl said. "Or if not something modern, then a reasonable facsimile."

READING GROUP GUIDE

1. What was your first impression of Liesl, as a leader, as a parent, as a woman? Did your opinion change throughout the book?

2. Everyone except Liesl is extremely reluctant to involve the police. What do they fear? What are the consequences of that fear?

3. Liesl often has to swallow her feelings to get along with her colleagues and family. Have you ever been in a situation where you felt like you couldn't be honest about what you felt? What impact did that have? How does Liesl's isolation affect her search for the Plantin?

4. The Peshawar facsimile at the book fair makes Liesl uncomfortable. Do you think reproductions of rare books or art cheapen

the original? What do you see as the difference between a facsimile and a forgery?

5. The characters at the library spend their days surrounded by priceless books. Was there a title in the library's collection that especially moved you? Which of the books would you have stolen to keep for yourself?

6. Francis is a complicated character, especially from Liesl's perspective. Were you rooting for him? Did you think he deserved Max's suspicion? How did Liesl's feelings about him shape your impression?

7. Liesl mentions having "never had more authority and less control in my life." What's the difference between authority and control? Have you ever been in a similar position?

8. One of the barriers that prevented Miriam from seeking treatment for her depression was the possibility of people calling her "crazy" for it. How has mental health stigma shifted throughout your life? Where is it most persistent?

9. Vivek ends the book carrying a lot of guilt for his inability to help Miriam. What do

you think happens to Vivek after the end of the book?

10. Hannah points out that there's a difference between putting your name forward for a promotion and doing your work well and hoping people will one day notice. Where do you fall on that scale? How do these competing theories shape the workforce, especially in how men and women are evaluated at work?

11. Of Detective Yuan's list of noncommercial motivations for theft — revenge, thrill, passion — which did you think was most likely? Who did that make you suspect?

12. When the thief was revealed, what were your thoughts? How well do we know the people around us? Do we know more or less once they leave us for good?

13. Would you take the chief librarian position in Liesl's place? Do you think her final decision was the right one?

A CONVERSATION
WITH THE AUTHOR

What was the inspiration for *The Department of Rare Books and Special Collections?*
I've worked in libraries for a long time, so that had a lot to do with my decision to set the book in a library. But what I really wanted to explore was the character of a woman who was older than a traditional protagonist in fiction. I had just become a mother when I started writing the novel and I had heard older women in my life say that at some point as a woman, you just become invisible. I became obsessed with that idea — the way that women are seen, or not seen, through the different stages of their life.

How have your own experiences in libraries shaped this book?
When I was a graduate student I worked in a rare books library, and it was one of the

coolest experiences of my life. The librarians had the most fascinating backstories (Soviet defection, love affairs with ballet dancers — and that's just one woman's out of the bunch), and they spent every day surrounded by treasure. Writing the book was a way to spend more time in that place, even if it was just in my imagination.

The final chapters of the book read almost like a love letter to libraries and books. How would you describe the role of an ideal library?

Isn't every library an ideal library? When I was a kid, I spent half my life in my little community branch that was scarcely larger than a corner store, but they had dozens of Nancy Drew novels and back issues of *Spin* magazine. It was perfect. As an undergrad I would use a study carrel to nap between classes. It was perfect. When I lived overseas I would go to the British Museum on my lunch break and peer through the window at the papier-mâché ceiling of the great reading room where Oscar Wilde and Virginia Woolf used to do their work. Perfect. Now I take my son to the sort-of-smelly children's section of our local branch in a 150-year-old former postal station and we sing our hearts out to "Baby Shark" with the children's librarian. Perfect, perfect, perfect.

Speaking of past and future, the dating of the Peshawar manuscript is quite the controversy here. Which do you think is a greater responsibility, preservation or understanding?

The goal of preservation of cultural property is to aid in understanding. But that understanding shouldn't come at the expense of preservation. There's a certain amount of hubris in that, isn't there? In thinking that you are equipped to extract all of the meaning from a thing, that you have no responsibility to leave the thing for the people who come after you. In the case of Rhonda's project to date the Peshawar, there was care and respect for preserving the Peshawar manuscript as her team sought to understand. I wouldn't have let them do it without that care and respect!

What draws you to crime fiction as a writer? As a reader?

Plot, plot, plot, plot, plot. As a reader, I love the feeling of *needing* to turn the page. As a writer, committing and solving crimes gives my characters something interesting to do. If left to my own devices, I would write snappy conversations between characters in cool locations and nothing would ever happen.

More than one of your characters struggles with their mental health. Do you think the stigma attached to mental health is decreasing? Do you have any advice for people who are struggling?

I think little by little the stigma is decreasing. But I worry that while people now understand that mental illness is illness, not a character defect, they are still unsure about how to support the people in their lives who may be suffering from mental illness. So my advice is not for people who are struggling with depression or other mental health challenges, it's for those who aren't. My advice is to seek resources from your local health authority so that you can be a supportive partner, coworker, employer, or friend.

Which books are on your bedside table these days?

It's a big pile! But if I push aside the overdue library books, there are a few that stand out. There's *Mort sur le Nil,* a translation of Agatha Christie's *Death on the Nile* that I'm using to practice my French. I'll be able to say "She's been shot!" before I can successfully order dessert *en français.* I'm also savoring *Where the Wild Ladies Are* by Matsuda Aoko. It's a collection of short stories that are retellings of Japanese folk tales and ghost stories. They're moody and spooky and feminist and surprising. Lastly, I just read Rumaan Alam's *Leave the World Behind* in one sitting. At one point it stressed me out so much I threw it across the room. I'm keeping it close so I can eventually reread it.

ACKNOWLEDGMENTS

I'm everlastingly indebted to my agent and fairy godmother, Erin Clyburn, for finding a home for my book and answering my thousands of questions. Thank you to Anna Michels at Sourcebooks for her excitement about the book from day one and to Heather VenHuizen and Kelly Lawler, the creative team who turned the idea of my book into something beautiful I can hold in my hand. And to Kimberly Glyder for the beautiful cover design. For the incredible publicity, marketing, and sales folks who made sure that my book made it into the hands of readers — there are too many of you to name but I'm forever in awe of your creativity and energy.

Many thanks are owed to everyone at the University of Toronto Libraries, my professional home, with particular gratitude to the welcoming and wise and endlessly interesting staff of the Thomas Fisher Rare

Book Library who welcomed me there: Anne Dondertman, Luba Frastacky, Phillip Oldfield, Pearce Carefoote, Natalya Rattan, Elizabeth Ridolfo, Graham Bradshaw, Susan Chater, Linda Joy, John Shoesmith, Tom Reid, Jennifer Toews.

For providing the precious minutes of childcare that allowed me to write this book, thank you to Francine St. Pierre, Bronislawa Jurczyk and Carol Shapiro. And of course, thanks to my delightful little family, Matthew and Henryk Valentine, for being infuriating and distracting but always making me want to make you proud.

ABOUT THE AUTHOR

Eva Jurczyk is a writer and librarian living in Toronto. *The Department of Rare Books and Special Collections* is her first novel.